# Rejected
# Princesses

# Rejected Princesses

*Tales of History's Boldest*
*Heroines, Hellions, and Heretics*

## JASON PORATH

**DEY ST.**
*An Imprint of* WILLIAM MORROW

**DEY ST.**

HarperCollins books may be purchased for educational, business, or
sales promotional use. For information, please email the Special Markets
Department at SPsales@harpercollins.com.

FIRST EDITION

Library of Congress Cataloging-in-Publication Data
has been applied for.

ISBN 978-0-06-240537-1

16  17  18  19  20    RRD    10  9  8  7  6  5  4  3  2  1

*Dedicated to my mother,*
*the strongest woman in the world.*

*You carved a space for yourself*
*out of a world that offers*
*strong women no quarter.*

*Then, out of everything you could*
*have been, you chose to be my mom.*

*I hope I can live up to you.*

# Contents

# Introduction

here's a list of stories in your head. You know the one. It's the list schools give to girls: Amelia Earhart, Marie Curie, Rosa Parks, and so on. It's safe. It's censored. It's short. It's the list of amazing women in history.

But what of the untold stories? The uncompromised ones? The uncomfortable ones? The rejected ones?

That's where this book comes in.

## Who Rejects the Rejected?

Let's get the obvious out of the way: if you're expecting a collection of pitched-and-rejected ideas for animated movies here, you're out of luck. I didn't pitch any of these as movies. To my knowledge, nobody has. Heck, most of the women covered here aren't even princesses. "Rejected Princesses" is less a description and more a question: *Why don't we know about these women? Where are their movies?*

I mean, think back to history class. You learned about male figures running the gamut from Abe Lincoln to Genghis Khan. And on the female side? The aforementioned short list. And that list was not a foregone conclusion: it's not like history lacks for strong-minded women. But at some point, our society collectively decided that people like Elizabeth I and Cleopatra VII are fine, but rebels, hellions, and warlords? Not so much. And when someone like Harriet Tubman does sneak onto the list? The unpalatable parts of her story, the bits "not suitable for children," get left off.

Now, as you read this book, some of you will bristle a bit and say, "Well, that's obviously not suitable for kids." Okay, sure—but where is that line? Ancient Greek children had Zeus impregnating women while in the shape of various animals. Norse children heard about Odin plucking out his own eye for wisdom. Inuit children got a lot of talk about genitalia in their folktales. (Seriously, look them up. Inuit stories can get pretty weird.) Kids are flexible. Kids can handle more than we think.

What's "suitable for kids" defines what sort of kids we as a society want. And right now, the girls society wants are the ones who can fit on a short list—while the list for boys is without borders or end.

If girls can be anything, let them be anything.

This is a book for any girl who ever felt she didn't fit in. You are not alone. You come from a long line of bold, strong, fearless women. Glory in that.

This is a book for anyone who ever underestimated a girl.

## Where'd This All Come From?

I hadn't planned to start this project.

It all began with a lunchtime question posed to my DreamWorks Animation coworkers: *Who is the least likely candidate for an animated princess movie?* Over an hour, we tried one-upping each other with increasingly inappropriate suggestions (most inappropriate: Nabokov's *Lolita*). Throughout, I kept suggesting obscure warrior women I'd learned about from Wikipedia binges, like Angolan freedom fighter **Nzinga Mbande** or tank-driving Soviet **Mariya Oktyabrskaya**. None of my coworkers had ever heard of them. I thought that should change.

By the end of the conversation, I knew this needed to exist. I had almost no artistic training to speak of (I was a very technical sort of animator), and no background as a historian, but I did the best I could. After I left DreamWorks, I put a handful of entries online, to see if there would be any reaction.

There was. In short order, www.rejected princesses.com made Reddit, Huffington Post, Buzzfeed, NPR, and newspapers around the globe. I got a book deal. And here we are.

Throughout this project, I've been asked one question more than any other: "*Why?* Why are you, a random white guy from Kentucky, so interested in women's issues? Where'd this come from?" To which I have a simple reply. And it's one that I want you to keep in mind as you read this book, as you gaze upon hilariously mismatched art styles and subject matter. Keep it in mind as you chuckle and automatically dismiss these stories as unsuitable for kids. The reply is: *Why not?*

## What We Know and How We Know It

At some point, the following scene is going to happen.

In a bookstore, someone will pick up this book. Not recognizing a lot of the names in the table of contents, they'll flip to an entry they do know—maybe **Joan of Arc** or **Elisabeth Báthory**. And they'll spot something they think is wrong. And they'll put down the book and say, "How can I trust anything in this book if this one thing is wrong?"

Which is a shame, for a couple reasons. First of which is that they'll be missing out on a lot of great stories. But second is that it shows a common misunderstanding of how history works—because history is not an unchanging record of facts and figures. History changes. It shifts and evolves, as does our understanding of it.

One example of many: Textbooks for decades held that James Watson and Francis Crick discovered the structure of DNA. Wasn't until years later that it came to light that they'd based much of their work off that of a largely uncredited woman named Rosalind Franklin. Does that make everything else in the textbook incorrect? Of course not! The textbook is a product of its time and the knowledge available when it was written. And this book is the same.

Know that a lot of love and effort has gone into creating *Rejected Princesses* and making it a valuable (and entertaining) resource. I may not be a trained historian, but I've done my damnedest to treat these stories right. And really, what else can you ask?

Here's hoping you enjoy. I certainly have.

# Hold Up a Second!

## YOU SHOULD KNOW WHAT YOU'RE ABOUT TO READ

Unlike what you may be used to reading, **this book doesn't pull punches**. It's not censored. Sometimes there's rough content.

Not every entry is suitable for every reader (despite the cartoony demeanor).

To help you know what's a good fit for you, this book provides **helpful guide markers**.

As the book goes on, the icons change from green to yellow, then to red. The way to think about these divisions is, how much evil are you comfortable with in the world?

• Green is simple. Good beats evil, the world is moral. Think PG.

• Yellow is more complex. No black and white, just shades of gray. Think PG-13.

• Red requires maturity. You must be your own moral guide. Think R.

Additionally, look out for these **icons** that tell you what's in an entry.

## On to the stories!

# Khutulun

## (1260–1306, MONGOLIA)

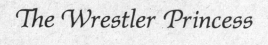

## The Wrestler Princess

Staring at you from the opposite page is none other than Khutulun, princess of 10,000 horses, the pride and glory of the Mongol Horde.

A bit of background on the Khans' Mongol Empire—it was, for the time, as big a deal as deals got. At its height, it stretched from China to Europe and the Middle East, making it, at the time, the largest contiguous empire in human history. The whole thing was started by Genghis Khan (maybe you've heard of him), who unified a number of nomadic tribes under a single banner. While he did bring many advances to the regions he conquered (religious tolerance, increased trade, meritocracy), you probably know him more for his reputation as a brutal dictator. Certainly it was the defining characteristic of his reputation back in the day too.

And it was not undeserved. Here's an example: Genghis once conquered the neighboring Khwarezmian Empire. Right after taking control, he decided to erase it from existence, burning towns to the ground and killing everyone in its government. He went so far as to divert a river through the deposed emperor's birthplace, wiping it off the map. These were the sorts of things he was known for, and it was these warlike traits that he passed down to his descendants.

Well, Khutulun was his great-great-granddaughter.

By 1260, the year Khutulun was born, the Mongol Empire was starting to fray at the seams and civil war was imminent. Some of the Khans, Khutulun's father Kaidu among them, favored the old ways of riding and shooting and other trappings of the nomadic lifestyle, while Kublai Khan—Kaidu's uncle—was more into politics, governing well, and other things that bored the average Mongol to tears. Eventually Kaidu and Kublai began outright warring against each other, in a conflict that would last 30 years. Throughout this, Kaidu relied on one person above all others, and, spoiler alert, it was not one of his 14 sons—it was Khutulun.

Growing up with 14 brothers, Khutulun had no shortage of testosterone around her at any given time. She grew up to be incredibly skilled in horsemanship and archery. Marco Polo, history's greatest tourist, described her thusly: "Sometimes she would quit her father's side, and make a dash at the host of the enemy, and seize some man thereout, as deftly as a hawk pounces on a bird, and carry him to her father; and this she did many a time."

Picture that. You're up against a horde of Mongolian warriors riding into battle. You're tracking the movements of this huge chunk of stolid soldiers, trying to read which way they're going. Suddenly, one of them—a woman, no less—darts out from the group, picks off a random person in your group, and runs back, before you even know what's happened. That's intimidating as heck.

But all of this paled in comparison to her skill with wrestling.

The Mongols of Kaidu Khan's clan valued physical ability above all things. They bet on wrestling matches constantly, and if you won, people thought you were literally gifted by the gods. Now, these weren't your modern-day matches, separated out by things like weight class and gender—anyone could and did wrestle anyone else, and they'd keep going until one of them hit the floor. This was the environment in which Khutulun competed. Against men. Of all shapes and sizes.

She was undefeated.

Now, okay, back up. How can we be sure of that? Well, according to Marco Polo (and this is corroborated by other historians of the time), Papa Kaidu desperately wanted to see his daughter Khutulun married, but she refused to do so unless her potential suitor was able to beat her in wrestling. So she set up a standing offer, available to all comers: Beat her and she'd marry you. Lose and you'd give her 100 horses. She ended up with 10,000 horses and no husband.

Now, in these sorts of texts, 10,000 is like saying "a million." It's shorthand for "so many I can't count them all"—you may also note that elsewhere in this book **Mai Bhago** fought 10,000 Mughals at Khidrana. While 10,000 may have been hyperbolic, it was, suffice to say, a truly ludicrous number of horses, supposedly rivaling the size of the emperor's herds.

Khutulun remained stubborn about marriage even as she got older and pressure mounted on her to find a mate. Marco Polo tells of a time when a cockier-than-average suitor challenged her. This guy was so confident that he bet 1,000 horses instead of the usual 100. Apparently he was a decent fella too, because Kaidu and his wife liked him. Khutulun's parents approached her privately and begged her to just throw the match. Just lose intentionally, they said, so you can marry this totally decent guy.

She walked away from that match 1,000 horses richer.

Unfortunately, due to her stubborn refusal to take a husband, people began to talk. Rumors began to spread around the empire that she was having an incestuous affair with her father. (These sorts of slanderous rumors, you will note, are a recurrent problem for many of the women in this book.) Realizing the problems her refusal to marry was causing her family, she finally relented and settled down with someone. Who, exactly, is subject to some debate, but whoever it was never beat her at wrestling.

Near the end of his life, Kaidu attempted to install Khutulun as the next Khan leader, only to meet stiff resistance—particularly from Khutulun's many brothers. Instead, a rival named Duwa was appointed to be Great Khan, and Khutulun's story here begins to slide into obscurity. Five years after Kaidu's death, Khutulun died under unknown circumstances, at the age of 46.

Afterwards, the Mongol Empire, particularly the more nomadic factions, began to crumble. Khutulun could be considered one of the last great nomadic warrior princesses.

After her death, she was forgotten for centuries. She only began her comeback in 1710, returning to historical prominence when a Frenchman named François Pétis de la Croix, while putting together his biography of Genghis Khan, wrote a story based on Khutulun. This story was called "Turandot,"* but it was greatly changed from the facts of her life. In it, the eponymous Turandot challenged her suitors with riddles instead of wrestling matches, and if they failed her challenge, they were killed.

Centuries later, in the early 1900s, "Turandot" was turned into an Italian opera—except, getting even further from Khutulun's actual history, the opera was about a take-no-nonsense woman finally giving in to love. Ugh. She has since appeared in the 2014 Netflix original series *Marco Polo*, where she is portrayed as slender and waifish when she was anything but.

Mongolia continues to honor Khutulun to this day. The traditional outfit worn by Mongolian wrestlers is conspicuously open-chest—to show that the wrestler is not a woman, in deference to the undefeated Khutulun.

## · ART NOTES ·

The scene is set at night as a reference to Khutulun's Turkish name of Aijaruc (used by Marco Polo), meaning "moonlight."

She wears a silver medal around her neck. This is a *gergee* (also known as *paiza*): a medallion given by the Great Khan that signifies the power of the holder. It was usually reserved for men. Most women instead used seals to signify their status—Khutulun is the only woman ever mentioned as owning a gergee.

Her outfit is not a wrestling outfit by any stretch, but Mongolian fashion is so fascinating and colorful that it had to be shown off. The outfit in question is based on a man's outfit, but given that Khutulun had many masculine qualities, it seemed in line.

The idea for her pose was inspired by portraits of noblewomen sitting demurely with their hands in their laps.

---

* It's possible that the story was based off Turandokht, a historical Persian princess from the seventh century. Jack Weatherford, an anthropology professor who's studied the Mongols as much as anyone, claims the la Croix version is based on Khutulun. Muddying all of this yet further are modern-day online claims that Turandokht was part of *1001 Arabian Nights*, along with **Marjana**. She was not; Turandokht was instead in the similarly titled *1001 Days*, which was la Croix's compilation.

## KHUTULUN

The background is filled with horses and yurts—the Mongols of Kaidu's tribe almost certainly slept in yurts. Well, technically, the Mongolians called them *gers*, but this author loves the word *yurt* (which is Russian). Apologies, ancient Mongolia. It cannot be helped. Yurt. Yurt yurt yurt.

They are, of course, on the Mongolian steppe. The wrestling match described by Marco Polo actually happened in a palace, but capturing Khutulun's nomadic nature was more important. Also, moonlight.

# Tatterhood

## (NORWEGIAN FAIRY TALE)

## The Princess Who Rode a Goat

nce upon a time, there were a king and queen who had no children. The queen's biological clock was ticking something fierce, so she took in a girl to raise. Everything was pretty cool!

Then one day, a beggar woman and her little girl came by the castle. The queen's adopted daughter began to play with the beggar girl, even bringing her up to the queen's quarters. The queen was not pleased and told the beggar girl to bugger off. The beggar girl quickly responded that her mother was capable of magic and could help the queen have children of her own if she wanted. This was undoubtedly hurtful to the adopted daughter. Jerk move, beggar girl.

But the queen was impressed by the impassioned rant of this random underage trespasser and summoned the beggar woman to her quarters. There, she asked if what the woman's daughter had said was true, but the woman demurred and said that her daughter was prone to making up stories. The beggar girl then took the queen aside and whispered in her ear, "Get my mom plastered—then she'll help you out!"

And so, before long, the queen had the beggar woman three sheets to the wind and ready to do her bidding. The beggar woman gave the queen some instructions: Before you go to bed, bring in two pails of water, wash yourself in them, and then throw the water under the bed. The next morning, there will be two flowers, one beautiful and one ugly. Eat the beautiful one, but leave the ugly one be.

It is at this point that the story ceases to mention the adopted daughter. Poor adopted daughter. You deserved better.

So the queen did as instructed, and, as you might expect, the next morning there were two flowers. She chowed down on the pretty one, and it was mind-blowingly delicious. So delicious, in fact, that she couldn't help but down the ugly one as well. It was . . . less than delicious.

Soon thereafter, the queen became pregnant, and she gave birth to the ugliest baby on earth. This baby came out with a wooden spoon in its hand, riding a goat. Presumably the labor was equally horrifying. As soon as she was out the baby cried, "Mama!"

"If I'm your mama," said the queen, "God help me mend my ways." The queen was also kind of a jerk.

"Oh, don't worry," said the hideous, spoon-wielding, goat-riding baby, who could somehow also immediately talk. "You're about to have another girl, who's better-looking."

True enough, she did! Out popped another girl, who was lovely and sweet and everything the shallow queen had hoped she would be. From that point, the twins were inseparable. The older goat-riding twin they called Tatterhood, because she wore a ratty hood everywhere. The nurses repeatedly tried to seal her away in various parts of the palace, but the beautiful younger sister couldn't bear to be separated from her.

Their childhoods were pretty standard, simple stuff, until they were approaching their tween years. That was when, one Christmas, they heard a terrible clattering about the palace. Tatterhood asked the queen what was making the noise, to which the queen answered, "Oh, it isn't worth asking about."

It was actually a pack of trolls and witches. They were celebrating Christmas in the traditional way set forth by Christian doctrine: by breaking everything in someone else's house. Apparently they did this regularly, to the point where the queen did not even deem it worthy of conversation.

Tatterhood grabbed her wooden spoon and, ignoring the pleas of her mother, went out to drive off the witches and trolls. She told her family to seal up the room while she beat the snot out of their uninvited guests. Judging from the ensuing cacophony of shrieks and groans, she did a pretty good job of it. However, the younger sister, who could not bear to be separated from Tatterhood, opened the door a crack to see what was going on—and *pop*! A witch instantly replaced her head with that of a calf.

She ran back into the room on all fours, mooing loudly. Tatterhood, having driven off the unwanted guests, saw what had happened. She was frustrated, telling her mom and sister, "Come on, guys! You had *one job*! Sigh. Fine, let's go, sis, I'll fix this mess."

The two set sail after the trolls and witches in search of the younger sister's head. They did so alone—no sailors, no help, just the two of them (and a goat) crewing a massive boat. When they got to the witches' castle, Tatterhood quickly spotted her sister's head and snatched it away. This brought the attention of the witches, who swarmed her. However, after getting repeated head-butts from the goat and smacks from Tatterhood's spoon, the witches gave up and let her go.

Tatterhood got back to the boat, swapped her sister's cow head for her actual head, and the two sailed off into the sunset.

Now, this is where the story should end. It doesn't, but it should. If you're reading this to a child, stop now. But for completion's sake, and if you are intent on having disappointing ends to awesome stories, here you go.

The sisters wound up in a faraway kingdom. Upon their arrival, the widowed king

instantly fell for the beautiful sister, but she wouldn't marry him unless he found a match for Tatterhood too. So the king set Tatterhood up with his son, who was . . . less than enthusiastic at the prospect of marrying a famously ugly goat-rider. But without much of a choice, he agreed, and soon he and his dad were off to the church with the two sisters.

On the way, Tatterhood asked him, "Why don't you talk?" to which the prince sulkily replied, "What should I talk about?" She suggested, "Well, why don't you ask me why I ride upon this ugly goat?" So he did. And she answered, "This is no ugly goat, but the most beautiful horse a bride ever rode." And sure enough, it was.

They repeated this exact line of conversation for her spoon (which became a wand), her hood (which became a crown), and her face (which became ten times more beautiful than her sister's).

She was beautiful all along, she married a shallow douchebag, her sister became her mother-in-law, and they lived happily ever after, blah blah blah, terrible ending.

So, seriously: adventures. They sailed off for more adventures. That's the new official story. It'll be our secret.

## · ART NOTES ·

As this is a Norwegian fable, Tatterhood is here depicted standing over Norwegian-style trolls—themselves inspirations for the tall-haired troll toys popular in the 1980s. No witches are seen in the picture mostly because witches get a bad rap. There are a lot of very nice witches out there.

# Agnodice

## (4TH CENTURY BCE, GREECE)

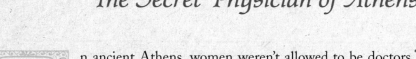

## The Secret Physician of Athens

In ancient Athens, women weren't allowed to be doctors,* which resulted in some problems. Male physicians had some pretty strange ideas about female anatomy—a popular theory posited that the uterus would regularly just get up and mosey around the body, wreaking havoc as it went. With such spot-on medical knowledge ruling the roost, many women understandably had reservations about trusting their local medical professionals.

Agnodice was not having any of that.

Fed up with seeing women risk life and limb because of stubbornly ignorant doctors, Agnodice decided to become a doctor herself. She cut her hair short, moved to Alexandria, Egypt (where women were part of the medical community), and started studying. By the time she came back to Greece, she was a full-fledged professional—but knowing that women weren't allowed to practice, she started posing as a man.

Agnodice soon became a hugely popular gynecologist, although her method of getting new patients was . . . unorthodox. When she approached a woman who was going into labor and was subsequently turned away for being a man (since only women helped women through childbirth), Agnodice simply hiked up her robes, flashing the unsuspecting pregnant woman. Wowed by the sudden revelation of the physician's genitalia, the woman generally agreed to take on Agnodice's services. And for a while, everything was great!

Unfortunately, Agnodice's success brought her enemies, which led to her being put on trial. Her fellow physicians (all male), smarting from lost business and thinking her male, accused her of seducing her clients (and, in a classy follow-up, charged said clients with "playing sick" to cheat on their husbands). They put her on trial before an all-male court, whereupon she repeated, to great shock and some delight, her time-honored tradition of surprise sex organ revelation.

However, flashing the court didn't achieve the desired effect, and the subsequent deliberations focused on the severity of her crime—one punishable by death. But just as it looked as if her goose was well and truly cooked, her salvation arrived in the form of her

---

* Well, not for its entire history. As a practice, it flipped back and forth from okay to not okay multiple times throughout the centuries.

clients. Storming the court, a crowd of women forcefully praised her ability as a doctor, while simultaneously browbeating those who sought to string her up.

In the end, the legion of surprise witnesses was victorious: Agnodice was let free, and the law was amended to allow women to practice medicine in Athens.

Agnodice's story, now the better part of 24 centuries old, is nigh-impossible to verify. Several aspects of the story seem implausible. For one thing, the "sudden reveal skirt flip" was a popular feature of many contemporary myths. For another, Agnodice's name means "chaste before justice"—which seems a bit on-the-nose for someone's actual name. But regardless of what is true and what is exaggeration, the story of Agnodice served as inspiration for women throughout ancient Greece and continues to do so today.

# Te Puea Herangi

## (1883–1952, NEW ZEALAND)

## The Reluctant Royal Who Became
## the Maori's Greatest Leader

ost little girls, at some point in their childhood, want more than anything in the world to be a princess. Te Puea Herangi, who technically was one, wanted to be anything but.

To say that Te Puea was a difficult child would be the understatement of the century. Born into the Maori royal family of the Waikato district, she behaved with anything but refinement. Bossy to the point of cruelty, she'd order around adults and beat other kids with sticks because she knew she could get away with it.

This behavior only intensified when she entered her teens. Believing herself to have tuberculosis and not have long to live, she shirked her royal responsibilities and began a hedonistic binge that lasted for years. She cut herself off from her family and began dating a number of men (including *pakeha* [non-Maori]),[*] drinking heavily, and constantly fighting.

And then she turned it all around.

After her uncle personally appealed to her to rejoin her community, Te Puea returned and began mending fences. Despite facing resentment from those around her for her past behavior, she became a model citizen, ceasing her drinking habits, dressing in sackcloth, and working seven days a week—a schedule she'd keep for the rest of her life. Her work efforts were varied and included:

- When World War I broke out, she refused to let the New Zealand government conscript her people for a war that didn't concern them. When the government overruled her and began conscripting Maori men by force, she'd travel to the training camps and sit outside, giving them encouragement. She made similar efforts during World War II, raising money for the Red Cross rather than supporting the war effort.

---

[*] One boyfriend in particular stands out: Roy Secombe, whose family had set up New Zealand's first brewery. He was less than charitably described by his relatives as a man whose only contribution to the family business was that he was alcoholic.

- After a flu epidemic, she arranged homes for 100 orphans, set up makeshift clinics (as most Maori did not trust pakeha-run hospitals), and started making plans for permanent ones.

- Realizing Maori towns desperately needed revitalization in an area away from the damp marshes that were breeding grounds for illness, Te Puea raised funds to buy and develop a new settlement. She supervised the cutting of trees, laying of cement, and cultivation of farmland. She kept meticulous finances and even levied taxes. Her efforts paid off spectacularly: cases of illness dropped significantly, and the Maori became much more economically self-sufficient.

Having been raised with bitter, difficult memories of the 1860s war against the pakeha, Te Puea decided the best thing was to bury the hatchet once and for all. In a very controversial (yet practical) deal, she accepted a suboptimal amount for reparations, just so that her people could move on.

She worked hard to build better relations between Maori and pakeha. Feeling that Maori could show the pakeha what was good in them, and vice versa, she smoothed over numerous cultural misunderstandings, particularly over the amount of worker leave required for Maori funeral rites (at least three days, sometimes much more).

Lastly, Te Puea stayed ever vigilant that no one would ever repeat the mistakes of her childhood. She tried abolishing smoking and drinking among her people, to moderate success. She was strict to the point of demanding, especially with her many adopted kids (she was never able to have any of her own). Nevertheless, she was widely mourned when she died, her funeral rites lasting a week. The media, calling her "the greatest Maori woman of our time," hailed her as "Princess" Te Puea—a title that was usually used by pakeha but never by Te Puea herself, who disliked it to the end.

# Moremi Ajasoro

## (12TH CENTURY, NIGERIA)

## *Spy Queen of the Yoruba*

The kingdom of Ife had a problem. Prosperous and green, its full storehouses had rapidly become the envy of its neighbors, the Igbo.* So the Igbo hatched a plan to steal from the Ife—unable to take on their neighbors by force, the Igbo instead dressed up as Egungun, messengers from the dead.

Now, you may be saying to yourself, *Oh, come on, who would actually fall for that sort of thing?* Well, imagine otherworldly heaps of cloth and color, with no discernible head, limbs, or human form. Look up pictures if you have the time (this book will still be here). Now picture hundreds of those running out of the forest at night, screaming and hitting people with sticks.

It's little surprise the Ife ran for the hills when the "Egungun" raided them.

After months and months of this, an Ife princess named Moremi Ajasoro began to ask questions. "Why do they need food if they're spirits? Where do they go?" Although it was utter heresy to confront the spirits, especially for a woman, Moremi insisted on staying put during the next raid.

True to form, the Igbo came again, and the Ife all ran away—save Moremi. The Igbo, impressed by her bravery and beauty, brought her back to their city, where she was married to their king. There she learned that they were just men in costumes made of tree fiber. She played the dutiful wife for many months, learning the Igbo ways. Finally, feeling that she had learned enough, she got the king drunk on palm wine and escaped.

The journey back to Ife was long and fraught with peril. She spent the nights up in trees, trying to avoid wild animals. After many days on foot, she made her way back, where she was reunited with her true husband, Oranmiyan. And they devised a plan.

When the Igbo came on their next raid, the Ife greeted them with torches, setting their (very flammable) costumes on fire. The Igbo were utterly unprepared and ran back into the forest. They never returned.

The story does end on a bittersweet note, however. Prior to initially confronting the Igbo, Moremi had asked the river god Esimirin for his favor to stop the raids. Once she and her

---

* These Igbo seemingly have no connection to the modern-day Igbo people of Africa. Some sources spell the modern-day tribe's name as "Ugbo."

tribe had driven off the Igbo for good, she proceeded to sacrifice all manner of animals to Esimirin, but nothing would satisfy the river god—save Moremi's son. So she dutifully offered him to Esimirin. However, instead of drowning in the river, the boy miraculously stood up, just as a great glowing vine rose up to the sky. He climbed up it and disappeared into the sky, now under the protection of the sky god Olorun.

## Was Moremi Real?

The story of Moremi comes from Yoruba oral tradition, and many of its figures—notably Moremi's husband Oranmiyan—are demonstrably real historical figures from around the 12th century. While certain aspects, notably the parts about the river god, are of course suspect, the base of the story is probably true. Oranmiyan was well regarded as a successful king, having conquered much land to expand Ife territory. It's likely that the Igbo people of the story were previous occupants, driven to the margins by an invading people.

In some versions of this story, the Igbo king Obalufon II is actually the rightful heir to Ife. In this version, he'd been driven out by the warlord Oranmiyan, and at the end of the story Moremi uses her political sway to get him back on the throne, marrying him in the process. This then ushers in a new era of peace.

Regardless, Moremi's story is widely celebrated to this day—many schools and institutions bear her name, and the annual Edi festival commemorates her story with a monthlong feast.

As a side note, the Yoruba fell on hard times in the 1800s, after a series of wars devastated their population and slavery scattered them across the globe. One of their main opponents in all of this? The kingdom of Dahomey, which you can read about in this book in the entry on **Agontime**.

# Sybil Ludington

## (1761–1839, UNITED STATES)

### The True Midnight Rider

uring some of the darkest days of the American Revolution, a courageous patriot risked life and limb to alert the rebels to the approaching British. This hero rode at breakneck speeds on a rain-slick night through dangerous territory, evading enemy soldiers and brigands to rouse the Americans against the menace at their doors.

Paul who? We're talking about Sybil Ludington, a 16-year-old girl.

Sybil was the daughter of Colonel Henry Ludington, local commander of the rebel troops in southeastern New York. Although she was young, she'd had lots of experience with danger. When a royalist named Ichobod Prosser sneaked up to her family's house with 50 men, intending to capture her father, Sybil enacted a plan straight out of a kid's movie. Lighting candles throughout the house, she ordered her siblings to march in front of the windows in military fashion, creating the impression of untold numbers of troops guarding the house. Prosser fled.

So when, months later, an exhausted messenger came to the Ludington house late at night with the news that the British had taken the nearby town of Danville, Sybil stepped up to serve. Since her father needed to stay put and organize the patriot army once they were summoned, and the weary messenger was unfamiliar with the area, Sybil was the only one able to locate and rouse the nearby patriots.

This was not an easy ride. Not only was the territory wooded and treacherous, but it was home to many bandits. Nevertheless, Sybil took off on her horse Star, armed with nothing but a stick. Sure enough, she was accosted by a "skinner," who tried knocking her off her horse. She fended him off with her stick and was on her way. She went on to ride around 40 miles over three hours.

By contrast, a certain other someone famous for a midnight ride only went 12 miles across well-worn streets and was caught by British loyalists at the end of it. Ahem.

In the end, Sybil's spirited yells spread the word far and wide. Come morning, Colonel Ludington had an army at his gate, ready to go.

Scream like a girl indeed.

# Kurmanjan Datka

(1811–1907, KYRGYZSTAN)

## The Tsarina Who Kept the Peace

**K**urmanjan's life didn't go as expected. The daughter of an ordinary shepherd in a Kyrgyz tribe, she was married off early in life to a man from a neighboring tribe. Had things gone as expected, she would have had some kids and lived an unremarkable life, and you would not be reading about her.

Instead, she ended up running an entire country and standing up to Russia. And it all started with her divorce.

At that time, divorce was about as well regarded a life choice for women as marrying a horse. When the recently married Kurmanjan reappeared at her father's house, having run away from her husband, Kurmanjan's father lost it. Exclaiming that she was possessed by the devil, he pulled in the local *datka* (general or governor), Alymbek, who happened to be passing by, to mediate. Kurmanjan was not about to give in, though.

"Is my husband of marriageable age?" she asked. "He was a grandfather when I was a child."

"Well," Alymbek replied, "it's Allah's will that you should marry."

"No, this is my father's will. He wanted 20 sheep and some silver, and he sold me for it. Allah would want me with someone my own age."

"Maybe your husband has a young soul. Don't judge a book by its cover."

"Why should I start a long journey on a limping horse?"

At this point, the village elders were losing their minds with rage. Alymbek, on the other hand, was laughing himself silly. To everyone's surprise, he granted the divorce—and soon thereafter married Kurmanjan himself.

She proved a great match for Alymbek, saving his life on multiple occasions. Alymbek was an ambitious man, hell-bent on uniting the 40-plus tribes of Kyrgyz peoples under one banner and finally driving out the Khans, who'd been ruling them for years. This regularly put the couple in danger to such an extent that Alymbek and Kurmanjan made a promise: if she sent her silver-handled horse whip to him, he would drop everything and head to her side, no questions asked.

So one day, while Alymbek was out scheming in the big city, he received her whip and rode back to her side—only to find her just hanging out, saying that she missed him. As she cooked him dinner she said that she'd overheard that some men were aiming to assassinate him. He responded with some old-timey misogyny: "It is not for nothing that people say a woman's mind is shorter than her hair. I respect you as a mistress, but could a sheep teach a mountain goat to leap through the air? It is better for you to do housework. The female eagle should watch a nest, the male should fly in the sky. I am going [back to the city] in the morning!"

He then passed out. Because she'd drugged his tea.

She proceeded to wrap his comatose body in a tarp, toss him in a cart, and sneak past the legions of assailants now looking for him. The following day he awoke in a yurt outside of town, assuming he'd had too much to drink the previous night. She kept him there several more days, using a combination of flattery, guilt trips ("it's our anniversary!"), and flat-out bribery ("I have a great gift for you, but you can only get it tomorrow!").

After several days, one of Alymbek's servants arrived to inform him of the attempt on his life—and how it'd been thwarted by his wife. Kurmanjan explained that in handling all the tribe's trade deals, she'd secretly assembled a massive spy network—which informed her of an imminent attack on her pigheaded husband. Because Kurmanjan was rad like that.

Aghast, he exclaimed, "You saved my life!"

"I promised you a great gift, didn't I?"

Eventually, despite Kurmanjan's best efforts, Alymbek was assassinated. Immediately thereafter, in a surprise move, the Khans, who'd subjugated the Kyrgyz tribes, summoned her to appear before them—to interview her to be his replacement as Datka. The conservative Khan leaders were somewhat shocked by what they saw.

"Are you actually Muslim?" they asked. "You wear no veil."

"Veils are for covering shameful things. Does my face look shameful?"

She got the job.

The Khans installed Kurmanjan mostly because they thought a female ruler would keep things peaceful. They were wrong.

In short order, she consolidated various Kyrgyz tribes in opposition to the Khans, working both political and military angles. While her troops staged mountain pass ambushes on the Khans, she skillfully used her double life as a politician to block new taxes. Simultaneously, a petition quietly snaked its way to Russia, asking for the Kyrgyz to be accepted as Russian citizens, which would free them from the Khans. Kurmanjan was playing many games at once.

Eventually the Khans fell apart, and the Russians began annexing the area. While some Kyrgyz started fighting Russia, afraid that they'd be subsumed into Russia, Kurmanjan didn't. Seeing the Russians' immense technical advantage—they were in tanks while her people rode horses and hurled wooden spears—she sued for peace. It was primarily through her negotiations that the seeds were laid for modern-day Kyrgyzstan—a nation culturally and politically independent from Russia today.

It wasn't easy. Many Kyrgyz continued to bristle at Russian interference and being treated as second-class citizens—few more than Kurmanjan's son. After killing a border guard, her son was sentenced to death, a penalty that outraged many Kyrgyz. For a second, it looked like the fragile Russian alliance was about to fall apart.

Kurmanjan, now an older woman, traveled to her son's scheduled execution. But instead of calling for action against the Russians, she stood stoically by to watch the proceedings—only to see the hangmen bungle the job.

Seeing the noose slip off his neck, she yelled to her son to put the rope around his neck and show them how it was done. He did. And thus died like a gangsta.

Kurmanjan eventually died of old age, a rare feat for a military commander. After her death, Kyrgyzstan achieved independence and commemorated it by building a Kurmanjan museum, putting her face on its currency and stamps, and, in 2014, producing her own live-action movie—the biggest-budget production in Kyrgyzstan's history.

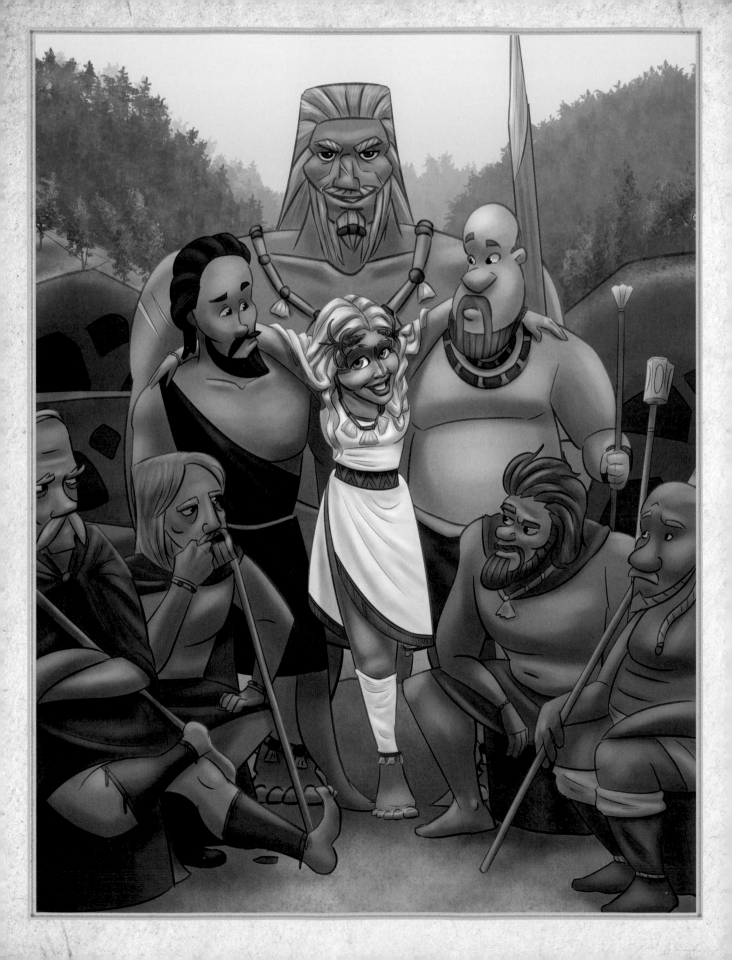

# Andamana

## The Lady Who Laid Down the Law

dmit it: somewhere, deep in your heart of hearts, you regret not knowing more about the indigenous people of the Canary Islands. Maybe you always meant to spend an afternoon online learning about the Canarios*' early legal system. Perhaps you thought about googling the greatest queen of these little-known people living off the northwest coast of Africa. But you didn't. And you have to live with that, day in and day out. Knowing full well that your every friend secretly holds you in utter contempt for your disgusting cultural illiteracy.

But it's okay. Your long nightmare of shameful ignorance is soon to end.

In the 1300s, the Canarios were a fractured bunch. Living an isolated Stone Age existence, they were messily divided into villages that traded and bickered with each other in equal measure. Part of the reason for this friction was that laws were different from village to village and even case to case.

Punishments, fees, and the like were decided ad hoc by wildly inconsistent magistrates. It was, as you might imagine, a suboptimal system of government.

Well, one woman got fed up and took matters into her own hands. Andamana, a wise lady living on Gran Canaria Island, started dispensing advice and settling disputes, just like the judges, but with one major difference: she didn't charge for her services. She quickly grew so popular that her village chief called a council meeting to discuss her power grab—only to have her crash the meeting herself, insult them, and dare them to point out a single time she'd been wrong. They couldn't.

From there, Andamana got more ambitious. She established a set of consistent laws that punished bribes and eliminated personal interpretation on the part of officials. Although these laws were a hit in her village, she soon learned other villages were not as enthusiastic when she began receiving the decapitated heads of her messengers in reply to her suggestions.

This didn't stymie Andamana. She next approached Gumidafé, the island's fiercest warrior, with an offer: her hand in marriage in exchange for his help in laying down the law. He

---

\* They are often also called the Guanche people, although that designation technically only applies to one of the islands. But it's a useful term to know if you want to look up more information to combat your inexcusable Canarian ignorance.

jumped at the opportunity, and their combined forces began sweeping across Gran Canaria in a torrent of justice and legality. Also butt-kicking. But mostly justice.

Her reign as the first queen of a united Gran Canaria was long and strife-free. Her descendants continued independent rule until the 1400s, when the Spanish came a-conquerin'. The Canarios didn't go gently, though—they held off both the French and the Spanish for many years, thwarting numerous conquest attempts with a great combination of brawns, brains, and badass rulers.

## · ART NOTES AND TRIVIA ·

The Canarios were said to be pretty enormous. Some European accounts describe men who were 9 and 14 feet tall, although math was likely not a key competency for the authors of said accounts. An anecdote survives about a Canario wrestler who dared a Spaniard to make him spill a single drop of wine as he slowly raised a glass to his lips. The Spaniard proceeded to fail hard.

While outwardly similar to Europeans, the Canarios were actually most genetically similar to the Tuareg people of northern Africa (see the entry on **Tin Hinan**)—even though they have relatively light skin and blond hair! Anthropologists currently think they sailed to the Canaries or were dropped off by some other seafaring people and then, for reasons unknown, seemingly forgot how to make boats. Truly, we live in a world of mystery.

The sitting council member with the finger in his mouth is practicing the traditional whistling language of the Canarios. Their original language has died out, but their whistle-based communication was adapted to work with the language of their foreign invaders. It continues to this day in the form of Silbo Gomero, the world's strangest form of Spanish communication.

Although the clothing of the Canarios was pretty simple, they would occasionally decorate themselves with flowers and the like (as seen in Andamana's hair). The flowers in the illustration are, of course, indigenous to the Canary Islands.

They primarily lived in caves like the ones visible in the background.

# Mary Seacole

# and Florence Nightingale

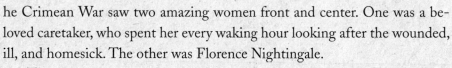

## The Odd Couple of Crimean Nursing

he Crimean War saw two amazing women front and center. One was a be-loved caretaker, who spent her every waking hour looking after the wounded, ill, and homesick. The other was Florence Nightingale.

These two mothers of modern nursing, despite their limited interaction in life, make a classic odd couple: Florence Nightingale was a buttoned-up, by-the-book Victorian who put her stock in measurements and results, whereas Mary Seacole was a loud, cheery Jamaican who swore by folk remedies and the occasional swig of liquor.

Mary started life in the hustle and bustle of Kingston, Jamaica. With her interest in medicine piqued by her mother, Mary would practice a blend of folk and Western remedies on cats, dogs, and dolls as a child. Her sunny disposition and quick wit were to be her defining traits. Famously, when at a banquet she was given a backhanded compliment on her fine character-istics despite her race,* she replied, "Seeing how all you white people act, I'm glad I'm not!"

Florence, by contrast, was born into upper-class British society and was expected to be-come a wife and mother. She loudly bucked this expectation† by announcing that she was instead pursuing nursing—a plan that, to her family, was roughly equivalent to joining the circus.

Mary spent her early years as a traveling businesswoman, but then changed course to nursing when she met her lifelong nemesis: cholera. In her writings, she referred to cholera in personal terms, describing her efforts at calling its bluff and physically fighting it. It ravaged many of the places where she lived and eventually frustrated her so much that she broke one of the greatest social taboos in her fight against it. After a one-year-old died of cholera, she bribed a gravedigger to let her examine the child's body to try to learn more about the disease.

---

* Mary's racial identity, as with so much else about her, doesn't fit neatly into a box. While many in modern times refer to her as black, she referred to herself as yellow, as did many others. She was Creole and possibly had a white father. While she did suffer from the racism that suffused the times (most overtly from Americans), she considered herself British above all else.

† How loud? Breaking-off-a-nine-year-courtship-just-because-it-would-interfere-with-her-nursing-career loud.

Meanwhile, to hear Florence describe her profession, God Herself had prescribed her calling. After some travels abroad, Florence had felt more strongly than ever that she needed to help people. She took a job at the Institute for the Care of Sick Gentlewomen, but it was just a prelude to her achievements in the Crimean War.

The Crimean War, a conflict that basically consisted of world powers picking over the bones of the Ottoman Empire, was a dirty affair. Conditions on the ground were so filthy that disease proved deadlier than the war itself. Once reports of this situation made it back to England, an entire generation of women were inspired to head to Crimea and offer help—including Mary and Florence.

Florence was first on the ground and instantly improved conditions. Within a year, she had helped bring down the death rate from 42 percent to 2 percent by improving procedures and petitioning the local sanitary commission to actually do its job. None of this was easy—during much of her time there she slept in a crowded room with 14 other people. Her wanderings at night among the wounded by lamplight would earn her the title "Lady of the Lamp." By all accounts, she nearly killed herself from overwork.

Mary had a harder time getting to Crimea. She described cheerily "laying siege" to the British secretary of war with the aim of joining the nurse corps, but was ultimately unsuccessful. Why, exactly, is lost to time, but given that she was old, eccentric, and black (characteristics that disqualified other applicants), it's not a stretch to imagine these were the reasons. Undeterred, she decided to open a British hotel in Crimea, near the war front.

It was here that Mary met, and came into conflict with, Florence. Mary aimed to dispense comfort above medical care, providing nutritious meals, free tea, and a comfortable, homey atmosphere. She charged for virtually everything she provided, which included alcohol—a substance that the temperate Florence abhorred. As one might imagine, her provisions, combined with her sunny disposition, made Mary quite popular among the soldiers. Florence, on the other hand, grew to dislike Mary so much that she started describing her hotel in terms reserved for brothels.

Florence's characterization of Mary is unfair—far from merely being a purveyor of entertainment, Mary put herself in danger on a terrifyingly regular basis. She would run into combat zones, delivering sustenance while literally dodging bombs. When an ammo supply exploded, injuring many soldiers, Mary's first instinct was to run directly into the melee.

Although she possessed a generally good business sense, in the end Mary's oversympathetic heart betrayed her. On top of dealing with constant theft, she went into severe debt from liberally taking IOUs from her "boys"—army officers who would leave without repaying her at the end of the war. Without the backing of any larger agencies or wealthy benefactors (of which, it must be said, Florence had both), Mary went bankrupt.

Florence flourished after the war. She used her prominent role in Crimea as a springboard to establishing nursing as a respected profession and solidifying modern ideas of hygiene. So next time you wash your hands after going to the bathroom, or talk to a nurse who says you should do so more often, thank Florence.

Mary met her postwar financial straits with characteristic cheeriness. When asked in a court proceeding on her debt what class of debtor certificates she possessed, she quipped, "First, to be sure! Am I not a first-class woman?"

Eventually Mary's financial situation did stabilize, although in fits and starts. She wrote a successful autobiography—the first by a British black woman, making her arguably the most famous black woman of the Victorian age—but its sales were ruined by the outbreak of the Indian War of Independence.[*] During this war, as well as the later Franco-Prussian War,[†] Mary once again attempted to lend her nursing services, but she was hindered by Florence in both cases.

In an appropriately titled letter labeled "Burn," Florence wrote to a member of Parliament that anyone who would employ Mary would enjoy "much kindness—also much drunkenness & improper conduct, wherever she is." Unsurprisingly, Mary didn't get the job.

Therein lies the root of the modern take on the relationships between Mary Seacole and Florence Nightingale as being one of conflict. When Mary's story was introduced into British textbooks, many viewed it as taking away from Florence's story—which, really, it shouldn't. Is the world so small that it can't accommodate the story of a pioneering iconoclast nurse and an enterprising caretaker? While they clearly didn't get along in their lifetimes,[‡] the traditions they represent do not have to forever be at odds.

---

[*] A conflict largely fueled by the actions of **Rani Lakshmibai**, also featured in this book.

[†] If Mary had gone to the Franco-Prussian front, she very well might have met future archaeologist and French fashion icon **Jane Dieulafoy**, also featured in this book.

[‡] Florence even spread the rumor that Mary had an illegitimate child named Sally, although there's scant evidence of that and Mary never mentioned Sally in her writing.

# Gráinne "Grace O'Malley" Ní Mháille

(1530–1603, IRELAND)

## The Pirate Queen of Ireland

There has never been anyone else like Grace O'Malley in the history of Ireland. An honest-to-God combination of queen and pirate, she spent most of her life performing, in her words, "maintenance by land and sea." Basically, she impounded ships, extorted money, burned down castles, and generally ran the Irish waters for decades.

Known in her native Ireland as Granuaile, Gráinne Mhaol, and a terrifying variety of increasingly confusingly spelled names, she was born into one of Ireland's only seafaring clans, the O'Malleys. She took quickly to the water, despite her father's protests. As the legend goes, when her dad told her that her long hair was unsuitable for work on a boat, she showed up with a shaved head—earning her the nickname Gráinne Mhaol, or "Grace the Bald." From there, she just kept racking up additions to her legend:

- When her first husband was killed in battle, the invaders went on to pillage his castle, where she was staying. She greeted them in traditional Irish fashion, by stripping off the lead roof, melting it, and pouring it on their heads until they rather sensibly buggered off.

- After a nearby clan killed a close confidant (and possible lover) of hers, Granuaile waited until the clan went on pilgrimage. Ever the holy woman, she then swooped in, killed every last one of them, sailed to their ancestral home, and seized it.

- When the Earl of Howth refused to give her lodging (as he was supposed to, since she was a fellow clan leader), she kidnapped his grandson. She turned down all ransom offers until the earl finally relented and offered her lodging.

- She eventually remarried, to a man she chose for politics as opposed to love. At the end of the first "trial year" of the marriage, she locked him out of his own castle and took it for herself. (They later reconciled.)

MATURITY 1

- According to legend, she ran a cable from the mast of her main ship through a castle window and tied the other end to her bedpost. That way she would know if someone was making off with her boat.

- When she gave birth to her son Toby, it was while sailing one of her (squalid, unsanitary) pirate ships—hence her son's nickname, "Toby of Ships." The very next day her ship was attacked by Algerian pirates. She put down her baby, jumped out of bed, grabbed a musket, and joined her men in the battle.

- Granuaile was jailed by British authorities for two years. Once she left prison, she was immediately assaulted by a small army of sailors seeking revenge for earlier clashes with her. She overpowered them all and sailed off.

That last point, her clash with England, was a harbinger of the main conflict of her life. Ireland at the time was a divided collection of 60 squabbling countries, a fact the English were quick to exploit. By playing the tribes off one another, slowly the English began to establish their own power base. In response, Granuaile and her husband united a huge number of clans under one banner and resisted the English. Contemporary documents describe her as "nurse to all rebellions in the province for this forty years."

The back-and-forth between her and the English governor Richard Bingham became increasingly brutal. Bingham orchestrated her second husband's death. She killed two dozen of his soldiers and burned down a number of castles. He burned her lands, killed her cattle, and got one of her own sons to turn on her. She took to the sea and started living as a nomadic exile. The final straw came when Bingham discovered her extensive network of secret ports and impounded most of her fleet.

At this point, when Granuaile was in her sixties and living on the lam, she concocted an amazing plan: she sidestepped Bingham and met with his boss, Queen Elizabeth. The meeting between the two elderly queens is, in itself, the stuff of legend. When Elizabeth offered the barefoot Irish pirate queen a silk handkerchief, she is said to have used it and then thrown it into a fire. Noting the horrified faces of the English court, O'Malley remarked that in Ireland they did not carry dirty things around with them.

The meeting got Granuaile everything she wanted: orders for Bingham to leave her alone, official dispensation for her to run Irish waters, lower taxes, and—as a special treat—the privilege of delivering the news to Bingham personally. And so, at 65 years old, Granuaile began pirating again, and she continued to do so until her death.

## · ART NOTES AND TRIVIA ·

The baby at Granuaile's side is using a handkerchief as a bib—a reference to both young Toby's tender age and his mother's general disrespect for Queen Elizabeth's finery.

The cliffs in the background are modeled after Ireland's famous Cliffs of Moher, which Granuaile actually held in her dominion. They may be more familiar to some movie-watchers as the Cliffs of Insanity from *The Princess Bride*.

Granuaile is seen here wearing a dress, despite its general impracticality on a seafaring vessel, because it was likely what she actually did wear. Not just because it was proper for a queen, but because even the men of the time wore similar outfits (i.e., kilts).

The practice of a "trial year" for a marriage was not uncommon in olden Ireland, nor was divorce. At the end of the trial marriage, it was traditional for women to get back some of the dowry they'd brought into the arrangement. This was precisely the main reason why Granuaile took her second husband's castle for herself—since it was her second marriage, she was not allowed a return on her dowry, so she took one for herself.

# "Stagecoach" Mary Fields

### (1832–1914, UNITED STATES)

## The Baddest Postal Worker
## in the Wild West

"Stagecoach" Mary Fields was not anyone's first choice for a babysitter.

At six foot two inches and in her fifties, Mary Fields was famous across Montana for many things—smoking cigars, getting into bar brawls, fighting off wolves to deliver the mail, habitually packing a pistol under her apron, and having a specially granted legal exemption allowing her to drink in saloons—but raising kids? Not so much.

Which is really quite unfair. She loved children, and they loved her back. Even before she started offering her services as a babysitter for $1.50 a day, she had a long history of working with children. Both in her early life as a slave and her post-emancipation life as a free woman, she worked with nuns, helping with household chores and looking after little ones. Whenever she celebrated her birthday—twice a year, since she didn't know the date—the town of Cascade, Montana, would shut down the schools so she could treat the local kids to a party.

But to many adults and even some children, Mary was no more than her roughest edges. Echoing the more pointed public sentiment on her, one child wrote in an essay that she "drinks whiskey, and she swears, and she is a republican, which makes her a low, foul creature."*

All of which was true, save the foul creature bit. While Mary was a warm and loving person, she also liked to get her drink on and wasn't about to take lip from anyone. For example, she worked at the local mission for over ten years,† during much of which time she served as the foreman for its construction efforts. Some construction workers didn't take well to working for a woman—so Mary quickly resolved the situation by punching the dissenters in the teeth. This rancor escalated until she was fired. According to legend, the bishop had to let her go after finding bullet holes in his laundry from one of her construction worker duels.

Once she left the mission, she tried several other jobs. She tried emphasizing her kinder nature by setting up a restaurant. Unfortunately, it went under within a year, because she'd serve meals to anyone, even those unable to pay.

---

\* It is lost to time as to what grade the kid got on said essay.

† And got paid for none of it. Booooooo.

After the restaurant, she became a postal carrier, one of the first women in the nation to do so. This was an utterly terrifying job. The temperature in Montana could dip to 45 below zero, and snowstorms would force Mary to leave her coach stranded in the snow, heft the mailbags over her shoulder, and walk upwards of 10 miles to town. On one occasion, a blizzard overtook her and she had to walk back and forth all night to keep from freezing to death. On another, she was attacked by a pack of wolves and her vehicle was knocked over—so she stayed up all night, fighting them off. But she never missed a delivery in her eight years on the job.

And this was while she was in her sixties, mind you.

In her seventies, Mary's life quieted down some, but not much, when she retired from postal work and started a laundromat. Still essentially kind, she spent much of her time growing bouquets of flowers for the Cascade baseball team, giving them to players who made home runs—but she'd also slug anyone who had a bad word to say about the hometown team. When a laundromat customer neglected to pay his $2 bill, she, by now a senior citizen, knocked him flat with one punch and declared his laundry bill paid.

Years after her death, Mary Fields was eulogized by fellow Montana resident Gary Cooper, one of the biggest movie stars of the time, with a glowing biography reprinted across a number of magazines. In it, he described her, quite accurately, as "one of the freest souls to ever draw a breath, or a .38."

## · ART NOTES ·

Mary's regular uniform, as depicted here, was all men's clothing, save an apron and a skirt.

In the background, you can see a heap of dead wolves around a knocked-over stage-coach, as well as the laundromat customer, flat on his butt.

The chicken is a callback to her time with the nuns. During that period, she was in charge of 400 chickens. One day, she found that a skunk had killed 62 of her brood, so she in turn killed it with a hoe and carried it to the mission, a mile away. When the bishop asked, "Did the skunk spray you?" Mary replied, "Oh no, Father, I attacked and killed him from the front, not the rear."

# Yennenga

## (EARLY 12TH CENTURY, BURKINA FASO/GHANA)

## *The Warrior Who Just Wanted to Have Kids*

nce upon a time, there was a princess of the Dagomba named Yennenga.* Her father, the king, was utterly delighted with her—and why wouldn't he be? She was a powerful warrior and a skilled leader of the royal guards, so brave she was described as a lioness "with stubborn chin and flowing mane."† She made his granaries and treasuries overflow with the goods brought back from her raids. She was so beautiful that praise singers compared her to an "open parasol" and a "gingerbread palm." She was so perfect, in fact, that he could not find a single man worthy of her: each suitor who came by, he decided, was too fat, or too thin, or too smart, or too dumb, or . . . you get the idea.

But Yennenga was a teenager. And what do teenagers do? They rebel.

Yennenga's rebellion took an unusual form: a huge field of okra. After planting the vegetables, she let them go bad, untended in the open. She then brought her father to the rotting field of produce and said, "This is what you're doing to me. I just want to settle down and marry, just want to hear a child laugh. But I'm withering on the vine." Her father listened closely, taking her viewpoint under careful consideration, and then did what fathers since time immemorial have done with rebellious teens: locked her in her room.

Shortly thereafter, Yennenga fled on horseback, dressed as a man. After riding for weeks, she came across a solitary elephant hunter named Riale, who, thinking her a man, welcomed her into his hut. They sat up for days, talking like fellow elephant-hunting bros. However, her disguise didn't hold up forever, and once the truth was revealed, Riale let her in on a secret of his own: he too was runaway royalty. His father, king of the Mande, had been killed by Riale's brother in a coup. Rather than take on the odorous task of killing his own brother, Riale had run away to live in exile.

Shortly thereafter, the two fell in love—after all, how could Yennenga have resisted a

---

\* Her full title was Yennenga the Svelte, which doesn't quite have the same ring to it.

† In her honor, as the story goes, the Mossi people—the tribe her son starts at the end of the story—refuse to attack lions.

guy who hunted elephants with nothing but javelins and arrows? They named their son Ouedraogo ("Stallion"), after the flight his mother had taken from her homeland.

When Ouedraogo turned 17, Yennenga decided that he should meet her father—his grandfather—so that he might have a connection to his ancestors. In spite of the 20 years that had passed, Yennenga was scared that her father might still be angry at her . . . or worse yet, not remember her! But when they saw each other, it was like no time at all had passed, and her father welcomed her back with open arms.

Ouedraogo learned much from his grandfather, who taught him "a thousand and three things." The first thousand things, every ruler knows. Part of the standard ruler introductory kit. The last three, though? To see beauty in the world and say it is ugly; to get up in the morning and do what you cannot do; and to give free rein to your dreams, because those who dream too much become victims of their dreams.

Ouedraogo founded the first Mossi kingdom in what is modern-day Burkina Faso, and his sons started many more tribes—all of which recognize Yennenga as their common ancestor. To this day, both Ouedraogo and Yennenga are common names in Burkina Faso, and a great many streets and buildings are named after Yennenga herself.

# Annie Jump Cannon

## (1863–1941, UNITED STATES)

## The Astronomer Who Heard the Stars Calling

nnie Jump Cannon's middle-class Victorian-era biography could have easily gone something like this:

- Mom teaches her piano.

- She gets a high school education.

- Marries some dude.

- Babies *everywhere*.

- The end!

But thankfully for the field of astronomy (and humanity at large), Annie led a less conventional life:

- Mom says "screw piano" and sneaks Annie up to the attic to stargaze. By her teens, Annie has memorized a working map of the night sky.

- Seeing how much she likes school, her parents send her to college (!).

- When some beaus come callin', Annie nopes off to study astronomy in grad school.

- Stars *everywhere*.

- The beginning!

Annie's story begins in earnest around age 33, when she became a Harvard Computer. The Harvard Computers were an all-female team of astronomy analysts who worked for Edward Pickering in the early 1900s. As the story goes, Pickering, as head of the Harvard Observatory, became so fed up with a (male) grad student's incompetence that he hired his maid to prove that even she could do better—only to find out that she was a bona fide genius. After that, he hired only women, reasoning that they were better at detailed work.

At the time, though, they were largely referred to as "Pickering's Harem." Sigh. Early 1900s academics, you suck.

Annie quickly became a phenomenal astronomer. Tasked with classifying stars based on a huge catalog of astronomic spectography, Annie quickly realized that the classification system they were using was woefully inadequate—so she made her own. Whereas previously all stars had been lumped into categories of A, B, and C, she came up with the classification system of O, B, A, F, G, K, M, R, N, S,* which has been remembered for years now with the mnemonic of "Oh, be a fine girl, kiss me right now, sweet." By 1910, Annie's system had become the de facto standard, and with minor modifications, it remains so to this day.

Annie became scarily good at her job. At the peak of her career, she could classify three stars per minute, which led to her cataloging upwards of 350,000 over her lifetime. For reference's sake, Williamina Fleming, the aforementioned bona fide genius, cataloged only 10,000. Not only was she fast, but Annie remembered all of her work. When offhandedly asked for a photo of a specific star, she instantly knew, out of tens of thousands of plates, the exact one to pick up (Plate I 37311).

As her career expanded, Annie became involved in the women's suffrage movement and served as an ambassador for professional women everywhere. She gave talks at the World's Fair in Chicago and fought tooth and nail against the stereotype of female astronomers as just astrologers and horoscope readers. She never retired and kept working—seven days a week, mostly for the criminally low rate of 25 cents an hour—until she was 76, at which point heart disease took her life.

Part of the reason for Annie's amazing astronomical skills was that she was almost totally deaf. A nasty bout of scarlet fever permanently damaged her hearing in college, but she used this to her advantage. The relative silence, she'd later say, allowed her to concentrate more fully on her work. While some biographers claim her hearing loss had a negative effect on her social life,† any effects were only temporary. In later years, with the help of a powerful hearing aid, she held regular dinner parties at her house, an utterly charming villa she dubbed the Star Cottage.

Near the end of her life, with World War II on the horizon, Annie summed up her worldview in one of her last interviews: "In these days of great trouble and unrest, it is good to have something outside our own planet, something fine and distant and comforting to troubled minds. Let people look to the stars for comfort."

---

* All of which differentiates stars based on the spectrum of emissions they provide—from which we can tell how hot they are, their composition, and the like.

† One, Nancy Veglahn, presumes that Annie's deafness was a big factor as to why she never married—because it happened just as she was hitting a marriageable age. She was nevertheless considered pretty and popular, so how much of an effect it had seems to be up for debate.

## · ART NOTES ·

The scene here is a bit of a mishmash of Annie's life. The observatory is based off a Peruvian one she worked with, producing some of her most important work (although she never visited), but the telescope is from later in her career. The women in the background didn't do their work at the observatory, and almost certainly didn't work by lamplight, but they did illuminate much that was unknown to humanity.

Speaking of the Harvard Computers, some notable ones include:

· Williamina Fleming (standing with book): Pickering's ex-maid and leader of the Computers. Deserted by a crappy husband, she devised the first star classification system and cataloged around 10,000 stars.

· Henrietta Swan Leavitt (seated at the end of the table on the right): Also a deaf astronomer! She devised a method for calculating the distance to very faraway galaxies, and Edwin Hubble himself said she deserved a Nobel Prize for her work.

· Antonia Maury (seated, getting poked by Williamina): Had a big disagreement with Pickering over classification systems and ended up leaving the Computers. Hence she's got kind of a snarky look at Williamina's comments.

· Pickering himself is holding the ladder for Annie.

# Wilma Rudolph

(1940–1994, UNITED STATES)

## The Olympic Runner Who Beat Polio

 f anyone ever had the cards stacked against them, it was Wilma Rudolph. Born in the segregated southern United States, Wilma was the 20th of her father's 22 children. With her parents' annual income never topping $2,500, she lived in utter poverty her entire childhood. She made dresses out of cloth sacks, used candles and outhouses in place of electric lights and plumbing, and had to take a Greyhound bus—where she was forced to sit in the back—50 miles to the nearest hospital.

It was a trip she had to take often. Before the age of seven, she had contracted scarlet fever, measles, mumps, whooping cough, pneumonia (twice), and, worst of all, polio. The disease took away her ability to walk, forced her to miss her entire kindergarten year and much of first grade, left her in leg braces until the age of 11, and instilled in her deep seated feelings of inadequacy.

Consider how unlikely it was, then, that by the age of 20 this little girl would become a three-time Olympic gold medal winner. After becoming an unwed teen mother.

But it happened.

For all the setbacks life handed her, Wilma had one key strength: her family. After Wilma's disabling bout with polio, her family took turns massaging her legs until she could walk again. When she started running competitively, they cheered her on—and gradually she became so good that scouts took notice. When she became pregnant (the father, her high school sweetheart, initially took no responsibility), the family kept it secret, and her sister Yvonne would raise the baby so that Wilma could focus on her athletics.

Wilma competed in both the Melbourne (1956) and Rome (1960) Olympics. Prior to Melbourne, she didn't even know what the Olympics were. She'd never been on an airplane, let alone traveled out of the country. Although she didn't take home any gold medals, she did return with a fervent desire to win. Four years later, win she did—taking gold for the 100-meter dash, 200-meter dash, and 4-by-100-meter relay.

The reaction to her victories was overwhelming. Not only was Wilma the first American woman to ever win three gold medals in track and field, but she'd also beaten the Russians at the height of the Cold War—establishing herself as one of the first famous black female athletes in the world. She met President John F. Kennedy, Vice President Lyndon B. Johnson, and the pope; starred in newsreels sent around the country; and even appeared on Ed Sullivan's variety show. There was also a TV movie of her life story starring Cicely Tyson and a young Denzel Washington.

Wilma quickly used her newfound fame for good. When her hometown of Clarksville, Tennessee, put on a parade for her return, she made her attendance contingent on the parade being integrated. This condition put her in direct conflict with the governor, who'd run on a strict segregationist platform—but in the end Wilma prevailed.

It was not all celebration thereafter, though. Wilma's track and field teammates, feeling slighted, eventually turned on her. Before one banquet, they hid her hair care products, so she had to appear without her hair done. Later they intentionally threw a relay match in Britain, running slower than they could—only to see Wilma pour on the speed in the last leg and narrowly eke out a win. Gradually, feeling that her peers saw her as a rival or a threat, she retired from running, reunited with her high school sweetheart, and settled down.

Her post-Olympics life was one of setbacks and disappointment. She'd won her medals in the era before sponsorships for athletes, and without a lot of knowledge of the world of entertainment and agents, Wilma had no idea how to parlay her victories into other opportunities. She moved her family around often and worked a series of menial jobs. Moreover, her fame proved only temporary insulation against racism: a white man spit on her children the same day Martin Luther King Jr. was shot.

Nevertheless, she stayed strong. In her autobiography, she never shared her failures, only her successes. Even as she struggled toward the end of her life—after divorcing her husband because he wanted a "traditional" subservient woman, she would face poverty once again—she never complained. She kept striving, all the way to the end.

Wilma Rudolph died of brain cancer at age 54, happy with her life of ups and downs. "The triumph can't be had without the struggle," she said. "And I know what struggle is."

## · ART NOTES ·

The image is, left to right, a timeline of Wilma Rudolph's life—escaping the polio leg braces, leaving her newborn child with her sister, winning the Olympics, and becoming a worldwide star.

# Alfhild

## (5TH CENTURY, DENMARK)

### The Viking Who Became a Pirate

Our story begins in typical Rapunzellian fashion: the beautiful princess Alfhild, chaste to the point of covering her face so as not to incite lust, was living locked away from the rest of the world.

Guarding her from gentleman callers were a viper, a snake, and several hundred guards. Get through, the rules went, and she'd be yours. Fail, and your noggin would be repurposed as a furnishing no Viking home could do without: heads on pikes.

Enter the son of King Sigar: Alf, hunky fella and dashing hero type. Wearing bloodstained hides to whip Alfhild's reptilian sentinels into a frenzy, he quickly dispatched the snakey duo with a red-hot poker and a spear. After all, everyone knows the surest way to a maiden's heart is by sneaking past her guards, breaking into her room unannounced, and brutally slaughtering her childhood pets before her eyes.

To his credit, Alfhild's dad didn't give her away just like that. In a display of paternal virtue rare for the time, he let her choose if she wanted to marry the first man to successfully run the gauntlet of doom. After consulting with her mom (who warned her against letting Alf's good looks influence her decision), Alfhild chose option C: donning men's clothing, running away from home, and becoming a pirate.

For the next several years, Alfhild led an all-female band of pirates, looting and plundering (as any virginal and chaste shieldmaiden would). She became such a nuisance that several Danish expeditions were launched to stop her, but none returned. So great was her renown that, upon meeting her, a newly captainless crew of sailors quickly accepted her as their new leader.

By the time Alf caught back up with Alfhild (he'd been stalking her all this time), her fleet had grown much larger than his. Undeterred (and not wanting to seem like a coward around women), Alf boarded her ship and began wantonly stabbing people. It was only after Alfhild's helmet was knocked off that he realized the terrifying warrior in front of him was, in fact, the object of his obsession. He wrapped his arms around her and the battle was over.

The rest of the story goes in a manner typical for its sexist historian scribe Saxo Grammaticus. According to Saxo, Alf and Alfhild marry, she starts wearing women's clothing again, they have a kid, and Alfhild is never heard from again.

But just because they were not recorded does not mean she didn't go on to have other adventures.

# Calafia

## (16TH-CENTURY SPANISH MYTH)

### *Griffin-Riding Muslim Queen of California*

op quiz! California was named after:

A. John Gideon California, a 15th-century pilgrim who founded an orphanage for gay socialist orphans.
B. A Native American word meaning "unaffordable rent."
C. A griffin-riding Muslim warrior queen from an island of black Amazons.

The correct answer is C. Meet Calafia, queen of California.

Calafia is introduced at the tail end of *The Labors of the Very Brave Knight Esplandián*, an adventure novel that was the *Harry Potter and the Chamber of Secrets* of 1500s Spain. In it, the titular Esplandián, a capital-C Christian warrior, ventures across the world in a fire-breathing serpent/boat, fighting the pagan (read: Muslim) menace. This leads to a climactic battle at Constantinople that draws out all the greatest warriors of the Muslim world—including Calafia.

Calafia was from the island of California, a gold-rich nation described as being somewhere near the Indies.* The cave-dwelling inhabitants of California were women warriors who raised the island's native griffins (mythical bird/beast hybrids described as depicted in the art, purple dots and all) to both carry them into battle and kill and eat any man in sight. Virtually the only male Californians were ones kidnapped from nearby islands and held in slavery. The Amazons killed most of the male children shortly after birth.

The author of this novel was not, shall we say, a stickler for historical accuracy.

Calafia arrives late in the story, crushing the entrenched Christian defenders of Constantinople by having her aerial forces gift them with impromptu skydiving lessons. This quickly turns into a comedy of errors once the Muslim ground troops subsequently charge the walls, only to also be murdered by the man-eating griffins (who are more anti–Y chromosome than anti-Christianity).

Calafia sheepishly stops making it rain men and proposes that the war be settled with one-on-one fights between the leaders of both sides.

---

* This is the source of modern California's name—people kept searching for this mythical golden land. Even the name ties into the Islamic roots (*Caliph*-ornia, get it?).

## CALAFIA

From there, the story dissolves into godawful fan fiction. Calafia's messenger returns, going on at nauseating length about Esplandián's stunning good looks, which leads Calafia to meet him in person so she can go on about it herself. Calafia acquits herself fairly well in one-on-one combat but is defeated. Then she sits around waiting for Esplandián to marry her. When he doesn't, she marries his uncle, converts to Christianity, and happily goes off to conquer more islands around California. The story ends by saying that to list her continued exploits would make for a never-ending story.

Seems to this author that perhaps it's time someone continued chronicling those exploits.

# Keumalahayati

## (16TH–17TH CENTURY, INDONESIA)

### The Widow Admiral of Indonesia

By the time the sultan of Aceh came asking her to lead his navy, Keumala-hayati* was ready. The descendant of the first sultan of Aceh and the daughter of a line of naval admirals, Keumalahayati had already long been working in the sultan's armed forces. After her soldier husband had been killed by the Portuguese, she'd banded together all her fellow war widows and started the Inong Balee: the "Widow's Army." They operated out of their own superhero headquarters fortress (the "Widow's Fort") and fought the Portuguese at every opportunity.

But now that Keumalahayati was being given command of the naval fleet, it was time for the first female naval admiral in the modern world† to step up her game. She had a lot of work ahead of her.

Aceh at the turn of the 17th century was in a precarious position. Located at the northern tip of Sumatra, Aceh was a natural gateway to the rest of Indonesia and a target for foreign powers, notably the Dutch and the Portuguese. Compounding matters was the sultan's age: he'd taken the throne in his nineties, and attempts to dethrone him were as regular as the setting of the sun. In fact, it was his general distrust of men that led the sultan to seek Keumalahayati's aid. It's a good thing he did.

The first major crisis of Keumalahayati's career came in 1599, with the arrival of two of Holland's worst diplomats, the brothers Cornelis and Frederick de Houtman. They had already made a disastrous name for themselves by insulting a neighboring sultan and go-ing on to pillage nearby villages. They soon got into a heated battle with Keumalahayati‡ in which she—and her 100-galley-strong fleet—got the better of them. She killed Cornelis in the fighting and took Frederick prisoner, forcing him to make the world's first Malay-Dutch dictionary.

In the years that followed, Keumalahayati made it abundantly clear that Aceh was not

---

* Usually referred to as Keumalahayati, she was also called Laskamana (Admiral) Keumalahayati, Malahayati, or just Hayati.

† The first is generally considered to be Artemisia I of Caria, who fought on the side of Xerxes I and was quite possibly the namesake of **Artemisia Gentileschi**.

‡ Which, some sources say, may have been sparked by deliberate misinformation given to the Acehnese from an ostensible Portuguese ally. Those wily 16th-century Portuguese!

to be played with. When a Dutch admiral robbed and sank an Acehnese merchant ship, Keumalahayati began attacking Dutch ships and arresting their crews on sight. After two years of this, the Dutch royalty finally relented. Prince Maurits of Holland sent out ambassadors with official apologies and levied a substantial fine on the merchant-robbing admiral. This was a fresh start in friendly relations between the two nations: for the first time, Aceh sent ambassadors to Holland, making Maurits look all the more prestigious to his European neighbors.

By the time Britain came around to visiting Aceh, the reputation of the Acehnese navy had spread so far that the British didn't even try forcing their way in and instead worked diplomatically from the start.

According to legend, Keumalahayati died in battle against the Portuguese. Her name has become synonymous with boats in Indonesia—one of their chief warships today is called *Keumalahayati*—and the Inong Balee live on as a contemporary all-female guerrilla force that agitates for Aceh's independence from Indonesia.

# Marie Marvingt

## (1875–1963, FRANCE)

### *The Fiancée of Danger*

re you the sort of person who got mad when you learned Mozart composed his first symphony at age five? Do kids who graduate from college before they're old enough to drive make you angry?

Prepare to get furious.

Here's a short sampling of Marie Marvingt's long athletic career:

- Swam four kilometers by age four and was hailed as France's best female swimmer by age 31.

- Learned gymnastics with the circus and could ride a horse using secret inaudible commands.

- Dominated the 1908–1910 Olympics in skiing, ice skating, luge, and bobsledding— all of which helped promote the ski school she'd opened, the first ever accessible to civilians.

- Became proficient at cycling, tennis, golf, polo, jujitsu, boxing, shooting, fencing, swimming, mountain climbing, and ballooning.

- Finished 36th in the 1908 Tour de France, although she wasn't even allowed to officially enter.

- Scaled Dent du Geant, a treacherous mountaineering feat that only two people, both men, had accomplished before her.

- Sailed a balloon from Paris to England in the middle of a storm, almost dying multiple times. When she did land, it was by crashing into a tree and getting tossed out (she was fine).

- In 1910 won the Medaille d'Or for All Sports from the French Academy of Sports. Yes, she won a medal for all sports. Every single one of them. Hers was the only one of these awards ever given.

Mad yet? Well, buckle in, we're barely halfway through her résumé.

Marvingt was intensely focused from a young age. Her mother died when she was very young, and with Dad busy looking after her infirm brother, Marie had to step up to run the house. When she was 22, her brother died, and she vowed she would never marry. Instead, she became, as she'd later title her autobiography, *The Fiancée of Danger*.

After hitting her mid-thirties, Marie began to drift away from sports and into aviation, the interest for which she became best known. She started flying a scant seven years after the Wright brothers' test at Kitty Hawk, operating experimental planes that could charitably be described as flying death traps. Despite crashing several times (an inevitability in those days), she became the third woman in the world to get a pilot's license. Next Marie did what any upstanding citizen with an incredibly dangerous, unproven piece of new technology might do: she joined the war effort.

Although most of her efforts in World War I revolved around developing the first flying ambulances (earning her the nickname the "flying **Florence Nightingale**"), that was far from her only contribution. After spending several weeks in disguise as a foot soldier at the front, she carried food to troops on skis, helped with evacuations, trained as a nurse, assisted in wartime surgery, and invented a surgical suture device.

Then Marvingt became the first female bomber in history, flying missions over German territory. For this, she earned the Croix de Guerre, one in her endless collection of medals.

And the list goes on!

After the war, she spent decades publicizing the idea of aerial ambulances. This was not a matter of simply appearing in the newspapers upon occasion: she went to upwards of 3,500 conferences over the rest of her lifetime—around 70 per year, or one every five days.

Even after Marvingt settled into old age, she continued to impress everyone around her. At age 86, she biked from Nancy to Paris—a 400-kilometer journey—in the dead of winter, for fun. She would regularly stroll into expensive restaurants and pay her bill with autographs (a trick that **Josephine Baker** would pull years later, sometimes at the same restaurants). She studied law and medicine, achieved fluency in four languages, and became an accomplished singer, actress, author, painter, and sculptor.

She died in a nursing home at age 88. She was so long-lived that in an interview two years before her death, Marie joked around about how she kept delaying city plans for a museum dedicated to her by stubbornly refusing to die. Every few days, she said, "Somebody has come to look in and see if Marvingt is still around, and if they can start work on the museum. This has been going on for a long time. They are starting to lose interest."

They didn't, though. Marie Marvingt was hailed as "the most extraordinary woman since **Joan of Arc**" and held up as one of France's greatest heroines. To this day there are streets, buildings, schools, aviation awards, and flying clubs named after her.

# Iara

## (BRAZILIAN LEGEND)

### Brazil's Lady of the Lake

aybe you're familiar with mermaids as lovesick sea dwellers who just can't get enough of hunky air-breathers. Maybe you have even read the unsanitized versions of said stories featuring, say, the besotted protagonist essentially stabbing herself repeatedly so the handsome prince will like her. (Spoiler: does not work, do not emulate.)

Well, the story of the Brazilian mermaid Iara is nothing like that.

Iara was the pride of her Amazon-dwelling tribe. The daughter of the group's spiritual leader, Iara grew to be the best warrior of them all—courageous, kind, strong, and (as virtually every single history ever written about women feels inclined to mention) beautiful. In short: she was a total boss, and everyone liked her.

Everyone, that is, save her two brothers, whom she overshadowed by virtue of being far more awesome. Upset by this, they decided to handle their problem with mankind's traditional go-to solution: murder. The only catch was, they knew they couldn't take her, even two-on-one. So they waited until she was asleep, reasoning that two alert soldiers would be stronger than one unconscious one.

They were wrong. They were so, so wrong. As soon as they got near her, she jolted awake and killed them both in self-defense. She might have still been half-asleep.

Afterwards, her father, unaware that her brothers had tried to kill her first, and apparently deaf to her cries of "they started it," led the rest of the tribe on a hunt for her. Although she eluded them for quite some time, eventually they caught up to her and tossed her into a nearby river, where she drowned. Bummer.

But even underwater (and dead), she was still making friends! The fish there thought she was pretty cool, so they transformed her into a half-fish, half-human person—the first of an entire branch of river-dwelling mermaids called Iara. When men chanced upon Iara, usually in the afternoon, they would be so overcome by her beauty (or singing voice) that even if they somehow managed to escape, they would literally go insane. What happened to the men if they didn't escape changes in different tellings. In some versions, Iara would drown them and even eat them. In others, they would join Iara's aquatic harem, and she'd treat them pretty well! Life could suck more.

The legends are unclear about what would happen if a woman chanced upon Iara. Presumably, a curt head nod.

The tale of Iara is, in all likelihood, an intermingling of European myths, local monster stories, and river goddess worship. The European myths are probably obvious to most everyone reading this. The monster in this case can be tracked back to the Ipupiara, a crazy-looking 15-foot-tall sea monster that terrorized 1500s Brazil. The river god worship is a bit harder to track down, but as far away as Venezuela you'll find the story of Iara conflated with that of Maria Lionza, a tapir-riding, vulva-wielding beast queen.

(This author would like to think he's the first person to ever write "tapir-riding, vulva-wielding beast queen," but he's probably not.)

## · ART NOTES ·

Since the myth is associated with the Tupi people, Iara's face paint and tattoos are modeled after theirs.

In the stories, her hair is often described as green because of algae.

The setting is the actual river she's reported to live in.

Her fish half is based on the look of a Brazilian guppy. They have such beautiful fins!

# Jane Dieulafoy

(1851–1916, FRANCE/PERSIA)

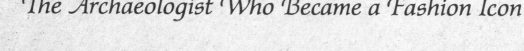

## The Archaeologist Who Became a Fashion Icon

**M**ost of the women in this book achieved their life's work without the aid of (and sometimes despite the interference of) a man. Jane Dieulafoy, one of the most successful archaeologists in history, was not such a woman. On the contrary, she shared all her adventures—excavating cities, roughing it in the wilds of Persia, and even fighting in wars—with her partner, equal, and soul mate: her husband, Marcel. Not that most of her contemporaries knew this, as she disguised herself as a man for much of her life abroad.

Jane came from conventional beginnings. Born into a bourgeois French family, she received her education at a convent and got married as soon as she graduated. Her husband, Marcel, was a worldly engineer who enjoyed travel.

Jane's conventional life ended with her wedding. Her husband enlisted to fight in the Franco-Prussian war, and, disguising herself as a man, so did Jane. They spent their honeymoon on the front lines, shooting at enemy tanks. Thankfully, the war ended soon, and before long they were back home in Toulouse. Although neither ever wanted to set foot on a battlefield again, both longed for adventure, and to that end they started planning a trip to Persia (present-day Iran).

To describe their trip as grueling would give a bad name to gruel. For two years, the pair logged over 3,700 miles on horseback. They slept on rocks, battled fevers, endured horrific rainstorms, experienced dire poverty, dodged angry wildcats and boars, and fought off recurrent head lice. Most remarkably, they somehow stayed married. Their goal was the ancient city of Susa. The seat of several ancient civilizations (notably several started by successors of **Tomyris**'s headless foe, Cyrus the Great), Susa had by that point been abandoned for so long that it had almost passed into the realm of fable. Marcel's aim was to prove that Western art owed a debt to Eastern art. Jane's was to pursue her interest in history. Neither was a trained archaeologist, but they proved to be quick studies. Many of the techniques they would soon pioneer became the foundation of modern archaeology.

They did finally reach Susa, and the importance of the work they did there can scarcely be overestimated. In short order, they unearthed a massive relic—26 feet by 200 feet long—called the Lion Frieze. That was followed by ancient urns, coins, and lamps, replete with ivory and opal. Soon word of their dig spread, bringing in such a colossal number of workers that they had to hire round-the-clock security to keep an eye on the dig.

And in charge of this small village of 300 hired hands stood Jane. Still disguised as a man, she regularly appeared with archaeological equipment in hand, a rifle on her shoulder, and a horse whip at her side. She was the first to break ground at the dig, and she defended their findings tooth and nail.

When it came time to transport some of the pieces back to French museums (many can still be seen in the Louvre), she and her husband camped out with the excavated treasures around the clock. The artifacts belonged in a museum, and they were hell-bent on making sure they made it there.

Once back in France, Jane was an instant celebrity, as was Marcel, though to a lesser extent. The two of them received many accolades and honors, and Jane became one of the first women to receive a cross from the Legion of Honor. Intellectual salons and newspapers across the nation buzzed about her short-cropped hair and her male wardrobe. Having now permanently eschewed women's clothes (and having received special government dispensation to do so), she became a minor fashion icon.

Many at the time assumed that, because of her appearance, Jane was a lesbian. However, there is no historical evidence to support the theory. She remained fiercely steadfast and, by all accounts, passionately in love with Marcel for her entire life. Despite her atypical presentation, she was in many ways quite traditional. When a female journalist, bored with her own husband, asked Jane's opinion on leaving him for a life of adventure, Jane replied: "Divorce works against women, it annihilates them, it lowers them, it takes away their prestige and their honor. I am the enemy of divorce. . . . I only wish to show that happiness comes from doing your duty towards others and not from satisfying your wishes and whims. The best way to love your husband is to love his soul, his intelligence and also the highest expression of himself, namely his work in the world."

The journalist left in tears.

The Dieulafoys' later careers were stymied by their newfound celebrity. With the authorities now aware of Jane's gender, the Persian government barred the couple from returning to Susa (although the real culprit may have been Jane's angry letter chastising the government for taking so long to get back to them about reentry). With a return there closed off, Jane found success in literary pursuits, and one of her more popular novels (a historical drama set in Susa itself) was turned into a famous opera. She even banded together with other female authors to start the Prix Femina, a literary prize awarded by women.

The Dieulafoys continued their archaeological work to the end of their lives, digging in Morocco, Spain, and Portugal. It was at one of these sites that Jane contracted a fatal case of amoebic dysentery from the dirty water. She died in Marcel's arms. She was 65. They had been married for 45 years.

# Tin Hinan

## (C. 4TH–5TH CENTURY, ALGERIA)

### The Queen Who Put Men in Veils

I n 1925, a massive tomb was excavated in the northern Algerian town of Abalessa. In it rested a skeleton popularly identified as the mother of one of the most unconventional tribes on earth—the Tuareg, a nomadic people who afforded their women the highest liberties and covered their men in electric blue veils. According to the tribes of the area, there, proudly adorned in her resplendent jewelry, was their leader and progenitrix, "she of the tents": Tin Hinan.

The history of Tin Hinan is a fractured one that has been mostly passed down through oral tradition. Most Tuareg agree that she left her tribe in Tafilalet (modern-day Morocco) and, alongside her servant Takama, journeyed into the Sahara, one of the most hostile environments in the world. She found an oasis at the Ahaggar Mountains and then brought in her people from Tafilalet. There she established a peaceful social order, formed commercial trade routes, and made a prosperous new nation.

Beyond that, the story of Tin Hinan changes dramatically in each telling. Related Imazigh (Berber) tribes claim she was a woman named Tiski al-Ardja, which translates as either "Tiski the Sweet-Smelling" or "Tiski the Lame." "Lame" was no judgment on her character: Tiski was said to be unable to walk without assistance. Corroborating this story is the fact that the skeleton found in the Algerian tomb thought to belong to Tin Hinan had evidence of a spinal deformity that would have caused a limp.

Some anthropologists and historians point to the matriarchal culture of the Tuareg today as evidence of Tin Hinan's influence. The men of the Tuareg strike an unfamiliar dichotomy: fierce warriors, they also wear veils, braid their hair, and apply makeup before meeting women. Women, strikingly, select their sexual partners (of which they can have many without stigma) and pass their family names to their husbands, and their wealth and possessions are inherited by their daughters. Women dominate politics, and the sultan elected by the tribes is said to represent the queen.

Unfortunately, we may never know all of the story behind Tin Hinan. The 1925 excavator of the Algerian grave was Byron Khun de Prorok, a man vilified in archaeological circles as an incompetent grave robber. It's uncertain, judging from his long history of archaeological blunders, how much of his account of the discovery should be believed, especially as regards the original condition of the tomb and the question of whether any treasures might have "walked off." Despite protests from the Tuareg, de Prorok took the bones and treasures back to the Ethnographical Museum in Algiers, where they remain on display to this day.

Sadly, today the traditional values of the Tuareg are in decline, as civil wars and drought have forced them to move to cities, where a patriarchal social structure is the norm.

## · ART NOTES AND TRIVIA ·

Tin Hinan is assumed to be a title rather than a proper name. Translations include "she of the tents," "the nomadic woman," and "she who comes from afar."

She is wearing the jewelry she was found with: seven gold bracelets on her left arm, and seven silver on her right. Additionally, she was said to have ridden a cream-colored camel, pictured lying down, exhausted.

Some fringe writers, chief among them L. Taylor Hansen, theorize that the Tuareg actually fled the fabled Atlantis. Some Tuareg apparently believe this as well.

Historian Lyn Webster Wilde, in her book on the origins of the Amazon myth, supposes that the Tuareg matriarchal streak may be a holdout of female-centric Bronze Age societies.

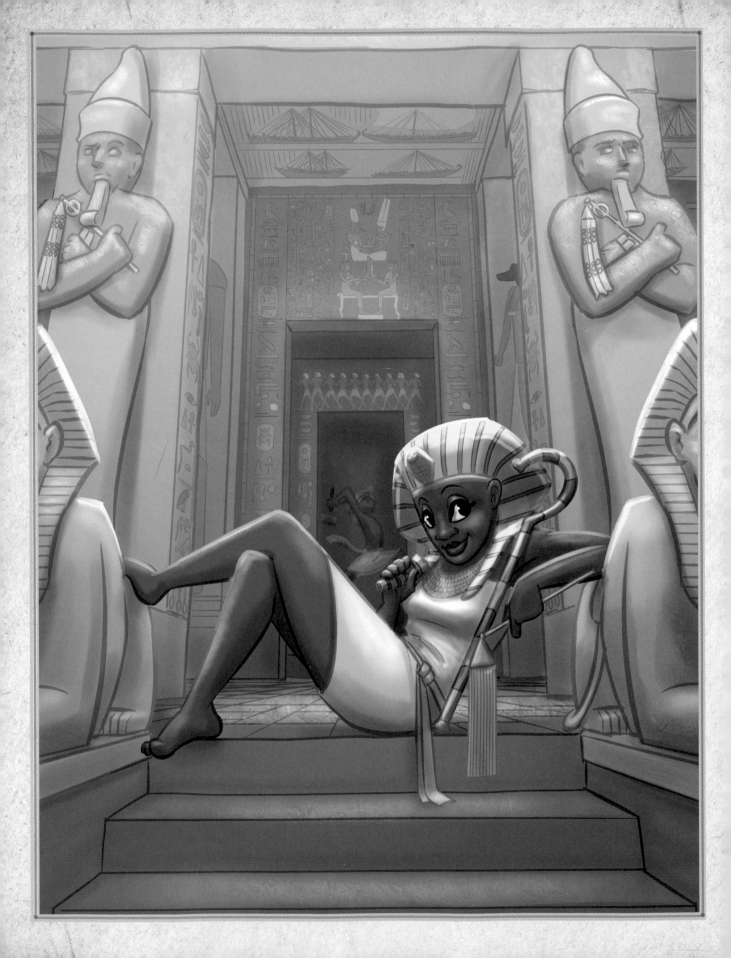

# Hatshepsut

## (1508–1458 BCE, EGYPT)

### The Unforgettable Pharaoh

orget Cleopatra, King Tut, or Nefertiti—Hatshepsut was quite possibly the greatest pharaoh in history. She didn't come to power through assassinations or war, nor did she even engage in violence. She just ruled brilliantly.

You'd be forgiven for not knowing about her, though. Thanks to a sustained campaign by her successors to erase all traces of her (more on that in a bit), it was not until fairly recently that she came back to prominence. She was rediscovered because her time in power saw such an incredible proliferation of architecture, statues, and art that it proved impossible to scrub mention of her from everything. So many of her artifacts have survived to the present day that almost every major museum in the world has at least one artifact from her reign. New York's Metropolitan Museum of Art has an entire room devoted to her.

All this out of a reign of only 22 years, 1,500 years before the birth of Jesus.

In fact, speaking of Jesus—you know the myrrh that the wise men brought to his birth? That gift was almost certainly made possible by Hatshepsut's import of myrrh to Egypt, in the first recorded attempt to transplant foreign trees. While this may not sound impressive on its face, she had brought them in from the land of Punt*—an act that, for the time, was akin to going to the moon. This was just one of the many nigh-miraculous acts she pulled off in order to legitimize her claim on the throne.

Like many ancient female rulers, Hatshepsut was never meant to be in power. She ascended to rule when her father and brothers died suddenly and the heir to the throne was too young to rule. She spent much effort on her own PR—besides the aforementioned trip to Punt, she oversaw the creation of multiple statues of herself as pharaoh (in various androgynous guises, including with the pharaoh's false beard). These building efforts culminated in a 10-story-tall stone obelisk that displayed her official history. In it, she is portrayed as divinely conceived and the rightful ruler as appointed by the gods. Essentially she was saying, "I've always been king."

Eventually, she stepped aside, and the young ruler Thutmose III—with whom she'd, strictly speaking, been co-ruling, although she'd been doing everything herself—went about establishing his own legitimacy. A large part of that was taking credit for all of Hatshepsut's accomplishments by attempting to erase her name from everything. This *damnatia memoriae* went on for decades, but he could never erase her entirely.

---

* Generally assumed to be somewhere in the vicinity of modern-day Somalia.

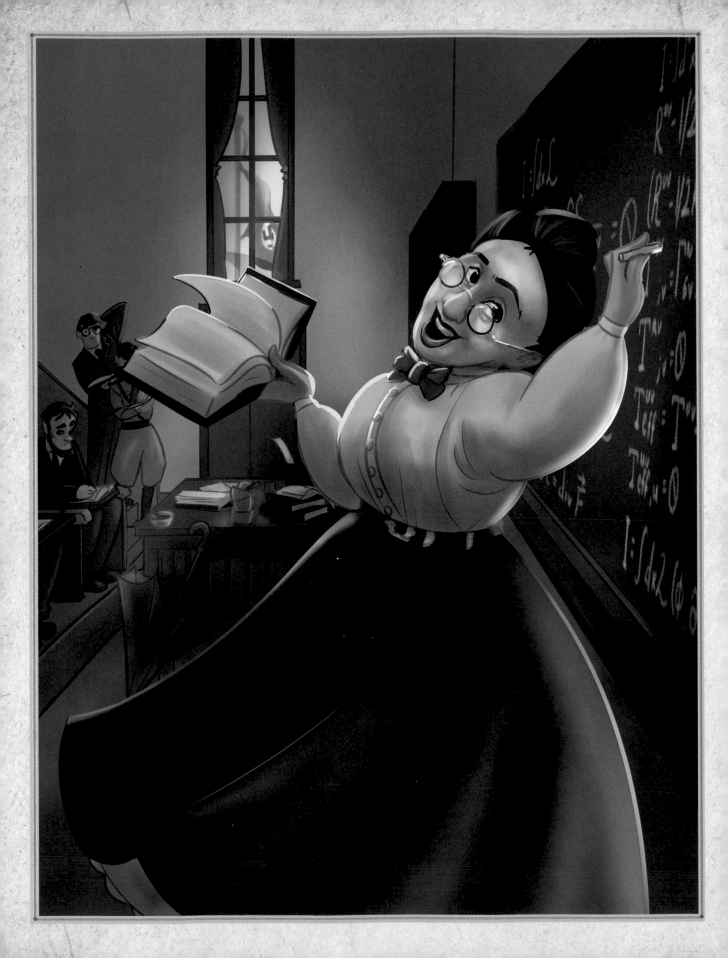

# Emmy Noether

## (1882–1935, GERMANY)

## The Most Important Mathematician
## You've Never Heard Of

f you had told German mathematicians in the late 1800s that their field would be radically upended by a woman—let alone a chubby, boisterous, life-long bachelorette who wouldn't even get paid for her work for most of her life—you would have been laughed out of the room.

Come the 1920s, they wouldn't be laughing.

To say that Emmy Noether revolutionized the field of mathematics is almost an understatement. Noether's theorem became the bedrock foundation of a new generation of physics and calculus by proving symmetry and conservation across physical systems. While the specifics are too complex to discuss in depth here, suffice to say that Albert Einstein himself described her as "the most significant creative mathematical genius thus far produced since the higher education of women began."

Emmy was an improbable candidate for such a label. Although her father was the brilliant mathematician Max Noether, in her childhood she showed no particular facility with academics. Nevertheless, she stayed the course, going on to attend university classes, although, as a woman, she could only sit in on them. She was one of only two women out of a total of 986 students. She was eventually allowed to matriculate, graduate (summa cum laude even!), and go on to work—without compensation.

Her employer was the Mathematical Institute in Erlangen, where her father had also worked. There she taught classes, although her teaching style was, well, different (more on that in a bit). She loved talking and collaborating with her fellow mathematicians, and they loved talking with her. Many tried to help her secure a post that would pay, but she was always turned down because of her gender. One ally famously objected to the university's gender segregation, saying, "This is a university, not a bathing house." It was to no avail.

To be fair, as a teacher, she was tremendously difficult to follow. Whereas you might expect a math teacher to work out proofs using formulas and equations, Emmy took a more philosophical approach. She avoided doing any calculations, instead keeping more to abstract thought and theorems—in much the same way **Ada Lovelace** constructed theoretical models in her head. Her teaching was so conceptual that it often drove away classroom visitors, leaving her to crow: "The enemy has been defeated; he has been cleared out!"

Because of her limited income, she lived a very spartan life. She ate the same plain meal every day and lived in an untidy student apartment. Her outfits, described as having all the fashion of a country clergyman, were usually a mess. She was often covered in food stains, her blouse was usually rumpled, and her hair would always come undone in the middle of class. She was famous for carrying around a broken umbrella—because she never bothered to get it fixed. Some female students tried helping her out but could never get a word in edgewise.

Noether was fiercely protective of her students. A eulogy for her said she would take personal offenses with a laugh, but blow her top if you attacked "Noether's Boys."* She'd spend her little spare money on helping her less fortunate students and even opened her house to some (an act that would later come to haunt her). Even when some of her students wore Nazi uniforms to their lessons, the Jewish Noether continued teaching them regardless.

The rise of the Nazis spelled the end of Noether's time in Germany. Some students had her expelled from the boarding house where she lived because of her interest in Russian mathematics—they said they did not want to live with "a pro-Marxist Jew." When Prussian government officials found that she had offered her apartment as a meeting place for leftist students, they worked to have her fired.

Her work was even dismissed by extremists who wanted to separate the field into Jewish math and Aryan math. Yeah—that was a thing.

Sympathizers such as Albert Einstein brought her to the United States, but her time was short. Two years after coming to the states and getting work at Princeton University and Bryn Mawr College, Noether was diagnosed with ovarian cancer. She died during an operation, and her cremated ashes were interred on the Bryn Mawr campus.

Her eulogists were a who's who of the world of mathematics. Albert Einstein's moving testimony, describing her contributions as "unselfish" and "significant," was published in the *New York Times*. Others lovingly paid tribute to her giving, peculiar nature. Hermann Weyl described her as "warm like a loaf of bread" before admitting that "no one could contend that the Graces had stood by her cradle."

However, there can be no greater tribute to Noether than her place in the reference books. Long described in her lifetime as "the daughter of Max Noether," Emmy would be represented differently shortly after her death. Her famous father, as well as her other mathematician relatives, came to be cited in relation to her—the most prestigious member of an already prestigious family.

---

* As her students were called—contrast this with the "Pickering's Harem" that **Annie Jump Cannon** found herself in!

# Ka'ahumanu

## (C. 1768–1832, HAWAII)

## *Honolulu's Queen of Controversy*

I t's said that, on a long enough timeline, we become the very thing we once hated. Exhibit A: Ka'ahumanu.

The favorite wife of Kamehameha (the Hawaiian king who unified the islands under a single government), Ka'ahumanu came into her own only after she became a widow. At her urging, Kamehameha had created, before he died, the new position of *kuhina nui*—a co-regent akin to prime minister. The first person appointed to the new position was, as you can probably guess, Ka'ahumanu. Her first order of business: helping out women.

At the time, Hawaiian culture was ruled by religious Tabus, superstitious rules that often kept women in a subservient position. The least-beloved of these Tabus was one prohibiting men and women from eating together. So, as the most powerful woman in the country, Ka'ahumanu regularly broke out a banana and started eating it in the presence of the new king, Liholiho (making him quite uncomfortable). Soon thereafter, she worked up enough political alliances to strong-arm the king into abolishing that Tabu by publicly eating with her.

She didn't stop there. She went on to forcibly destroy as many Tabus and religious idols as she could, although this led to some short-lived civil wars (which she, of course, won). By the time foreigners began to arrive in earnest, Hawaii was basically an atheist nation. With food plentiful and rules minimal, Hawaiians spent most of their time chatting and relaxing on the beach.

Their main form of entertainment was gossip, and few people's lives were better fodder than Ka'ahumanu's. While having multiple lovers was no big deal at the time, Ka'ahumanu brought this practice to a new level: at one point she kidnapped and forcibly married the king of Kauai—and his son. She dealt with jealousies and scheming rivals with a level of political craft that was second to none. The Hawaiians loved it.

Foreign missionaries, however, were not so comfortable with Hawaii's lifestyle of idle joy and casual infidelity. Several New England pilgrims, led by Hiram Bingham, were intent on bringing this "fortification of Satan's kingdom" into the light. They were aghast that Hawaiians had no jails, no jobs, no religion, no chores, and no clothes. Ka'ahumanu let the Mirthless (as the Hawaiians referred to Bingham's group) teach literacy, which proved useful, but was less interested in religion: "We will accept no new gods," she told them. "The gods brought only sorrow and unhappiness to our people."

Everything changed when Ka'ahumanu suffered a series of personal losses. Her beloved husband, the aforementioned captive king, died suddenly. He was followed shortly thereafter by King Liholiho, who, on an impromptu visit to George IV in England, sickened and died, along with most of his party. Lastly, Ka'ahumanu's younger husband, the son of the captive king, left her.

Suddenly, Ka'ahumanu was running things on her own. In her grief, she turned to Christianity.

Gradually, the Tabus that Ka'ahumanu had abolished were replaced by new ones. Clothing became mandatory, hula was outlawed, and loud displays of emotion—a Hawaiian trademark—were prohibited. This led to yet more civil strife, which Ka'ahumanu again quashed with her master statesmanship. When would-be assassins met to discuss killing her, she sent a messenger to tell them that she knew about the plot, that she was home without any guards, and that if they had the guts they should just do it now. Instead, they gave up.

Ka'ahumanu died in 1832. Dispensing with the traditional wailing and clamor usually associated with the deaths of rulers, the Hawaiians respected the wishes of their melancholy matriarch and let her be buried silently, as missionary custom dictated. But according to legend, after the funeral a select group of traditionalists, under cover of night, sneaked her body onto a canoe to reinter it far away . . . in the old ways.

## · ART NOTES ·

Ka'ahumanu is here depicted rebelliously eating a banana while simultaneously wielding Kamehameha's spear (and symbol of authority). While her body is turned toward her husband, her head is turned to the missionaries.

On the left side, we see Hawaiian women idly playing cards, a pastime that drove the missionaries nuts.

On the right, we see the missionaries covering naked beachgoers. In the background, amid many felled trees, is a church. The trees are indicative of all the sandalwood that was harvested for trade with foreigners (approaching on the boats).

Behind Hiram, a volcano is erupting, with explosive force similar to his sermons. This represents the wrath of the old Hawaiian gods, particularly the volcano goddess Pele. Under Ka'ahumanu's reign, a woman named Kapiolani, recently converted to Christianity, rebelliously entered a sacred volcano and took Pele's offerings to prove the old gods had no power. It was a big deal at the time.

Scattered on the ground around Ka'ahumanu are chipped and broken idols of Hawaiian gods.

# Katie Sandwina

## (1884–1952, AUSTRIA/UNITED STATES)

## *The Strongest Woman in the World*

ax Heymann met his wife in unusual fashion. A circus acrobat in peak physical condition, Heymann entered a wrestling competition. Beat the opponent and win upwards of 100 German marks, they said. How hard could it be? The wrestler, after all, was a 16-year-old girl.

The next thing he remembered was the blue sky that filled his vision as he was being carried out of the ring by his opponent. She would later become his wife: Catherine Brumbach, better known as Katie* Sandwina.

He shouldn't have felt bad—nobody else ever beat her either.

Katie was almost predestined for a life as a strongwoman. Herself born of the circus, she was the child of two giant circus performers (her father was six foot six, her mother six feet tall). Katie began performing as young as two years old, doing handstands on her dad's arm. She grew to be a towering beauty and made a name for herself as an undefeated wrestler—until she met the strongest man in the world.

At the time, the man who laid claim to that title was a Prussian-born weight lifter named Eugen Sandow. His usual M.O. was to strut about in a fig leaf and sandals, showing off his impressive physique. The two came face to face in New York City after Katie, trying to expand her act, publicly issued a challenge for any audience member to lift more weight than her. To her shock and dismay, Sandow strutted forth from his seat and began to match her weight for weight. Eventually, she lifted 300 pounds over her head—and Sandow could only get it to chest level. She had won.

Overnight her life changed. The news made headlines across the country. She quickly took the name "Sandwina" as a tribute to Sandow (or perhaps a barb) and changed her circus act from wrestling to feats of strength. Some of her amazing accomplishments were:

• Juggling 30-pound cannonballs.

• Using husband Max as a surrogate rifle while running through various martial positions.

• Lifting horses . . . yes, horses.

---

* There's some evidence that she spelled her name "Kati," but most biographies have it "Katie."

- Balancing a carousel and 14 riders on her shoulders.

- Lifting a half-ton cannon onto her back.

- Bending iron bars and breaking iron chains.

- Lying on a bed of nails with an anvil on her chest—and having people hit her with a sledgehammer.

But far from being a masculine figure, she was seen by popular media as the epitome of a new kind of woman. They lavished attention on her measurements and height, the latter accentuated by her heeled boots and piled-up hair. She appeared even more feminine after giving birth to her son Theodore—even though she was performing tricks like the bed of nails up to and including the day she gave birth. The fawning press dubbed the child "Superbaby" and swarmed Katie for mothering tips. By two years old, he weighed 50 pounds—almost double the weight of an average baby.

Katie's popularity gave her latitude and power to support causes she felt strongly about, and the one she put much of her weight behind was women's suffrage. She became vice president of the suffrage group at Barnum & Bailey Circus, and many write-ups referred to her as "Sandwina the Suffragette."

Although Katie had an impressively long career with the circus, she eventually retired, at age 64, still doing the same tricks she'd done her entire career. Afterwards, she opened a restaurant in Queens, New York. Her duties included running the restaurant, performing the occasional circus act for old times' sake, and acting as bouncer. Often the inebriated men she'd toss out of her establishment returned and apologized after sobering up. Throughout this second act of her career, she maintained her girlish charms, tossing men out the door with nails painted and perfectly styled hair.

She died of cancer in her late sixties, the only battle she ever lost.

# Gracia Mendes Nasi

### (1510–1569, PORTUGAL/ITALY/TURKEY)

## The Savior of the Jews

One of the cornerstones of being Jewish throughout the centuries has been the secure knowledge that someone, somewhere, is trying to kill you. Few instances of this bloodlust were more successful than the Inquisition. Far from being unexpected—despite what British comedians might have told you—the Inquisition was the outgrowth of a slow escalation in mob violence over many years. Spreading from Spain to Portugal, and eventually to Rome, the Inquisition was an almost inescapable force of terror for Jews.*

Almost inescapable, but not totally. Enter Gracia Mendes Nasi, to whom much of the world's current Jewish population owes their existence.

Born Beatriz de Luna,† Gracia was one of the Portuguese *conversos*—Jews who were outwardly Christian but practiced Judaism in secret. This was a smart move. Jews in those days were blamed for a laundry list of the world's ills: causing plague, poisoning wells, eating babies, you name it. The mere accusation of Judaism was enough to set off a witch hunt, and thousands were regularly dragged through the streets, crucified, and set on fire in impromptu pogroms.

However, the incalculable wealth of Gracia's family made them less vulnerable to said attacks. With the Catholic Church exercising a ban on moneylending, Jews occupied an important role in European society, functioning as merchants and financiers where others couldn't. Gracia's silver-trading family, in particular, was welcomed by the Portuguese crown as one of only 600 Jewish Spaniard families granted indefinite asylum from the Spanish Inquisition. Gracia's family was so rich that at one point they provided over half of the Portuguese crown's income. They were even able to purchase special protection from the pope himself. They were not easily dismissed.

The crown turned a blind eye to their Jewish heathenism only for so long, though, and

---

* And others, particularly Muslims! It isn't germane to this particular entry, but for a look into some of the effects that Ferdinand and Isabella had on the Muslim world, check out this book's entry on Moroccan pirate queen **Sayyida al-Hurra**—who, given her extensive nautical purview, might very well have had dealings with Gracia!

† Beatriz de Luna was her Christian name, which she went by most of her life. Gracia Nasi was the Spanish equivalent for her Hebrew name. Interestingly, "Nasi" is a Hebrew title meaning "prince," arguably making her a princess.

after the death of her merchant/rabbi husband,[*] Gracia took the reins and moved to Antwerp. She proved a natural at the job of merchant. Along with her brother-in-law Diogo, she swiftly established shipping routes across much of Europe, which she also used as an underground railroad. Alongside legitimate goods, she smuggled Jews from Iberia to Antwerp to Venice, and finally to the Ottoman Sultanate, where they'd be safe. She spent her free time visiting convents and creating a secret network of safe houses and messengers. When Diogo died, Gracia was fully ready to take on the responsibilities of their vast mercantile/smuggling empire by herself.

The opposition she faced upon stepping into the spotlight was intense. While the various political attempts to seize the Mendes fortune were easily enough handled by bribes, she had more trouble fending off attempts to seize her daughter Ana's hand in marriage—and with it, her daughter's inheritance. When one man offered to marry Ana off to a Catholic, Gracia privately considered having him beaten for the suggestion. When Queen Mary, sister of Holy Roman Emperor Charles V, insisted repeatedly on marrying off Ana to a Catholic nobleman, Gracia said to Mary's face that she would rather drown.

From there, Gracia only grew bolder. With the Inquisition officials bearing down on her, she left open ledgers around the house in Antwerp, making it look like she was coming back, and quietly moved to Venice. She began using her Hebrew name in public and funding the Jewish arts, particularly the translation and publication of Hebrew texts. Eventually, she moved to Constantinople, where she organized Jewish boycotts of Italian businesses from afar. She even tried establishing a fledgling Jewish state in modern-day Tiberias, Israel.

Gracia's herculean efforts to shelter her people did gradually take their toll. In making enemies of so many monarchs, she found her ability to collect on debts compromised as the amount spent on bribes increased. Compounding matters was her sister Brianda,[†] who, feeling cut out of the picture, acted out by revealing Gracia to be a secret Jew and working with Inquisition figures to arrest her (it didn't stick). By the end of her life, Gracia's vast fortunes had dwindled significantly, although she was still quite wealthy.

None of this stopped Gracia from providing for her people until the end. In her final years, she established homes for the poor, constructed synagogues and schools, and even fed and sheltered sick and destitute Jews.

She died in Constantinople in 1569 and was promptly forgotten for centuries. It was not

---

[*] Her husband, Francisco Mendes, was simultaneously a rabbi of the Portuguese Jewish community, a successful pepper and silver merchant, and quite possibly Gracia's uncle. Um . . . yeah.

[†] Brianda had been married to Francisco's brother Diogo—yes, two sisters married two brothers, who were possibly also their uncles. It's confusing. Anyway, after Diogo's death, he left the family fortune to Gracia, because she was clearly a boss. Brianda, who was far less capable, carried a chip on her shoulder about it her entire life and was a pain in Gracia's tuchus because of it.

until the 20th century that her story once again came to light. Since then, Gracia Mendes Nasi has been heralded in lectures, museums, and books (like this one!).

## · ART NOTES AND TRIVIA ·

Gracia is here depicted showing her Christian side outwardly to the camera, while hiding her Jewish coins (silver) throughout. There are 18 coins scattered throughout the picture, what with 18 being a lucky number in Judaism. See if you can spot them all!

The book on the table is the Ferrara Bible, whose translation and publication she's suspected to have funded.

The map in the ledger denotes the location of Tiberias, the site of her Zionist efforts.

Compositionally, all elements in the picture point toward Gracia, indicating her importance at the center of a vast web of disparate elements.

Her clothing is primarily blue and white, in a nod to the colors of the Israeli flag.

The account covered in the open ledger is *taglit*—the Hebrew word for "birthright" (and the name of a program financing Jews worldwide to make a trip to Israel, as Gracia did). As the "client" in her ledger, she's scratched out the Hebrew word for "sister" and written in "daughter," indicating where she was putting her efforts. The ledger is opened, of course, to page 18.

# Sayyida al-Hurra

## (C. 1482–1562, MOROCCO)

## The Pirate Queen
## Who Ruled the Mediterranean

o this day, no one knows Sayyida al-Hurra's real name.

Which might initially sound a bit odd—you'd think an Islamic pirate queen who ran Morocco for 30 years and repeatedly repelled Spanish invasions would be a *little* memorable—but the fact is, nobody dared use anything but honorifics when speaking of or to her. Not only was she a governor (*Sayyida*), but she was also the last woman to hold the title of *al-Hurra* (thought to mean "sovereign woman").*

Sayyida came to power against a backdrop of conflict. Born in the kingdom of Granada, she was forced to flee as a child when the Spanish monarchs Ferdinand and Isabella drove the Muslims out of Europe with bloody force. Swearing revenge, she escaped to Morocco, which was itself in a precarious position, its borders being nibbled away by all surrounding kingdoms. But Sayyida's family integrated quickly: her father became ruler of the independent region of Chefchaouen, and Sayyida eventually married the sultan of Tetouan, al-Mandari II.

Sayyida took to the realm of politics swiftly. A highly educated woman, fluent in both Arabic and Spanish, Sayyida helped her husband not only in ruling Tetouan but also in military operations against the Spanish and Portuguese. The gender dynamics between Sayyida and her husband were totally atypical for the time—they shared diplomatic responsibility instead of he, as husband, having complete control. There are records indicating that, if anything, Sayyida was more in charge of the military than the sultan himself. On several occasions, he even implored her to soften her approach. A neighboring governor, referring to Sayyida's bellicose personality, dubbed her "The Iron Lady of the Arab-Muslim World."

She earned two more titles after her husband died in 1518—al-Hakimat Tetouan ("ruler of Tetouan") and Barbarossa Tetouania ("Barbarossan pirate of Tetouan"). Upon taking the reins from the late sultan, Sayyida befriended Barbary pirates. This was no minor relationship: piracy not only became the foundation of much of Tetouan's economy but was also one of the

---

* Some of the historians who make this claim also suspect that her birth name was either Fatima or A'isha. Given the prevalence of those two names in the region (see the entry on **A'isha bint abi Bakr**), there's a decent chance of that being correct for virtually any woman of the era.

chief tactics in her wars against the Spanish and Portuguese. Sayyida rebuilt Tetouan for this purpose, with massive docks to house her fleets, winding roads to trap invaders, and walls to stymie her enemies. Before long, Tetouan was one of the key seats of power in the region.

Sayyida's piracy paid off handsomely. Tetouan flourished from the influx of stolen goods, and the Spanish and Portuguese, with their expansionist efforts stopped in their tracks, were forced to negotiate with her. Sayyida's policy of taking captives—including the wife of the governor of Portugal—compelled the Spanish and Portuguese to forge numerous bilateral agreements for the release of their people.

In one of her crowning achievements, she remarried, to the Moroccan sultan Ahmed al-Wattassi—and made him travel to her for the privilege. This was unheard of, and the first time in Moroccan history that a marriage ceremony took place in the bride's home. Then, instead of moving to be with her husband, Sayyida stayed in Tetouan to continue her reign.

In 1542 a group of individuals (including her stepson, by some accounts) deposed her, and from there, her story is lost to the mists of time. She died 20 years later in her father's province of Chefchaouen.

# Matilda of Tuscany

(1046–1115, ITALY)

## *Defender of the Pope*

 ost women could not make kings kneel before them. Then again, Matilda of Tuscany was not most women.

From the time she was a young girl, Italian-born Matilda had a singular, clear interest: kicking butt for God. While her mother and sister busied themselves with sewing and housework, Matilda started training with spears, battle axes, and swords. Which isn't to say she eschewed more sedentary pursuits—she spoke four languages and was hugely literate at a time when most rulers could not even write their names, and her skill with embroidery was widely celebrated. Of course, said celebration was largely from the court of William the Conqueror, owing to her sending him a handmade flag to commemorate his, well, conquering—but still.

This military preoccupation served Matilda well, considering the turbulence of the age. Conflicts between the Roman popes and the German-led Holy Roman Empire—struggles that boiled down to "church versus state"—led to nonstop warfare across Europe, to which Matilda's family was hardly immune. She would see her mother tossed into prison and her father murdered by poisoned arrow.

By the age of six, Matilda was formally in control of the family holdings. She relinquished full control only when she entered an arranged marriage at the age of 23. That state of affairs, along with the marriage itself, was temporary.

The husband in question was the unfortunately named Godfrey the Hunchback, whom Matilda haaaaated. According to one (likely apocryphal) story, she showed up to their wedding night with her hair newly shorn, wearing a frumpy nightgown, and basically told him, "God says we gotta do it, so let's get this over with." Although later legends would portray her as a virgin (more on that in a bit), she did consummate her marriage to Godfrey. However, they never had any children who lived past childhood.

Their marriage got even worse when they ended up on opposing sides of a war. The event that finally pushed Matilda to take up the sword was brazen even by the standards of the time: on Christmas Eve, a bunch of German assailants attacked the pope, beat him up, and unsuccessfully tried to drag him to Germany.

Let's repeat that: The pope got jumped. At the Vatican. On Christmas Eve. By people who tried to kidnap him.

Eleventh-century Europe was a rough place.

So Matilda started fighting for Pope Gregory VII, and her husband for the pope's enemy, Henry IV. The couple separated, and Godfrey was assassinated shortly thereafter (not by Matilda's hand—he'd ticked off another entirely different set of powerful people). In the absence of an heir, Matilda regained control of her family's wealth and land. She promptly used them to raise armies to fight for her pope.

Her support came just in time, because Gregory VII had just tossed gasoline onto the fire by excommunicating Henry IV. This was the 11th-century equivalent of dropping a nuclear warhead: basically, if Henry IV did not repent, in the eyes of his pope-friendly subjects, he would be an illegitimate ruler within a year. The official word of God made it clear to Henry's subjects that it was their right—nay, duty—to start smashing everything in sight.

Things got more and more heated. The pope tried getting to Germany to negotiate a replacement for Henry IV, and Henry IV tried to stop him—only to be thwarted time and time again by Matilda's forces.

Eventually, Gregory VII holed up in Matilda's fortress at Canossa, largely considered to be invulnerable. This brought Henry to his knees, literally. He approached Canossa, asking Matilda to put in a good word for him with the pope.

She made him wait outside. In rags. For three days. In one of the coldest winters on record.

This would be such a landmark event that the phrase "come to Canossa" became synonymous with "caving in." Even though Henry's repentance was nothing but lip service—even receiving official absolution, he continued opposing the pope militarily—he never lived down his defeat.

In the decades to come, Matilda steadfastly held out against the increasingly overwhelming power of Henry's forces. Even after Gregory VII passed away and she was virtually the only defender of his successor, she held strong, refusing every compromise that might end the conflict. Her finances became so dire that she melted down 709 pounds of gold and silver in her treasury to keep up the war effort. She even married a man less than half her age—a marriage arranged by the pope—to shore up support.

Her persistence paid off. Although she did rack up some significant military victories (notably ambushing and massacring some of Henry IV's troops in the middle of the night), in the end she just outlasted everyone. Henry IV, the "antipope"* Henry had backed as an alternative to Gregory VII, Pope Gregory VII himself, and Gregory's successor all died, while Matilda

---

\* That's the actual term used in historical instances where competing popes have risen up against the establishment pope—see Manfreda Visconti in **Pope Joan**'s entry. Sadly, the term does not refer to a pope made of antimatter, as awesome as that would be.

soldiered on. Once the entire generation of people waging the conflict had passed, Matilda accepted a compromise of sorts from Henry IV's appropriately named successor Henry V and laid down her sword. In return, Henry V dubbed her Imperial Vicar Vice-Queen of Italy.

By this point, Matilda was a legend. Her image had been bandied back and forth by both sides. The papist forces held her up as a virginal "daughter of God," while her enemies claimed that she was the pope's mistress. Some biographers extended her legend back to her childhood, claiming she was leading an army of 400 archers by the time she was 15 (possible, but unlikely). Others were not such fans. Henry IV's biographer, Bishop Benzo of Alba, described her as *os vulvae*, which roughly translates to "cunt face."

Her fiery spirit stayed with her to the end of her days. At age 69, while she was in Mantua being treated for gout, the townspeople rose up against the local magistrate in rebellion. Annoyed by this sudden clamor, she threatened to lead an army against them if they didn't quiet down. They did.

# Moll Cutpurse

### (1584–1659, ENGLAND)

## London's Queen of Thieves

uick, pop quiz! A woman in Shakespearean-era England, on trial for stealing, theft, cross-dressing, and pimping, shows up to her trial blindingly drunk, still wearing men's clothing. Does she:

A. Get a hefty fine?

B. Have her hand branded to indicate she's a thief?

C. Become the main character of a popular stage play?

D. All of the above?

The answer is D. Meet Mary Frith, alias Moll Cutpurse.

Moll was a notorious character from a young age. As early as age 16, she was caught stealing and then set to be shipped off for reformation of her character. Once the ship left port, she jumped overboard and swam to shore.

Once settled back in London, she became known as the "Roaring Girl," a play on the term "roaring boys"—bar-brawling drunks who were the soccer hooligans of their day. Early in her career, she stole purses from passersby while they were distracted by her accomplices (hence "Cutpurse"), but later in life she grew into a sophisticated elder stateswoman among thieves.

As London's unofficial queen of thieves, Moll's range of services expanded tremendously. Not only could she arrange escort services for anyone who asked—male or female—she could also retrieve stolen items. Should some ne'er-do-well (say, an escort hired through Moll) relieve you of a precious heirloom, Moll could get it back to you. For a price, of course.

As the years passed, her personal life became more colorful. In addition to her everyday male uniform, she began wearing an array of daggers, swords, and (presumably for contrast) flowers. Her house—maintained by three maids—was awash in mirrors and home to numerous parrots and mastiffs. Legend has it that each of the dogs even had its own bed and that Moll would tuck them in each night after feeding them hand-prepared meals.

However, Moll's most infamous stunt was likely her daring ride across London in men's clothing. In this case, "daring" is literal—she was challenged to parade herself across the city in full defiance of ordinances against female-to-male cross-dressing. Not only did she do just that, but she did so atop the famous "counting horse" Marocco, a performing animal that could dance, play dice, and, of course, count.

Now, how much of all this is actually true? Probably not much. We know from her numerous court cases that she was indeed constantly in trouble with the law. We know she regularly took the stage during performances of the play about her own life (*The Roaring Girl*) and played the lute—amusing the crowd and angering the authorities. The rest, though? Folklore. Much of it stems from her "autobiography," a document roughly as trustworthy as Moll herself.

## · ART NOTES ·

Moll is here situated onstage at the Fortune Theatre, a contemporary of the Globe Theatre (where Shakespeare's works were performed). She's joined by a mastiff, an exotic bird, and Marocco the counting horse (in glasses, so you know he's smart), all fighting the authorities.

She's got flowers tucked in her cap, as was the style of the time, and is, of course, dressed in men's clothes. Strewn about her are the cut purses from which she derived her name, and you can see T-shaped scars on her hand—from the punishment for her thievery.

# Nellie Bly

(1864–1922, UNITED STATES)

# and Elizabeth Bisland

(1861–1929, UNITED STATES)

## The Journalists Who Raced Around
## the World in 80 Days

he idea was simple: beat Phileas Fogg.

At the close of the 19th century, the mild-mannered hero of Jules Verne's *Around the World in 80 Days* loomed large in the public imagination. With the European colonization of much of the world, such a speedy circumnavigation of the globe—once a flight of fancy—seemed increasingly possible. The only thing left was for someone to actually do it.[*]

Two someones, actually.

Nellie Bly (real name: Elizabeth Jane Cochrane) was famous before she ever began the trip: two years earlier, she'd faked insanity to be admitted into an asylum on Blackwell's Island (now known as Roosevelt Island in New York City). There for 10 days, she reported on filthy conditions, abuse bordering on torture, and inmates who found themselves admitted owing to no more than an inability to speak English. Her work resulted in increased oversight and a massive increase in the mental health budget by the government.

She went on to write more stunt pieces. She exposed a corrupt lobbyist, ending his career. She trained as a boxer. She bought a baby to expose the white slave trade. She identified a rapist carriage driver who'd bought off the police. She became so popular that imitators began edging in on her turf. And then, in 1889, she came up with her biggest stunt yet: she was going to go around the world in less than 80 days.

She just didn't know she'd be racing against someone else.

---

[*] The reality is that someone had already beaten them to the punch. In 1870, entrepreneur George Francis Train had made the trip in 80 days, possibly inspiring Verne's Fogg. Train also engaged in odd feats, like only speaking to children and animals (after deciding adults had nothing to say), espousing a diet of only fruit and chocolate, and running for president, during which time he shook hands with himself instead of other people. It is the position of this author that George Francis Train is a true American hero.

Elizabeth Bisland was the polar opposite of Bly. A statuesque, genteel woman from a desperately poor background in Louisiana, she'd made her name in journalism through sheer force of will. Arriving in New York City with just $50, she worked for four newspapers simultaneously, writing for 18 hours at a stretch. Living by the idea that "after the period of sex-attraction has passed, women have no power in America," she put more stock in work than fame—making her one to never refuse an assignment.

And so, when her editor came to her with the challenge of beating Nellie Bly in a race around the world, despite her misgivings about the piece being mere fluff, Bisland had her bags packed in 30 minutes.

Nellie traveled impossibly light: she took one small gripsack. That was it. She wanted to combat the notion that women needed tons of luggage.[*]

But for all the effort Bly put into countering that stereotype, she was stymied in combating the idea of feminine frailty: new to traveling by boat, she was seasick three times the first night. She landed in England and was quickly off to France, where she met Jules Verne. In a necessarily brief meeting, Verne was outwardly kind, but in private he disparaged her.[†]

Quickly becoming accustomed to the fast-paced travel, Bly nevertheless managed to have the occasional bit of fun. In the Suez Canal, she played assistant to a local magician, despite knowing how his tricks worked. When a stuffy Englishman—a trait/nationality pairing she was to find increasingly common and frustrating—demanded to know why she didn't just expose the magician's trick, she replied that she wanted to see the poor hardworking man get his money.

Bisland's trip did not start nearly as auspiciously. Heading west while Bly went east, the first leg took Bisland on a special mail train through the Midwest. There she found herself at the mercy of a train conductor calling himself "Cyclone Bill." Bill would fling them through mountain passes so fast that sparks would fly from the wheels and the sides of the train would lift into the air and then slam down. Ignoring pleas to slow down, Bill got them to Ogden, Utah, on time, wandered into a bar, and was never seen again.

After that, things went fairly smoothly. Bisland made it to the West Coast, and then to Japan and Hong Kong, without incident. Stressed to make the best time possible, she lamented her inability to see the sights. She wrote of her fleeting glimpses of kabuki plays, Sikh policemen, and, unfortunately, giant rats. By Christmas, she'd made it as far as Singapore.

---

[*] Bisland took three bags. Still fairly light for the time.

[†] He wrote privately, "My God, what a shame to see such a clever woman treated so badly by nature. As thin as a match, neither bottom nor bosom!"

By this time, the competing newspapers sponsoring the two women were ramping up their publicity. The *New York World*, Bly's patron, opened up a contest asking readers to predict Bly's arrival time to the second—a game that attracted seemingly every lunatic amateur numerologist in America. Bisland's sponsor, *Cosmopolitan* magazine (yes, that *Cosmopolitan*), spent most of its efforts trying to rope its competitor into a bet over who'd arrive first. It was unsuccessful.

Bly, still blissfully unaware that she even had a competitor, bought her only souvenir from the trip: the world's most ill-tempered monkey, whom she named McGinty. Over the course of the journey, this foul hellbeast would fight shiphands, maul a stewardess, and generally make enemies wherever it went.

In Asia, Bly suffered a number of misfortunes. First, her ships were delayed owing to mechanical failures and weather. Second: she had a stalker. A lovesick sailor followed her around the boat for days, blind to her indifference (and deaf to her claims to be engaged to the ship's captain). Things came to a head when he proposed to jump overboard with her and drown them both. The captain, thankfully, intervened, and her suitor gave her no trouble after that.*

Around Christmas, Bly finally received word that she was in a race with Bisland. Shortly thereafter, her progress ground to a halt when the boat was caught in a typhoon. The superstitious sailors, feeling McGinty's presence was to blame, wanted to throw the monkey overboard. She did not allow it.

Bisland blasted through the Middle East without incident and was on to France when she ran into bad news: she'd missed her next connection. As the travel agent who'd boarded her train told her, because of delays caused by an anal-retentive Italian customs agent, the top-of-the-line steamship that she was to board next was not able to wait for her.

Scrambling to put together an alternative route, Bisland eventually hopped on a train to London. What she didn't know was that the steamboat *was* actually waiting for her. The travel agent had given her false information. His identity, and the identity of whoever gave him his orders, was never determined.

Now in a race she feared she'd lose, Bly too was facing impossible setbacks. Finally back on American shores after a brutal journey, she found that the entire Western rail system was shut down by the largest snow blockade in the history of the United States. Eastern California reported drifts up to 20 feet deep, and Nevada drifts were 30 to 60 feet deep. Dozens had already died, and some train passengers—including a correspondent for the *World*—escaped dire fates only by skiing to safety.

---

* The captain wanted to throw him in chains, but Bly was against it. In the end, she resolved to simply not spend any time alone and unprotected.

Bly's salvation came from her employer's willingness to spend a ludicrous amount of money. In order to bypass the snow by sending her on a southern route through New Mexico, the *World* chartered a train and made sure it was given the right of way ahead of everyone. This included pulling stunts like sending the train over a barely finished bridge. The ploy worked, but proved hugely costly—more so than the rest of the trip combined.

On January 25, 1890, 72 days after she'd left, Nellie Bly arrived back in New York City to thunderous applause. She'd beaten Bisland.

The remainder of Bisland's trip saw one calamity after another. After arriving in London, she found out that the ship she'd planned to take had been swapped out for a much slower one, owing to mechanical problems. Compounding this was the worst Atlantic weather in years on the return journey. She arrived in New York on January 30, having still beaten the 80-day deadline, but definitely in second place. Her editor went on the attack, blaming Bisland but also claiming that the *World* had sent the rogue travel agent who threw off her trip. Even after *Cosmopolitan* filed a lawsuit, the truth was never uncovered.

After her win, Bly's fame skyrocketed to new heights. The clothes she'd traveled in became a fashion trend. Kids were named after her. She had her own board game, her own songs. She went on the talk circuit. She was now one of the most famous women in the world.

But with fame came a dark side. Finding herself unable to do undercover work because of her fame—and finding the niche filled by her numerous imitators—she switched to fiction writing, but did not succeed at it. Soon at odds with the entire publishing establishment (and depressed besides), Bly left New York.

At 31, Nellie married a 73-year-old millionaire. She took over his metal manufacturing plant and became an inventor and leading industrialist. However, she proved a less-than-savvy businesswoman, and employee embezzlement sank the company. In her final years, she dabbled in journalism and charity work before dying at age 57 of pneumonia.

Bisland took a very different path. At the height of the American press's interest in her, she moved to London. There she settled into the intellectual circles she'd always adored and met her husband. They were together for 30 years, during which time she made her living writing books, including early feminist critiques. After her husband became ill, Bisland began volunteering as a nurse, then went on to offer nursing help during World War I. She too died of pneumonia, in 1929 at age 67. She was buried in Woodlawn Cemetery in New York City—the same resting place as her onetime rival, Nellie Bly.

# Trung Trac and Trung Nhi

## (1ST CENTURY CE, VIETNAM)

## *The Sisters Who Stomped China*

ay back in 40 CE, Vietnam was in one of the toughest spots in its history. Conquered by China 150 years earlier, it had recently been put under the purview of the cruel Su Ting.* The new governor levied heavy taxes, violently quashed dissent, and was, by all accounts, putting together a strong case for being Asia's biggest sentient butthole. In the words of a 15th-century Vietnamese poem, "all the male heroes bowed their heads in submission; only the two sisters proudly stood up to avenge the country."

The sisters in question were Trung Trac and Trung Nhi. The daughters of a local lord, they had every reason to hate the Chinese. The sisters Trung had been oppressed by foreign overlords their entire lives, and their suffering had recently come to a head when Thi Sach, the beloved husband of Trung Trac, died at the hands of the Chinese.

Overcome with rage, the sisters gathered together tens of thousands of soldiers—many of whom were led by other female generals—and expelled the Chinese. Among their lady allies were Le Chan, whose family had been killed when she refused to marry Su Ting, and Phung Thi Chinh, who gave birth in the middle of battle. According to legend, after having her baby, Phung strapped it to her back and continued fighting. In all, the Trung forces took 65 strongholds from the Chinese.

Thereafter, the Trungs established a new kingdom, with Trung Trac on the throne. They abolished the cruel laws and onerous taxes they'd previously lived under, but their rule, sadly, was short-lived. The Chinese general Ma Yuan came back three years later with an enormous army and overwhelmed the fledgling Vietnamese nation. The Trungs either died in battle or committed suicide, depending on the source.

In fact, the story about the Trungs, the earliest folk heroes of Vietnam, changes rather a lot depending on the source and has evolved significantly over time. Early versions stressed that their motivation was primarily to avenge Trung Trac's husband and made them so frustratingly modest that multiple people were required to encourage them to take the reins. Su Ting's level of villainy is also highly variable, ranging from merely raising taxes to sacrificing

---

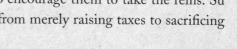
* Known as To Dinh in Vietnamese tellings. Ma Yuan is known as Ma Vien in Vietnamese.

his own children to save his own life. Modern versions, especially ones published after Vietnam's 1976 reunification, emphasize how everyone in Vietnam, including the Trungs' mom, got in on the revolution—a call to arms to get behind the same cultural identity.

Regardless of the specifics of the actual history, the sisters Trung are some of the first Vietnamese figures in recorded history, and some of the most highly revered. Moreover, as their role has expanded in the popular consciousness, they've become perennial idols to Vietnamese girls everywhere—and a reminder to everyone that a pissed-off woman is nothing to trifle with.

# Yaa Asantewaa

## (C. 1830–1921, GHANA [ASANTE CONFEDERACY])

## *Queen Mother of the Golden Stool*

he war started because of a pair of pasty English butt cheeks.

Said cheeks were attached to Sir Frederick Hodgson, colonial administrator for the Gold Coast and culturally illiterate scumwad. The setting was a meeting between him and the Asante Confederacy. After nearly a century of conflict between the British and the Asante, Hodgson deftly extended a diplomatic bridge of understanding by demanding to rest his sweaty rear on the Asante's most sacred cultural artifact, the Golden Stool. He graciously barked, "Where is the Golden Stool?! Why am I not sitting on it at this moment?!"

After the meeting (in which he was not allowed to sit on the stool that represented the very soul of the Asante), many of the shocked Asante leaders left wordlessly. Not so with Nana Yaa Asantewaa.* Shouting that she would not listen one more second to the British, she laid down a challenge to her fellow leaders: "If you, the chiefs of Asante, are going to behave like cowards and not fight, you should exchange your loin cloths for my undergarments."[†]

The war[‡] against the British started five days later, with Yaa Asantewaa in charge of the armies.

The British absolutely had it coming, as their relations with the Asante Confederacy represented the most despicable nadir of their worldwide colonial efforts. Years earlier, after multiple wars, Prempeh I (the head of the Asante Confederacy) had begun working with the British wholeheartedly, agreeing that the Asante would become a British protectorate. Far from welcoming this news with open arms, the British replied with a series of baffling and brutal acts: they arrested Prempeh I and his closest 30 advisers, exiling them 4,000 miles away in the Seychelles. The British then refused to hear from any Asante-hired lawyers.

The English brutishness continued well beyond these acts. They actually dissolved the Asante Confederacy, destroying the hard work that had brought together its component nations. In subsequently negotiating treaties one on one with each of the subnations, the British

---

* "Nana" was an honorific title used across Africa. See also entries in this book on **Nanny of the Maroons** and **Nana Asma'u.**

† Varying accounts are given for her actual wording. Bottom line, she was calling them wimps.

‡ The British generally called it the Asante Uprising, while the Asante referred to it as the War of the Golden Stool or, more popularly, the Yaa Asantewaa War.

inflamed old hatreds and turned the factions against each other. The British went on to give missionaries free rein to proselytize, wrecked the Asante economy,* and demanded compulsory (read: slave) labor from the Asante on work projects designed by and for their foreign overlords.

A telling example of the British opinion of the Asante came in a newspaper editorial from 1873. The author said that, "if by any lucky chance [the British governor] manages to catch a good mob of savages in the open, and at a moderate distance, he cannot do any better than treat them to a little Gatling [gun] music."

Yaa Asantewaa was acting far differently than most Asante women in her desire to fight. While women were highly respected in Asante society, they usually served as diplomats and judges. Their traditional contribution to war was to perform ritual dances and shame war-dodgers into suicide with insulting songs (a tradition reminiscent of the "sitting on a man" custom detailed in **Nwanyeruwa**'s entry). For a woman to take control of Asante armies, for the first time in history, was to shame the entire country's men into fighting. It was a testament to the Asante's true hatred of the British.

Much to the shock of the British, Yaa Asantewaa's warriors thoroughly trounced the colonialist soldiers. Although the British were much better armed and trained, the Asante took tremendous advantage of the terrain. They would stage ambushes, snipe from trees, and, most effectively, stage blockades. The Asante routinely built massive wooden structures that the British could not shoot through. From behind these walls, the Asante would fire their rifles through small openings, then lie flat on the ground and reload—leading the British to return fire at the wrong area.

Unfortunately, the blockades, while a great source of strength, also had severe downsides. Limited mobility and a fractured communications system made each blockade an island unto itself. The blockade commanders could not easily signal for reinforcements, coordinate attacks, or go on the offensive.

For five months, from April to September 1900, the Asante fought the British in earnest. They laid siege to the capital city of Kumasi for a month and a half, cutting telegraph wires and freeing prisoners. However, when British reinforcements arrived in mid-July, the tide turned. On September 30, the Asante fought their last major battle and were defeated. Although the British conquered the Asante, the Golden Stool remained hidden for decades.

---

* This was done in several ways. One was by opening up the country to free trade with its neighbors, thus flooding it with foreign labor and merchants. The other was by abolishing slavery—which, while unassailably the moral thing to do, caught the Asante off guard and made it difficult for them to compensate economically. They were hardly the only African economy of the time to rely heavily on slaves—see the entry on **Agontime and the Dahomey Amazons** for another example.

After the war, Yaa Asantewaa was captured and exiled to the Seychelles, where she died 21 years later.

Her legacy has evolved in the years since. Ghana (the location of the former Asante Confederacy) was the first African nation to declare independence from England, and its government latched on to Yaa Asantewaa's image as a national symbol. In their rush to venerate Yaa Asantewaa, Ghanian politicians have smoothed over many of her rougher edges. She is portrayed as only fighting for the confederacy as a whole, with little mention of her intention to position her subnation of Edweso over others after the fighting. As with so many political figures in so many nations before her, the historical record has rarely gotten in the way of political maneuvering.[*]

Her fame has spread even beyond the borders of her native Ghana. All over the world, but particularly in the United States, as historian T. C. McCaskie points out, black women have taken to identifying with Yaa Asantewaa, with some even going so far as to name themselves and their children after her. Across the Internet, people sell T-shirts and posters depicting her, and white men who've never even been to Ghana include her in books about unconventional heroines.[†]

## · ART NOTES AND TRIVIA ·

The gourd and spilled water here are a reference to Yaa Asantewaa's practice of pouring out water for magic rites to give her troops an advantage in battle.

Her outfit is based on the ceremonial war dress *(batakarikese)* that she's seen wearing in one of the few surviving pictures of her.

Although she did apparently raise and fire a gun in one of the early meetings of chieftains, most assume she did not actually participate in battle, instead handling the logistics and strategy from a distance.

---

[*] This rush to canonize her is nowhere more evident than in 2000's centennial celebrations of the Yaa Asantewaa War, detailed in first-person detail by T. C. McCaskie. As part of that extremely fractured event, the government opened a Yaa Asantewaa museum, which housed many of the surviving artifacts of her life. A scant four years later, the museum burned down in a fire that McCaskie hints was started intentionally. In McCaskie's estimation, the truth of Yaa Asantewaa's life and motivations was devoured, quite literally, to further various political ambitions.

[†] And then talk about themselves using insufferable third-person perspectives.

# Gertrude Bell

### (1868–1926, IRAQ [MESOPOTAMIA]/ENGLAND)

## *Mesopotamia's Uncrowned Queen*

After World War I, as the Ottoman Empire crumbled and Britain began drawing new borders for the Middle East, the administrators hit a snag. The British barely had any maps of the area, and nobody could say with real confidence what tribes lived where, or with whom they had ongoing feuds. Into this mess came an unexpected champion, bringing detailed maps and a nigh-encyclopedic knowledge of the region: explorer/archaeologist/badass Gertrude Bell, described as "one of the few representatives of His Majesty's Government remembered by the Arabs with anything resembling affection."

Before the war began, Gertrude Lowthian Bell had already lived a life utterly alien to most women of that time. She'd adventured on horseback for years through the Bedouin camps, royal palaces, and bustling marketplaces of the Middle East—always by herself, save for the helpers she'd hire. And this was after a short career as the world's greatest female mountaineer, during which she was successful enough to have a Swiss mountain (Gertrudespitze) named after her. The woman who would come to draw the boundaries of Iraq and fiercely safeguard the artifacts of its history even became an adviser to none other than Winston Churchill. She was, to quote one biography, "the most powerful and respected woman of the British empire."

Bell did not come from humble origins—far from it. Born into England's sixth-richest family, this "social hand grenade" didn't allow anyone or anything to hold her back. In the Victorian era, when doctors warned that too much thinking would hurt a girl's brain and make her barren (claims that date back to **Christine de Pizan**'s heyday centuries earlier), she not only went to college but also received the highest academic marks possible. She would berate male teachers when she felt they needed it and made herself a hero to her female friends.

After graduation, Bell fell in love with the Middle East and would spend almost two decades traveling there extensively. She accrued some serious skills: fluency in Arabic (in a myriad of dialects), Farsi, French, and German; proficiency in Hindustani and Japanese; expertise in cartography and archaeology; and mastery of photography. Between 1905 and 1914, she took almost 7,000 photos with her trusty (if finicky) Kodak camera, capturing on film for the first time numerous landmarks that had never been mapped or visited by Westerners. She was beloved by virtually every local she met, many of whom took her to be a literal queen. When she was given a rare hostile welcome and held hostage by one powerful tribe, she demanded to be let go and they did just that.

In such a lifetime of accomplishments, Bell's early career in mountaineering could almost be overlooked were it not for her unbelievable achievements in that arena. In an era before specialized clothing and gear, she scrambled up rocky cliffs in only her undergarments and showed unreal calm in hazardous circumstances: for instance, when she was trapped by an avalanche for more than a day and sure she would not make it down alive, she kept her cool and somehow escaped.

Despite her rough-and-tumble lifestyle, she kept a very feminine appearance. Unlike her contemporary **Jane Dieulafoy**, she never wore pants or attempted to disguise her gender—instead, she flaunted it. Although often residing deep in the desert, she was up to date on fashion and even kept a collection of fine china available for meals with dignitaries. Which is not to say she was squeamish: she did not flinch at drinking muddy water or local delicacies like camel's milk.

Bell's relationship to her own gender was, however, fairly complicated. Frustrated by the lack of serious concern by the women of the British aristocracy ("the devil take all inane women," she wrote), she was very active in anti-suffrage circles. While she thought herself the equal of any man, she did not feel all women were. And despite her unconventional activities, she personally was quite socially conservative. Both times she fell in love in her life she refused to break the rules of propriety. Her father forbade her to see the first man; the second was trapped in a loveless marriage that Gertrude refused to violate, despite the husband's desire to do so. Gertrude died a virgin.

Around 1915, she put her energies toward the formation of the nation that would become Iraq. Recruited to the position of Oriental secretary by the British High Commissioner of Iraq, Bell was the only woman in a cabinet of men. She was clearly one of the most experienced on the cabinet. A young T. E. Lawrence, better known as Lawrence of Arabia, once tried impressing her with his accomplishments. She responded by calling his methods of archaeology "prehistoric" and taking him under her wing to show him how things should really be done.

While in that post, she continually pushed for the Arabs to be self-governing. While she did advocate a colonialist approach (she was a product of her times), she wanted Britain's influence to be indirect. To this end, she wrote massive documents, papers so clever that the newspapers were shocked to discover a woman was behind them. About this, Bell wrote to her father with characteristic snark that the press found it "most remarkable that a dog should be able to stand up on its hind legs at all—i.e., a female write a white paper. I hope they'll drop that source of wonder and pay attention to the report itself."

Things didn't go exactly as she'd hoped. Because she butted heads with everyone—she was shunned in the dining halls and not kept in the loop on important cables—her advice was often ignored and the resulting borders for Iraq were a compromised mess. She bemoaned the installation of the Sunnis instead of the Shias, knowing the chaos that would erupt down the line. "Muddle through!" she wrote. "Why yes, so we do—wading through blood and tears that need never have been shed."

After the outlines for Iraq had been agreed upon, she was given a new task: training the new nation's first leader, Prince Amir Faisal. On the one hand, Faisal was a brilliant choice to unite disparate tribes, as he was able to trace his lineage to the Prophet Muhammad, but on the other hand, he was a terrible fit. He'd never lived in Iraq, he spoke a foreign dialect of Arabic, and he had little to no cachet with the local tribes. Bell brought him up to speed and included lessons on how to deal with businessmen and influence tribal councils. It was in this advisory work that she became known as the "uncrowned queen of Mesopotamia."

Concurrently, she expended a huge amount of energy in preserving the cultural history of Iraq. She founded the Iraq National Museum and became its first chief curator and director of antiquities. In 1924 she even drafted Iraq's "Law of Antiquities," which set a groundbreaking precedent in the world of archaeology and ended the looting that had plagued the field. For an example of the sort of plundering Bell fought, read the entry on **Tin Hinan**, whose grave was opened a year later, in 1925.

Unfortunately, her life after Faisal came to power was empty. With her major goals achieved (after a fashion), Bell took stock of her life. Her financial resources were strained, and she'd essentially become a social pariah because of her strong opinions. Whatever other projects she wanted to take on next would surely be difficult to impossible to accomplish. Days before her 58th birthday, she was found dead, an empty bottle of sleeping pills next to her.

Gertrude Bell was mourned by people the world over, from Britain to Iraq. Perhaps the most fitting testimony came in one obituary: "At last her body . . . was broken by the energy of her soul."

# Eustaquia de Souza and Ana Lezama de Urinza

## (1639–C. 1661, BOLIVIA)

### *The Valiant Ladies of Potosí*

otosí, Bolivia, was a rough town in the 1600s. It was the kind of place where innocent people couldn't go out at night for fear they'd be mugged—by the magistrates of the town, no less! It was just the sort of environment that cried out for a hero. For justice. For vigilantes.

Enter two 14-year-old girls.

Eustaquia de Souza and Ana Lezama de Urinza were sisters who'd grown up very sheltered. Ana's parents had died early in her life, and she'd been adopted by Eustaquia's family. Tragedy struck a second time when Eustaquia's mother and older brother died too. After that, Papa de Souza was not taking any chances and kept the two young ladies locked away from danger as much as possible.

Unfortunately for the father, Ana and Eustaquia were plenty good at finding danger on their own. While their brother had been alive, they'd eagerly watch him train with sword and gun. Now that he was gone, whenever their father was traveling, they would train themselves. Because what could possibly go wrong with two untrained (and unsupervised) preteens going at it with sharpened blades and unwieldy firearms?

Eventually, they decided to make use of their newfound knowledge. They waited until late one night and snuck out dressed as (incredibly stylish) men. Soon after their jaunt began, they met a man named Diego Melgarejo, and their slick outfits and staggering amount of weaponry immediately convinced him to join them. When they finally told him they were women, he was impressed, confused, and a little frightened. All of these feelings were about to magnify for poor Diego.

Soon the trio ran across a crowd of the thuggish town magistrate's servants. The head servant demanded that they hand over their money and arms. Eustaquia did so, after a fashion: she unloaded a bullet into him, killing him immediately. Everyone stood in shock for a moment until Ana, not to be outdone, fired her gun. Then the trio took off. The town government was outraged and began a search for the servant's killers.

In spite of being the subject of a manhunt, Ana and Eustaquia decided to go out again. They wrote to Diego, cajoling him into joining them, to which he replied, "You're crazy! No way." They then sent another letter, this time calling him a coward and (weirdly enough) a woman. That seemed to work, and he agreed to join their gang again, as long as they avoided danger.

So on the eve of San Juan, the three went out again, and for a while it was a great evening. They went to a nearby plaza, where they played and sang music. It was only when they stopped to tune their instruments in a doorway that they ran into trouble. Four men approached them and told them to scram. Diego was perfectly ready to do so, but Eustaquia wasn't having it. After a short argument, she tossed the guitar to poor Diego (who ran and hid) and leapt into battle.

It was a bloody fight, with the men outnumbering the women two to one. When Ana was wounded in the chest, Eustaquia hit Ana's assailant so hard in retaliation that she broke his shield and wounded his hand. In the end, both girls were wounded heavily, but their opponents came out much worse: one died, and another was close to it. Gradually, the neighborhood watch began arriving, and everyone fled the scene.

In the weeks that followed, the girls hid their injuries from their father, convalescing in their rooms. (Presumably, they played the "Dad! I'm on my *period*!" card frequently.) When Dad finally insisted on sending in a doctor, they demanded the doctor be female—and they immediately inducted her into their little conspiracy.

After two months, they were ready to go out on the town again. Diego respectfully declined this time with, "Screw that noise, you gals are nothing but trouble."

It was a moot point anyway. As soon as the girls gussied up for their third outing, their dad found them. He was not amused. In no time he made the lockdown they'd been on look like after-school detention, grounding them for the rest of their lives.

They escaped, of course, tying ropes to their windows and running across rooftops. They then used poor Diego to procure weapons and men's clothing before disappearing to Lima, where they became accomplished bullfighters and well-loved socialites.

Eventually, their father, who searched for them until the end of his days, died, with his last wish being that they become nuns. They agreed, but never followed through. Ana was injured while bullfighting and died. Shortly thereafter, Eustaquia died too, ostensibly of a broken heart. They willed their money to Lima, their servants, and their trusted sidekick, Diego—who received not only 1,000 pesos but also all of their flashy outfits.

## · ART NOTES AND TRIVIA ·

The way the duo are described in that story would suggest, to the people of the time, that they were lesbian lovers. Writers of fan fiction, fire up your word processors.

Sadly, the historicity of the story is questionable. The sole source, Bartolomé Arzáns de Orsúa y Vela's *Tales of Potosí*, is hit-and-miss with its accuracy, to put it mildly.

# Mary Bowser

## (19TH CENTURY, UNITED STATES)

### The Spy Who Set Fire to the Confederate White House

**B**y late 1864, Confederate president Jefferson Davis was about ready to lose his mind. Somehow, despite taking every precaution, information about troop and supply movements kept ending up in the hands of the Union. Little did he know that his enemy was right under his nose—as it was unimaginable to him that Ellen Bond, his slow-thinking, illiterate slave, was actually a highly educated secret agent with a photographic memory: Mary Bowser.

Bowser's story, one of the greatest espionage feats in history, is interwoven tightly with that of one of her closest friends, Elizabeth Van Lew. Bowser, born Mary Jane Richards, grew up as a slave to Van Lew's family, but not for long—Van Lew, a staunch abolitionist, emancipated Bowser when Mary was just three years old. From then on, the two became inseparable. Even after Bowser traveled abroad,* she decided to come back to the Van Lew home in Richmond, Virginia. However, since Bowser's return was technically illegal (blacks who'd left to be educated in the free states or abroad weren't allowed to return), Bowser pretended to be Van Lew's slave again. It was a ruse that would soon become useful.

In the years Bowser was traveling, Van Lew had gotten seriously involved in Union underground efforts, building a 50-foot-long room in her attic crawl space to hide soldiers and sympathizers. Considering the political climate of the town, this was beyond dangerous. The women of Richmond would collect the bones of Union soldiers to show to their children. A children's math book of the time contained the question: "If one Confederate soldier kills 90 Yankees, how many Yankees can 10 Confederate soldiers kill?" Prison guards would regularly shoot Union prisoners for sport. Van Lew was playing with fire.

But as much peril as Van Lew was in, Bowser was soon in far more. Van Lew organized the installation of Bowser—with her ability to memorize images at a glance and recall entire conversations overheard in passing—as a servant for Jefferson Davis's wife, Varina. The virulent Confederate hatred toward blacks made this an incredibly hazardous proposition. Even Varina, the First Lady of the Confederacy and one of the most powerful women in

---

* Including a four-year trip as a missionary in Liberia. Elizabeth made sure Mary traveled in first-class instead of steerage. They were such besties.

Richmond, had been ostracized because of the mere suggestion that she was part black. If Bowser made a mistake working in the Davis household, she was sure to be tortured and killed.

Bowser's methods of communication with the Yankees were subtle in the extreme. When she had urgent messages to convey, she would hang a red shirt on the clothesline. Then she would take one of Varina's dresses in for alteration, having sewn messages to the inside of the lining. The seamstress would convey the message to Van Lew or another agent, who would often pass it on in code. Van Lew was partial to poking out holes in the letters of books to spell out secret messages. Her brother would send invoices with specific items as code for military information—370 iron hinges for 3,700 cavalry, 30 anvils for 30 batteries of cavalry, and so on.

Come January 1865, the jig was up. Davis had arrested another spy in the ring, a baker to whom Bowser would also sometimes convey information. Knowing she was about to be uncovered, Bowser fled, but not before leaving one last good-bye present: a massive fire in the Confederate White House, which she set in the basement. It failed to burn down the entire house, but Bowser was able to escape to Van Lew. From there, she fled north on a horse cart in one of the most harrowing disguises imaginable: being covered completely in layers of horse manure.

Bowser's later life falls into the vagaries of history. Many of the records of Civil War espionage were destroyed to protect those involved. It is thought that she returned south and became a teacher, working in Florida and Georgia. She also wrote memoirs that were kept secret by her descendants, for fear of reprisal. Unfortunately, they were permanently lost to history when they were mistakenly thrown out in 1952.

## · ART NOTES AND TRIVIA ·

In the doorway stand Varina Davis and Elizabeth Van Lew. Van Lew is picking at Varina's sleeve, possibly encouraging her to get it tailored.

The book in Bowser's hand has a small pin sticking out of it, a reference to one of Van Lew's methods for passing messages. Another one involved invisible ink that could only be read when combined with a special acid!

The out-of-control fire is, of course, a callback to Bowser's attempt to burn down the Confederate White House.

The flag on the wall is the actual Confederate flag—its first version, at least. The better-known stars-and-bars design was the battle flag of the Army of Northern Virginia. It was later adopted by Southerners and became synonymous with the Confederate states.

### The "Crazy" Adventures of Elizabeth Van Lew

Elizabeth Van Lew experienced no shortage of danger herself during the war. As suspicion of her Union sympathies grew, the prestige and protection afforded by her family name gradually gave way to her new reputation as a pariah. Faced with this new public level of scrutiny, she resorted to the only action she thought could excuse her behavior: pretending to be insane. She became known to the citizens of Richmond as "Crazy Bet."

Her feigned lunacy was hardly a bulletproof shield, though. Her neighbors threatened to shoot her, strangers tried grabbing her off the street, and she started to check every night behind the bed for someone waiting to abduct her. She took to wearing peculiar dresses and stuffing her cheeks with cotton to make herself unrecognizable, and she kept her spy documents within arm's length so that she could quickly destroy them if need be.

After the war, Van Lew, having spent much of her family fortune on helping the Union, was left a destitute outcast in Richmond. With much of the city still shunning her company (some considered her a witch), she took work as a postmaster general for a while to make ends meet. In her later years, she relied on donations from Bostonians and the family of Paul Revere. She died in 1900 and was purportedly buried standing up, facing north.

# Pope Joan

## (9TH CENTURY, VATICAN CITY)

### The Pope Who Gave Birth

A curious thing happened in 856 CE. During a procession from St. Peter's Basilica to the Lateran Palace, the pope doubled over. The line of attendants stopped the march immediately and tended to their spiritual father—only to find "him" to be, in fact, a spiritual mother. The pope had given birth in the middle of the street. According to legend, Pope Joan, as she came to be called, either died on the spot or was subsequently beaten and killed by an angry mob.

How in the world could this happen? Joan, the Vatican discovered, was a lovestruck woman who'd secretly entered the church disguised as a man in order to be with her lover. She turned out to be extremely intelligent—medieval historian Martin Polonus describes her as "advanced in various sciences" to the point where "none could be found to equal her." And in 854, following the death of Leo IV, she was unanimously elected Pope John VIII.

The aftermath of her exposure as a woman was wide-ranging and brutal. The cardinals whom she'd deceived were tossed into a dungeon, where they all languished and died. The papal processions from then on avoided the spot where she'd given birth. Future popes were made to sit on a specially fashioned chair with a hole in the bottom so that their genitals might be inspected—to prevent a recurrence of a female pope.

There was just one problem: none of this ever happened.

Not that the faithful of 13th- and 14th-century Rome would question the validity of this story. With most convinced of the legend of Pope Joan, it was not until 1451 that the tale—which had first appeared 200 years earlier—would begin to be questioned. As has now been all but conclusively proven, Leo IV's reign gave way almost immediately to that of Benedictus III. (John VIII did exist, but was a different person than represented in the story.) Pope Joan is a fictional figure.

(Weirdly enough, popes did sit on a commode-shaped Roman birthing chair. One even still exists, housed in the Louvre. The most rational explanation on offer for its shape seems to be that it was old and Roman, and thus squatting on it somehow gave popes legitimacy.)

All of which brings us again to the question: How did this story come about? In a word: Protestants. In three: Protestants hated Catholics. In order to chip away at the power of the Catholic Church, the Protestants of the period repeated this legend endlessly. Their point was that the existence of an illegitimate female pope revealed Roman corruption and destroyed any claims of an unbroken divine succession dating back to St. Peter.

By the 1600s, belief in Pope Joan was scant, with only a handful clinging to the tale—mainly those who claimed that her baby (a) was still alive, (b) was the Antichrist, and (c) was waiting behind the scenes to destroy the world. Nevertheless, Joan's story persists to the present day, and she has become the subject of movies, songs, tarot cards, historical novels, and some unbelievably tedious historiographical books. Her birth name has been reported by various sources as Agnes, Gerberta, Joanna, Margaret, Isabel, Dorothy, and the surpassingly mellifluous Jutt. Not sure where Joan came from.

Now here's the twist: there actually *was* a historical female pope. She just wasn't named Joan. In the late 1200s, a woman named Guglielma, frustrated at women's exclusion from the church, began a rival, feminist sect of Christianity. She anointed one of her disciples, Manfreda Visconti da Pirovano, as popess, first in a line thereof. Unfortunately, the sect was short-lived, and Popess Manfreda was burned at the stake in 1300.

# Nwanyeruwa

## (EARLY 20TH CENTURY, NIGERIA)

## *Peacekeeper of the Igbo Women's War*

ontrary to the connotations of its name, the Igbo Women's War* was nonviolent—think less "warfare" and more "nonstop block party." A party, that is, that almost shut down the British colonial government in Nigeria. Accustomed to having a say in government matters, the women of Nigeria, in danger of losing their say due to British law, reacted in traditional fashion. They started, en masse, "sitting on a man": singing, dancing, yelling, and ridiculing government officials all day and night. The protest that drew in over 10,000 women all started with just one: Nwanyeruwa.

In November 1929, Nwanyeruwa was just trying to hold things together in her family. The Great Depression's effects had just spread to Nigeria, driving down the price of their exports. Compounding her difficulties was the recent death of her daughter-in-law. So when a local government official levied taxes on Nwanyeruwa (although women had never had to pay in the past) and then tried strangling her when she objected, she went to complain to his superior, Warrant Chief Okugo.

Unfortunately, Okugo was no help. He blamed Nwanyeruwa for starting the conflict and for dirtying his messenger with palm oil. (She'd had some on her hands when fighting him off.)

Nwanyeruwa replied by mobilizing the town's women, who then started "sitting" on Okugo: loitering outside his house 24 hours a day, playing music, and dissing him in song. Okugo reacted in utterly insane fashion—first chucking a spear into a woman's foot, then shooting a pregnant woman with an arrow (she miscarried), and finally setting his own house on fire and blaming it on the women, attacking anyone who tried to put it out.

Shockingly, these acts did not settle down matters in the slightest.

Soon thereafter, the protests spread. In many nearby towns, the combination of hatred toward the British-appointed warrant chiefs and fear over women's taxes boiled over, and women began protesting. Nwanyeruwa's group, lacking official channels through which to lodge their many complaints, took to the streets. They marched on the offices of the administration that had ignored them, continuing to sing their nonviolent yet inflammatory

---

\* Also known as the Aba Women's Riots.

songs ("If it were not for the white man we would have killed Chief Okugo and eaten him up").

When, weeks into the protests, their actions were still being dismissed as feminine hysterics, the women went beyond the pacifist tactics espoused by Nwanyeruwa. They attacked European stores, banks, and courts and knocked down telegraph poles and cut wires (much like **Emmeline Pankhurst**'s suffragettes); they even freed prisoners from the jails, but they never harmed anyone.

The British government was not nearly so measured in its response. On December 13, a frightened British medical officer ran over and killed two women, then fled. When over 15,000 women, outraged over the killings, began again attacking European property, British soldiers opened fire into the protesters, killing more than 50 and wounding over 50 more. The British burned entire villages as punishment.

Thereafter, the colonial authorities relented in their plans to tax women and curtailed the power of the warrant chiefs. Thus ended the Igbo Women's War, one of the first major challenges to British authority in West Africa. From there, Nwanyeruwa disappeared into the mists of history.

## · ART NOTES ·

Nwanyeruwa is seen here robbing Okugo of his red cap, an Igbo symbol of leadership.

The scars on the people in the scene are traditional for many tribes in West Africa. Be forewarned if you decide to research this custom further: while very striking, some of these scars can be quite extreme.

In reality, Nwanyeruwa and Okugo would probably be at least 10 years older than this. While their birth dates are uncertain, they are both described as old.

# Mary Lacy

(1740–1801, ENGLAND)

## The Runaway Who Built Ships

t 19, Mary Lacy's life took a strange turn. Literally. At six in the morning, dressed in men's clothing, Mary sped off from her family home in an unplanned direction, intent on living a life of adventure instead of that of a house servant. As it turned out, the direction she'd chosen brought her to Chatham, where she soon began serving in the navy on her majesty's spectacularly named ship *Sandwich*—as a man named William Chandler.

Mary had been a lively sort from her childhood. In her youth, she'd ride horses without saddle or bridle, pushing them as fast as they could go. When warned she would break her neck, she'd reply, "Neck or nothing!" The beatings and admonishments of her parents did nothing to dampen her spirit. In her teens, she took to sneaking out at night to attend secret dances. Her decision to run off at 19 was less a rash decision than it was the culmination of years of mischief.

Ships in those days had a reputation for being some of the most rough-and-tumble places around, and the good ship *Sandwich* did not disappoint. Mary became apprenticed to the ship carpenter, who, as a semifunctional alcoholic, beat her regularly and paid her a pittance. Additionally, being small for a sailor, she made enemies of the admiral boys-in-training. It was only after she challenged one of their best scrappers to a fistfight—and won—that she gained respect.

Mary spent many years at sea, across several ships, posing as a man. This was not as difficult as one might think. Her main adaptations were feigning ignorance of basic housekeeping ("How do you make a bed?") and using heaps of profanity. As for her monthly cycle? She was among sailors, one of the populations most prone to venereal disease. As a rule, they did not ask many questions. The last step, though, was the hardest: she needed a girlfriend.

Mary's sexuality is a bit of a question mark. Although early in her autobiography she remarks upon being smitten by a man, later on she mentions seducing (and being seduced by) a number of women. Her chief biographer, historian Suzanne Stark, theorizes from her analysis of the language used in the text that the passages that portray Mary as more heterosexual were added by someone else and that she was closer to the homosexual end of the Kinsey scale than 1700s England would have been comfortable with. In any event, she became quite the ladies' woman, bedding numerous women, including her superior's mistress (!).

It was only after she'd been gone for many years that she finally sent word to her family that she was alive. In a letter that comes across as more sheepish than genuinely remorseful, she instructed them, with no explanation, to address any replies to "William Chandler" and signed off as "your undutiful daughter." Eventually, after being gone almost eight years, she visited her family in Kent. While it was a joyous reunion, it led to a crisis.

One of the more loudmouthed family neighbors who'd witnessed Mary's return soon thereafter moved to the town where Mary was working—and outed her as a woman to several of her shipmates. Her fellow workers spoke to Mary about it, but she held her ground, and somehow they came away convinced she was not just a man, but a man's man. Nobody ever doubted her again.

In 1770, she got her certificate as a shipwright, the first ever given to a woman. Sick with rheumatism by then, she powered through and worked 12- to 17-hour shifts, sleeping on the planks of disassembled ships, until she was physically incapable. At that point she retired and collected a pension—under her real name.

Applying for her pension as Mary Lacy hadn't been her first choice. She'd tried as William Chandler but suffered endless delays. It was only after revealing the truth of her gender that she finally made headway: indeed, her annual pension of 20 pounds was granted almost without delay.

From there, her story becomes impossible to track. While her official autobiography has her marrying a Benjamin Slade, many, including Suzanne Stark, consider that information suspect. Historian Peter Guillery makes the case that she moved in with a female lover, became one of the first female architects, and built her own house. Historian Olwen Jonklaas finds that scenario less likely and puts forward substantial evidence that she did marry, have a child, and settle down to a quiet life in Deptford.

Given the uncertainty of her post-shipwright life, it might be best to do as Mary did and choose your own adventure.

## · ART NOTES ·

Mary Lacy is here portrayed working on the ship, in the state of poverty in which she spent most of her life—with dirty clothes and no shoes. Behind her, nursing a bottle of booze, is the carpenter to whom she was apprenticed. On board the ship are the admiral boys-in-training with whom she tussled early on. Down on the docks you can make out a number of women waving handkerchiefs at her.

# Josefina "Joey" Guerrero

## (1918–1996, PHILIPPINES)

## *The Leper Spy of the Philippines*

eprosy* is vanishingly rare today—so rare that you're far more likely to come across a joke using this affliction as a punch line than to meet someone actually suffering from it. But in the 1930s it was anything but funny. Contracting leprosy meant a lifetime of ostracism and pain, and then eventually death.

Nevertheless, some managed to rise above the stigma of the disease and even use it to their advantage.

Exhibit A: Josefina "Joey" Guerrero.

Twenty-three-year-old Joey was diagnosed with leprosy during a terrible era in Philippine history. Lepers were treated as subhuman and often quarantined in filthy colonies. Those who weren't shipped off would suffer worse degradations. In Manila, for example, lepers had to ring bells as they walked so that others could avoid them—an aural scarlet letter. But this was not the worst part of Joey's fate: three weeks after her diagnosis, Japan bombed Pearl Harbor and subsequently invaded the Philippines.

Her initial distrust of the Japanese quickly blossomed into quiet rebellion. A turning point came early when some Japanese soldiers propositioned her while she was out in public with several of her friends. Her demure, understated response was to repeatedly bludgeon the soldiers with her umbrella and run off. That night one of the friends came to her in secret and asked if she'd be willing to join the locals' resistance. With the nearby leprosarium suffering even further neglect under Japanese rule, Joey agreed. Thus began what she came to call her "quiet war."

Her initial missions were low-key. She would sit in her apartment and count all the incoming and outgoing Japanese forces at the military base across the way. She eventually surpassed expectations—for instance, by noting which squadrons were dirty, she was able to surmise where they'd been. She started visiting some of the American POWs, smuggling notes in and out using all manner of vessels: scooped-out fruit, hairbands, even hollowed-out shoes.

She and her husband† conducted spy work for three years and proved so skilled at it that

---

* Also known as Hansen's disease. Some organizations agitated for the phasing-out of the term "leprosy," owing to the stigma associated with it, but given that the disease has become rare, easily treatable, and less stigmatized, this book will use the better-known term.

† The couple had a daughter. Age two at the time of Joey's diagnosis, she was sent away to live with her grandparents so as to not contract leprosy.

they were eventually recruited into some of the highest levels of the resistance. They were even brought to resistance headquarters: a secret cave hidden behind movable boulders.

Throughout all this, Joey's untreated disease progressed, until no amount of clothing could conceal it. She would routinely get horrified reactions everywhere she went, and nobody was more horrified than the Japanese soldiers.

One day she was called into the rebels' fort again and given the most difficult mission of the entire campaign. The American forces, she was told, were soon launching a major offensive, but they faced an area covered in land mines. The resistance had mapped out a safe path for them, but they needed to get the info to the Americans quickly—the US forces were 50 miles away, coming in three days, and on the opposite side of some of the most dangerous areas of the country.

So Joey put on her shoes and started walking. Alone. In revealing clothing.

Her fashion sense worked wonders. When she came to Japanese checkpoints, the guards were so disgusted by her appearance that they just let her pass—never realizing that she had a map taped between her shoulder blades.

For two days straight she walked, day and night, through sniper fire and mortar shells. Even though she was so malnourished, sleep-deprived, and sick that she was barely able to stay upright.

When she arrived at the coordinates for the American camp, 50 miles from her starting point, she found that the Americans had moved—and set out to walk another 25 miles.

When she eventually found the US forces, she was so weak that she couldn't even eat the pancakes and coffee they offered her—even though it was the first offer of real food she'd had in years. Then, to top it all off, she had to make her way back through territory that had become even more dangerous. At one point she hid behind an American tank, only to have it immediately explode. Somehow she managed to make it back unscathed. The Americans also made it through the mine field, and soon thereafter the war was over.

After the occupation ended, Joey immediately volunteered as a nurse for the wounded, but quickly proved too ill to work. She was sent to the nearest leprosarium, only to walk into a vision of hell. The facilities had been completely ignored for three years, and the rotting shacks were awash in people sleeping in their own waste. Within weeks, 600 more people were transferred to the facility, tipping the situation past the breaking point. Joey again took matters into her own hands.

Writing to journalists, the daughter of the president of the Philippines, and friends in the US military, Joey directed a spotlight on the leprosarium. Within months, everything changed. The entire facility was transformed with an infusion of modern drugs and newly implemented sanitation standards.

But all of this came too late for Joey. Her condition had progressed to the point where she needed treatment at a top-notch medical facility, which could only be found in the United States. However, the United States had a strict policy of not admitting foreigners with communicable diseases.

Until, that is, the attorney general himself stepped in and used his special wartime powers to allow Joey into the country for treatment. Thus, in 1948, she became the first foreign leper allowed into the United States. She was greeted by a crowd of 400 in San Francisco, including many of the soldiers she'd helped in the Philippines. After giving her the US Medal of Freedom, they sent her to Carville, Louisiana, for treatment—and there she was eventually cured.

Joey stayed in the United States from that point onward, becoming a major figurehead in the fight against the stigma of leprosy. After a pitched battle over her right to stay in the country that involved the intercession of three senators, she gained citizenship. She moved to San Francisco, became a journalist, got a master's degree in Spanish literature, and worked as a Peace Corps volunteer in Niger, Colombia, and El Salvador. She eventually remarried* and died at the age of 68 in Washington.

---

* What became of her husband and young daughter is seemingly unknown. Nothing written about her after the 1940s mentions her Philippine family. Her name at the end of her life was Joey Guerrero Leaumax, and her obituary notes no immediate survivors.

# Chiyome Mochizuki

## (16TH CENTURY, JAPAN)

## The Matriarch Who Ran a Ninja Academy

 here are eight ninjas in this picture.

Not that you'd know it to look at them—which was kind of the whole point of Chiyome Mochizuki's schemes.

Chiyome was a noblewoman who lived in one of the most violent periods in Japanese history (it wasn't called the Era of Warring States for no reason). Towns were destroyed, and soldiers killed with such terrifying regularity that virtually everyone was one degree of separation from a murder.

Chiyome was no exception: she lost her husband in one of the bloodiest conflicts of the time, the Battle of Kawanakajima. After that, she came into the care of her husband's uncle, one of the most famous, powerful, and highly regarded feudal lords to ever live: Shingen Takeda.

And Takeda had plans for Chiyome.

In short order, with Takeda's blessing, Chiyome set up camp in the village of Nazu to help the female victims of war. The province was awash in orphans, widows, runaways, and lost girls, and Chiyome found it in her heart to take them in. She quickly gained a reputation as a kindly woman who provided a foster home for the less fortunate. All she asked in return was that her boarders work for their room and board . . . as ninjas.

You see, Chiyome's foster home was, in actuality, a secret training camp for female ninjas (*kunoichi*). She would train them to pass themselves off as shrine maidens, serving women, and geisha in order to secretly gather information on Takeda's enemies. She ended up with between 200 and 300 agents in all, forming one of the largest and most powerful spy agencies in all of Asia.

As kunoichi, these women rarely saw combat. On their behind-the-scenes battlefields, they planted rumors to sow confusion and dissension, snuck into secret areas, and used their feminine wiles to charm men. Not that they were untrained in the martial arts—since Chiyome's family were longtime members of the Koga Ryu school of ninjutsu, it is assumed that she taught her kunoichi many of the same martial arts techniques used by their male counterparts.

Little else is known about Chiyome herself. In fact, about all one can concretely say is that she existed—the rest is oral history. Her involvement with Takeda was kept a secret for most of their lives, and little was ever revealed. Even the date of Chiyome's death and how she died are unknown. The question of whether kunoichi even existed—and if so, what they actually did—was a matter of no small debate for much of Japanese history. All of the lore surrounding kunoichi and Chiyome can easily fall into the realm of mystery and rumor. But this much is true: Chiyome Mochizuki had such a fearsome reputation that we are still talking about her 500 years later.

## · ART NOTES AND TRIVIA ·

Chiyome (in purple) is displaying the *hikimayu* style of the time—noblewomen would pluck out their eyebrows and paint on large smudges in their place. Were her mouth to be open, her teeth would undoubtedly have been painted black, as that was also a style common to the era (called *ohaguro*).

The geisha on the right is passing a note to Chiyome. Technically geisha did not exist in this era—Chiyome would likely have employed *yujo* (prostitutes whose work had no platonic component, unlike that of geisha), *shirabyoshi* (dancers who wore male garb), and *miko* (shrine maidens, seen outside in the back).

The pronunciation of Chiyome's name is indeterminable from how it's written. Some think it's pronounced Chi-yo-jo.

---

## Japan's Greatest Warlord: A Woman?

The man whom Chiyome's kunoichi would have spent the most time spying on was Takeda's enemy, the warlord Kenshin Uesugi—who, if you believe one contemporary Japanese historian, was actually a woman.

Let's be clear: said historian, Yagiri Tomeo, is kind of a nut. He's posited any number of bizarre conspiracy theories that have been discredited, but when it comes to Kenshin, he brings forth some evidence that is not as easily dismissed:

- Kenshin had severe stomach cramps on a monthly basis, around the 10th of the month. He actually scheduled his military campaigns around this.

- Kenshin's cause of death was recorded as a form of uterine cancer—by a doctor who made virtually no mistakes in the rest of the book in which this information is found.

- When the Uesugi were forced to relocate, they reportedly took Kenshin's remains with them and refused to tell even the shogun where he was interred. This rules out DNA testing.

- Kenshin's personal tastes and appearance were consistently described in feminine terms, which, given the extreme subtleties of the Japanese language, is actually a bigger deal than it might seem.

- Kenshin was the only man allowed by the shogun to wander among his harem.

- Kenshin never married and never had children (although he did adopt).

Why would Kenshin pose as a man? According to the law of the time, a clan's leader had to be a man or the shogun could divide up the clan holdings and give them away.

All that said, it's tremendously unlikely. Kenshin had three older brothers, thus obviating any need for his parents to present a daughter as a son. Given the records of the time, it would be very hard to hide Kenshin's birth sex or rewrite it later. The most obvious explanation is that Kenshin was intersex, but even that is subject to debate.

# Nana Asma'u

## (1793–1864, NIGERIA [SOKOTO CALIPHATE])

## *The Princess Who Loved Learning*

**I**f you lived in western Africa during the 1800s, you were in *jaji* territory. Roaming across the land in their telltale hats, the jaji were notorious gangs of women. Under the orders of their leader, Princess Nana Asma'u, these take-no-crap ladies would wait until you were home, burst into your house, and educate you to within an inch of your life.

Yes, the jaji were itinerant female teachers.

The jaji were born out of Nana Asma'u's love of education. Fluent in four languages and well versed in many more, the princess of the Sokoto Caliphate translated books, wrote her own, and read everything she could get her hands on. Early in her life, she came to the conclusion that learning without teaching is empty. Thus, jaji.

The jaji were a clever idea. Tasked with the goal of bettering women's place in society, the jaji tailored their curriculum to the average woman. They used mnemonics and poetry to teach their largely illiterate students in the comfort of their own homes—often as they took care of household duties. They taught the basics of reading and writing, with the Qur'an as their source.

Now, it is entirely possible that "wandering bands of female teachers" would not be the first image to pop into your mind when you think about an African Islamic state—which is a shame. The Sokoto Caliphate, birthed in (and maintained by) bloody conflict around the interpretation of Islamic law, was the largest nation in Africa for almost 100 years. It held women in high regard—Nana Asma'u herself served as court adviser, sending orders to governors and debating foreign scholars. She advanced the idea that the search for knowledge is a religious imperative, and that women should be able to move about freely for just that purpose.

Unfortunately, in recent years, the Sokoto Caliphate (and Nana Asma'u along with it) has figured in the cultural zeitgeist mostly as a "precursor" of sorts to the horrific gang of ignorant murderers known as Boko Haram. This group, whose name translates to "Western education is forbidden," aims to end the influence of Western cultures in Africa and start their own caliphate. Citing as inspiration the work of Nana Asma'u's father, who founded the Sokoto Caliphate, these thugs made worldwide headlines in 2014 for kidnapping 276 schoolgirls, inspiring the "Save Our Girls" social media campaign.

Nana Asma'u deserves to be remembered in a more positive light.

# Julie "La Maupin" d'Aubigny

### (1670–1707, FRANCE)

## The Sword-Slinger Who Burned Down
## a Convent to Bang a Nun

At the top of the list of history's greatest rascals is undoubtedly "La Maupin," Julie d'Aubigny: sword-slinger, opera singer, and larger-than-life bisexual celebrity of 17th-century France. Her life was a whirlwind of duels, seduction, grave robbing, and convent burning so intense that she had to be pardoned by the king of France twice.

La Maupin (her opera name, which this book will use, since nobody's 100 percent sure her real name was Julie) had a real piece of work for a father. As the man in charge of training Louis XIV's pages, her father would fence nonstop during the day and hit up gambling dens, bars, and brothels in the evenings. Given the seedy circles in which he ran, it should be little surprise that his main ideas for daddy-daughter bonding time were (a) teaching her how to use deadly weapons and (b) using said weapons to drive off any potential suitors.

This paternal embargo on genital contact backfired when our heroine found a loophole: shtupping her dad's boss, the one guy her dad couldn't challenge to a duel.

When said boss became frustrated with La Maupin's increasingly wild ways, he arranged her marriage to a mild-mannered clerk, thinking that might settle her down. She responded in the only sensible manner—by taking an itinerant swordsman as a new lover and leaving home to wander aimlessly through France.

She earned her living through singing and dueling demonstrations, usually dressed as a man—a fashion she'd maintain throughout her life. She was already so skilled with the sword (quickly surpassing her new lover) that audiences sometimes would not believe that she was actually a woman. In fact, when one drunken onlooker proclaimed loudly that she had to be a man, she tore off her shirt, providing him with ample evidence to the contrary. The heckler had no comeback.

If La Maupin had one overriding flaw, it was an allergy to boredom. In fact, she soon dumped the wandering swordsman, pronounced herself tired of men in general, and seduced a local merchant's daughter. The merchant, desperate to separate the two, sent his daughter to a convent—but again, our heroine found a loophole. La Maupin joined the convent herself and started hooking up with her intended in the house of God. Shortly into their convent stint, an elderly nun died (from natural causes, it would seem), and La Maupin reacted the same way anyone might: by disinterring the body, putting it in her lover's room, and setting the whole convent on fire.

The two ladies ran off in the confusion and enjoyed a long elopement. After three months, La Maupin got bored, dumped her nun lover, and ran off into the night.

For this bout of shenaniganery, La Maupin was sentenced to death. In response, she approached her first paramour (her dad's boss) and, through his influence, convinced Louis XIV (who by this point had his hands full with **Hortense and Marie Mancini**) to pardon her. The king did so, and La Maupin took advantage of her new lease on life by running off to Paris and joining the opera.

And this was all before she was 20! Makes you feel like an underachiever.

Her behavior grew only more outrageous when she became an opera singer—basically the rock stars of the day. In true theater major fashion, she alternately sparred with and slept her way through her stage contemporaries, and audiences loved her for it. Here are three stories to exemplify her time in Paris:

- Another opera singer, named Duménil was a notorious trash-talker, and his main target was La Maupin. She responded by ambushing him, pushing a sword in his face, and demanding a duel. When he refused (on the grounds that he was a wimp), she beat him with a cane, stealing his snuffbox and watch. The next day she caught him complaining that he had been assaulted by a gang of thieves. She called him a liar and a coward, threw his watch and snuffbox at him, and declared that she alone had architected his ass-beating.

- One night while she was out carousing on the town, a particularly ardent man named d'Albert began crudely hitting on her. She'd just finished singing for the crowd, and he let loose with the one-liner "I've listened to your chirping, but now tell me of your plumage"—the 17th-century equivalent of the come-on "Does the carpet match the drapes?" She was, shall we say, unimpressed. In short order, she got into a fight with him and two of his buddies, won, and ran her sword clean through his shoulder. She felt a bit bad about that, so she visited her impaled victim in the hospital and hooked up with him anyway. Although the relationship only lasted a short while, they apparently became lifelong friends.

- She attended a royal ball (thrown by either Louis XIV or his brother) dressed as a man. She spent most of the evening courting a young woman and thus earned the ire of three of the woman's suitors. When La Maupin pushed things too far and kissed the young lady in full view of everyone, the three challenged her to a duel. She fought all of them—outside of the royal palace, mind you—and won. According to some accounts, she actually killed them. This entertained Louis XIV so much that he pardoned her from any punishment.

Actually, La Maupin didn't get off scot-free for that last one. The anti-dueling laws of the time were becoming increasingly severe, and even though the king had basically pardoned her (musing that the law governed men but didn't say anything about women), she still was forced to run off to Brussels until the heat died down. While in Brussels, she (surprise) took another lover, this time the Elector of Bavaria. The two grew apart in short order. Apparently the Elector was a bit alarmed when La Maupin stabbed herself onstage with an actual dagger, as part of a theatrical performance. When she was offered 40,000 francs to leave on good terms, she threw the coin purse at the Elector's emissary and started swearing at the poor man. In some versions, she also kicked the emissary down the stairs.

After that, she returned to Paris and died five or six years later of unknown causes at the age, as best anyone can tell, of 37. Her life story was thereafter reported in a number of articles, usually in the pearl-clutching, vapor-having tone a high-society woman might use to describe the bride of Satan. Several of these stories claimed that La Maupin had a massive change of heart late in life, became religious, and (re-)joined a convent. Given that these articles seemingly only exist to use her life as a morality tale, it's best to take them with a brick of salt. It is generally agreed, however, that she spent the final years of her life reunited with her husband and lived fairly peacefully.

That's right, she was technically married through it all. Don't worry if you forgot about that detail. This author did too. Heck, so did she, from the sounds of it.

## · ART NOTES AND TRIVIA ·

The picture is meant to evoke the sense of La Maupin running madly through France, leaving a trail of chaos in her wake. The lights coming from the house suggest spotlights and the authorities looking for her.

Her design is consistent with what is known about her looks: that she had blue eyes, light skin, dark curly hair, an aquiline nose, an athletic build, and, apparently, perfect breasts.

As was French fashion around the time, she has a beauty mark on her face. Depending on where you placed the mole, it would communicate something different. La Maupin's means "passionate," which seemed appropriate.

Her story, although endlessly recounted as verbatim truth, is difficult to verify—and the sources themselves are somewhat suspect. It's entirely likely that much of the story is hyperbolic at best, but that doesn't stop it from being a rollicking good time.

# Nanny of the Maroons

## (C. 1680–C. 1750, JAMAICA)

### The Mother of Us All

Let's face it, the story of much of the 1700s and 1800s was one of the European powers using the world for target practice. Innumerable are the queens and kings of the rest of the world who met violent and undeserved ends at the ends of European muskets.

Queen Nanny* of Jamaica's Windward Maroons was no such figure. For Nanny kicked in the Brits' teeth. Repeatedly.

First, some background on the Maroons. When Jamaica was being settled by Europeans, they would routinely bring slaves over from Africa. Just as routinely, said slaves would escape and run off to other parts of the island, often in huge numbers—we're talking up to 300 people at a time walking off the job. This resulted in two large communities of Maroons (escaped slaves): the western-side (Leeward) Maroons and the eastern-side (Windward) Maroons, led by Nanny.

In a shocking turn of events, the British weren't too cool with communities of escapees who routinely raided their settlements and freed their slaves. And so the British set in motion their time-honored tradition of killing their former servants, both bodily and in reputation. While the former did not prove very effective, as you will soon see, the latter served to significantly muddy the waters. So keep in mind that much of what we know about Queen Nanny is a combination of Jamaican oral history and centuries-old smack-talk from angry racists.[†]

This is what we do know for sure: Nanny stomped the British. Records on both sides show entire British platoons[‡] being wiped out for every one or two Maroon casualties. How did the Maroons achieve this? According to the histories, they had several methods—see if you can tell where facts start becoming legends:

---

\* You may at this point be saying to yourself, "Nanny is not a name." You are correct! But not in the way you might think. In this case, Nanny is probably short for Nanani—a combination of *nana* (a term of respect) and *ni* ("first mother," another term of respect). Nanny's actual name may be lost to time. See also the entries on **Nana Asma'u** and **Yaa Asantewaa**.

† When it came to the Maroons, the British literature characterizes them as bloodthirsty misogynist savages (despite the fact that they were, and are, ruled by women). One particularly notable jerk, Edward Long (1734–1813), wrote that one of their women could marry an orangutan and it would be no dishonor to the simian.

‡ The Maroons never actually killed the entirety of a platoon. Instead, they would leave one person alive to go back and tell the others what had happened.

- Nanny set several lookouts throughout the island with cow horns (*abeng*) that they could blow to communicate the number, distance, and armament of oncoming British troops. This communication would move across the island quickly, giving the Maroons upwards of six hours to prepare for any assault.

- The Maroons manipulated the entryway to their town to the point where people could only approach one at a time, in single file. Combined with the advance warning, the British were basically sitting ducks.

- Nanny would camouflage her soldiers in tree branches and vines, teaching them to stand still and slow their breathing for long periods of time. One British record states that their troops would come to a clearing, hang their coats on a tree, and promptly be decapitated by the same "tree" a couple minutes later.

- She would set out a cauldron that boiled without fire and cast several herbs into it. The British, upon encountering it, would pass out from the fumes and fall off a cliff.[*]

- She could catch bullets and throw them back at the British with deadly force. This led to the modern-day Jamaican saying to chastise selfish people, "Granny Nanny didn't catch bullets for you alone." British chroniclers of this legend, in their characteristic sophistication, claimed that she caught bullets (and tossed them back) with her buttocks. Stay classy, y'all.

- When the Maroons ran low on food, Nanny procured more through magical methods that were part "Jack and the Beanstalk," part Hanukkah: when her people were near starvation, she planted several pumpkin seeds, and they grew into full-fledged pumpkins almost overnight.

Regardless of the boundary between fact and fiction, the Maroons remained undefeated, and after almost two decades of warfare the British negotiated a peace treaty. Although she is mentioned in the negotiations, Nanny didn't sign the peace treaty (one of her headmen did),[†] and from there she falls into the fog of history.

---

[*] Specifically, some Jamaicans have pointed to the churning caused by two nearby rivers merging as a potential source of the "Nanny's Pot" legend. She and the other Maroons were known to be gifted herbologists, so the idea of them cooking up some incapacitating agent out of local plants is totally not out of the question.

[†] Karla Gottleib, one of the primary historians who's looked into Nanny's story, supposes that this was because Nanny didn't trust the British but saw the necessity in a peace treaty. Sure enough, in one of the least shocking plot twists in history, the British walked all over the treaty shortly after ratifying it. They relocated the entirety of the Leeward Maroons to Sierra Leone and in 1842 tried revoking the rights of all remaining Maroons to their land. Jerks.

One of the most mysterious facets to Nanny is her origin. Oral tradition describes her as Ghanian royalty and says that she arrived in Jamaica a free woman with a retinue of slaves.[*] Some tellings paint this series of events as Nanny sending herself by boat to the New World in order to rescue her kinsmen. Various tellings describe her as having one sister and up to five brothers.

After her death, her legacy lived on. Her face adorns the Jamaican $500 bill, and her name graces any number of schools, offices, and towns. The Windward Maroons, still mostly governed by women, live in Moore Town, formerly known as New Nanny Town. The site of the original Nanny Town, abandoned around 1743, remains a sacred site for the Maroons. Superstition has it that any *bakra* (white person) who tries entering the area will get lost, fall ill, or die. Seeing as this actually happened around a dozen times in the 19th and 20th centuries, it would seem there's something to it.

---

[*] An oft-overlooked aspect of the Maroons was that despite being escaped slaves themselves, they kept slaves. They integrated some of the people they freed from British plantations into their community, while others they took as slaves. History is complicated!

# Xtabay

## (MESOAMERICAN MYTH)

## *Siren of the Yucatán*

**B**efore you continue reading, look at the art. Gather your initial impression. Got it? Good— remember that.

Now, if you've heard of Xtabay, you probably know she's a demonic temptress who lures unsuspecting (read: horny) men to their deaths in fields of Yucatán cacti. She's another variation on the Siren myth, like **Iara**. You may then ask, "Why is she in this book? We already have a Siren entry!" The answer is the part most people don't know about: Xtabay's backstory.

A long time ago, in an Edenic little village, there lived two beautiful Mesoamerican girls: Utz-Colel and Xkeban.* Utz-Colel was chaste and pure, virtuous to a fault. Xkeban was . . . not. She was quite open with her favors, so to speak. She liked the fellas, you could say. Not shy around the menfolk, if you know what I'm saying.

Madonna/whore complex. I'm talking about the Madonna/whore complex.

However, things were not as simple as all that. Xkeban's wide-ranging affections extended to helping the homeless, the sick, and the poor. She'd sell the gifts suitors gave her to raise money for the less fortunate. Utz-Colel, by comparison, took her virginal austerity to extremes, refusing to even smile at the less fortunate. Helping the downtrodden wasn't exactly on her social calendar.

One day a sweet perfume began wafting over the village. Tracking it to its source, the villagers, to no small shock, found Xkeban dead in her house. Utz-Colel didn't believe for a second that the smell was actually emanating from Xkeban: she reasoned that since Xkeban had been so "dirty" in life, she could only emanate a mighty stink in death. She continued thinking this even after Xkeban was buried and sweet-smelling flowers† sprang from her grave.

*I'm gonna make twice as fragrant a corpse, just you watch*, thought Utz-Colel.

Eventually the day came for Utz-Colel to make good on her vow: she died a virgin and was praised for her lifelong chastity by admiring neighbors. But as soon as she was buried, a

---

* While these may sound like flowery exotic names, in the original language they lose some of the poetry—Xkeban means "sinner," Utz-Colel means "good woman," and Xtabay means "female ensnarer." Mayan books of baby names were apparently not much fun.

† These flowers were called Xtabentún. It's also the name of a liquor company. Honestly, Xtabay would probably make a pretty good name for a liquor company. Like, Xtabay Microbrewing? Who wouldn't drink that!

stink to end all stinks issued forth from her burial plot. This was a debilitating stench, an odor to reduce hardened souls to tears, to make the most vivacious pray for death, to make everyone wish for deliverance unto a world without scent. It done stanked up the place, y'all.

The origin of this fetid, fulsome funk? The Tzacam flowers now growing from Utz-Colel's grave.

Now dead (or possibly transformed into a Tzacam flower, it's a little ambiguous), Utz-Colel mulled over her life. Thinking that Xkeban had only done so well in death because her lifetime of sins had been so sexy (and thus, apparently, the best sins of all), Utz-Colel decided to emulate her sister's lustiness in her own afterlife. However, lacking the emotional honesty that Xkeban brought to her love life, Utz-Colel became the Xtabay—a demon who waits under the ceiba tree, combing her hair with the spines of the Tzacam flower until she can seduce and kill wayward men.

## · ART NOTES ·

The girls are seen next to their respective flowers. Utz-Colel, in the foreground, has a pattern of spikes in her jewelry that mirrors the spikiness of the Tzacam flower.

# Tomoe Gozen

### (1157–1247, JAPAN)

## The Samurai Who Made Samurai Flee

**I**f you know anything about samurai, you probably know that they aren't big on backing down. Battling to the death? Sure. Charging into certain doom? Absolutely. Ritual suicide? Race you to the knife closet.

But going one-on-one against a woman whom the history books describe as "a match for any god or demon?" No thank you.

Such was the hard-earned reputation of Tomoe Gozen, one of the only female Japanese warriors (*onna-bugeisha*) of medieval times. She grew up as the foster sister of Yoshinaka Minamoto, a samurai general with an eye on the shogunate. When the two reached adulthood and Yoshinaka began looking for lieutenants for his army, Tomoe was one of the first on the list. By that point, she'd won a reputation as a "warrior who could stand alone against a thousand," mostly by winning a crap-ton of fights (that's 9.7 buttloads for those of you on the metric system).

Now, it should be noted that Yoshinaka himself was not burdened with, shall we say, an excess of competency—leading one to question how much of his success was due to savvier associates such as Tomoe. Described as a "wild barbarian," the would-be shogun made an early attempt to introduce himself to the aristocracy by burning down the emperor's house, decapitating 100 of its defenders, and parading their heads around town. This was generally perceived as downright unneighborly.

With the help of Tomoe and his other lieutenants, Yoshinaka did eventually become shogun, but soon thereafter he had to flee from a rival's invading forces. After a long-delayed departure (Yoshinaka dallied so long his servants literally started killing themselves outside his room to get him to leave), he left with 100 samurai. Charging through dozens of skirmishes, the force was a scant dozen people by the time they exited the city. Tomoe was one of those twelve. She was unscathed.

As they fled through the forest, Tomoe ran into a fearsome enemy general named Hatakeyama. Instead of running away, she continually charged at him, dodging his every attack. Her handiwork soon made it apparent to him that "this is no woman, this is a demon at work." Given the potential shame from his imminent loss to a woman, Hatakeyama decided the most honorable thing to do was to run away—because not only was Tomoe definitely going to kill him, she would ruin his entire family name in the process.

He wasn't wrong, as his fellow general Uchida proved shortly thereafter.

Upon finding Tomoe, Uchida ordered all of his soldiers to attack her, before eventually deciding to confront her himself. Determined to prove he was stronger, he walked his horse right up to hers and began grappling with her from the saddle. Almost immediately, he was outmatched. So he grabbed a knife, only to have her knock it away, yelling, "I am the combat instructor you need!"

She then grabbed him by the faceplate, slammed him onto her horse's pommel, and cut off his head. This did not do wonders for his family's honor.

Despite Tomoe's heroics, Yoshinaka's cause was lost, and he ordered her to retreat. After refusing to do so for several more skirmishes, she finally obeyed—but not before decapitating another enemy general on the way out, for good measure.

What happened to Tomoe after her days on the battlefield is unknown. One source claims she became a Buddhist nun, and another that she married an enemy general and had a family. The latter is less plausible (her life span barely matched up with that of the general named) and was probably dreamed up by someone who wanted to claim relation to her. Can you blame them?

## · ART NOTES AND TRIVIA ·

Although she mostly wore a helmet, after her fight with Hatakeyama, Tomoe let her hair down and put on a white hat. The design here is based on hats from Japanese horseback archers.

Traditionally, her armor is portrayed with brighter colors, and Tomoe herself with far more makeup. This armor design is based off a surviving coat of female samurai armor. Such armor was put on like a kimono, to preserve feminine modesty.

The pattern on her shoulder pads (it looks like three commas in a circle) is also called *tomoe*. Which may explain why she was called Tomoe. It was considered rude to refer to a woman by her given name. "Gozen" was an honorific title given to many Japanese women of ancient times.

Tomoe has her own Noh play, which is no small feat: there are only around 200 such plays in existence, and only 18 are devoted to the tales of warriors.

The number and names of Tomoe's opponents differ based on the source. In some versions, she only fights one man, Honda no Moroshige (mentioned earlier as the man she decapitated on her way off the battlefield). In other versions, she's given two other fights, against Uchida and Hatakeyama, whom she kills and lets go, respectively.

The historicity of Tomoe's existence is (surprise) disputed by many scholars. While her story shows up in two major Japanese historical documents, said documents have variable historical accuracy. It is perhaps best to take the finer details with a pinch of salt.

# Empress Theodora

## (C. 497–548, TURKEY)

## The Concubine Who Conquered Constantinople

any of the women in this book were bad-mouthed in their lifetimes, but few experienced gossip taken to the hyperbolic levels accorded Theodora. Prior to becoming consort to Justinian I, emperor of the Eastern Roman Empire, Theodora had come from one of the lowest rungs of society: she was a prostitute. But she rose above her origins through force of will, becoming one of the most influential—and controversial—empresses in history.

Theodora entered the world of sex work early in life. When her father, a bear trainer, died,* Theodora's mother was left with little source of income. Theodora started working as an actress, a profession in those days that was nearly synonymous with sex worker. She proved quite popular, telling dirty jokes and taking onlookers' flirtation in stride. Her most famous stage act was to dress as Leda—a woman from Greek mythology whom Zeus, in the guise of a swan, impregnated— and have specially trained geese nibble barley grains off her body. She was a decidedly raunchy gal.

Everything changed when she became mistress to Hecebolus, a governor of North Africa. After traveling with him to his homeland, Theodora found herself unexpectedly dumped, stranded a huge distance from her native Constantinople. So she turned to sex work to finance her trip back home. Upon returning, though, she had a religious conversion and swore off sex work permanently. She became a wool spinner near the palace, and it was in that role that she met Justinian.

Justinian was smitten by Theodora instantly. Wowed by her intelligence and ability to quote orators, he actually rewrote the laws of the land in order to allow him to marry her. She was equally enamored of him, insisting on banishment and harsh punishment (like being tossed into the sea) for those who were proven to have been plotting against him. Despite vicious rumors to the contrary, all evidence points to the two being faithfully monogamous to one another their entire lives.

Theodora took to the role of empress quickly. When an earthquake ravaged Antioch, she sent lavish gifts to help the citizens rebuild—and did the same numerous times for other cities

---

* Yes, he trained bears. For the circus. Where they fought people and other animals. This author hopes it was as cool as it sounds.

experiencing natural disasters, like drought and famine. Against her husband's will, she sheltered the religiously oppressed and talked Justinian into easing up on them. When Justinian contracted the Black Plague and was bedridden, she even took charge for a time.

Much of Theodora's energy was spent on bettering the lives of women, in particular sex workers. She expanded the rights of women in divorces, established the death penalty for rape, gave mothers guardianship over their children in the case of divorce or the death of their husbands, and forbade the killing of wives for adultery. At one point she summoned all brothel owners in Constantinople, lectured them, and then bought all of their girls from them.* She then sent the newly freed girls back to their parents. When the brothels reopened soon after, she again tried shutting them down. Eventually, she built a convent called Metanoia ("repentance"), where ex-prostitutes could support themselves.

But for all the good she did for women, she was inarguably cruel to bureaucrats, keeping them waiting for interminable amounts of time. She schemed viciously against those who irritated her, causing the downfall of several key figures in Justinian's government—among them, his finance minister and some of his best generals. Unwilling to chide her too much, Justinian never stopped her. Unfortunately, this was a key factor in causing some of his biggest plans, such as the recapture of Rome and the Western Roman Empire, to fall apart.

Theodora's tough tactics made her a target for many, but for none more so than the scholar Procopius. In his *Secret History*, he makes the following outrageous claims:

- She would go to parties with 10 men, sleep with all of them, then sleep with another 30, and still be unsated.

- She would have abortions regularly and then boast of them in public.

- She had a massive spy network that she would use to kidnap and kill her opponents.

- She wished her nipples had holes so that she could use them for sex as well.

- She would run into the bridal chambers of the just-married on their wedding night and arrest the groom, just because she could.

- She was, in fact, a demon whose head left her body at night to vex the citizens of Constantinople.

---

* Admittedly, at one gold solidus per girl, she paid dramatically under market value, which was around five times that. According to Procopius, though, this did not go as intended—many of the girls went right back to sex work, and some whom she moved into her Metanoia convent killed themselves. Take this account with a pinch of salt, though: Procopius was a pretty angry guy.

- Other demons would come to her while she was having sex with clients, and she'd kick out her johns to have relations with said demons.

- She actually caused the earthquakes and floods for which she gathered aid.

In short, he was not a fan. His *Secret History* did not come to light until centuries later, by which time Theodora was unable to defend herself (or have Procopius banished). Not that it caused much of a stir—historians generally see the bitterness of the *Secret History* as saying more about Procopius than Theodora.

After she died of cancer in 548, she left behind a policy of religious tolerance within the Christian faith, a rebuilt Constantinople, and a grieving Justinian I.

## · ART NOTES ·

Theodora is here pictured offering a hand to a sex worker, in reference to her work on their behalf.

On the left side are some bureaucrats, who are both waiting for her (one has a handy hourglass wristwatch) and being attacked by her trained geese. On the right is Justinian I, coughing from the plague, in the palm of her hand.

The Hagia Sophia, seen behind Theodora, is one of the iconic symbols of Constantinople (modern-day Istanbul) and was rebuilt under her leadership. It does not have its four famous minarets here, as they were added later.

# Rani Lakshmibai

## (1828–1858, INDIA)

### The Rebel Queen of Jhansi

I n 1857, India got an unlikely icon in its struggle for independence from the British: a 28-year-old widowed mother of one. Within a year, she was leading thousands into an all-out war against British colonialists—often while carrying her child on her back.

Lakshmibai's story starts in the heart of India, in the city of Jhansi. The ruler of the city, Gandaghar Rao, had spent years creating stability from political upheaval, in both the city and surrounding areas, and was eager to create a line of succession. To that end, in the grand Cinderella tradition, he picked the young Lakshmibai* from obscurity, married her, and soon had a child with her.

Except things didn't go as planned. Their child died in infancy, and Rao became gravely ill. On his deathbed, Rao adopted a second child, Damodar, to be his heir. Then, one day short of Lakshmibai's 26th birthday, Rao died.

From there, the Rani† of Jhansi's problems only increased. The British East India Company, which had helped stabilize the region, had made an agreement with Rao's predecessor to let any of his descendants rule—but they didn't accept this adopted child as a legitimate heir. Lakshmibai argued her case like a veteran lawyer, poring over case studies and producing legal precedents, but was ultimately overruled. Jhansi was annexed, its military disbanded, and Lakshmibai's royal court reduced to near-poverty.

Now, this was just one in a lengthy list of things the British‡ were doing to piss everyone off. A sampling of other offenses includes:

• Installing corrupt officials who would flagrantly steal from Indians.

• Outlawing Hindu rituals and banning access to certain temples.

---

* Possibly very young. Many sources say Lakshmibai (or Manikarnika, as she was named before marriage) was actually born in 1835, which would have placed her around age seven when she married. Rao would have been 29. Other historians think it more likely she was born in 1828, making her a somewhat-more-sensible (but still uncomfortable) 13.

† Rani is a title, like Queen.

‡ Here "British" should be taken to mean "British East India Company," the megacompany/nightmarish capitalist endgame that effectively represented the British government in India for most of the century.

- Establishing a slaughterhouse to kill cows, considered a sacred animal, in the middle of the city.

- Giving the predominantly Hindu infantry a new rifle that could only be reloaded by chewing through a bag doused in pig and cow fat. This weapon, the Enfield rifle, is a low-water point in both weapon design and multicultural understanding.

It should not be a huge surprise, then, that Indians began rebelling against the British. Lakshmibai had no part in the initial uprisings, but behind the scenes she began consolidating a power base for a larger entry into the conflict. She proved phenomenally good at this—within the span of two years she had established a mint, started manufacturing cannons, brought in soldiers of all faiths and backgrounds (including bandits who'd previously raided her lands), and established a first-rate spy network.

But she was not a standard-issue warlord by any stretch of the imagination. For one thing, her rule was marked by tremendous mercy and sympathy. She exempted the poor from taxes and had a thousand coats made for them. She sold her jewelry to pay her soldiers and ate only gruel.

She also integrated women deeply into her plans. She taught her female subjects sword fighting and horsemanship and led them in target practice—she herself was an expert in all three. During the sieges to come, the women who didn't ride alongside the men would repair Jhansi's walls at night, hidden under dark blankets. They also made platforms for the cannons and supplied a steady stream of cannonballs and gunpowder. Jhansi under Lakshmibai had a staggeringly egalitarian workforce.

Simultaneously, Lakshmibai remained a devoted mother to her adopted son, Damodar, whom she called Ananda (joy). She made him eat his vegetables and study hard, admonishing him to fight the British with pen and paper. By all accounts, he had quite the happy childhood, largely oblivious to the fact that his mother was conducting a war.

(And who says women can't have it all?)

Unfortunately, Lakshmibai's wartime compatriots weren't operating at her level. During the months following her declaration of war ("I will not give up my Jhansi"), time and time again her allies would snatch defeat from the jaws of victory. Much of the blame could be laid at the feet of the astoundingly incompetent Tatya Tope,[*] a bumbling rebel leader whose baffling military blunders caused the author of this book to audibly curse, repeatedly, while researching this entry. In the end, despite almost always outnumbering and often outgunning the British, Lakshmibai's forces were usually defeated.

---

[*] Tope was one of several neighboring leaders who brought their armies and military expertise to Lakshmibai's David versus Goliath rebellion. Tope himself was apparently quite popular, for reasons that are not at all evident to this author.

Eventually Lakshmibai had to abandon Jhansi, fleeing on horseback with Damodar strapped to her back—an image that has become her primary depiction.

The Brits were indescribably monstrous in all of this. A wandering ascetic later described the entire city of Jhansi under British rule as a cremation pyre. Indian women would drown themselves and their children to avoid a worse fate at the hands of the British soldiers. The British outlawed funeral rites and left 5,000 to 10,000 dead in the streets. Perhaps this was wartime hyperbole, but even if you only follow the British sources, it's undeniable that the British committed war crimes.

Lakshmibai regrouped and kept fighting for months, but sadly, she eventually died in battle. She was shot while leading the cavalry in a charge against the British. As she lay dying, she instructed her companions to pay the troops by selling her belongings, to look after her son, and to not let the British defile her body. They cremated her on the spot and took Damodar into hiding.

In the years following, the British regained control of Jhansi, but it was not to last. The British East India Company was dissolved the same year Lakshmibai died, and India threw off Britain's shackles for good a century later— a movement that Indian spy princess **Noor Inayat Khan** would aspire to assist. Rani Lakshmibai is now revered as a national hero of India. Her name and likeness grace universities, statues, songs, movies, parks, and even a military regiment.

## · ART NOTES AND TRIVIA ·

There's a lot going on in this illustration.

While most images depict Rani Lakshmibai riding into battle, the truth is that she was a peace-loving person. So here she is prepping for the inevitable while her son plays and her poorer subjects are handed coats in the background.

The jeweled sword and the diamond choker are both historically accurate artifacts of hers. The choker, specifically, was one of the few things she kept to the end of her life, as it was a present from her husband. The moon symbol on her forehead is a mark she was known to use regularly. The symbol on her forehead clasp is Shiva's third eye, as she was a Shiva devotee. She has no other jewelry, as she'd given most of it away.

The horse handing her a coat of mail is her favorite horse, Sarangi, whom she befriended when she pulled a nail from his side.

The background line of elephants (and the two "helping" with the planning) are a reference to a story from her childhood. As it goes, when denied an elephant ride, she proclaimed that she would one day own many elephants. She did—and one of them was actually trained to hold a chandelier at dinner functions.

Tatya Tope can be seen in the background, walking off from the planning table while whistling idly. Ugh. He's the worst.

The flatbread on the table behind her is a reference to the Chapati Rebellion. Early in the Indian rebellions of 1857, Indians started passing out massive amounts of flatbread (*chapati*) throughout all of India. This completely freaked out the British, who were convinced it was a form of secret communication, and one that was faster and more efficient than any they had. The British seized every flatbread they could find, but never found any hidden messages. In the end, it may not have been a secret communication at all, but a superstitious effort to ward off cholera.

The woman in the background dressed similarly to Lakshmibai is a woman named Jhalkaribai. When Lakshmibai fled Jhansi, Jhalkaribai posed as her, leading the English on a wild goose chase. She came from the lower castes (Dalit) and was raised as a boy—and has become a hero for modern-day Dalits.

The city of Gwalior, site of Lakshmibai's last stand, was where **Phoolan Devi** would be imprisoned many years later.

# Mariya Oktyabrskaya

## (1905–1944, RUSSIA)

## The Tank-Driving Widow

hen the stars are all burned out and human beings are but fairy tales told by robots, somewhere there will be a list of the toughest women who ever lived. And near the top will be Sergeant Mariya Oktyabrskaya, the first woman to win the Hero of the Soviet Union Award, and her tank, Fighting Girlfriend.

During World War II, Mariya's husband, Ilya, an army officer, was killed in action. Mariya mourned his loss in traditional fashion—by selling all of their belongings to buy a tank. She then wrote Stalin the following letter: "My husband was killed in action defending the motherland. I want revenge on the fascist dogs for his death and for the death of Soviet people tortured by the fascist barbarians. For this purpose I've deposited all my personal savings—50,000 rubles—to the National Bank in order to build a tank. I kindly ask to name the tank 'Fighting Girlfriend' and to send me to the frontline as a driver of said tank."

Stalin wrote back quickly and said yes.

Initially, the army was skeptical of Mariya's ability to handle a tank. However, in training she quickly proved that she could drive, shoot, and throw grenades with the best of them— skills she'd picked up from her late husband, with whom she'd presumably had some interesting dates.*

On her first outing in the tank, she outmaneuvered a group of German soldiers, killing 30 of them and taking out an anti-tank gun. When her opponents shelled her tank, immobilizing Fighting Girlfriend, she got out—in the middle of a firefight—and repaired the damn thing. She then got back in and proceeded to kill more Germans.

During all this combat, she wrote a letter to her sister describing her time in the war: "I've had my baptism by fire. I beat the bastards. Sometimes I'm so angry I can't even breathe."

In the end, she was felled by a mortar round when she climbed out of her tank in the middle of yet another firefight to repair Fighting Girlfriend. She was awarded the highest

---

* She'd spent some time as a nurse in the military and had served on the Military Wives Council, so it's also possible she picked up some skills elsewhere.

honor in the Soviet military and is buried in one of the nation's most sacred cemeteries. Her likeness was reproduced on stamps, cards, and newsreels to promote the war effort.

## · ART NOTES ·

The vehicle depicted is a T-34 tank, the actual model of Fighting Girlfriend.

The Fighting Girlfriend logo was on the side of the turret, just out of the cropping of this picture.

The German soldiers used many different color tracer rounds, but red was among them.

The planes in the background are PE-8 Petlyakov Soviet bombers.

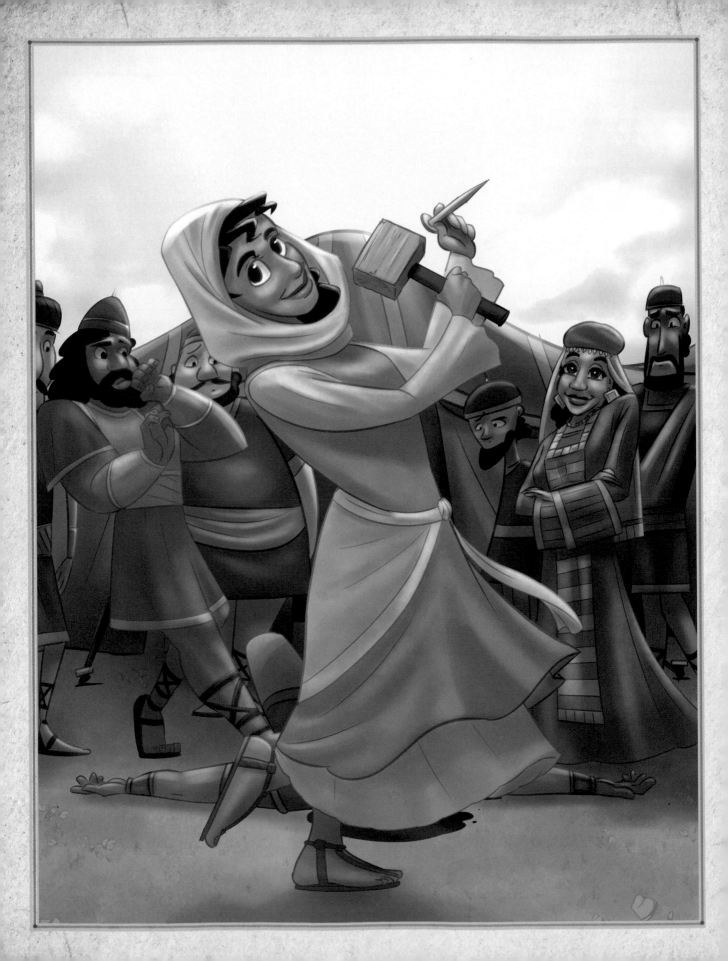

# Yael

## (C. 13TH CENTURY BCE, KINGDOM OF ISRAEL)

## *Hammer Time*

et's jump back to biblical times. Like, early Bible. Old Testament. Some of the earliest material to make it into the Old Testament, in fact: the story of Yael.

To set the stage: The Israelites had been having some tough times due to, you guessed it, another bad guy.* The villain of this story was a general named Sisera, who'd been a capital-D Douchebag to the Israelites for 20-odd years. According to some sources, he could yell loudly enough to kill wildlife and had a beard so manly he could use it to catch fish. While he'd clearly made some odd choices from the superpowers list, he was nevertheless no one to mess around with.

And yet, messing around with him is exactly what happened! A judge named Deborah, leader of the Israelites, decided to take Sisera on, and rounded up a general† to take him out. But as she departed with the army to take out Sisera, she warned the general: "The honor will not be yours, for the Lord will deliver Sisera into the hands of a woman." The general likely thought Deborah meant herself. She did not.

Deborah and the gang busted Sisera's army so bad he turned tail and ran—which is where our heroine Yael comes into the picture. Sisera fled to the neighboring Kenites, who weren't interested in taking sides in this whole Sisera-Israel business. Specifically, he went to the tent of Heber and his wife, Yael. She, being a hospitable sort, invited him right in and offered him some milk, a blanket, and seven successive rounds of passionate sex to tire him out.

That last part is an interpretation of the phrase "falling down at her feet" as an old-school sexual euphemism. At least one scholar even takes it to read as Sisera trying to rape Yael, so take any mention of sexy times in this story with extreme suspicion.

As soon as Sisera fell asleep, Yael cemented her reputation as a world-class host by grabbing a mallet and driving a tent spike through his skull. Some interpretations have her doing so while he was still awake and on his feet. In any event, Yael was less than chummy.

Afterwards, things went swimmingly! Peace reigned for 40 years, and Yael was hailed as the most blessed woman of all the tent-dwellers—beating out any number of more conventionally mannered contenders for the title. All in all, not bad work.

---

\* To be fair, the Israelites had just gotten back to doing unspecified "evil in the eyes of the Lord" after their last hero bit the dust, so they sort of had it coming? Those Old Testament scamps!

† Named Barak, after the United States president. Okay, maybe not.

# Wallada bint al-Mustakfi

### (C. 1000–1091, SPAIN [ANDALUSIA])

## The Princess Who Put the Slam
## into Slam Poetry

In the medieval Islamic world, one of the quickest routes to fame was poetry. Considered an elegant way to meditate on the nature of divinity and the universe, Islamic religious poetry elevated the discourse of every conversation it touched, raising even the most mundane subjects to lofty heights.

And then there was all the other poetry. The love poems. The battle poems. The poems that were more roast than reverence. And here's where we meet our heroine.

Princess Wallada bint al-Mustakfi was the toast of Cordoba. Witty, charming, skilled in both song and verse, she delighted everyone with her intellectual salons and poetry competitions.

Her intelligence was matched only by her boldness. She chose her own lovers, refused to wear a veil, and spoke her mind freely. When a judge accused her of being overly loose with her affections, she not only wrote a poem telling him to mind his own business, but she had it embroidered onto her dress:

> I am fit for high positions, by God!*
> And I am going my way, with pride!
> I allow my lover to touch my cheek
> And bestow my kiss on he who craves it.

Her most infamous writing, however, stemmed from her turbulent love affair with court poet Ibn Zaydun. They composed poems that were the literary equivalent of making out in public. They became the "it couple" of Cordoba, attracting both admirers and detractors. One, vizier Ibn Abdus, was so jealous of their relationship that he set about trying to destroy it—and succeeded when he caught Zaydun cheating on Wallada with Wallada's favorite slave.

What followed was some truly scorched-earth poetry. Wallada wrote that "you know I am the clear, shining moon of the heavens, but, to my sorrow, you chose instead a dark and

---

* According to professor of Jewish studies Marla Segol, this was a direct attack on the Qur'an's claim that women were "one degree lower than men."

shadowy planet." Zaydun, seeing Wallada now in the arms of Abdus, responded, "You were to me nothing but a sweetmeat that I took a bite of and then tossed away the crust, leaving it to be gnawed on by a rat." She, suitably outraged, ended the feud by outing him as bisexual in one of her most famous pieces:

> Because of his love for the rods in the trousers, Ibn Zaydun,
> In spite of his excellence,
> If penises were palm trees
> He would become a woodpecker.

Now, it's worth examining her sometimes-peculiar invective. If one can set aside the homophobia and racism of the era (which is quite a big if—seriously, Wallada, you were doing so well there for a second), one can find a surprisingly clever literary reference. In evoking the image of phallic palm trees, she's referencing popular works of the time, such as Ibn Sina's "Hayy ibn Yaqzan"—in which two men retire to the utopian paradise of al-Waqwaq, where naked women with exposed genitalia grow on trees.

No, really. Look it up.

The rancor between Wallada and Zaydun eventually grew so out of control that her father imprisoned and banished Zaydun—in part due to pressure from Abdus, who later claimed all of Zaydun's belongings, and in part due to the accusations of homosexual activity, which was a crime at the time, although one rarely punished. Zaydun eventually returned and rekindled a romance with the princess, albeit short-lived. Then he moved to Seville, never to return.

As for Wallada? She lived with Ibn Abdus the rest of her life, although they never married. She died in 1091, having taught poetry and run her salon for many years. Nine of her poems survive, of which eight are related to Zaydun, five being less than flattering.

## · ART NOTES AND TRIVIA ·

Wallada was famously described as blond-haired and blue-eyed, which was considered quite exotic. Her ethnicity is somewhat indeterminate: one source claimed her mother was an Ethiopian servant of her father.

Her defiant poem is embroidered onto her sleeves, in Arabic.

# Ada Lovelace

## (1815–1852, ENGLAND)

## *Enchantress of Numbers*

I magine your crazy uncle tells you about a machine he's building out of Legos. No, he hasn't finished (or even started) it yet, but it is going to be great! Pump in some steam and a couple index cards and it will solve any math problem in the world. The only thing is, he wants you to write a user's manual for it. Even though it doesn't exist. But he'd be happy to describe it to you!

Welcome to the life of Ada Lovelace.

Ada's life got off to an off-kilter start when her mother, deathly afraid Ada might become a debauched poet, began schooling her in mathematics. Her mother's characteristically histrionic fears were not totally unfounded: Ada's father was the "mad, bad, and dangerous to know" poet Lord Byron, who had years earlier rocked English polite society with a series of scandals. Fearing his degenerate love of wordplay might be genetic, the divorced Lady Byron (referred to by Lord Byron as the "Princess of Parallelograms" in their courtship) early on began steering her daughter toward a life of virtuous calculus.

Although Lady Byron did inspire quite the interest in math, she could not fully temper Ada's innate hooliganery. Ada refused to sleep in beds, argued with every adult she met (one described an encounter with Ada as "conversational litigation"), declined to learn basic etiquette, and wrote long, funny, sarcastic letters. At age 12, she laid out extensive designs to build a steam-powered flying machine and only abandoned her plans when Lady Byron guilt-tripped her into stopping: Lady Byron claimed it would disturb her own precarious health.

And here we find the first major obstacle to Ada's ascension to math goddess: her hypochondriac mother. From reading Lady Byron's letters, one gets the impression that Ada's mother was almost constantly bedridden for around 30 years. Her medical "treatments" rotated between leeches, cupping, and eating ludicrous quantities of meat—which she would then vomit, usually over the side of a boat, so as to protect her feminine modesty. Lady Byron's writing (of which there is no shortage) is a nonstop stream of health reports, breathless gossip, and complaints about Lord Byron, even decades after his death.

The responsibility of caring for her mother hampered some of Ada's desires, but it was hardly the only family-related impediment. At age 22, she married William King-Noel (better known as Lord Lovelace). Her husband was a kind man who fully encouraged her interest in mathematics, but being a public figure whose work demanded Ada's high-society involvement, he made serious demands on her schedule. Moreover, they eventually had three children together, so that also took up just *a little* bit of time.

However, even the intense social pressures of high-society England never kept Ada restrained for long. In her late twenties, she began regularly abdicating her maternal and wifely duties in order to associate with rogue intellectuals—and no contemporary was more of a rogue than Charles Babbage.

Babbage, the "crazy uncle" of the introductory analogy, was an infamously eccentric inventor with one of the shortest attention spans on record. His primary claim to fame was the Difference Engine, a complex machine with about half the functionality of a modern-day calculator. Despite receiving a great deal of attention and funding for the device, he never finished it, because he got distracted by a newer idea: the Analytic Engine, essentially history's first computer.

In spite of Babbage's excited talk and hand-waving, not many people understood the thinking behind the Analytic Engine—except for Ada. She took to the idea quickly and began translating mathematical treatises with the aim of helping Babbage develop the machine. In addition, she wrote a long document, the "Notes," on how to program for it. She referred to this document as her "child"—which should give you a sense of where her head was.

But in fairness, by this point her head was all over the place. Partly because of her own illnesses and partly because of her mother's histrionic nature, at this point Ada's diet primarily consisted of laudanum, wine, and opiates. Her writing from this period reflects this regimen: one week she's sensibly describing algorithms, and in the next she's describing herself as a fairy or a prophet charged by God with unveiling the secrets of the universe using math.

Yes, she went full mad scientist.

Her final years saw her life spinning more wildly out of control. Even as she wrote prophecies of the computing revolution (many of which would come to pass, albeit over a century after her death), she was also regularly abandoning her family and using her mathematical prowess to unsuccessfully gamble on horse races. Eventually, the health problems that had clouded her life for years caught up to her and she became confined to bed. She spent her last months making peace with her loved ones before passing away from cancer at the age of 36.

It is tempting to think of the contributions she could have made had she been born in a different time, or if she'd had a better support network, or if she had lived longer. Although later historians have questioned how much impact her writing had on Babbage, her genius is beyond question. She programmed for a machine that didn't exist, and never would. Think about that—she successfully envisioned an entirely theoretical machine and wrote history's first software program, all in her head. The mental acuity required to do that beggars belief.

Thankfully, she is remembered in the present day. One of the first programming

languages ever created was named ADA in her honor. Modern-day technology companies such as Adafruit and Ladyada bear tribute to her in their names. And every October millions celebrate intellectual women on Ada Lovelace Day.

## · ART NOTES ·

Ada's mother, Lady Byron, can be seen here fainting into the arms of Ada's long-suffering husband, Lord Lovelace.

Ada has her hand on a copy of the Difference Engine, although none were completed in her lifetime.

Entering in the doorway is Charles Babbage. A lockpicking enthusiast, he is eyeing the door as a challenge. In fact, Babbage was so avid a lockpicker that he at one point interviewed the famous French thief Eugene Vidocq on the subject. Babbage came away unimpressed, remarking, "To my great disappointment, I found him not at all strong upon that question."

# Laskarina Bouboulina

(1771–1825, GREECE)

## Heroine of the Greek War of Independence

f you will, take a second to run through the standard list of adjectives you might use to describe babies. Chances are you're thinking of "cute," "sweet." Maybe "cuddly"? Possibly even "loud" or "stinky." Whatever words come to mind, it's unlikely the word "badass" is one of them. This is understandable, as few babies can really lay claim to being badass. "Badass" should be reserved for truly extreme infants, like those born in prison.

Laskarina Bouboulina was a badass baby.

Bouboulina's badass beginnings were due to the politics of the time. For centuries, Greece had been under the rule of the Ottoman Empire—a fact that didn't sit well with a large number of Greeks, Bouboulina's father included. For participating in one of the many failed attempts at overthrowing the Ottomans, her father had been locked up in Istanbul. It was on a visit to said prison that Bouboulina's pregnant mother went into labor, and several hours later Bouboulina took her first breath in a Turkish prison cell. She was to take after her father.

Her path from jailbird to revolutionary wasn't a straight road by any means. The first part of Bouboulina's life was, on the whole, rather conventional. She married twice (not at the same time!), and both husbands were seafaring merchants. Each was killed in battle with Barbary Coast pirates, leaving her with an enormous fortune and unheard-of free agency by the age of 35.

While many in her position might have blown their savings or fallen prey to nefarious hangers-on, Bouboulina did just the opposite. She took the reins of the family finances and started investing like a pro. Said investments, which grew her wealth even more, included partnerships in several ships. Said vessels would turn out to be good investments in the realms of both finance and butt-kicking.

This level of control was not achieved without some difficulty. Early on, the Ottomans tried to lay claim to her late husband's wealth, through dubious legal antics. In response, Bouboulina put on her diplomacy hat and played several factions against each other (including Russia). This years-long political game ended with Bouboulina the victor—she charmed a sultan's wife into officially declaring the money Bouboulina's in perpetuity. Remember this, it will come up later!

Eventually Bouboulina grew in influence to the point where she was inducted into the Filiki Etairia, or "Friendly Society," a Greek secret society dedicated to overthrowing the

Ottoman Turks. She was the only female member of the group. In that role, she used her fine upstanding reputation to smuggle arms and ammunition. She hid the weaponry all across her home island of Spetses, like the world's deadliest squirrel.

Because arming an entire landmass worth of people evidently wasn't enough, she also commissioned a full-fledged warship. If the Ottomans asked, she said she was just building a merchant vessel—albeit one with 18 cannons. When a local brown-noser tried to rat her out, she bribed her way to safety. Part of the bribe involved wisely getting the brown-noser booted off ~~Lethal Scavenger Hunt Island~~ Spetses.

And so, when the Greek War of Independence began in 1821, Bouboulina was at the front of its navy, commanding the warship *Agamemnon* and seven other ships. She laid siege to a number of Ottoman strongholds, chief among them Tripoli and Nafplio. She had her own army—the Brave Young Lads—and personally commanded their attacks against the Turks.

The war was incredibly brutal. The Ottomans wiped out entire islands of people—around 100,000 were killed or enslaved in the taking of Chios alone. The Greeks were no less brutal in their tactics: once they took Tripoli, the revolutionaries spent three days killing around 25,000 of its inhabitants.

Bouboulina brought a sense of mercy to this brutality, at great personal risk. As her fellow revolutionaries sacked Tripoli, she rushed to the sultan's palace in order to save the lives of the sultan's wife, children, and harem. In so doing, she was repaying the support of the sultan's wife from years prior (told you it would come up later!). She didn't have to—her side definitely held the upper hand, and sparing the lives of the Ottoman ruling class was certainly not high on the Greek priority list. But Bouboulina did what she thought was right. She held nothing back in the war: within two years virtually her entire fortune was gone. But at the end of it, so were the Turks.

Unfortunately, the years after the war were not kind to Bouboulina—or to Greece, for that matter. The country, though free from the Turks, rapidly sank into a series of civil wars. During one of said upheavals, Bouboulina was arrested for her political opinions, and she was eventually exiled to Spetses. Once released, she prepared to head back to war, this time with Egypt, when she was shot dead in a family dispute.

Her son had eloped, and the bride's family was none too pleased. Bouboulina got involved and met her end. No one ever confessed to shooting her.

She has returned to prominence in the years since her death. Not only has her likeness been featured on the drachma, on postage stamps, and in movies, but her descendants remain heavily involved in politics and the military. In fact, one of the main World War II resistance groups based in Greece was named Bouboulina—and led by her descendant Lela Karayianni to boot!

# Ching Shih

(1775–1844, CHINA)

## *Princess of the Chinese Seas*

In 1809, the Chinese government sprang a trap. They were gunning for a group that had taken control of its southern waters, the Red Flag pirate fleet. Blockading the pirates in a bay, the authorities laid siege to them for three straight weeks with an overwhelming amount of firepower. In the end, the Red Flags strode out through a graveyard of government ships, largely unscathed. At the head of the Red Flags stood one of the most fearsome pirates in history—Ching Shih, a former prostitute turned leader of over 70,000 men.

Getting accurate information on Lady Ching (alias Cheng I Sao) is a bit difficult. Nobody knows much about her early life. Even the name Ching Shih isn't her own: it translates to "widow of Ching," Ching being her late husband and the commander of the Red Flags before her. We do know that before her husband died, he (and by extension, his fleet) was so renowned that the emperor, in an early attempt at curbing his piracy through bribery, gave him the title "Golden Dragon of the Imperial Staff," effectively promoting him to the rank of prince—and thus, one could argue, obliquely making Ching Shih a princess.

When her husband died unexpectedly, Ching Shih took on the family business, assuming control of the Red Flag fleet. According to legend, following her husband's death, she summoned the scattering fleet captains and announced: "Under the leadership of a man you have all chosen to flee. We shall see how you prove yourselves under the hand of a woman."

She was a leader unlike any they'd had before. Where her husband had been brash and loud, she was quiet and calculating. Soon after her rule began, she took a charismatic man named Chang Pao as her husband and installed him as head of the fleet. This proved a savvy move for a number of reasons. Chang Pao had been her husband's right-hand man (and lover . . . and adopted son . . . yeah, it's a bit weird) and was widely respected among all the pirate fleets. Moreover, Chang Pao was an illiterate fisherman's son (he'd been taken by the pirates as a child and received little to no schooling) and was likely easy to manipulate.

Under Chang Pao's rule (and Ching Shih's guiding hand), many rowdy pirate fleets united beneath the Red Flag banner, and the Red Flags soon eclipsed all other pirate groups in size. Every single ship, no matter how small, was given an edict from Ching Shih that all were to learn and obey. This outlined an incredibly hardcore code of conduct:

- Ching Shih okays all attacks beforehand. Disobey, and you're beheaded.

- You give all loot to your superior, who distributes it afterwards. Disobey once, you're beaten severely. Disobey twice, you're dead.

- Don't desert your post or take shore leave without permission. Disobey once, we cut off your ears (since you clearly weren't using them) and parade you around. Disobey twice, you're dead.

- Rape a female captive, off with your head.

- Have consensual sex with a female captive without permission from the boss, you're headless and she's taking a swim with a lead weight.

- If you want to have sex with a female prisoner, you take her as your wife. You are faithful to her. You treat her well. Or we take your head.

- Oh, and don't use the word "plunder." Instead, say "transferring shipment of goods." It just sounds nicer.

It is telling that one of the primary sources of information on Ching Shih's life was a Westerner she'd imprisoned for three months while setting up his ransom.

Under the leadership of Ching Shih, the Red Flags were unstoppable. As previously remarked, the Chinese government (with the help of the Portuguese) made a concerted effort to isolate and kill her in late 1809. That didn't happen. When the government sent "suicide boats"—ships loaded up with straw and explosives, set on fire, and launched at the pirates— the Red Flags extinguished the flames, repaired the ships, and incorporated them into their fleet. In the end, the pirates lost 40 people and not a single ship. So humiliating was the government's loss that the leader of the government expedition ended up falsifying the official reports to make himself look better.

Eventually, the government's persistent interference became too troublesome for even Ching Shih, and she put up her swords . . . but here, too, her genius shines through. Instead of merely negotiating amnesty by informing on her shipmates, she spent months bargaining with the government—at one point even giving herself over as a hostage to ensure her shipmates' safety. The end result: she actually retired. The government gave over a big chunk of cash, canceled all warrants for her arrest, and made Chang Pao a lieutenant in the Chinese navy (giving Ching Shih official status as a capital-L Lady in Chinese society). One of Chang Pao's first acts? Using the government forces to destroy all their old pirate rivals.

According to most sources, Ching Shih spent her final years running a brothel and gambling den. She died at age 69, a wealthy and widely respected woman.

# Christine de Pizan

## (1364–C. 1430, FRANCE)

### Literary Architect of the City of Ladies

At the age of 25, Christine de Pizan faced a crisis. Already reeling from the death of her physician-astrologer father, she received word that her beloved husband had succumbed to the bubonic plague. Suddenly deprived of support (and income), and with three young mouths to feed, she had few options. With the courts unwilling to give Christine her husband's back wages or property (creditors even seized some of her property!), she faced the last resort of so many women of the time: entering the convent.

But Christine did not become a nun. Instead, she picked up a pen and became the hardest-working woman in France—a woman who enraptured queens and tricked kings, went toe-to-toe with the intellectuals of her day, and developed into one of history's greatest defenders of her gender.

Christine's move into the role of breadwinner, while entirely within her abilities, was emotionally exhausting. Well educated by an intellectual father who "took great pleasure from seeing" her "inclination to learning," Christine was, skills-wise, well disposed to become a writer. Mentally, though, the transition was devastating. In one poem, she described herself as a passenger on a boat struck by catastrophic weather, who had to take the helm amid nigh-suicidal grief. She went on to speak of this moment as one in which an anthropomorphized Fortune switched Christine's gender by repeatedly touching her body—a passage that surely launched a thousand dissertations.

Regardless of Christine's personal gender politics,* her prolific outpouring of work not only proved successful but also soon established her as one of France's premier intellectuals. She began her career with uncontroversial love poetry designed to attract patrons. Once her finances were more in order (and her children were older), she took an abrupt left turn into the areas for which she became best known: French politics and the defense of women.

With France knee-deep in the Hundred Years' War against England, Christine de Pizan tried her best to prevent the unstable political situation from erupting into all-out civil war. To avoid this, she continually pointed to the menace of the English in an attempt to galvanize the country in one direction. In her *Book of Deeds of Arms and Chivalry* (yes, she wrote a book on

---

\* Most seem to agree that this was a rhetorical device rather than a reorientation of her gender identity.

warfare!), she even warned the French to take the threat of England's archers seriously. They didn't, and five years later they faced catastrophic losses at Agincourt, owing in large part to English archers. These losses would prove instrumental in the rise of **Joan of Arc.**[*]

Christine's most lasting legacy came in her literary uplifting of women. Disgusted by a contemporary's misogynist depiction of her entire gender,[†] she started a public quarrel over women's place in literature—one of the first debates of its kind. To give some context, here was an educated woman standing her ground at an advanced intellectual level, in an era when it was thought that knowledge would make women sterile and that females were "empty thing[s] and easily swayed."

Her frustration over the treatment of women led to one of her greatest masterpieces, *The Book of the City of Ladies*, in which she stages an extended defense of her gender and builds a metaphorical city out of exemplary historical women. Amazons and skilled women are the gates and foundations, morally upright women the buildings, and saints and martyrs the lofty towers. *The Book of the City of Ladies* was a beautifully illustrated illuminated manuscript, the creation of which Christine oversaw, employing only other skilled women.

At the end of her career, Christine had written thousands of pages, a staggering output considering the manually laborious nature of writing in medieval times. She established herself as one of the premier female intellectuals of human history and provided a role model for generations of women.

## · ART NOTES AND TRIVIA ·

Christine de Pizan is seen here constructing a model "city of ladies" out of the women in the other entries in this book.

The presence of a dog is historically accurate: she appears in one of the illustrations of *The Book of the City of Ladies* with a cute little white dog at her feet.

There is one person in this illustration who is not a woman. This person bears a striking resemblance to this book's author.

---

[*] Christine was, in fact, one of Joan of Arc's biggest fans. Christine's last work was an ecstatic poem praising Joan. This poem is one of the only surviving reactions by a contemporary woman to Joan's life!

[†] This would be Jean de Meun's contribution to the *Romance of the Rose*, where he portrays women as deceptive cheats and gives men advice on how to outwit them. It had all the progressive views on gender you'd expect from a 14th-century pickup artist manual.

# Harriet Tubman

## The American Moses

or most people, the first words that spring to mind when they hear the name Harriet Tubman are probably "Underground Railroad"—which is a shame, since those words should be something more along the lines of "unstoppable force of nature." For Tubman, a smuggler, nurse, spy, general, and modern-day Moses, was one of the toughest women in history.

Harriet (birth name: Araminta Ross) was born into plantation life slavery, but decided after 27 years to free herself. One can hardly blame her. Her upbringing had left her body a mass of scars due to daily whipping sessions. Her most notable scar was received from a lead weight that was thrown at her, cracking her skull. Probably because of this injury, she suffered narcoleptic symptoms her entire life, often falling asleep mid-sentence. Luckily, she was able to balance her disadvantages with two amazing qualities—borderline-inhuman stamina from all the backbreaking labor and a burning hatred of slavery.

Nobody knows much about the first few years of Harriet's freedom. It's likely she was aided by a nascent Underground Railroad, but with the need for secrecy at the time, little information survived as to the particulars of her escape. It is known that she left the plantation without warning anyone, including her parents, siblings, and husband. She covered 90 miles in her journey to Philadelphia, probably on foot, by sleeping in forests during the day and avoiding slave catchers at night.

Once in Philadelphia, however, she made a startling choice. Instead of continuing northward to safety or even settling into a simple life there, she joined the Underground Railroad in the most dangerous capacity of all. She became an "abductor," or someone who would sneak into the southern United States, where slavery was legal, and personally extract slaves from their bondage.

Harriet was possibly the most skilled abductor of all—even though, as an escaped slave, she was in far more danger than any of her white colleagues. Making the situation even riskier was the fact that, working by herself, she smuggled out groups of slaves instead of the more customary one or two at a time. The anecdotes from this period of her life are awe-inspiring:

- She led around two chickens on a leash. If she saw one of her former slave owners—not an uncommon occurrence, as she'd been rented to many in her childhood—she would pull the leashes, causing the chickens to squawk and allowing her to hide her face as she ducked down to deal with them.

- She carried around newspapers, pretending to read, even though she was illiterate. This fooled more than one slave owner into thinking she was someone else.

- She would sing aloud to herself as she walked, choosing songs that could signal to escaped slaves within earshot whether it was safe to come out.

- Harriet carried a loaded revolver nearly everywhere she went. One of the only times she used it was when an escaped slave, exhausted from the journey, threatened to turn around and head back. She put the gun to his head and forced him to continue. A week later, he and the rest of the group were free.

- Another notable occasion for using her gun came when she was in the wilderness smuggling a group to safety. Isolated from civilization and suffering from a painful tooth infection, she used the revolver to knock out her entire top row of teeth.

- She disguised herself as an old woman and sneaked into a courthouse to rescue an escaped slave about to be sent back south. She forcibly yanked him out of the bailiff's grip and rushed him down the stairs, even as cops beat her half-unconscious. When he was recaptured and put in a judge's office, she and several others rushed in and got him out a second time, even as bullets were flying overhead.

A solid decade of these escapes, during which she smuggled out almost her entire family,[*†] earned her the moniker "Moses." An intensely religious woman prone to visions, Tubman would often have premonitions of oncoming patrols and stop her groups in their tracks.

For reference's sake, in recent years there's been a popular fictional character with almost the same danger-detecting abilities. You may have heard of him. His name is Spider-Man.

---

[*] All except two of her sisters, whom she was never able to save, and her husband, John. He, having been born free, refused to go. In the year between her escape and her first return to smuggle out family members, he remarried. The two never had children (well, kind of—see the next footnote) during their relationship and ostensibly had a difficult marriage. Harriet nonetheless kept his name and remained faithful to him until his death.

[†] Officially, Harriet never had any children, but there is some murkiness surrounding her "niece," Margaret Tubman. Margaret's daughter would in later years claim that Harriet had actually kidnapped her mother from a happy family. However, the two apparently had a very happy and close relationship, and many contemporary accounts remark on their physical similarities. This has led some historians to put forward the idea that Margaret was, in fact, Harriet's daughter and had been raised, for reasons unknown, by others for the first part of her life. In this hypothesis, Margaret's father is presumed to be either John (in which case, Harriet would have been pregnant during her escape) or a white slave owner, who presumably forced himself on Harriet (Margaret was described as having light skin).

He is not real. Tubman was. She was also illiterate, uneducated, narcoleptic, and unstoppable.

When the Civil War broke out, Tubman made a beeline down to South Carolina—the heart of the South—to assist the Union army. She first worked for them as a nurse and was later put in charge of an entire scouting group. Her work was quite controversial, however: the question of whether the Union army should accept black recruits at all was the subject of much debate, but having a black woman in a position of power was unheard of. Luckily, she got a chance to prove herself—as did many black recruits when Union ranks were opened to them in 1863.

Also in 1863, Tubman guided three steamboats on a nighttime raid of southern plantations along the Combahee River. This was unbelievably daring: the area in question was rife with underwater mines, and the shores of the river were home to some of the most elite forces of the Confederacy. But Tubman, by befriending local slaves, mapped out all the mines and led a successful raid. They seized thousands of dollars in supplies, torched a number of plantations, and rescued nearly 800 slaves* in one night, without suffering a single casualty.

Unfortunately, life was not as kind to her after the war. Despite her status as a war hero, Tubman began to suffer discrimination as early as the train ride back to her home, now in New York. Faced with a conductor who didn't believe her military-issued ticket was the genuine article, she was forcibly removed from her seat and tossed in one of the rear cars. This was no small struggle: upwards of four people were brought in to remove her, and her arm was broken in the process, an injury that took months to heal.

She lived out the rest of her life doing humanitarian and women's suffrage work, putting almost every dollar she earned toward helping others. She therefore spent most of her later years in poverty—exacerbated by the government taking over three decades to pay her for her service during the war. Ever the one to think of others, one of her last statements to those visiting at her deathbed was, "I go to prepare a place for you."

The same year Harriet Tubman died, Rosa Parks was born.

---

* One of whom brought onboard two pigs contemptuously named "Jefferson Davis" and "Beauregard" (after Confederate general P. G. T Beauregard).

# Anne Hutchinson

(1591–1643, UNITED STATES)

## New England's Rebel Preacher

ere is a list of things the Puritan leaders of early Boston disliked, in ascending order of hatred: cold weather, Native Americans, Protestants, women talking back, Satan himself, and Anne Hutchinson.

The heroine of this story was guilty of falling into at least two of the last three categories. Although if you'd asked the magistrates running her trial, they'd claim she fell into all three.

Let's take a step back to the Boston of the 1630s. The first thing to know is that it was crazy religious, with heavy emphasis on crazy. Everyone knows that the Puritans left England to practice their religious beliefs, but often the beliefs themselves are glossed over. Well, no more, dear reader! I present to you some of the fine religious freedoms put forward for 17th-century Boston:

• Women were not allowed to wear fur, lace, or colorful cloth.

• All women were required to wear veils.

• Public funds paid for church.

• Church attendance was mandatory.

Now, some of these "freedoms" became laws, while others (veils) were just debated, but the fact of the matter is this: here was a community of people who put "ministers" at the top of their list of supplies for the one-way trip to America.

In the middle of this hotbed of holiness sailed Anne Hutchinson. Anne, despite a total lack of formal education, nevertheless knew the Bible so well that she argued with a preacher the entire voyage over. In this regard, she took after her father, a clergyman who so frustrated the Bishop of London that he was put on trial for blasphemy. During the trial, he further needled the bishop until the man exclaimed, "Thou art a very ass, an idiot, and a fool." In her approach to legal defense, Anne would follow in her father's footsteps.

Anne went about her work quietly and cleverly. Instead of directly ministering to whoever would listen, she began a women-only study group—to which the male powers-that-be were totally blind. Further, she took advantage of the church's mandatory sermons: the town preacher would pose thought-provoking questions in church, and Anne would actually provide answers in her group.

In short order, her growing popularity put her on the radar of the local magistrates. By this point, she was doing "study sessions" twice a week, and women were bringing their husbands, who in turn started asking pointed questions in church. The governor, John Winthrop, was not a fan: he thought that Anne was a witch, and that the devil had taken over her soul and was using her to subjugate men by establishing "the community of women" to foster "their abominable wickedness." So yeah, she wasn't on his Christmas card list.

Winthrop put her on trial, but it was there that her true cleverness shone through. After the panel's initial bloviating, Anne calmly asked what she was on trial for. She knew it couldn't be for contempt, since she, as a woman, had no public role. She couldn't be disenfranchised because she couldn't vote. Even her most visible crime, leaving church in the middle of a sermon, was easily characterized as "feminine distress"—a tactic that stopped the menses-fearing panel of men dead in their tracks.

In this way, she turned her weaknesses into strengths, which only complemented her tremendous physical endurance. The weather during her trial was deathly cold—literally, someone had frozen to death just the week before. The courtroom had no fireplace (although the magistrates were given beds of heated coals). Anne was made to stand the entire time. And she did all of this while pregnant with her sixteenth child. Yep, sixteenth.

The best part? She *crushed* it. As the trial predictably fell into a game of quote-the-Bible, this uneducated woman debated a panel of Cambridge-educated lawyers into silence. She argued so hard that she actually fainted in the middle of the trial, only to begin arguing again as soon as she was revived. In the end, the only point the panel could make was that her behavior was not "comely in the sight of God."

Unfortunately, it is at this point that Anne's arrogance got the best of her: she began to lecture the panel on the Bible, in full view of everyone.

Historian Eve LaPlante argues that no matter how Anne's trial went, her ensuing banishment was a foregone conclusion from the beginning. But even if that isn't true, her high-profile schooling of the panel of magistrates certainly didn't exactly make them turn the other cheek.

After the trial (and a short house arrest), Anne left Boston and walked (still pregnant, mind you) 40 miles to a new city. Several years later, she and her extensive family were all, save one, killed in a horrific Native American raid, in a tragic case of mistaken identity. This act is made all the more tragic by the fact that she had publicly opposed raids on nearby Native American tribes while in Boston—and more importantly, she had convinced a huge number of would-be soldiers to oppose them as well.

The magistrates decided that the root cause of the problem was a shortage of preachers. To remedy that, and to prevent future Anne Hutchinsons, they founded a college: Harvard University.

# Petra "Pedro" Herrera

## (LATE 19TH CENTURY–EARLY 20TH CENTURY, MEXICO)

### *The Soldadera Princess*

entle reader, staring at you from the illustration for this entry is Colonel Petra "Pedro" Herrera: Mexican revolutionary, demolitions expert, and leader of an all-female brigade that boasted hundreds of women.

Here's the Mexican Revolution in one oversimplified paragraph: It's the 1910s. President Porfirio Diaz is being a jerk. Revolutionaries (Pancho Villa, Zapata, others from the "Bad Boys of the Revolution" calendar series) pop up and say, "Hey, stop being a jerk and step down already." Bam, war.

Most of the *soldaderas* (women embedded with the armies) were covering the minutia that the "let's go fight already" soldiers hadn't thought through—like eating. With the war swallowing up town after town, increasing numbers of women and children joined up with the growing armies, although not always by choice—some were straight-up kidnapped. The end result made the armies appear to journalists of the time like "an immense picnic."

Petra Herrera, though, was not about to cook or clean. Petra was there to kick butt.

Disguising herself as a man (Pedro) in order to be eligible for battlefield promotions—a commonplace tactic among female soldiers of the time—Petra established her reputation with the revolutionaries through solid leadership, good marksmanship, and, you know, blowing up bridges. Eventually, she became so popular that she dropped the "I'm a man" pretense. Afterwards, she started wearing braids and fighting under her own name. By 1914, she was a captain under Pancho Villa, commanding 200 men.

Her crowning achievement was to sack the city of Torreón—in the biggest fight in the war to that date—which gave Pancho Villa access to heavy artillery, a half million rounds of ammunition, and armored rail cars. And yet, Herrera was not given much, if any, credit for her work. Now, mind, she's not mentioned in the official documentation on this, but according to another soldier in the battle, "she was the one who took Torreón, she turned off the lights when they entered the city." And yet, she was not promoted to general afterwards.

In response, Herrera said, "I'm out." She left Villa's forces and made her own—an independent all-female brigade. By the end of the war, it was estimated to comprise around 300 to 400 women. She looked after her women like a mama bear. A mama bear with a rifle and ammo bandolier. Petra wouldn't let men sleep in her camp, and she enforced that rule by staying up late and using any male soldier who disobeyed as target practice.

At the end of the conflict, she asked again to be made a general and was denied. She was made a colonel, and her brigade was disbanded. Soon after, she was killed by a band of drunken men while working as a spy.

As cool as she was, Petra was not unique in being an amazing soldadera. There were so many distinguished women in the Mexican Revolution, it's hard to pick just one to represent them. Some others:

- Petra Ruiz (who also disguised herself as a male named Pedro) was nicknamed "Echa Balas" (Bullets) and was known for her temper as well as her skill with knives and guns. One account tells of soldiers arguing over who would be first to rape a young girl, only to have Ruiz show up, demand the girl for herself, and upon winning her, let her go.

- Rosa Bobadilla, when widowed by the war, took up arms and fought in 168 battles— surviving them all.

- A woman named Chiquita rode into an enemy camp, saying she was a trained nurse. Hours later, she was skipping town, having stolen papers, documents, and maps.

- When US president Woodrow Wilson sent an army into Mexico, 13-year-old Elisa Grienssen rallied the women of Parral to kick them out. They surrounded the American commander (who was apparently already leaving, but taking his sweet time with it), throwing rocks and sticks and shouting, "Viva Villa, Viva Mexico!"

Unfortunately, for most of Mexico's postwar history, soldaderas were largely memorialized through folk songs that didn't do them justice. In the most famous of these songs, "La Adelita," the eponymous Adelita follows the army because she is in love with the sergeant. Although certainly that sort of thing happened, love wasn't exactly the prime motivator for Petra "make me a freakin' general already" Herrera.

## · ART NOTES ·

Because Petra dressed as a man for much of her career, she is seen here in a period-accurate officer's outfit. She has an officer's sword and characteristic ammo bandolier and is unfurling her braid from her hat in a nod to her "guess what? I'm a lady" reveal. Her revolver is a copy of the one that Emiliano Zapata used (a Mexican Smith & Wesson replica).

The soldaderas below her are in outfits more typical of the standard soldadera representation. Together, their different tones comprise the colors of the Mexican flag.

The setting is an actual Mexican bridge from the time, but it was clear on the other side of Mexico from where she operated (mostly Durango and Chihuahua).

# A'isha bint abi Bakr

### (614–678, SAUDI ARABIA [ARABIA])

## Mother of the Believers

Hoo boy. Here we go.

It's safe to say that A'isha bint abi Bakr is one of the most controversial figures in all of Islamic history. The youngest and most beloved wife[*] of the Prophet Muhammad is, on the one hand, the source of a huge percentage of Islamic teachings, a model for spirited women everywhere, and a revelatory figure for the Prophet himself—and on the other hand, she is a divisive military leader at the center of an Islamic schism that has persisted for 1,300 years and counting.

A'isha was the daughter of the Prophet's best bud, Abu Bakr, a man who, like A'isha, was either Allah's anointed messenger or Satan's slimiest scoundrel, depending on who you ask.[†] After the Prophet's death, Abu Bakr was next in line to lead the Muslim people. While he would have probably been at the top of the list regardless, his personal stock had been bolstered greatly through his daughter's marriage to the Prophet—and her status as the Prophet's favorite wife.

Let's get this out of the way up front—A'isha was young when they married. Way too young. Most sources claim she was six when engaged and nine when married, although some claim she was as old as 12 or 14. While that's hardly atypical for most cultures in human history (it's standard for many women covered in this book), it sounds shocking today. But seeing as this issue has been debated endlessly in virtually every medium in human history, not to mention that it has little to do with who A'isha actually was, this book is going to leave it at that.

So what kind of a person was A'isha? In a word: lively. In her youth, she was not slow to remind her fellow wives that she was the Prophet's favorite, that she was the only one who'd been a virgin when married, that the Prophet got revelations only in her presence . . . you get the point. Bottom line: she was clever, quick-witted, and all too happy to let you know it. But as she matured, especially in the years following the Prophet's death, she came into her own as a leader.

---

[*] Well, best beloved after the death of Khadija, the Prophet's first wife. Khadija is the only one with whom he had children.

[†] In fact, let's call the pro-Bakr folks "Sunnis" and the anti-Bakr folks "Shiites." Because that's what they're called. Now those news reports about the Middle East make a little more sense, right?

One of the biggest turning points in A'isha's personal evolution was an episode called "The Incident of the Lie."* Following a raid the Prophet led on a nearby tribe, A'isha was accidentally left behind. She had left to look for a necklace she'd dropped, but she weighed so little that when her servants hefted up her carriage onto a camel, they didn't realize she wasn't in it. Stranded in the desert, she got help in rejoining her husband from a strapping young lad named Safwan. Whereupon rumors quickly spread that she'd cheated on the Prophet with Safwan.

Now, these rumors were bogus. Various people, including relatives of the Prophet's other wives, were jockeying for political power,† and the rumors originated from them. With nobody defending her (not even her parents), and unable to prove her innocence herself, A'isha was totally isolated. The Prophet, unsure whom to believe, at one point consulted his son 'Ali, who counseled him to ditch A'isha: "There are many women. You can easily replace one with another."

'Ali was so convinced A'isha was lying that he at one point beat her servant in an attempt to get the truth. Suffice to say, A'isha and 'Ali did not get along.

In the end, A'isha's reputation was salvaged by a deus ex machina—literally. The Prophet got word from Allah that she was innocent. The rumor-spreaders were punished,‡ A'isha got pissed off enough to literally build a wall between her apartment and 'Ali's, and that was that. Or . . . not.

Matters grew even more complex after the Prophet's death. Nobody was quite sure who should lead next, and eventually 'Ali was made leader—a move A'isha could not have disagreed with more.§ This culminated in a clash between her supporters and his, known as the Battle of the Camel: the first episode of Muslim-on-Muslim violence in history. Although she personally led 3,000 men into battle (on a war camel!), A'isha was eventually overcome and ceded authority to 'Ali.

This conflict became the basis of a major break in Islamic tradition. Some followed A'isha and took her many subsequent teachings—as favorite wife, she knew the Prophet's private

---

* This could also be translated as "The Incident of the Slander." (Or is it libel now that it's being written down in this book?)

† To be fair, A'isha *totally* played this game too. When one of the other wives got hold of some honey that the Prophet liked, A'isha and yet another wife pretended it smelled horrible so that the Prophet wouldn't spend so much time with the honey-dispensing wife. Things occasionally got very catty in the Prophet's household.

‡ With 80 lashes, ouch. Allah: not cool with gossip.

§ The particulars are *way* more complicated. While A'isha was on a spiritual journey to clear her head, Uthman, the third Islamic leader after Muhammad, was assassinated and 'Ali was put in charge. Already not much of a supporter of 'Ali, and further incensed that he didn't execute Uthman's killers, A'isha eventually declared him unfit to rule and led an army against him. Again: massive simplification, but that's the gist.

customs better than anyone—as the basis for the religion. The others felt that she and her father had lied to everyone and tried to usurp power from 'Ali, who was the rightful successor. People fight about it to this day (see the footnote on Abu Bakr a few pages back).

Complicating the matter further is the fact that none of this was written down until 150 years later! Who knows what changed over a 15-decade-long game of telephone? By the time the story was put to parchment, the social standing of Muslim women was in a very different place. Anecdotes such as A'isha's explosive reply to someone's implication that women, dogs, and donkeys all could break prayer—"are you calling women *dogs*?!"—was not given the same cultural weight. Some stories were taken as legitimate, and others were dismissed.

According to most sources, A'isha spent the remainder of her life teaching, nursing, mediating, and advocating for women. In all, she left 2,210 *hadiths*—the teachings that are the bedrock of Islamic tradition—placing her as the fourth most prolific *hadith* imparter. Her lessons ranged from proper prayer technique to admonitions for men to wash their genitalia, to passionate anti-cootie rhetoric—basically saying that men could in fact eat, drink, and pray around women while they were on their period.

Obviously, this book cannot hope to comprehensively cover a figure as hotly debated as A'isha. There are many stories and anecdotes that could easily flip her (or 'Ali, or Abu Bakr, or almost anyone) from hero to villain and back. This author highly recommends that anyone with an interest in further particulars of A'isha's story read up on their own. While entire libraries of books have been written on her, the bibliography in the back of this book lists a few to help you get started.

## · ART NOTES, OR WHY DOESN'T SHE HAVE A FACE? ·

You may have heard that Islamic tradition can be very particular about depictions of their holy figures. In modern times, holy persons are often portrayed with either light or golden fire obscuring their features or just a big golden dot over their face. Here, the spilled golden ink—spilled by two dueling hands, each seeking to literally reframe A'isha's image—serves that purpose.

The unfinished golden borders around the image are mirror images of one another—except one side is all vines and blooms and the other is all fire, symbolizing how one side holds her as a positive influence, the other as a negative one.

Half the crowd is enraptured by A'isha's teachings (or call to action?), and the other half—not so much. This represents the Sunni/Shi'a split.

The camel on the left side of the image is a reference to both A'isha's steed at the Battle of the Camel and the animal who carried her sleeping quarters away in the Incident of the Lie.

The dogs on the right side of the image are a callback to the Parable of the Dogs of al-Hawab. In some traditions, their barking at A'isha as she led forces to the Battle of the Camel was indicative of her doing the wrong thing.

# Olga of Kiev

## (890–969, UKRAINE)

## The Saint Who Set Fires with Pigeons

The story of Princess Olga starts in a familiar manner: her husband is killed, their heir is too young to step up, and so Olga steps in. In this case, her husband, Igor, had been gruesomely killed[*] by the Drevlians[†] for overtaxation and general being-a-jerk-itude. Assuming Olga would be overwhelmed by the pressures of ruling, the Drevlians demanded that she marry their Prince Mal, thus effectively transferring the throne to the Drevlians.

The Drevlians were wrong. They were so, so wrong.

But they didn't appear to be at first! Olga timidly acquiesced to the marriage, and even offered a suggestion to cement the Drevlians as the new overlords in everyone's eyes. "Come back tomorrow," she said to the 20 emissaries before her, "and have the citizens of Kiev carry you to me."

So they did as she suggested and were soon being carried through Kiev like big, manly, conquering babies. When the Drevlians came to the throne room, the Kiev citizens proceeded to unceremoniously toss them into a hidden pit they'd dug overnight. Olga then asked, "*How you like me now?!*" as she started scooping shovelfuls of dirt on them, burying them alive.

Next she sent a message to the rest of the Drevlians, asking that their wisest citizens accompany her as she journeyed to meet her new Drevlian husband. When the elite Drevlians came to Kiev, she said, "Oh, you must be tired from the long journey! Here, rest a bit, take a bath." Once they all went in the bathhouse she'd prepared, she locked the door and set the bathhouse on fire.

And she wasn't done! Having murdered all the Drevlian upper crust, Olga next invited the remainder of its citizenry to a funeral feast to mourn her late husband, Igor. When asked where the high-class Drevlian emissaries were, she replied, "They're right behind me." She then got the unsuspecting Drevlian revelers drunk and killed over 5,000 of them.

At this point, the Drevlians began to wise up. When Olga appeared at their gates with a massive army next, they threw up their hands in surrender. "Good lord, lady," they said, "what do you want?! Furs?! Honey?! Whatever it is, we'll give it to you, just stop already!"

---

[*] According to one source, the Drevlians bent over two birch trees and tied Igor's legs to them. The killers then let the trees spring back to their normal state, tearing him in half.

[†] A Slavic tribe, now either extinct or subsumed into other ethnicities, courtesy of Olga.

"Oh, really?" she said quizzically. "Well, I don't want anything. If you're willing to have peace between us, then just give me a little tribute. Simply send me some doves or pigeons as a token of your good faith."

Relieved, the Drevlians obliged. Olga promptly tied bits of burning sulfur to each of the birds and sent them back home, thus setting every house in the Drevlian capital on fire at the same time. When the Drevlians tried escaping, she either killed or enslaved them.*

And here's the kicker: she's an honest-to-God Christian saint. As the first ruler of Rus to convert to Christianity, she widely proselytized the religion and helped establish a foothold for it in that corner of the world. She was then canonized as Holy Equal to the Apostles. Yes, that's right: in the eyes of the Church, Olga of Kiev, possibly the only person to burn a city to the ground with pigeons, is on par with any of the 12 disciples of Jesus Christ.

Now, her deeds are almost certainly hyperbolic propaganda—for one thing, the area talked about didn't have any birds that would live in roofing—but it's really *fun* propaganda.

---

* According to legend, **Khutulun**'s great-great-granddad Genghis Khan used the same tactic when sacking the fortress of Volohai centuries later.

# Agontime and the Dahomey Amazons

## (19TH CENTURY, BENIN)

## The Fiercest Women in the World

**I**n the 1800s, in present-day Benin, there was a kingdom called Dahomey. If you've ever heard any horror stories about African cannibalism or human sacrifices, they likely stemmed from tales of Dahomey. Although the bloodthirst of the Dahomeys was massively overstated, they were undeniably aggressive. In fact, a huge portion of the Dahomey economy stemmed from selling their conquered into slavery.

This includes one of their queen mothers, Agontime.

Ousted in a coup and shipped off to Brazil, Agontime was seemingly destined to disappear into the fog of history. However, her story took an unexpected twist: she was found and brought home. The ones who brought her back were quite possibly accompanied by Dahomey's elite warriors—famed and feared worldwide.

Those warriors were the Dahomey Amazons.* And they were all women.

But we're getting ahead of ourselves. To really appreciate the tale of Agontime and the Dahomey Amazons, one must first understand a bit about Dahomey itself. Much of Dahomey's culture was built around a religious love of symmetry. The Amazons themselves were a female counterpart to male fighting units, although usually better trained. This symmetry extended even to the ruling class—for each king, there was a queen mother (*kpojito*), who held equivalent, but different, power. While kings would largely make the final decisions, the kpojito controlled what the king knew and who got to see him.

The power of Dahomean women extended beyond that. Women could divorce men, but not vice versa. Royal women could take whatever lovers they wanted, including married men, but men could not do the same. New mothers were given a guarantee of three months of maternity leave that could extend to 12. While the new mother was taking care of her new child, the other women of Dahomey would chip in and provide for her and the rest of her family.

Not that any of these practices made the headlines in the European press, who chose

---

* "Amazons" as a term is virtually the only word we have to describe this corps of women—the European observers who wrote of them apparently never asked them what they called themselves.

instead to focus on the Amazons themselves. One of the recurring descriptions would detail their facility with traversing thorn hedges. At the time, most smaller African villages were protected by eight-foot-tall barriers of sharp thorns. A British officer described them thusly: "I could not persuade myself that any human being, without boots or shoes, would, under any circumstances, attempt to pass over so dangerous a collection of the most efficiently armed plants I had ever seen."

One minute later, the entirety of the barefoot Amazons had run headlong through the thorn wall.

Some descriptions:

- Induction into the Amazon corps involved cutting your arms, pouring blood into a human skull, mixing it with alcohol, and then drinking it.

- Amazons could imitate bird calls expertly and used them as a method of sending signals to one another in the field.

- Many would grind their teeth to points and hang the skulls of their enemies around their waists.

- Many considered themselves men, chanting, "As the blacksmith takes an iron bar and by fire changes its fashion, so have we changed our nature. We are no longer women, we are men."

- However, Amazons were not fully considered men until they had disemboweled their first enemy.

How much of this is factual is a matter of some debate. Many of these reports come from observers brought in specifically to witness displays arranged by the king. Others fought the Amazons in pitched combat and had every incentive to paint them in an unflattering light[*]—to this day, if you search for pictures of the Amazons, the first thing you'll find is probably a picture of one holding a decapitated head. Nevertheless, the fact that the scores of independent eyewitness accounts all detail virtually the same points over and over lends the claims significant weight.

The Amazons largely died out due to a series of wars against the Egba and the French in the late 1800s. Stubbornly clinging to outdated military technology and techniques, the Amazons were gunned down in droves as they rushed their enemies.

---

[*] And to be fair, there were a *lot* of things to dislike the Dahomeans for. As previously mentioned, they were ruthless, bloodthirsty, and heavy into slavery. By the standards of conventional morality, even if you only believe a small amount of the historical record on them, they are borderline indefensible.

But let's not forget Queen Agontime.

Shipped off to Brazil, Agontime spent 24 years as a slave, likely near São Luís de Maranhão. By 1823, the king who had exiled her had himself been ousted by King Gezo. Gezo considered Agontime his mother, although she may have been a non-biological relation. Once returned to Dahomey, Agontime, by her very presence, helped legitimize Gezo's claim to the throne. In fact, she only took the name Agontime after coming back: the word is from a phrase literally meaning "the monkey has come from the country of the whites and is now in a field of pineapples."

The details of her rescue are scant. Some convincingly claim that she was in fact never recovered. Her retrieval, if factual, was likely conducted by two of Gezo's male attendants independent of assistance from the Amazons. In the end, though, her return—or rather, the story of it—served more as a symbolic truth than a historical one. To the people of Dahomey, it represented not only a victory over the cruel king who had sold her into slavery in the first place but the ability of their Gezo to achieve the impossible.

And if the facts of the case are going to be that loosely interpreted, who's to say that an elite squad of Dahomey Amazons did not, in fact, bust Agontime out of a plantation and escape with her through unfamiliar Brazilian jungle, killing slavers as they went? Not this book, certainly.

## · ART NOTES AND TRIVIA ·

There are two Amazons hidden on the left and right sides of the image—one is in a tree, situating herself to snipe off the pursuing Brazilians. This was a technique the Amazons regularly employed in battle.

The gold adornments on the head of the closest Amazon were symbols of distinction within the Dahomey military and can be found in several historical depictions of the Amazons.

# Mata Hari

## (1876–1917, FRANCE)

### The Double Agent Who Wasn't

et's get this out of the way up front: Mata Hari wasn't a spy.

"But," you might exclaim, "she was tried as one! And executed!" Continuing, this fictional you would then say, "I don't know much about her, but 'Mata Hari' is practically a synonym for 'sneaky lady-spy'! It's like I don't know anything anymore! My world is falling apart!"

First off: Calm down, hypothetical person. It will be okay.

Her story begins with an unhappy marriage. Mata Hari, born Margaretha Zelle, was a woman of few prospects. Impulsively wed early in life to an abusive womanizer who gave her little more than grief, bruises, and syphilis, she spent her formative years as his captive in everything but title.* When she finally escaped, she found herself in Paris with little education, fewer contacts, and almost nothing to distinguish her from the crowd save the fact that she'd spent several years in the Dutch Indies.

In the end, she smartly leveraged that one fact to reinvent herself as Mata Hari: exotic Indonesian princess and burlesque dancer.

"But," you the rhetorical audience person now stammer, "that's ridiculous. How could anyone believe her?" Well, many didn't. But understand that most Europeans knew little of the Dutch Indies. (As you'll soon find out, pasty white **Princess Caraboo** pulled the same trick.) Also, her skin tone was somewhat dark—sufficiently so that many in the Indies had assumed she was a native. So when she invented a sultry "dance of seven veils" and branded herself as the "eye of the day" (as "Mata Hari" translates to in Malay), audiences ate it up. She quickly became one of the most popular acts in Paris, and then one of the most popular across Europe.

Yes, it was shameless cultural appropriation. But Mata Hari was doing the only thing she could to get out of a bad situation.

For about 10 years, life was good. Mata Hari had both money and the affections of men in abundance, things she'd sorely been lacking for the first half of her life. Her attempts at greater

---

* This is not much of an exaggeration. She attempted to divorce him, but the case was thrown out. Over three years, he would on various occasions beat her, wave a gun in her face, spit on her, and tell her, "Go to hell, bitch," while frequently sneaking out to see prostitutes. After she left, he took out a newspaper ad telling merchants to not sell anything to her. His name was Rudolf MacLeod, and regardless of his other possible merits, it is the position of this author that he was a real crap sandwich.

credibility were stymied by the Parisian elite, who held her (and her largely untrained dancing) in low esteem. She found refuge in feeding her more dubious traits—being a profligate spendthrift and unrepentant flirt. It was through a combination of those two pastimes that she entered the world of spying.

"Wait," you now shriek uncomfortably loudly at me, "you said she wasn't a spy! You lied to me! And just when I was opening myself up to your peculiar yet reckless style of storytelling!"

Get down from that table, invented reader persona. She wasn't a spy—or at least, not much of one, as you are about to see.

With the advent of World War I, Mata Hari's career as a dancer went into decline. Partly this was a matter of her age—she had been a novelty of the stage for a decade, and age was starting to take its toll in a career that demanded youth—but the increasing conservatism of the age played a larger part. Immigrants of all stripes were now viewed with intense suspicion, and even foreign nannies were subject to relentless interrogation. A shifty traveler such as Mata Hari, with influential lovers across the globe, would inevitably be suspected of being a spy.

Which is not to say she had no connection to the world of espionage—but here her story turns into a bit of a "he said, she said" arrangement.

In 1916, she met with Georges Ladoux, head of French counterespionage. To hear her telling, he asked her to do some work for him: to get info from her international network of paramours. Although utterly bereft of training and less than enchanted by Ladoux and French intelligence,* she carried out the job, to some success. She uncovered information about U-boats in Morocco, secret fingernail ink crystals, and German code-breaking efforts. Her lack of training, however, shone through in her attempts to report back to Ladoux: she sent the information in unencoded letters to his work address, through the post office.

In Ladoux's version, he never approached her with work and instead suspected her from the start to be a German double agent. Having come into his position with a desire to publicly expose foreign agents, he worked tirelessly to uncover her true allegiance—which he did with a series of communiqués that he presented at her subsequent trial for being a German spy.

It is important, at this point, to note three things. First, said communiqués were clearly fabricated, likely by Ladoux, who wanted some high-profile victories. Second, several observers decried her trial as full of rookie mistakes, with one using the peculiar description of there not being enough evidence to whip a cat. Third, and most important, Ladoux was himself arrested for being a German spy a mere four days after Mata Hari's death.

---

* Having been harassed by the military for being a spy at virtually every step in her travels—to the point where she slapped an officer across the face hard enough to draw blood—she opined thus to Ladoux upon meeting him: "Now this idiotic game has to end. Either I am dangerous, and in that case, you must expel me from France, or I am just a nice little woman who, having danced a winter, would like . . . some peace of mind."

Yes, Ladoux was a slimebag of staggering immensity.

Ladoux's faulty evidence and testimony were enough to convict Mata Hari of espionage and sentence her to death. She spent the last months of her life in a prison for prostitutes where the inmates lived in such squalid conditions that riots were a nigh-monthly affair. This, despite persistent public rumors that she bathed in milk and was awash in flowers and chocolates from admirers.

She was executed by firing squad at the age of 41. Some of her last recorded words were: "I know how to die without weakness. You shall see a good end!"

After her death, her image as a femme fatale extraordinaire became the de rigueur representation of her life. Many books and plays expanded on the small scandals of her life, ballooning her exploits to cartoonish proportions.[*] The not-insignificant detail of Ladoux's arrest for treason,[†] on the other hand, was kept secret for nearly a century.

## · ART NOTES AND TRIVIA ·

In the far background of the image is a statue of Shiva. In her act as a lost princess, Mata Hari would enact scenes of worship of the deity. Given the historical details that remain of her act, it is safe to assume she had scant knowledge of Hinduism.

Late in her career, Mata Hari attempted to enliven her act with the addition of live musical accompaniment. The leader of that band? Inayat Khan, father of World War II heroine **Noor Inayat Khan**, featured elsewhere in this book.

Although she often stripped nearly nude (usually with the aid of a flesh-colored body sock), Mata Hari almost never removed her brassiere. The reasons for this are subject to myriad rumors, but the most reasonable (and oft-cited) explanation was body image issues—despite being the most desired woman in Paris.

On the left side of the image, we have three tiers of people from her life. On the bottom is Ladoux, leading in a legion of French troops as he pulls the curtains on her. In the middle are the disinterested German political elites, with whom it's unlikely she had much interaction. On the top is her ex-husband, Rudolf, and their son—who, after a lifetime of custody battles between his parents, died at 21 of complications possibly related to his inherited syphilis.

---

[*] Typical examples have her seducing her headmaster at 16 years old, receiving chocolates and flowers in her jail cell from admirers, and, of course, virtually any slanderous sex act one could assign to a woman.

[†] Ladoux was never definitively proven to be a German spy, but he did run afoul of the law multiple times in the years following. He never returned to a position of prominence.

# Josephine Baker

## (1906–1975, UNITED STATES/FRANCE)

## *Queen of the Stage*

Virtually every culture has its variation on the Cinderella story, of a peasant girl lifted from poverty to royalty by the love of a kindly prince. But Cinderella was just a fable—Josephine Baker was real. And her prince was herself.

Born Freda J. McDonald in St. Louis, Missouri, Josephine had a tough childhood. As the one light-skinned (possibly half-white[*]) child in a desperately poor black household, she didn't fit in even at home. Put out to work as a maid by an exasperated mother, she suffered hideous abuse from her employers—from beatings to scaldings to sexual assault. Her only refuge was the theater, where she became "Josephine."

The theater was a perfect outlet for her intense energy. While Josephine's family certainly didn't appreciate her bringing snakes to funerals, and her first husband certainly didn't enjoy getting hit in the face with a beer bottle,[†] onstage her wild dancing and cross-eyed clowning netted her legions of fans. Her fellow performers were often not among those fans—she had no compunctions about bolting onstage when it suited her, upstaging whoever was mid-act. While her behavior was far from polite, standing out catapulted her to stardom.

Josephine made her name in Paris, where she danced in skimpy outfits in some of the same venues that **Mata Hari** had graced years earlier. She constantly traded up to higher-profile gigs, often betraying friends in the process.[‡] In a few short years, she was the first internationally famous black movie starlet, a distinction that brought with it enormous sums of money. According to one newspaper, she was the richest black woman in the world.

It's difficult to capture the eccentricity of Baker's life at its height. She owned countless animals—monkeys, cheetahs, a gorilla she dressed in human clothes and took for walks, even an ostrich that pulled her around in a carriage while she was on tour. She'd regularly visit the

---

[*] Nobody was sure who her father was. Given Josephine's notably light skin, many biographies assume her father was a white man. Baker, never having had a totally cordial relationship with her mother, was unsure herself. Josephine had issues with family.

[†] This was Willie Wells, whose marriage to Baker is rarely counted in official tallies, as it was illegal—she was 13 and he was 25. She hit him with a beer bottle after an argument over her being pregnant (she maintained she was, although she wasn't). Josephine had issues with boundaries.

[‡] Caroline Reagan, the woman who had brought her from the States to France, was especially badly burned. When Josephine left her show mid-tour, she ended up stranding Reagan and all her fellow performers in Europe with no way to get back home. Josephine had issues with friendships.

downtrodden of Paris and shower them with expensive gifts. She once crashed a new car, got out to sign autographs, and went home, leaving the wreckage for someone else to clean up.

Baker left even more wreckage in her love life. As befits someone who spent as much time as possible naked, she had untold scores of lovers, both male and female. After shows, she'd regularly take whoever struck her fancy to a hotel across the street, in full view of everyone. By the end of her life, she'd had four husbands,* two of whom were almost exclusively attracted to men. Almost. (As her son and chief biographer described it, she liked the challenge.)

After World War II broke out, Baker dropped everything and became a spy to help her beloved France. As an internationally famous woman with myriad connections, she was able to easily smuggle information across borders. Sometimes this was in invisible ink in the margins of her musical sheets, and sometimes she would just write on her hand.

The war lit a fire in her to do more with her life than perform, and she thereafter pursued the cause of civil rights fervently. She was the only woman to speak at the March on Washington, shortly before Martin Luther King Jr.'s "I Have a Dream" speech. This and other outspoken alliances (including a friendship with Fidel Castro) netted her a 1,000-page FBI file. She was determined to provide a shining example of racial equality and, unable to have children herself, did so by adopting 12 children of varying ethnicity—her "Rainbow Tribe."

This next chapter of her life—Baker as mother—was troubled. She bought property in the south of France, a grand fairy-tale castle that she was determined to make into a theme park.† But with her plans only half-baked at best, and her career stalling, she soon began to run out of money. Despite many donations from wealthy benefactors, she was eventually evicted.

In the twilight years of her life, she staged a number of comeback shows, including one before a packed Carnegie Hall. Then in her sixties and increasingly prone to injury, she was no less audacious—she wore fishnets and revealing outfits all the way to the end. She died of a brain hemorrhage at age 67, leaving behind a legacy that even Michael Jackson, Madonna, and Angelina Jolie combined could not hope to attain.

---

* Officially there were four. In reality, she had closer to seven, due to her often marrying one before divorcing the previous one. Josephine had issues with commitment.

† The Rainbow Tribe kids would have been one of the star attractions. She wanted them to be a symbol of the peace possible from the partnership of all races, but she vacillated wildly between mothering them far too much and not mothering them at all. Josephine had issues with her children.

# Dhat al-Himma

## (8TH-CENTURY ARABIAN MYTH)

## Woman of High Resolve

You know you're in for a treat when the name of a story's protagonist, depending on your translation, means either "woman of high resolve" or "she-wolf." You know it's going to be even better when you learn that she earned that title only after a period in which she was known as "calamity of the soul." The best is when you realize the story is thousands of pages long and yet she defeats bad guys in battle and rescues helpless men every couple of pages.

Dhat al-Himma was born into a rough situation. Her father and uncle, both high-ups in the Banu Kilab tribe (aka Kilabites—tragically, they did not fight tribes called Megabites or Gigabites), were arguing over succession. They had a bet that whoever had a boy first would gain control. When Dhat al-Himma (or Fatima, as she was initially named) was born, she was secretly given away because she wasn't male. Her father then claimed that Fatima had been a boy, but died, thus keeping a claim on the throne, at the expense of poor Fatima.

Soon thereafter, Fatima was taken captive by a rival tribe. However, she didn't kowtow to her new guardians. Instead of doing the normal activities expected of women, she busied herself with learning horsemanship (at one point she broke a wild horse just by shouting at it), forging weapons out of reeds, and practicing swordplay.

All of these skills came in handy when one of her captors began sexually harassing her. The first time he came by she complained to the tribal chief. The second time she chased him off with rocks and complained again—this time getting special dispensation to retaliate if he tried it again. ("I was just joking around," he retorted.) The third time she pulled him from his horse and killed him with his own sword.

This murder, committed in broad daylight, unsurprisingly brought forward a batch of new problems: namely, the harasser's family felt they were owed something for his death. Because the chief had okayed it, he was on the line for a thousand camels. It's at this point that Fatima comes to be known as "calamity of the soul."

"Chief," she said, "don't worry. Just give me some armor, a sword, and a horse, and I'll take care of things." Take care of things she did: soon she came back with 4,000 camels that she'd taken in a raid. Pretty quickly Fatima was put in charge of running raids.

Over the next several years, she became infamous for her raids, reunited with her father (after defeating him in battle and taking him prisoner), and rejoined the Kilabites. At this point, she came into the final evolution of her name, Amira (princess) Dhat al-Himma ("woman of high resolve")—which is likely a corruption of Delhemma, or "she-wolf."

Unfortunately, once she was reintegrated into her birth tribe, her uncle became hell-bent on marrying her off to Hadith, the son he'd managed to produce. Yes, he wanted her to marry her first cousin. Her level of enthusiasm for the match was somewhere between "nil" and "zilch." She told her father that "only my sword, my coat of mail, and my battle gear will lie with me," and if her father mentioned it again, she'd go live in the desert.

Hadith, apparently not being of the "no means no" school of romance, decided to challenge her in battle for the right to marry her. She beat him handily, knocking him off his horse. It was only after Hadith and his dad got a caliph to intervene with a religious argument that Dhat al-Himma was finally convinced. This was because she was extremely devout—for a period during her captivity, she was actually known as Shariha the Pious (she had a lot of names).

So she did get married to Hadith, but refused to even sleep in the same bed as her new husband. Hadith, being a grade-A a-hole, drugged, raped, and impregnated her. When Dhat al-Himma woke up, she was scorched-earth furious. She immediately tried to kill Hadith, and was only narrowly stopped by her father. She let Hadith go, but swore then and there to end his life.

Don't worry, it happened.

She gave birth to a mysteriously dark-skinned son, whom Hadith promptly disowned. She took her son, Abd al-Wahhab, under her wing and taught him martial arts, going so far as to disguise herself and attack him in the night (as you do). When she decided he'd become a great warrior, she let him loose to do his first great deed: kill his contemptible father and grandfather.

Told you it would happen.

From there, Dhat al-Himma went on to decades of adventures with her son and a trickster pal named Abu Muhammad al-Battal. She defeated countless warriors (male and female), disguised herself to sneak into enemy camps, and even endured numerous wounds and instances of torture. Her primary antagonist was a duplicitous judge named Uqba, whom she finally saw publicly executed.

Is the story of Dhat al-Himma fully true? No. But it isn't fully false either. Her story gets at the basic truth of the day and covers the transition from the Abbasid dynasty to the Umayyad. Was Dhat al-Himma real? Hard to say, but in the minds of the generations that grew up on her story, it didn't matter: she was an awesome, sword-slinging, pious heroine.

## · ART NOTES ·

Dhat al-Himma is here pictured swinging into battle. This was one of her trademarks—unlike her straightforward son, Abd al-Wahhab, she would sneak up on her enemies.

The knee to Uqba's face is dislodging a secret cross necklace, revealing him as a Christian. In contrast, Dhat al-Himma has a crescent on her helmet.

The wolf in the background quietly untying al-Wahhab and Battal seemed like an appropriate sidekick to someone whose name depicted her as a she-wolf.

Many of the mob attacking her are warrior women.

# Alice Clement

(1878–1926, UNITED STATES)

## Detective. Movie Star. Suffragist.

Chicago in the early 1900s was a rough town. With gangsters like Al Capone running the place, the populations of all manner of criminals surged, including one group that the police were unprepared to handle: women. With the public outraged over images of the all-male police force manhandling female shoplifters, fortune-tellers, pickpockets, and the like, the mayor ordered the cops to hire women.

Little did they know they'd get Alice Clement. A star detective who became one of their greatest assets—and one of their biggest headaches—their gun-wielding, jujitsu-practicing "female Sherlock Holmes" was unlike anyone they'd hired before.

Which isn't to say she started out like that. The environment they operated in was tremendously difficult on the new female employees. During training, a male policeman hazed them by tossing a white rat into their midst to see how they reacted (nobody moved). During a press conference, a reporter asked a sexist question, using old-timey slang for "arrest": "How would you make a pinch? Use tweezers?"

But Clement rose above it and made a name for herself as a uniquely female detective. The newspapers of the day engrossed themselves with descriptions of the massive wardrobe she used for undercover disguises. They delighted in descriptions of her sleeping with a gun under her pillow and traveling with shackles and handcuffs in her overnight bag, and they especially reveled in her unconventional personal life. By 1918, she'd divorced her first husband and remarried, having a female pastor perform the ceremony.

While Clement started her career by catching pickpockets—at one point claiming to have stopped a gang of them in which the average age was eight years old—her real glory came in combating "mashers." Mashers were a plague of sexual harassers rampant at the time. A typical example would be Joseph Withers, whose "acting school" included lessons on making a "knee skirt," which newspapers described as an "intricate achievement consisting in elevating the garment to the point mentioned." Clement tossed his butt in jail.

While she was very successful at arresting mashers, the legal system, in a depressing sign of the times, often found her at fault. Years into her life as a detective, when one of her arrestees was acquitted on grounds of entrapment, Clement retorted, "What would you expect from a jury of men?" Two years later, though, her patience had grown thin. When a judge dismissed yet another masher and blamed her for flirting with him, she hit the judge in the head with a blackjack, threatened to file a defamation suit, and announced she would not rest until she received an apology. It's unclear if she ever got one.

This was far from the only time that she got into fights with legal figures. By 1919, she'd become so famous in the newspapers for her daring arrests—they printed accounts of her many, sometimes fictional adventures, casting her in a similar mold as muckraking journalist **Nellie Bly**—that she wrote and starred in her own movie. *Dregs of the City* was a sensational look at a fictional Alice Clement saving a naive country girl from a shady opium den. But on the eve of its opening, the Chicago PD, annoyed by her showboating ways, prevented it from being released.

Clement's response was possibly the most audacious act in a life already dripping in chutzpah: she sued the city, earned a three-month furlough, and went on a road trip to promote the movie anyway.

This, shockingly, did not endear her to the powers-that-be, and in 1926 she was demoted to a menial post at the West Chicago police station. She left shortly thereafter and began a precipitous medical decline. Typical for Clement, who did not want anyone to see her weakness, she had kept her diagnosis of diabetes from even her close family. She died of the disease that year, December 26, 1926.

## · ART NOTES AND TRIVIA ·

The PSYCHIC sign (and the CLOSED sign underneath it) is a reference to a case in which Clement shut down a fraudulent psychic. She pursued the psychic alone into a building, only to quickly find a pistol against her chest. Smacking it out of the way, Clement ran to the back door to let in reinforcements and shortly thereafter apprehended her assailant.

In another case, she found a teamster who was beating a horse for no reason. After she informed him that she was a police officer and that he was to cease this animal cruelty, he responded by calling her a liar and threatening her. Clement proceeded to grab her revolver, slap him a half dozen times, and hustle him into a police wagon. Of the event, he reportedly said, "Gee, that dame packs an awful kick in her left."

As an outspoken and prominent suffragist, she was one of the few in the United States to meet **Emmeline Pankhurst**. One of the only surviving photos of Clement is actually a group photo with Pankhurst.

One of her cases saw Clement deducing that a young woman had not died randomly but had been murdered by her aunt. Clement figured out that the aunt had poisoned her niece's dulcimer strings, as she would lick her fingers between plucking the instrument. When Clement confronted the aunt, she killed herself in front of Clement with a pen knife.

# Shajar al-Durr

## (C. 1220–1257, EGYPT)

### The Sultan Who Ransomed a King

hajar al-Durr had quite the résumé: Muslim sultan who ruled in her own name, stopped the Seventh Crusade dead in its tracks, captured one of the most powerful monarchs in the world and ransomed him back to his own freakin' country, and, finally, died in rather embarrassing fashion when killed by a group of shoe-wielding assailants.

But that's jumping ahead. Shajar started life as a Turkic servant, purchased for the sultan of Egypt. Evidently she excelled in that role, as within a year she and the sultan were married with a child. For a while, life was pretty rad for Shajar.

Unfortunately, things took a turn for the crappy when the sultan became ill and died. He could not have picked a worse time to do it either: Louis IX of France had *just* begun invading Egypt as part of the Seventh Crusade, with the aim of toppling the sultan's dynasty and using Egypt as a springboard to sack Jerusalem. At this time, France was one of the most powerful countries in the world, and Louis IX was an intimidating ruler, beloved by his people.

So, with a dead husband and an invading army marching on Cairo, what did Shajar do? First she hid the fact that the sultan had died, by saying he wasn't feeling well and refusing to let anyone into his chambers. Then she quietly took the reins of the country and, with the help of her late husband's chief commander, prepped for war.

In short order, they stomped out the invaders and took Louis IX prisoner, in an incredibly humiliating defeat for the French. Louis IX had been so certain of his victory that at the beginning of his invasion he sent an incendiary letter to the sultan. This letter served absolutely no diplomatic purpose, but simply detailed how Louis was going to crush the sultan. Even if the sultan were to convert to Christianity, Louis crowed, he would still track him down and kill him "at your dearest spot on Earth."

Well, so much for that plan. Instead, the French forces, heady on a few minor victories, rushed into a town they thought was empty—only to be slaughtered by soldiers and townsfolk who were lying in wait. Concurrently, Egyptian soldiers had carried their boats over land and dropped them behind the French ships in such a fashion as to block French reinforcements. Then the Egyptians torched the Crusaders' ships with Greek fire. The Egyptians took Louis IX hostage and killed the majority of his forces. Thus ended the Seventh Crusade.

It is hard to state how soul-shattering this outcome was to the French people. To many, the defeat signified that God had forsaken them—some Crusaders actually converted to Islam afterwards. When word of the defeat spread throughout France, it spawned an uprising known as the Shepherds' Crusade: tens of thousands of farmers lost their minds, left their homes, and headed toward Egypt to rescue their king. They weren't big on organization, though, and within a couple months they were running around France throwing priests into rivers and setting things on fire instead. Mistakes were made.

In the end, Shajar al-Durr negotiated a treaty to return the captured monarch to his country for 400,000 livres tournois—about 30 percent of France's total annual revenue.

Stop and think about that. That would be like the president of the United States being captured while on a tour of Iraq, then ransomed back to the US for $5 trillion. That's borderline unfathomable.

And all of this was orchestrated by a woman. In a Muslim country. In secret. Over the first couple months of her rule.

Shajar did not stop there. Her next obstacle was Turanshah, the newly installed sultan of Egypt. By all accounts, Turanshah was a real gem—he drank openly and immediately began ungratefully antagonizing those who put him in power. In fact, one of his first acts was to replace those who'd installed him with his own henchmen. His to-replace list included Shajar, which was what we in the history biz like to call a "huge mistake."

In short order, Turanshah died in a series of violent acts so lengthy it would put Rasputin to shame. First, he was stabbed, so he fled into a nearby tower. Then the tower was set on fire, so he jumped out and ran for the river. Along the way, he took a spear in the gut, but somehow still made it into the river. There he was treated to a barrage of arrows from shore. Finally, one of the military commanders just waded out into the water and hacked him to death.

Afterwards, Shajar was officially instated as sultan. She was not, as tradition would assume, ruling in someone's stead. She was full-on sultan, with the support of the military. She minted her own coins and led her own prayers—both of which further solidified her legitimacy.

As you might imagine, some factions in Egypt were not cool with a lady on the throne. To pacify her enemies, she married her dead husband's former taste tester/accountant Aybek, and officially at least, Aybek became sultan. In reality, Shajar likely kept the reins while often sending Aybek away to deal with agitators. The particulars of this arrangement are debated, but most historians agree that Aybek was unpopular and probably chosen because multiple parties thought him easy to manipulate.

A few years into their marriage, Aybek decided to take another wife (his third) to help solidify his power. The details of what happened next change from account to account, but basically, Shajar was not cool with Aybek's triple-marrying and had servants strangle him in the bath. In one telling, she was there too, beating him and rubbing soap in his eyes.

Shortly thereafter, Shajar met her end. According to legend, Shajar was caught in the act of killing Aybek, imprisoned, and then executed by Aybek's first wife. The story goes that Shajar was beaten to death with wooden clogs by servants and her naked corpse was dumped over the wall of the city. This contrasts with the contemporary street-level account of what happened, where she slipped and fell while attempting to kill Aybek's son. In that version she is held up as a patriot acting on behalf of her country against the unloved Aybek.

The dynasty that Shajar started with her ascension went on to last for over 300 years and repelled Mongol and Crusader invasions until the rise of the Ottomans. The defeat of the Seventh Crusade dealt such a severe blow that after the failure of two more poorly supported attempts, the institution died out for good.

## · ART NOTES ·

Since Shajar al-Durr means "string of pearls," she is wearing one around her neck. She also has pearls on her rings.

Her kicked-up wooden shoe is a reference to the method of her grisly demise.

She's holding a coin, a reference to both her having her own coins and the ransom she got for Louis IX.

While Shajar's depiction was made in the absence of good source material, Louis IX is rendered pretty accurately.

# Amba/Sikhandi

## (INDIAN MYTH)

### Gender-Swapping Princess Out for Revenge

T he first mention of Princess Amba in the Indian epic *Mahabharata* is almost a footnote. She shows up when the warrior prince Bhishma, on the lookout for wives for his brother, heads to her *swayamvara* (husband-choosing competition). While there, Bhishma shows how macho he is by straight-out kidnapping Amba and her sisters (while yelling, "The wife is most dear who is stolen by force") and bringing them all back to his kid brother, presumably so he has options. Amba says, "But wait, I am already in love with another guy," and so Bhishma and his brother are like, "Well, okay, you can go, I guess," and she wanders off.

She doesn't show up again until around a million words later. That's not an exaggeration—the *Mahabaharata* is so unbelievably long that the Hare Krishna religion spun out of just 5 percent of the total thing.

When Amba does return, we learn what she's been up to. While Bhishma's been out kicking butts, leading to interminable passages about how cool he is, she's been picking up the pieces of her ruined life. You see, once she left captivity and reunited with her one true love, said genteel lover threw her out on her butt because he was a real turd burglar. The reason he gave was that she wasn't upset *enough* when Bhishma kidnapped her and thus was impure/unfaithful/infected with cooties. She pleaded with her dimwitted beau, but since his ears were packed tight with excrement, it didn't go anywhere.

From there, Amba set out on a path of revenge. Deciding that Bhishma, rather than her ex, was the bigger of the two jerkwads, she set her sights on him. Unfortunately, Bhishma was, as she would have known if she'd read any of the endless descriptions fawning over him, basically invulnerable. Kings wouldn't fight him, out of fear. Even Bhishma's teacher, who fought him for 23 days straight on Amba's behalf—at the end of which both he and Bhishma were full of arrows and still somehow walking, like human pincushions—was unable to defeat him. It boiled down to Bhishma's special god-given ability: he couldn't die unless he wanted to.

Frustrated upon hearing this, Amba turned to prayer. Now, this isn't go-to-church-once-a-week-type prayer. We're talking 12 years of fasting, standing on her toes, traveling to temples across the land, and meditating. It was so much that even the gods were like, "You might want to tone it down, lady." Some sages urged her to forgive and forget, to which she replied,

"No! I hate him. I want Bhishma to die, and I will never forgive him. . . . I have nowhere to stay and nowhere to go. I have no protection in all the worlds, and for that I would like to destroy those three worlds!"

There was one figure, however, who was very impressed by her devotion to murder: Shiva, the god of destruction. In return for her lifetime of asceticism, he told Amba that she would get to kill Bhishma in her next life as a man. She just had to wait.

She was not about to wait. As soon as Shiva left, she built a funeral pyre and walked into it.

She was reborn thereafter as Prince Sikhandi, who, to the bewilderment of his parents (whom Shiva had told they were going to have a son), had female sex organs. Nevertheless, they brought Sikhandi up as a boy, since you don't second-guess Shiva. In time, they even got Sikhandi engaged to a princess, who . . . was somewhat perturbed upon getting into Sikhandi's pants. A lot of high drama later (the princess's father decided to go to war over the matrimonial bait-and-switch), Sikhandi found a male forest spirit who agreed to swap body parts. Thus was Sikhandi given male genitalia and everyone was happy! Still keeping up?

Now Sikhandi joins Arjuna and his allies in the central story line, where they're in all-out war against Bhishma and his buddies. No matter how hard Arjuna and company fight, they can't seem to take their opponents down, because of Bhishma's invincibility. That is, until Sikhandi shows up. Riding out to Bhishma with the main character Arjuna hiding behind him/her, Sikhandi reveals himself to be a reincarnated Amba. Realizing his poor life choices and general pigheadedness, Bhishma sets down his bow and is promptly filled with arrow after arrow, "piercing him like winter's cold," until there is room for no more.

This is the climax of the entire 1.8-million-word story. After Bhishma goes down, although there are many other skirmishes, the tide turns in favor of the protagonists. While Bhishma's killing blow is attributed to Arjuna, even the book admits that he spent the climax hiding behind his friend Sikhandi, also known as Amba: the world's best transgender reincarnating suicidal revenge-seeking princess.

## · ART NOTES ·

Riding on the chariot to attack Bhishma (silver) are Sikhandi and Amba, Arjuna (ducking behind Sikhandi), and Krishna (driving the chariot). Lastly, there's the monkey god Hanuman, who actually at one point transforms into the chariot they're using. He's also the guy who shows up in the **Sita** entry to leap across all of India with a mountain on his back. Indian mythology is complicated.

# Khawlah bint al-Azwar

## Warrior Poet of Early Islam

Now, looking at the image for this entry, you may be asking yourself, "Is . . . is that an Arab ninja?" The answer is: yeah, kind of. Meet Khawlah bint al-Azwar: one of early Islam's greatest kickers of butt.

Khawlah's story begins with her brother, Dirar. These two children of a tribal chief were inseparable—everything that he'd do, she'd do. Fast-forward to adulthood, and you have two expert warrior/rider/nurse/poets (hey, they had a lot of interests). Dirar became such a powerful warrior that infamous military leader (and buddy of the Prophet Muhammad) Khalid ibn al-Walid recruited him to lead men into war against the Byzantines. Dirar did pretty well, fighting bare-chested like an '80s action star, until he was finally overpowered and taken hostage.

Khalid gathered 1,000 men and launched a rescue operation—only to find one was already under way. A mysterious soldier, dressed all in black and green, was mowing down Romans like grass . . . or, to use the colorfully strange description of the time, "it was like lightning striking the heads of two or four youths, then burning to ashes another five to seven."

After sowing fear (and death blows) among the Byzantines to the point that the survivors ran off, the mysterious knight attempted to blend into the crowd of Khalid's men and disappear—an attempt thwarted by the fact that the knight was completely drenched in blood, like "a crimson rose petal." After catching up, Khalid demanded to know the identity of the terrifying stranger.

It was, as you've probably guessed, Khawlah bint al-Azwar.

Khalid, who knew a good thing when he saw it, quickly integrated her into his forces, and she rode with him on other raids against the Byzantines. Often Khawlah rode solo, reciting poems while assaulting the Byzantines' rear guard, like Maya Angelou with a scimitar. After battles, she interrogated the survivors one by one, always with the same question: "Where is my brother?"

Eventually, they caught a break when Khalid thought to describe Dirar as "that bare-chested action hero guy," or something along those lines, and learned where he was being taken. Khawlah rode out with 100 fighters and ambushed Dirar's Byzantine captors (just as Dirar was reciting a poem—the al-Azwars were some serious Action Poets). Khawlah quickly freed him, killed a ton of Byzantines, and peaced out. Warred out. Whatever.

When next we hear of Khawlah, she'd gone back to being a nurse along with the rest of the women of her tribe—only to be captured unawares! Imprisoned by lusty Byzantines hell-bent on taking liberties with them, the women, all unarmed and most middle-aged, resigned themselves to their fates. Khawlah, not so much.

Paraphrasing, she asked, "Do you *want* to be these guys' property?! Where is your courage and skill I've heard so much about?!"

"Look, Khawlah," said one of the women. "We're plenty brave, but you know what would be useful against an army? Weapons."

"That's no excuse. Let's just uproot these tentpoles and pegs and kill them with those."

"By Allah! What a wonderful and appropriate suggestion."*

Bringing down the tent and circling into a defensive formation, the women began working their way out of the camp. In so doing, they shouted poems of rage,† as well as threats: "We have decided that today we will rectify your brains with these tent pegs and shorten your life spans, thus removing a spot of disgrace from your ancestors' faces."

After several forceful brain rectifications, the Byzantine leader ran out and tried to pacify the women in the most arrogant, mansplaining manner imaginable. He started by letting Khawlah in on a secret, one sure to put a smile on her face: that he was willing to marry her and be her master, and that he was quite the catch. All the Christian ladies wanted him. Additionally, he was rich and totally best buds with the Byzantine leader! Didn't that sound great?

Khawlah's verbatim response: "You wretched unbelieving son of an unchaste adulterer! By Allah! I will take this peg and gouge your eyes out. You are not even worthy of herding my camels and sheep, let alone claim to be my equal!"

If, at this point, you want to be best friends with her, you are not alone.

The women continued to hold off the Byzantines for some time (killing 30 in the process) until Khalid and Dirar arrived with reinforcements.‡ The Byzantine leader, claiming that he had somehow fallen out of love with Khawlah, handed her over to Dirar. Dirar replied, "Why thank you! Unfortunately, I have nothing to give in return except the point of a spear. So take it." And stabbed him to death.

---

* While the first three lines of this dialogue are paraphrased, this last one is too hysterical to change. Ancient texts have a hilariously understated approach to murder.

† "Himyar and Tubba's daughters are we / For us to kill you is quite easy / For we are the flames of war / We have for you great trouble in store." Old school diss tracks are just the best.

‡ Khawlah's sassy reaction to their appearance: "Took you long enough! Thank God we didn't actually *need* your help."

And then, as if that was not enough of a one-liner, Dirar dropped a verse from the Qur'an: "When you are greeted with a greeting, greet back better than that or at least return it equally." Stone cold, Dirar. Stone cold.

Khawlah continued on to fight in other battles, showing a level of endurance on par with a caffeinated rhino. When a squadron of male cohorts fled an overwhelming battle, she insulted them back into service, like a seventh-century **Mai Bhago**. When a squadron of women did similarly, she yelled, "Yes, flee! Your presence only makes us weak!" When she was hit in the head and bled so much that it was certain she was going to die, she rested a bit and then got up and started getting water for everyone, despite her gaping wound.

So here's to Khawlah bint al-Azwar: early Islam's unforgettable,* unstoppable warrior poet.

---

* Quite literally unforgettable—in modern times, she's become the namesake of many schools and military groups, including an all-female unit in the Iraqi military.

# Princess Caraboo

(1791–1864, ENGLAND)

## The Princess Who Faked It

 omething weird happened in rural England in 1817: They got a visitor. A princess. From the South Asian island of Javasu.

Not that it was easy to figure even that out. Princess Caraboo, as they eventually determined her name to be, didn't speak English. Or French. Or any other language that anyone knew. They eventually had to rely on the services of a visiting Portuguese sailor (who'd spent time in Indonesia) to help translate. Turns out she had quite the tale: After her mother had been killed by cannibals, Caraboo was kidnapped by Spanish pirates and then traded from boat to boat before escaping by eventually jumping ship—only to later wash up onshore nearby. Within months, she'd become quite the celebrity, a draw for visitors from all around and the subject of breathless newspaper articles.

If that sounds too incredible for you to believe, you're not alone. Even as Caraboo greeted people with her unique customs—performing her unique "salaam" gestures and dances, refusing alcohol, exercising with a homemade bow and arrow, and writing in an alphabet alien to everyone—her good-natured country hosts thought there was something fishy about this particularly light-skinned Asian princess. And they were determined to get to the truth of the matter.

They tried everything to get her to slip up. They listened by her bed for her to talk in her sleep. They would wake her suddenly to see if she'd speak English in her confusion. They left huge amounts of cash lying around the house to see if she'd grab it. When she was sick, they brought in a doctor who stood by the door and gave a fake terminal diagnosis, then watched for her reaction. Every attempt failed—she would just smile pleasantly, ignorant of any goings-on.

That is, until she got a little too famous.

After one newspaper article spread farther than usual, Caraboo's hosts were contacted by a woman who'd previously hosted Caraboo, until her guest suddenly ran off. The only discrepancy the previous host noted with her experience was that the princess had had no issues with imbibing alcohol while with her.

And with that, the jig was up.

Tearily, Caraboo admitted that her actual name was Mary Baker, and that far from being an Indonesian princess, she was a homeless runaway. Her history was beyond depressing: put out to work in her teens by her parents, she'd been mistreated to the point of suicide. For years, she'd wandered from home to home, working odd jobs or sometimes begging, staying with clergymen and thieves.

Eventually she married a sailor named Baker, who regaled her with stories about his time in Malaysia and Indonesia.

Her husband abandoned her shortly after getting her pregnant. When their child died in infancy, Mary began to wander the streets again, reinventing herself over and over. At first she pretended to be Spanish, then French, until she decided that her goal was to make a new start in America—for which she settled upon the identity of Princess Caraboo, with the ostensible goal of hustling up fare for a boat ticket. She made her act work by studying her visitors for context clues of what they expected her to sound like and playing on their vanities.

When her hosts finally sussed all of this out of Mary, their reaction was entirely unexpected: they bought her a ticket to America. Not only that, but they arranged lodging and booked her ticket under her maiden name, Mary Willcocks, so that she could travel anonymously and start a new life. She stayed in America for seven years, playing a version of her Princess Caraboo persona onstage to middling success. Eventually she remarried, returned to England, and lived a quiet life to the end of her days.

Astoundingly, the contemporary document that details her story went to extreme lengths to verify as much as possible. Everyone interviewed, including her parents, verified most of the details presented to them, then offered an entirely new aspect of her history—like that she'd taken up with a group of Romani people, or that her husband had died instead of running out on her. They all describe her as an imaginative yet harmless eccentric, with a seemingly malleable grip on her own history.

In the end, nobody knows the unvarnished truth about Mary Baker, alias Princess Caraboo. Which is just how she would have wanted it.

## · ART NOTES ·

Here Mary Baker is placing a portrait of her history as "Princess Caraboo" on the mantelpiece of her host, covering up her history as Mary Baker—which is itself covering up numerous other potential histories.

The outfit she's wearing is based on her descriptions of the "traditional dresses" of Javasu. Same with the depictions of her parents (seen in the Caraboo portrait).

# Anita Garibaldi

## (1821–1849, BRAZIL/URUGUAY/ITALY)

### Heroine of Two Worlds

**I**t is a rare woman who fights in a revolutionary war. Rarer still one who fights in two. Rarest of all is the woman who fights in three.

Meet Anita Garibaldi, who did just that. While pregnant.

Anita was born to a poor Brazilian family. At an early age, she began to delight her bold father and terrify her conservative mother by spending her time breaking wild horses instead of sewing and learning to cook. Her father died when she was young, but she soon proved that she carried on his fighting spirit: when a local boy tried to force himself on her, she whipped him in the face and sped off on her horse. He was scarred for life. Anita was just getting started.

It was to be a false start, though. At the outset of her adult life, she crippled her own freedoms with a terrible marriage in a big city. Her worrywart mother had spent years begging her to settle down, so Anita acquiesced and married a man who turned out to be an abusive drunk. She would regularly lock herself in her room to defend herself from his fits of alcoholic rage. She was 14.

At the same time Anita's life was taking a turn for the worse, so was Brazil. It had recently become independent from Portugal, which seemed totally positive—until it fell into an endless series of internal conflicts, including the incongruously-yet-adorably-named Ragamuffin War, which pit scrappy rebels (yay) against the Brazilian monarchy (boo). For Anita, two good things came out of all this. Firstly, her crappy husband volunteered to join the establishment forces and left home. Secondly, and more importantly, her true love came to Brazil: Giuseppe Garibaldi.

Giuseppe was the definitive bad boy of 1830s Brazil. For him, the Brazilian conflicts were just a warm-up, a practice war. His long-term goal was to drive out foreign interests from his native Italy—then a collection of many smaller countries—and unify the country under a single flag. To gain experience (and soldiers), he had left Italy for Brazil and started running the Ragamuffin rebels' navy. While his expertise and roguish good looks endeared him to Brazilian women nationwide, his "war, war, and more war" outlook on life understandably didn't win him much love from the mothers of said women.

This didn't much matter to Anita, who, against the wishes of her mother (and husband, and friends, and pretty much everyone—the pressure was intense), started an affair with Giuseppe. According to their memoirs, he fell for her at first sight, immediately blurting out "You must be mine" upon meeting her. Giuseppe Garibaldi: not the smoothest operator.

From this torrid start, their relationship took a turn into adult realms. They soon met clandestinely at an abandoned cabin late at night. With the lights low and a heap of straw waiting for them in the corner, they let their base urges take hold of them and gave in to their true desires. Which is to say, they started talking. Openly and frankly, they discussed their hopes, dreams, fears, and expectations, gaining a very clear understanding of what the other wanted. Didn't sleep together or anything.

You know, adult realms.

Anita thereafter joined him on his ship and immediately subverted the sailors' expectations by becoming an integral part of the crew. In no time, she learned the ins and outs of being a crew member, donned men's clothes, and even created a first aid station.

She got her hands equally dirty in battle. She started by running through gun and cannon fire to treat the wounded. In a later battle, when the monarchy's forces got the better of them, she manned the cannons herself, helped get the ship's ammunition onto shore, then set the remainder of the ship on fire.

In the Battle of Curitibanos, she was captured by the Brazilian monarchists while leading the rear guard. She soon broke out of captivity, sneaking into the forest. Over the next several days, she evaded enemy soldiers, forded a river, traversed rain forest and scorching desert—all without food—until she found her way back to Giuseppe. Once they were reunited, she helped protect the unit's horses from monarchist raiders, even besting a foe in hand-to-hand combat while they were both on horseback. She snatched his gun and threw him off his horse.

And she did all that while pregnant. (Guess they slept together eventually.)

From there, the couple moved on to Uruguay—partly because the Brazilian rebellions had devolved into political infighting in the new republic and further effort appeared useless, but mostly because Anita wanted a quieter life for their new child. Their baby had barely survived his first winter as the littlest guerrilla as they traveled through frozen wastes, with little to warm him but his father's breath.

Unfortunately, her hoped-for "quiet life" only lasted a couple months, as Uruguay, too, plunged into rebellion and Giuseppe got sucked in to lead the rebel navy. Compared to Brazil, however, their time in Uruguay was paradise. Anita had three more children, when she wasn't running the poorest section of the city of Montevideo. With the city under a prolonged siege from its enemies, Anita calmly organized its panicked residents, making the best of their skills and resources.

And in an ironic twist, Anita did indeed take up sewing, devoting huge amounts of time in Uruguay to the practice—but she was sewing rebel uniforms and flags. In fact, the outfit that gave Giuseppe's infamous Red Shirt soldiers their name? Courtesy of Anita.

Gradually, the Uruguay conflicts died down, and with the various Italian nations primed for revolution, the Garibaldis moved to Europe. Their reputation preceded them, and they

were greeted like royalty—some people would even smash open windows for a chance to get a clearer look at them. The leisurely life did not suit Anita, however, so she set herself to arranging field medics and first aid for the Red Shirts.

A combination of poor decisions and political infighting doomed the Italian rebellion shortly after it started. Soon Anita and Giuseppe left the kids with his mother and were on the run again. This time, though, they were up against an unimaginably strong enemy: at one point, the combined armies of four nations, totaling 65,000 soldiers, were chasing them. Time after time, they miraculously evaded their foes, but constant hunger and impending doom took its toll.

Compounding matters was the fact that Anita was pregnant with her fifth child, and on top of that, she had contracted malaria. Determined to continue fighting, she rode on through the fever, slashing at attacking soldiers from horseback. One later remarked, "Is that a woman or is it the devil?" The Garibaldis turned down offers of amnesty on principle and slogged from hut to hut, hoping to immigrate to the United States.

In the end, Anita could fight no longer, and she died in Giuseppe's arms—seven months pregnant, a month shy of her 28th birthday. She was buried hurriedly, for lack of time.

Giuseppe went on to escape Italy, only to return 10 years later for a successful rebellion that saw the formation of modern-day Italy. Upon his return, he arranged for Anita's body to be moved to Nice, to be given a proper funeral and interred with the rest of the Garibaldi family. There she rests still, an icon known in both South America and Italy as the Heroine of Two Worlds.

## · ART NOTES ·

The flag Anita is waving is that of the short-lived Riograndense Republic of Brazil, for which both she and Giuseppe fought during the Ragamuffin War.

Giuseppe's flag is one he adopted to represent Italy in mourning. The volcano at its center was to symbolize its soldiers ready to erupt forth.

The size of the navy in the background is symbolic of the odds they faced.

Giuseppe's outfit is the standard Red Shirts uniform, which Anita made.

Anita repeatedly made mention of Giuseppe's beautiful long hair. About the only fights they had were over her jealousy from the attention that other women would pay him. He once cut off all his hair so that she would feel better (which just made her feel worse).

For most of her life, Anita had but one dress, and it was incredibly shabby. Even her wedding ring was a cheap silver affair. Giuseppe was repeatedly offered tremendous riches in compensation for his various military successes, but to set an example for the troops, both he and Anita refused virtually all offers of aid.

# Tomyris

## (6TH CENTURY BCE, KAZAKHSTAN)

## *The Woman Who Headed Off the Most Powerful Man in the World*

 omyris was the widowed leader of the Massagetae, a semi-nomadic group living in Central Asia. Not much definitive is known about them (even their ethnicity is subject to debate), but a lot of the reported details (given by historians who are admittedly prone to hyperbole) are pretty colorful. In an awesome mashup of *Logan's Run* and *Soylent Green*, they regularly sacrificed their elders when they got too old—presumably so the resulting geriatric meat would be well seasoned when they subsequently devoured it. But the Massagetae would only cannibalize the healthier seniors. Everyone knows that eating a sick old person is only a momentary pleasure and bound to give you indigestion.

But while the Massagetae were enjoying their wrinkly long pig steaks, their neighbor Cyrus the Great was making plans to conquer them. Cyrus had founded the Achaemenid Empire and built it, through relentless military conquests, into the largest empire the world had ever seen. Big as it was, though, apparently it was not big enough for Cyrus. And so Cyrus was looking to expand with another hostile takeover—in this case, the Massagetae.

Cyrus began his attempts on Tomyris's holdings in the same manner as a Jane Austen villain: by proposing marriage. The widowed queen, however, was no blushing Regency ingenue and, seeing through his obvious scheme, laughed off his proposal. Cyrus took this jilting about as well as you'd expect from an all-powerful sovereign and went to plan B: declaring war and invading her country.

When word reached Tomyris that Cyrus was building a bridge across the river from her, she said, paraphrasing: "I'll take you on, but not on some bridge. We can either do this in my backyard or yours. You let me know."

Now, Cyrus was prepared to rumble on his side of the river, and he would have done so were it not for the terrible advice of one of his advisers, Croesus.* After all his other advisers had

---

\* It's worth pointing out that Cyrus (and, obliquely, Croesus) had already been defeated by a woman. Years earlier, Cyrus had invaded the Amyrgians and taken their king hostage. In response, the Amyrgian queen, Sparethra, raised an army of 500,000 people (40 percent of them women), crushed Cyrus, and rescued her husband. She later swore fealty to Cyrus (for unclear reasons) and helped Cyrus defeat Croesus in battle. Sometime after that defeat, Croesus and Cyrus became friendly—but not before Cyrus set Croesus on fire for a little bit.

already settled on a plan, Croesus stood up with another idea. "If you lose ground to this chick, everyone is gonna mad disrespect you. Besides, you know what chicks are like. Let them in your house and soon they're rearranging all your crap and getting their armies to take land for themselves. Bro up! Don't even tell her you're crossing the river to her side, dude!"

So Cyrus followed Croesus's plan and began his invasion, using some underhanded tactics. Cyrus built a bridge, crossed the river, and sent in his worst soldiers with an unusual siege weapon: a massive banquet. Tomyris's men soon found Cyrus's poor soldiers-turned-sous-chefs and murdered them. Subsequently, the Massagetae helped themselves to the abandoned feast and got blitzed on the wine—an intoxicant to which they'd had little previous exposure. Once the Massagetae were falling-down drunk, Cyrus valiantly moved in, slaughtering and imprisoning a great many inebriated opponents. Tomyris's son was one such prisoner.

As you might imagine, this displeased Tomyris. She wrote Cyrus again, calling him a bloodthirsty coward who let poison do his work. She ended her missive by commanding him to release her son and retreat. "Refuse," she said, "and I swear by the sun, the sovereign lord of the Massagetae, bloodthirsty as you are, I will give you your fill of blood."

From there things got worse: Cyrus ignored her message, Tomyris's son committed suicide, and Tomyris went after Cyrus. At the end of the ensuing battle—described by the historian Herodotus as "more violent than any others fought between foreign nations"—Tomyris was victorious and Cyrus was dead.

Afterwards, Tomyris filled a wineskin with human blood and ordered Cyrus's lifeless corpse brought to her. Cutting off his head and stuffing it into the wine sack, she proclaimed: "See now, I fulfill my threat; you have your fill of blood."

## · ART NOTES AND TRIVIA ·

Tomyris's outfit is based on depictions of the Scythians, of which the Massagetae were an offshoot. Fun fact: many of the Greek Amazon legends were based on the Scythians!

The background is the Araxes (Aras) River, the actual place where Cyrus crossed into Massagetae territory. You can see his bridge and towers burning on the right side of the image.

The cup Tomyris is holding is a skull cup—made from the top of an actual human skull. The peoples of her tribe regularly used the things. She was said to have made one from Cyrus's head.

The helmet on the table is Cyrus's helmet, as portrayed in almost every depiction of him.[*]

---

[*] This is one of several accounts of Cyrus's death—others claim he died under totally different circumstances. To this day, nobody is sure which one is correct. History is complicated!

# Emmeline Pankhurst

(1858–1929, ENGLAND)

## The Most Dangerous Suffragette

I am what you might call a hooligan."

So began Emmeline Pankhurst's 1909 speech to a group of women agitating for the right to vote. They laughed, hooted, hollered, and applauded the sentiment.

Pankhurst wasn't kidding. As the leading advocate for militant tactics in the British women's suffrage movement, she oversaw and encouraged widespread acts of property destruction (notably and purposely leaving people out of it). She and her followers broke windows, bombed houses, burned a train station, threw acid into mailboxes, cut phone wires, slashed a priceless piece of art, threw rocks at the Crown Jewels, and even shoved a hatchet (bearing the message VOTES FOR WOMEN) into the prime minister's carriage—all to get the vote. And they did so in proper British fashion: wearing pretty dresses and fancy hats.

Pankhurst was simultaneously an unlikely and inevitable leader for such a movement. She was born without much in the way of money or political connections and was borderline destitute for much of her adult life. However, politics and a fiery disposition were practically her genetic heritage.

Both her parents were activists, and her mother was from the ironically female-friendly Isle of Man: the first country in the world to grant women the right to vote. This, combined with her marriage to a scrappy young politician, pumped Pankhurst's willfulness to levels to which Steve Jobs could only aspire.

How strong-willed was she? In the span of a year and a half, she was arrested 11 times, only to be released within a couple days on medical leave each time. Said medical leave was necessary because after each arrest she would go on a combination hunger, thirst, and sleep strike. She refused to so much as sit down in her cell, instead pacing around in circles endlessly. When that became too much, she propped her arm up over her head in order to keep herself awake. When released, despite often being too weak to lift her head or arms, she would skip town, going off to give speeches all across the UK (and sometimes other countries). She got around in a special ambulance that her political organization bought for just such occasions.

Mind you, she was in her mid-fifties at the time.

These extreme measures were not her initial methods. She spent years with the Women's

Social and Political Union (WSPU) campaigning peacefully. But the British establishment (chiefly Prime Minister Herbert Asquith and future would-be war hero Winston Churchill) was brutal in response, beating and locking up many of her compatriots. When her increasingly violent tactics were criticized, Pankhurst shot back:

> Why should women go into Parliament Square and be battered about and be insulted, and, most important of all, produce less effect than when they use stones? We tried it long enough. We submitted for years patiently to insult and to assault. Women had their health injured. Women lost their lives. We should not have minded that if that had succeeded, but that did not succeed, and we have made more progress with less hurt to ourselves by breaking glass than we ever made when we allowed them to break our bodies.

One of the lost lives to which she alluded was that of her sister, who had died of heart failure after a particularly harrowing stint in prison. In response to women going on hunger strikes, the British authorities instituted a program of force-feeding, forcing unsanitary tubes into their noses, mouths, and, on rare occasion, vaginas and rectums. While Pankhurst herself was never subjected to force-feeding, she regularly heard its effects during her stays in prison. The memory of her WSPU comrades' screams, she said, never left her.

As the campaign for the vote became increasingly violent, the WSPU brought on a surprising corps of bodyguards—30 female jujitsu experts. They regularly used weaponry in fights with the police, notably inventing their own style of parasol-based self-defense in the process. They would hide their weapons, which included batons, billy clubs, and guns (loaded with blanks), under the mats of their secret martial arts schools.

At the height of her campaigning efforts, Pankhurst developed more and more creative tactics for fighting back. At one speech, delivered while a warrant was out for her arrest, Pankhurst stood on a stage decorated with flowers. When undercover police stormed the proceedings and climbed onto the platform, they found out the hard way that the flowers concealed a line of barbed wire.

At another speech, she strode out onto a balcony overlooking the street and announced to the crowd of onlookers, which included police: "I am coming out amongst you in a few minutes and I challenge the government to re-arrest me!" When the tiny woman walked out the door, pandemonium struck instantly. Police tried grabbing her, while the crowd of women pulled out Indian clubs (wooden bats shaped like bowling pins) from their dresses and began fighting the authorities. When the dust settled and the police had taken custody of the veiled woman, they realized that she was just a decoy: the real Pankhurst had slipped away during the fracas.

The efforts of Pankhurst and her allies came to an abrupt halt with the start of World

War I. Patriots at heart, the militant suffragettes rallied around the flag, volunteering their help to the war effort.

This made for odd bedfellows: one of Pankhurst's chief allies was wartime prime minister Lloyd George, whose country house the WSPU had bombed mere months earlier. It was a surprisingly successful partnership. The suffragettes proved a vital workforce and fund-raising group for the government. Pankhurst lobbied for their work to be compensated at pay equal to that of their male counterparts, to some success.

In 1918, due in no small part to the suffragettes' help with the war effort, Britain granted certain women over the age of 30 the right to vote—enough to quiet much of the movement.

In the absence of a good focus for her energies following the passage of women's suffrage, Pankhurst grew increasingly difficult and isolated. She had always been a borderline tyrant in her political life, regularly causing political schisms and excommunicating former partners, but after the war she brought this chaotic approach to her own family. Once her daughter Sylvia, who had long been a trusted lieutenant in the WSPU, had a child out of wedlock, the socially prudish Emmeline cut all ties with her. Sylvia joined her sister Adela, whom Emmeline had angrily (and successfully) suggested immigrate to Australia, on Emmeline's persona non grata list.

Emmeline died in 1928, after years of failing health. Her legacy remains a complicated one. While her presence at the time undoubtedly did much to publicize the cause of women's suffrage, it's uncertain how much effect, positive or negative, her actions had on the process. Nevertheless, she was an utterly unique figure, and a month after her death the vote was extended to all women over 21.

## · ART NOTES AND TRIVIA ·

The women in the image are dressed entirely in purple, white, and green—the colors of the WSPU. Additionally, Pankhurst herself is wearing a medal marked "H24"—a reference to her prison cell and the time she served. Everyone was ordered to dress as properly as possible in order to present themselves as "law makers, not law breakers."

The scene takes place outside of 10 Downing Street, the prime minister's office. This brawl did actually take place—first at the House of Commons, with 300 women, and several days later at Downing Street, with 200 women.

Other visible suffragettes here are jujitsu instructor Flora "the General" Drummond (on the back of the policeman, dressed in her military regalia) and Sylvia Pankhurst (wrestling a policeman to the ground on the left).

The jujitsu-practicing suffragettes referred to their martial art as "Suffrajitsu," which is pretty great.

# Marjana

## The Slave Girl Who Killed Ali Baba's 40 Thieves

Most people have heard of "Ali Baba and the 40 Thieves"—but it turns out that title is somewhat truncated. The rightful name, which includes the most crucial element of the tale, is "Ali Baba and the 40 Thieves Killed by a Slave Girl."

That slave girl would be Marjana.

The story starts with the familiar elements. Money-bereft pauper Ali Baba is out herding his goats when he spots 40 thieves riding toward him. Bravely hiding himself in a tree (leaving the poor goats to the thieves, the story notes), he witnesses the thieves approaching a rock. They intone "Open sesame," and the rock opens up, revealing their swanky hangout (awash in treasure and accented by a skylight—they clearly had great interior decorators). Once they leave, Ali sneaks in, steals a bunch of gold, and takes off.

Once he gets home, Ali Baba sets about burying his treasure. His wife insists on weighing it and visits Ali's well-off (but pretty shady) brother Qasim to borrow a scale. Qasim's wife coats the scale with sticky wax so that when it's returned to her a coin will be stuck to the bottom. She realizes Ali is now rolling in the dough and tells Qasim.

Qasim confronts Ali, extorts the location of the cave from him, and heads off to steal some gold for himself. Unfortunately, Qasim can't remember the password (he tries "Open barley" and various other grains) and is promptly killed by the returning thieves. They cut him up into four pieces to scare off future invaders. Realizing too late that his corpse is going to stink up their hangout, they leave it and head out to kill some time.

You may notice that nobody in this story is vaguely competent. That's about to change.

At the behest of Qasim's wife, Ali sets off to find Qasim—despite how terrible he'd been to his brother. Upon fetching Qasim's four-part corpse, Ali realizes he is in way over his head. So he prevails upon the one person he knows who can fix everything and who thankfully happens to be in Qasim's employ: his slave, Marjana.

Upon realizing her master is dead, Marjana immediately sets about making it look like he died of natural causes. The next day, she visits the local apothecary and asks for medicine for her poor, ailing, of-course-not-dead master Qasim. Soon after that, she approaches the apothecary again, this time even more upset, wailing that her master is so sick he cannot possibly leave the house. She makes sure a lot of people hear her doing this.

After that rumor has taken hold, Marjana approaches Baba Mustafa, a tailor in the marketplace. She bribes him to come to the house, sew up Qasim's four parts into one, and keep quiet about it. For good measure, she blindfolds him and spins him around, so he won't know where she's taking him. After bringing Baba Mustafa back, she performs cleansing rites on Qasim's body, arranges to get a coffin, and finds priests to carry out the burial.

Her plan works. Qasim is buried honorably, and Ali Baba takes Qasim's widow as a second wife. ("My wife won't be jealous," he says, a claim that is never verified.) Ali's family moves into Qasim's house, and Ali gives Qasim's business to Ali's hitherto-unmentioned son.

(No, it is never explained how and why Marjana knew to do all this. Maybe she had done it before? Maybe she had done it many times before.)

Meanwhile, the thieves realize someone absconded with their morbid house decor—someone who knows about their secret cave. They send one of their own into town to find out who.

Unfortunately for the Ali Baba household, said scout approaches the tailor Baba Mustafa immediately—and more unfortunately, Baba Mustafa turns out not only to be a total blabbermouth but also a total freak of nature when it comes to his sense of direction. The thief has not talked to Mustafa for 30 seconds before Mustafa brags that he is such a good tailor, he sewed up a four-part corpse the other day. When pressed as to where he did this, Mustafa can't rightly say, since he was blindfolded. However, when the thief blindfolds Mustafa again, he is able to remember the exact direction to Qasim's house, where he deposits the thief. The thief marks the house with white chalk and returns to his compatriots.

Marjana soon comes across the chalk. *That's odd*, she thinks to herself. *For good measure, let's just mark up all the other houses on the street with the same marking.*

When the thieves come by the next day, they cannot identify the correct house. They leave in a rage and kill the spy they'd first sent in for incompetence. They then send in a second spy, who repeats the steps of the first—bribes Mustafa, blindfolds him, gets led to Qasim's house, marks it up with a tiny red mark. Marjana finds the red mark and again marks up every house on the street. The thieves, stymied again, kill a second member of their group.

The captain of the thieves (the Thief Chief, if you will) realizes that his minions are, perhaps, not too bright—and that at the rate they're going, he's going to run out of henchmen. So he decides to take matters into his own hands. The Thief Chief bribes and blindfolds Mustafa, who by now is quite wealthy. Mustafa leads the Thief Chief to Qasim's house, and the Thief Chief proceeds to demonstrate his mental acuity by actually memorizing where it is.

He continues his mental gymnastics by hatching a plot: he has his underlings get 38 jars and 19 donkeys. He fills one of the jars with oil and the rest with his sword-wielding thug compatriots. He then disguises himself as an oil merchant and approaches Ali, asking to stay the night. Ali does not recognize him, and graciously allows him in. The Thief Chief sets up the 38 jars in the stables and instructs his men to wait the night in their cramped enclosures.

In the morning, he will toss some pebbles at the jars, at which point they are to cut themselves free and commence murdering.

The Thief Chief did not, of course, reckon on Marjana.

In the middle of the night, while prepping food and laundry for the next day, Marjana runs out of oil. One of the other servants suggests that it's fine to take a bit of the oil merchant's wares, so she decides to do just that. However, as she approaches the first jar, the thief inside whispers, "Is it time?" Putting together that (a) there is a guy inside, (b) he is here to kill them, and (c) the merchant is running the show, Marjana imitates the Thief Chief's voice and says, "Not yet." She does so with every jar until she finds the jar of oil.

She then boils the entire human-sized jar of oil and pours its horrifying contents into each of the 37 other jars, killing all the assailants in as gruesome a manner as possible.

Early in the morning, the Thief Chief tosses some pebbles at the jars of human barbecue, to no response. Finally, he casually saunters over and inspects the contents, only to be confronted with the reality that everyone he loves is dead and he is alone on this earth. He runs off. Marjana watches him go. Marjana has no need for sleep. Marjana has evolved beyond it.

When Ali Baba gets up, Marjana informs him that his garage is now full of toasty corpses. She also tells him that she thwarted two previous chalk-related attempts on his life as well. And then she serves him breakfast because, let us not forget, taking all night to murder three dozen trained assassins is no excuse for not getting your work done.

Ali sets her free on the spot. For unknown reasons, she chooses to stick around.

The Thief Chief, despondent from the macabre deaths of his friends, decides that he will get revenge on Ali Baba if it is the last thing he ever does. Disguising himself as a merchant again, he sets up shop in the town marketplace. Within a few weeks, he befriends Ali's son (remember him?) and starts plying him with gifts. In thanks, Ali's son invites the Thief Chief over for dinner at Ali's house.

Ali Baba, being a towering paragon of wisdom, once again does not recognize the Thief Chief. Marjana, however, does, largely due to blunders on the Thief Chief's part. When offered beef stew, he demurs, claiming that he does not eat salt or meat. Infuriated at having to now cook another meal for a surprise vegetarian, Marjana storms out of the kitchen, only to instantly recognize the merchant as the Thief Chief in a lousy disguise.

Thinking quickly, she puts on a dancer's outfit, tosses a tambourine to another slave, and starts dancing. She dances with a small dagger, which is not uncommon for belly dancers. At the end of the dance, she plunges the dagger into the Thief Chief's heart and keeps it there until he stops moving. Which is less common for belly dancers.

Ali and son are shocked, but when Marjana produces a dagger from the Thief Chief's belt and points out that he was the guy who'd tried to kill Ali a mere month ago, all is forgiven. Ali marries her to his son, retrieves the rest of the gold from the now-uninhabited cave, and all live happily ever after. Presumably with Marjana managing everything.

# Mai Bhago

## (LATE 17TH CENTURY–MID-18TH CENTURY, INDIA)

## *Savior of the Sikhs*

hen the dust cleared at the battle of Khidrana, one thing was clear: the Sikh religion had escaped extinction. This was due to the heroics of a ragtag group that came to the Sikhs' defense at the last minute—all of whom, save one, were now dead. That one? A woman named Mai Bhago.

But let's take a step back and look at the history of the Sikhs. You probably know that their men wear turbans, don't shave, and consistently get mistaken for Muslims by ignorant morons. Frustrating as that is, jerks attacking them for virtually no reason is something that Sikhs have had to live with for the majority of their religion's existence. Exhibit A: the Mughal Empire.

The Mughals were tough customers. Their founder, Babar, had quite the lineage himself: descendant of Tamerlane (an Uzbeki warlord known for constructing pyramids out of his enemies' skulls) on his father's side and grandson of Genghis Khan on his mother's. The Mughals carried on and refined this legacy. On the one hand, they did so militaristically, riding elephants into battle, redefining warfare, and expanding the empire until it encompassed all of present-day India and beyond. On the other hand, they also advanced literature, culture, and the arts tremendously. They built the Taj Mahal and giant libraries and had a tremendously multicultural empire. For more info on that, check out Akbar the Great, who—having brought together a huge number of disparate peoples, including the Sikhs, in a surprisingly peaceful, literary, and secular empire, especially for the time—definitely earned the moniker.

Unfortunately, by the time our story begins, the Mughals were being ruled by Aurangzeb, who was neither peaceful nor understanding. He was particularly aggressive toward the Sikhs, partly for religious reasons, and partly because the Sikhs weren't down with the caste system. In fact, the Sikhs were egalitarian in general and considered women equal to men.

Which brings us to Mai Bhago.

Mai Bhago lived in a peaceful rural town with her parents. She spent a lot of time with her dad, who, during their daddy-daughter hangouts, taught her what any good father should: how to be a devoted Sikh, how to ride a horse, and how to kill anyone who starts a fight with you. All of these skills came in handy just a few years later when the leader of the Sikh, Guru Gobind Singh Ji, founded the Khalsa—the warrior-saints.

You see, the guru before Gobind Singh Ji—and there were only ever 10 of these guys total—was executed by Aurangzeb when Guru Gobind Singh Ji was only nine years old. Rather than capitulating to Aurangzeb and living a quiet life, the guru ordered his followers to eschew the caste system, forsake their family names, be baptized as warrior-saints, and kick butt for the lord.

Mai Bhago was one of the first to get down on that.

The following years were very difficult on the Sikhs as the Mughals waged nonstop warfare on the guru. As tough as it was on him, it was arguably tougher on his warriors, holed up in fortress after fortress, eventually subsisting on nothing but nuts and leaves. After months of this, 40 of them, with heavy hearts, forsook the religion and left the Khalsa in order to return to their normal lives.

Mai Bhago was not on board with that decision. Upon hearing about the 40 deserters, she rode to every nearby city and convinced all the local women to refuse them hospitality. She even rounded up a group of women to take up arms in the deserters' place—telling the 40 to either stay behind and look after the children or sack up and fight. Suitably ashamed by this, the 40 deserters had a change of heart.

This happened just in time, because as the 40 (plus Mai Bhago) were riding back to the guru, the Mughals were making another assault on the guru's stronghold. The size of the army is difficult to determine from historical records, with the only source claiming the Mughals had 10,000 men, which seems a bit ridiculous. In any event, it is agreed that the Sikhs were massively outnumbered.

On December 29, 1705, the 41 Sikhs rushed in to cut off the Mughals anyway. They did several clever things leading up to and during the battle:

- They positioned themselves in front of the Khidrana reservoir, the only source of water for miles around, and defended it viciously.

- They laid sheets across bushes everywhere, giving the appearance of tents—and then hid nearby, ambushing the Mughals when they started attacking the empty "tents."

- They kicked up a colossal amount of dust, attracting the attention of the retreating guru—who proceeded to unleash an incessant barrage of arrows from a nearby hill upon the Mughals.

Eventually the Mughals, battered and thirsty, withdrew. All 40 of the deserters died in that battle, as did a large number of Mughal soldiers. Mai Bhago was the only Sikh survivor. From there, she became bodyguard to the guru. She outlived him and later died of old age. The Mughal Empire under Aurangzeb's leadership began a slow decline and petered out over a century later. The Sikh religion continues strong to this day. Mai Bhago's spear and gun can still be found in Sikh museums, and her house has been converted into a *gurudwara* (Sikh place of worship).

And lastly: although best known by the name Mai Bhago, technically her name, after she converted to the Khalsa, was Mai Bhag Kaur—Kaur being a surname all female Khalsa take, which roughly translates to "princess."

## · ART NOTES ·

Mai Bhago is depicted here wearing not just the traditional Khalsa clothing but that of the Nihang, an elite warrior Khalsa sect. This outfit includes a variety of bladed weapons (the guru was known to have five weapons on him at all times), electric blue robes, steel-wrapped turbans, and iron bangles about the wrist.

And yes, she is decapitating that guy.

Lastly: the Mughal being beheaded has period-accurate clothing, although his helmet is one of an infantryman and his outfit is that of a cavalryman.

# Hortense Mancini
## (1646–1699, FRANCE/ITALY/ENGLAND)
# and Marie Mancini
## (1639–1715, FRANCE/ITALY/SPAIN)

## *Divorce Pioneers of the Renaissance*

In the 1600s, few women were more famous than Hortense and Marie Mancini. For years, the gazettes of the time breathlessly reported on the Mancinis' defiant escapes from their abusive marriages and their subsequent court battles. As the sisters fled across Europe, escaping convent after convent, hiding in forests to evade their husbands' henchmen, the pair became feminist icons and pioneers of one of Europe's most revolutionary concepts: divorce.

Their story starts happily, with both Mancinis as young girls in the limelight of the French courts. Their uncle, Cardinal Mazarin, the chief minister of France, had gathered several of his young female relatives with the aim of marrying them off and solidifying the family's standings. Hortense and Marie dazzled the courtiers, and at the respective ages of 12 and 19 were the talk of the town.

Unfortunately, their uncle had exceptionally poor taste in men.

---

Marie's first love was one of the greatest figures in French history, Louis XIV. Their mutual romance was the stuff of epic poetry—from the moment Louis fell ill and Marie looked after him, they were practically inseparable. He loved her as intensely as she loved him. When Marie received a light bruise from bumping into his sword, he instantly threw it away, even though it was an expensive heirloom.

Their marriage was not strategically optimal for France. Cardinal Mazarin and Louis's mother, sharing a classic aristocratic view of marriage, combined forces to show the young lovers that life is supposed to be gray and horrible. They separated the two and married Louis off to another woman.

Even so, the two wrote letters to each other on a nearly daily basis. Gradually, however, the frequency of the letters declined and the frequency of courtier gossip ramped up. Finally, Marie, heartbroken and miserable, begged her uncle to find her a husband in order to silence the incessant mockery. This proved to be a really bad move.

Hortense also had a potential royal match early on. At the age of 13, she fielded a marriage proposal from the exiled son of the recently executed Charles I. Sensing that he had little in the way of future prospects, Cardinal Mazarin turned him down cold.

He was crowned Charles II, king of England, several months later.

Cardinal Mazarin then tried bribing him to reignite his interest with a truly ludicrous amount of money, but Charles II declined.

In the end, after rejecting a number of other suitors, Cardinal Mazarin arranged Hortense's marriage to Armand Charles de La Porte de La Meilleraye, Prince of Conti. Armand had refused Mazarin's offers of marriage to Hortense's various older siblings and cousins—he had, he professed, loved Hortense and only Hortense ever since he was 24.

Problem was, he was 14 years older than her. Yeah. You do the math.

At the age of 22, Marie married wealthy Italian prince Lorenzo Onofrio Colonna and moved to Rome. She hated Rome, immediately chafing against the restrictions Italian society imposed on women, saying that she felt like a slave.

Moreover, her new husband was, shall we say, overly ardent. Although he would later pull out all the stops to make her feel welcome, arranging fireworks, concerts, and festivals just for her, their initial meeting set a . . . suboptimal tone. Upon meeting her face-to-face, some of the first words out of his mouth were a demand to consummate the marriage. Despite the fact that they'd never met and that she'd been deathly sick almost the entire voyage from France to Italy.

It got worse.

Hortense, however, was undoubtedly in a more dangerous situation. Although her fortunes slightly improved when her meddling uncle died, bequeathing unto her a massive fortune, her husband, Armand, turned out to be insane.

This is not an exaggeration:

- He thought the angel Gabriel spoke to him in dreams.

- He warned farm families not to let brothers and sisters sleep in bed together.

- He told his milkmaids not to spend too long milking cows or churning milk because it was too overtly sexual.

- He forbade conversation and laughter in his house.

- He chipped the teeth of his servants to make them more homely.

These are pretty tame compared to the weird stuff he pulled later.

It should not be surprising that, when it came to Hortense, Armand bore the signature marks of an abuser: he forbade her to see her friends or family, constantly belittled her, and isolated her away from the city.

For the first several years, Hortense did not stand up to Armand, to the eternal consternation of her siblings. They even had four children together. But finally, Hortense had had enough and started to pursue the unthinkable: a legal separation.

Meanwhile, Marie fared slightly better during the early years of her marriage. Sure, Lorenzo showed her off like his favorite toy, going so far as to construct an incredibly ostentatious bed from which she could receive people who came to visit her after her first pregnancy. In spite of this, she established a world independent of him, producing elaborate plays and carnivals that were the equal of any in Europe.

But after giving birth to three sons in three increasingly difficult pregnancies, she too had had enough. Knowing that during this time one in 10 women died in childbirth, she insisted on "separation of beds"—basically, cutting off the conjugal aspect of their marriage.

This did not go over well.

Armand fought tooth and nail to keep Hortense with him, locking her in the house and physically blocking her escape. When she shoved him out of the way—no mean feat as he was a general in charge of France's military—he had her locked up in a convent.

At the convent, Hortense made a friend, Sidonie (who was herself attempting to divorce her husband). Together the two were absolute hellions: they put ink in the holy water, they flooded the nuns' beds, they attempted escape up the convent's chimneys, and they raced greyhounds around the building in the middle of the night.

After several years of being moved or escaping from one convent to another while pushing her case through the courts, Hortense came to a realization. Even if her separation—which had already become a cause célèbre in French circles—was successful, Armand's political influence would doom it in appeals.

So she ran away.

Disguising herself in men's clothing, she embarked on an arduous trip to Italy, traveling 250 miles on horseback in the first two days. Her outfit did little good—everyone recognized her as a woman, and the servant who came with her habitually called her "Madame."

Newly free for the first time in years, Hortense celebrated by taking a young squire as a lover. This romance was short-lived, as it displeased her new roommate and landlord: her sister, Marie.

For a time, the sisters were some of the biggest celebrities in Rome. Their salons were populated by the luminaries of the age, and their plays always debuted to packed houses. Portraits of the two sisters were such a hot commodity that people would fight duels over them.

Simultaneously, Marie's marriage was disintegrating. Although Lorenzo had kept mistresses from day one, he began to flaunt them even more openly, going so far as to impregnate Marie's best friend, Ortensia. Twice.

Infuriated by Lorenzo and emboldened by Hortense, Marie grew even more defiant. She took her own lovers. She swam in public rivers in the middle of the day. She wore masks to her carnivals, in clear violation of contemporary law. She dressed for one carnival as a controversial warrior maiden from her favorite story. The next, she dressed as the story's villain: a seductive sorceress whose name was virtually an epithet.

And then she found out her husband was planning to kill her.

Meanwhile, Hortense remained tethered to Armand. As she continued pressing the courts to allow for a separation, fighting her husband in the court of public opinion, she drove Armand closer and closer to the edge. He hired an army of mercenaries and lawyers to retrieve her, but she skillfully evaded every single one. All the while, she flaunted her freedom, publicly taking lovers in Rome.

Finally, in 1670, Armand lost it for good.

A huge part of the massive inheritance Hortense had received from Cardinal Mazarin was his art collection, one of the greatest in Europe. It included over 900 paintings by luminaries like Raphael, Caravaggio, and da Vinci, and hundreds of statues from Roman antiquity.

In 24 hours, Armand destroyed almost all of it.

He chipped the genitals off all of the statues with a pick. He took a bucket of black paint and splashed it on the nude paintings, to cover up their naughty bits. In all, he did around 400,000 francs' worth (about $17 million in 2014 US dollars) of damage before the king managed to throw him in prison.

Armand had issues.

So when offered the option of either reconciling with her husband and receiving Louis XIV's protection or receiving a small pension and remaining in exile, Hortense understandably chose exile.

It was to be a more difficult exile than she'd reckoned.

In 1671, Marie became deathly ill. Lorenzo seemed not to care, and Marie's maids soon found out why: they discovered an apparent plot by Lorenzo to poison her.

Soon thereafter, she fled Rome.

This was no small escape—she and Hortense put out word that they were off on a week-end trip, then crept away, in disguise, to a boat that took them up the Mediterranean.

Lorenzo was furious. Immediately, he sent out dozens of horsemen and a galley boat to intercept them. He wrote to the leaders of every neighboring country asking them to detain the women.

Marie and Hortense, now packing pistols, fought against every impediment tossed their way. When they were denied the rental of horses, they laid out bribe after bribe until someone relented. When one of Lorenzo's messengers caught up with Marie, she sat playing guitar and declining his every request in the form of song.

As Lorenzo's henchmen pursued them across the countryside, so too did Armand's.

---

Unfortunately for Hortense, because Armand's henchmen were significantly more cutthroat than Lorenzo's, she repeatedly had to separate from Marie. On one occasion, she fled into the woods when one henchman got too close, leaving Marie to cheerfully misinform him as to the direction her sister had taken.

Hortense found some protection under the Duke of Savoy, one of the many previous suitors her uncle had stupidly turned down. According to some accounts, she took him as a lover as a sign of gratitude. In Savoy, Hortense grew yet bolder. When she found out that one of her ladies-in-waiting was a spy for Armand, she threw the woman out. When Armand himself appeared and demanded to see her, she locked herself in her room and barred the door until he left. She began gambling, even crafting a special mask to conceal her tells.

Most boldly, she did something utterly unprecedented for noble women: she wrote her memoirs. By this point, the Mancini sisters had been so much the focus of court gossip, and their reputations so savaged, that Hortense felt the need to take ownership of her public image and set the record straight. She started the book with the declaration that "a woman's reputation depends on not being talked about"—and then proceeded to do just that.

Her memoir is one of the first written by a French woman without the cloak of anonymity. It became an instant hit across Europe, getting translated into English and Italian with lightning speed.

And then, in 1675, the Duke of Savoy died. Of poison.

---

Meanwhile, Marie had determined that her best course of action was to head to Madrid. She was unable to plan much for this journey, since Lorenzo's spies were watching her every move. Compounding her problems was the fact that much of Europe was in open warfare at this point and the route to Madrid was replete with bandits and combat zones.

Nevertheless, she headed out, only to be caught by Lorenzo's men in Belgium. There she was detained by a sadistic jailer, who bolted extra bars onto her windows and forbade her to speak with anyone, man or woman. Gradually word of her situation leaked out, and political pressure forced Lorenzo to free her.

When she finally made it to Madrid, she found it, too, crawling with Lorenzo's spies. Despite her growing popularity, Marie's attempts at solidifying new political alliances consistently ran afoul of Lorenzo's meddling. The move proved a worthless attempt at escape.

In 1675, she came across a copy of Hortense's memoirs. Then she found a copy of her own memoirs—except she'd never written any memoirs. She never found out who the impostor was, but it was clearly someone close to her. Even so, many of the details were wrong. Marie took special exception to her portrayal at the end as a poor helpless woman imprisoned in Belgium.

So she wrote her own memoirs. Just like Hortense, she set the record straight and took control of her public identity.

The book was also a massive success.

---

After the Duke of Savoy died, Hortense, sensing she was no longer welcome, headed to London. This, too, was a perilous journey. Entire villages along the European coast had been abandoned in the throes of war, and she was just one woman traveling alone. However, by this point Hortense had learned to effectively manipulate her public image, and she used this journey to portray herself as "Queen of the Amazons."

Once in London, she became the mistress of her old suitor, Charles II, and set up another intellectual salon. It proved quite popular, especially with the dice-playing set, who referred to it as a "gambling academy."

Hortense's romances were by no means limited to just Charles II during her 10 years in London. One of her other notable conquests was Charles's 14-year-old daughter, Anne of Sussex. The duo caused waves when they were found at night in a park, wearing nothing but their nightgowns. They were fencing. When Anne was forcibly separated from Hortense, according to rumor, Anne spent her days in bed, mournfully kissing a doll of her former lover.

After Anne, Hortense entered into a brief dalliance with the king of Monaco, which resulted in the temporary suspension of her pension from a jealous Charles. After that ended, she was embroiled in another scandal. Two of her admirers had fought each other in a duel, resulting in the death of the loser. The victorious party was one of the most bizarre men to ever be infatuated with Hortense: her 17-year-old nephew.

(No, she hadn't slept with him.)

All in all, Hortense's 10 years in London marked some of the happiest in her life. As a special favorite of the king, she enjoyed a privileged and peculiarly respected role in English society, insulated from the repeated lawsuits of her husband.

And then Charles II died.

Meanwhile, Lorenzo had been relentlessly continuing his attempts to have Marie thrown in jail, and he was finally successful. After some of the Spanish monarchs protecting Marie died, Lorenzo managed to send guards to toss her into the Alcázar fortress.

She went out fighting—literally. She stabbed her assailants with a knife. In return, they dragged her by her hair and tossed her into prison, where she remained for three months. During those three months, her son, whom she'd been trying to see for close to a decade, got married. She was not allowed to attend.

Finally, in 1681, after 20 years of marriage, she and Lorenzo were separated—but only on terms that preserved his public image. She was to enter a convent, and he a monastery. With both parties forbidden by religious edicts to engage in matrimony, their marriage could be annulled, thereby saving face for everyone involved.

The convent Marie entered was, by all accounts, more of a day spa than a prison. She was allowed to come and go as she pleased and even to keep pets. To mark the occasion, she got a spaniel. She gave it a gold collar, bracelets, and earrings.

---

Time and distance had not tempered Armand in the slightest. In a letter from the period, he starts out swearing that "menaces, prayers, rewards, punishments, the loss of fortune, or even of life itself" will never deter him from persecuting Hortense. He then, in the same letter, immediately pivots, promising, should she return to him, to be "the most humble, the most tender husband that anyone could ever imagine."

Unfortunately, without the protective umbrella of Charles II, Hortense's prospects diminished. She refused to leave London, but in the absence of any income and the presence of growing gambling debts, she had few options.

In the final year of her life she rapidly declined into alcoholism. Some claim that she became involved in a romantic triangle with her own daughter, vying for the attention of an English duke, but the available evidence is contradictory. In the centuries after her death, virtually every person she'd ever met—but especially her rapscallion friend Sidonie from the convent—was rumored to have been one of her lovers.

But even death does not bring an end to Hortense's story.

---

Shortly before his death, Lorenzo apologized to Marie for how shamefully he'd treated her. While Marie's writings indicate some lingering tenderness toward him, Lorenzo's own sister held no such feelings: upon his death, she declared that "he had lived like an assassin and a hedonist."

Marie lived another 25 years, during which time she freely wandered about Europe, finally able to do as she pleased. She died of a stroke in Pisa and is buried where she fell. Her tombstone merely reads thus:

MARIA MANCINI COLONNA, DUST AND ASHES.

The afterlife of Hortense's corpse reads like the blackest comedy imaginable. Upon her death, her creditors seized her body, quickly embalmed it, and had it arrested for failure to pay. In the end, the massive amount of money was paid out—by the one man determined to have her at all costs: her husband, Armand.

Armand then tossed her body into a cart and hauled it around northern France, taking it to all the places she'd hated going. It was only after four months, at the insistence of virtually everyone in his family, that he buried poor Hortense.

The effects of the Mancini sisters' lives were felt long after their deaths. By the time they had both died, women across England, France, and Italy were bringing divorce cases to the courts. The legal techniques that both Hortense and Marie had employed were put to the test by scores of women in equally desperate situations. Intellectual salons all across Europe were abuzz with debate over the justness of separation. And as women worldwide read the memoirs of the Mancinis, they began to consider the validity of writing their own.

## · ART NOTES ·

From left to right, we have: Anne of Sussex, Charles II, Armand, Hortense, Marie, Lorenzo, Louis XIV, and Marie's best frenemy, Ortensia.

Anne is clutching a doll of Hortense, and Armand is carrying a bucket of black paint.

The building from which they are racing is the old royal palace at the Louvre, since, for most of the story, Versailles hadn't been built yet. Much of the negotiation of their marriages was done through Louis XIV, so having the institution of the royal palace seemed fitting.

Marie is wearing a pearl necklace gifted to her by Louis XIV at the end of their relationship. She kept it to the end of her days.

Armand and Lorenzo are given color designs diametrically opposed to their wives—desaturated blues contrasting with the saturated reds and yellows. Louis XIV and Charles II, however, are given color palettes and clothing in line with (but subtly different from) Hortense's and Marie's. Anne's color scheme is a pale reflection of Hortense's, while Ortensia's is a mix of both Marie's and Lorenzo's.

Oh, and Hortense kept monkeys. Hence the monkey. She also kept parrots and black tetra fish. She was a little weird.

# Nzinga Mbande

### (1583–1663, ANGOLA [NDONGO])

## Mother of Angola

Nzinga Mbande began her political life as her nation of Ndongo (present-day Angola) was fighting off Portuguese invasion. Her brother, a by-all-accounts wimp, seemingly could not bend over backwards far enough for the Portuguese, and once he ascended to the throne the Portuguese tossed him in jail and took over. Nzinga approached the Portuguese and demanded two things: her brother's return, and the departure of the Portuguese from Ndongo. In a sign of disrespect, the Portuguese offered her no chair to sit in, instead providing merely a floor mat fit for servants.

In response, Nzinga ordered one of her servants to get on all fours, then sat on her as she would a chair. After the negotiations concluded, according to some accounts (more on that later), she slit the servant's throat in full view of everyone and informed them that the queen of Ndongo does not use the same chair twice. Shortly thereafter, the Portuguese agreed to let her brother go.

With her brother now safely home, Nzinga is said (again, more on that later) to have murdered him in his sleep, killed her brother's son, and assumed the throne herself—because if you're going to do something right, you better do it yourself. From there, she moved south, started a new country, conquered the ruthless cannibal tribe known as the Jaga, began offering sanctuary to runaway slaves and defector soldiers, and waged war on the Portuguese for 35 years.

Now, you may have noticed that this write-up has repeatedly used words like "supposedly" and "according to some accounts." As with many powerful historical women (as you've likely noticed by now in this book), Nzinga's tale is a mixture of fact and fiction, with the two difficult to separate. That she met with the Portuguese and sat on her servant's back is accurate. Furthermore, there is no doubt that she was a thorn in the side of the Portuguese, that she founded a new nation, and that she was a great leader.

Where her story begins to look suspicious is in the more salacious details. While some report that she murdered her brother, others report that her brother committed suicide. The slitting of the servant girl's neck is likely hyperbole. Other outlandish rumors, to be taken lightly, include:

## NZINGA MBANDE (CONTINUED)

- After killing her brother's family, Nzinga ate their hearts to absorb their courage.

- As a pre-battle ritual, she decapitated slaves and drank their blood.

- Nzinga maintained a 60-man-strong harem throughout her life. (This is regarded as more likely to be true than most of the other rumors.)

- The men in her harem would fight each other to the death for the right to share her bed for the night. (This one is more doubtful.)

- She also apparently dressed some of the harem like women.

- Conversely, she staffed her army with a large number of women warriors.

Fact, fiction, self-promotion, or smear tactics, it is hard to tell.

After Nzinga pushed down the Portuguese for decades (both militarily and economically, cutting off their trade routes), they eventually threw their hands up and negotiated a peace treaty. Nzinga died at the ripe old age of 81. There are statues of her all over Angola to this day.

## · ART NOTES ·

Nzinga's outfit and ax are derived directly from one of the statues around Angola.

She's wiping a bit of something red from her mouth as a reference to the blood-ingesting legends.

The servant she used as a chair was actually female, not male.

# Hypatia

(350 [370]–415, EGYPT)

## The Martyr Mathematician

Few women's legacies have been more of a political football than that of Hypatia of Alexandria. She was not only the first female mathematician in recorded history, but also an expert astronomer, philosopher, physicist, and overachiever. Unfortunately, Hypatia's death at the hands of a mob of Christian zealots in particularly grisly fashion turned her life story into a point of contention for centuries to come.

We don't know much about Hypatia, but we do know that, unlike a lot of women at the time, she was firmly in charge of her own life. By most accounts, she never married (although she turned down many proposals), instead becoming headmistress at the contemporary equivalent of MIT. She advised the town magistrates, who all agreed that she was pretty sharp. According to one account, she would regularly walk into the middle of town and engage random pedestrians in discussions about Plato and Aristotle, like the world's most hypereducated sidewalk busker.

The problem was, at the time Alexandria was politically unstable, and as a result, a lot of people wilded out on the regular. A months-long series of incidents (originally stemming from Jews dancing too much—seriously) had ended up with two sects at each other's throats. On one side, you had the town prefect, Orestes, who was basically trying to keep the peace. On the other side, you had the bishop of the town church, Cyril, who was trying to look after his own. Cyril had recently undermined Orestes's power by expelling all the Jews from the city. (They'd killed a bunch of Christians—and maybe burned down a church? It's complicated.) In any event, Orestes was all "respect my authoritah," Cyril was like "whatever," the two started butting heads, and thus: wilding out.

Hypatia got dragged into the middle of this mess when Orestes sought out her advice—because she was, as has been established, a capital-S capital-L Smart Lady. The mob under Cyril latched on to a rumor that Hypatia was prolonging the conflict by giving Orestes bad advice, so they did what mobs do: went to her house (in some accounts, her classroom), stripped her naked, and killed her. The translation here is subject to debate, but the instrument of her death was either roof tiles or sharpened oyster shells. Many of the "oyster shell" camp interpret the story as the mob using them to flay off her skin (ugh), apparently to prevent her soul from reaching the afterlife. Afterwards, her remains were burned and scattered around the city.

And this happened during Lent. Evidently these guys could give up meat for six weeks, but not murder.

After Hypatia's death, she became a figure for many groups that adapted her story to suit their agendas:

- **500s:** Byzantine historian Damascius: "She was the last Hellenic intellectual!"
  This guy claimed that Alexandria fell into an anti-intellectual slump almost right after Hypatia died. In reality, the intense intellectual climate there continued for a number of years, although Hypatia's life did mark its last peak. From his writings, you get the impression that Damascius was falling into the "back in the day everything was better, kids these days" fallacy. He also provides a really bizarre anecdote of Hypatia warding off a student who had a crush on her by waving her menstrual rag in front of him and saying, "I'm not so beautiful all the time." He holds this up as a symbol of chaste virtue, which is . . . well, different.

- **600s:** John of Nikiu: "She was the devil!"
  John of Nikiu corroborates the main facts about Hypatia's story, but also provides a lot of flavor text about her "Satanic wiles" and devotion to "magic, astrolabes, and instruments of music," adding that she had "beguiled [Orestes] through her magic." He characterized the mob lynching as the glorious eradication of the last remains of idolatry in the city. John of Nikiu was kind of a jerk.

- **1788:** Edward Gibbon: "Cyril was just jealous!"
  In Gibbon's telling, Cyril was jealous that everyone liked Hypatia. He also heavily implies that Cyril had a total crush on her and thus spread the rumor that incited a mob to kill her, taking the "be mean to the girl you like" tactic to ludicrous heights.

- **1853:** Charles Kingsley: "Catholics are awful, and I'll tell you why in my erotic fanfic!"
  Kingsley wrote a novel about Hypatia's life in which he sexes her up, makes her a hapless heathen-to-be-saved, and uses her story to rail against the Catholic Church. The book carries the distinction of being described by *The Oxford Companion to English Literature* as "ferociously racist."

- **1980:** Carl Sagan: "She was a pagan intellectual martyr!"
  Here's where the modern resurgence of Hypatia's fame largely began. What Sagan says about Hypatia in *Cosmos* (both the book and the TV series) is factually accurate, if a bit inflammatory. Where he gets a little outside the realm of straight fact is in characterizing the conflict as one of pagan intellectualism versus Christian mob mentality. This overlooks a couple things:

» Hypatia taught both Christians and pagans all the time. By all contemporary accounts, neither group had particular issues with her lessons. John of Nikiu's burn-the-witch hysterics came over a century later.

» The real conflict was between Cyril and Orestes, and they were both Christian.

» There's no actual evidence connecting Cyril to her death.

» Sagan also implies that Hypatia's death was a predecessor of the destruction of the Library of Alexandria, a claim for which there's not much support. (Most people date its destruction to partway through Hypatia's lifetime at the very latest, but probably centuries earlier.)

• **2009:** Amenabar: "One woman stands between civilization and chaos!"
There was a wildly exaggerated movie about her life called *Agora*, the trailer for which claims that she, uh, tried to unite all of mankind. It didn't do very well.

Basically, what you should take away from all of this is: being the wrong person, at the wrong place, at the wrong time, made Hypatia a victim of politics. It is entirely probable that her life would have been spared had she not been an intellectual, or not been a pagan, or not been a woman—but that's all speculation. What's sad is that, likely because of the vilification prior to her death, none of her works survive to the present day. While many of her students went on to make important contributions to mathematics and other scientific fields, we'll never know what Hypatia herself contributed.

## · ART NOTES ·

The setting is one of the classrooms where Hypatia might have taught—accurate as to the general floor plan. (The mob is entering from the side as opposed to the front door.)

The outfit she's wearing is a Greek tribon. It's supposed to be made of very poor cloth, signifying the philosopher's detachment from material things.

Hypatia's ethnicity is a bit of a question mark. She was ostensibly a Hellenic Greek in fifth-century Egypt, but it is entirely possible (some argue probable) that she was ethnically part Egyptian. (Her mother's identity is a mystery.) Her skin is thus an ambiguous tone, and the crowd is a varied mix of ethnicities, as a nod to the cultural makeup of the time.

Yeah, that student in the front is a callback to Damascius's charming tale.

# Jezebel

## (9TH CENTURY BCE, KINGDOM OF ISRAEL)

## The Most Maligned Woman
## in the Bible

I t's hard to find a woman more roundly despised than Jezebel: Israelite queen, makeup aficionado, and thesaurus entry for "slut."

This is totally nuts, because nowhere in the Bible is she mentioned as having sex with anyone, including her husband. Not even close! Does she worship gods other than the Jewish one? Yes, definitely. Make questionable real estate deals? Without a doubt. Get torn apart by dogs? Unfortunately, yes—this is Old Testament Yahweh* we're talking about here, the same guy who turns people into pillars of salt.† But have a fireman's calendar worth of dudes in her bed? Not so much.

So, here's the actual story of Jezebel, best as anyone can tell:

Jezebel, like a lot of women, first shows up in the history books when she gets married. In this case, she marries a guy named Ahab (King Ahab to you), who was considered a capital-G capital-W Great Warrior. Ahab and his dad had established a surprisingly stable kingdom in northern Israel after endless years of warfare and shaky government. (The predecessor to Ahab's dad spent seven days on the throne before getting assassinated.) By marrying Jezebel, Ahab is establishing stronger ties with Phoenicia, where she's from. This is a good thing!

The problems start when Jezebel makes her Israelite debut with around a thousand priests in tow and starts making a temple to two of her gods, Baal Shamem and Astarte. Neither of whom, you may notice, are Yahweh. This proves not to be a popular move with the Yahweh lovers in the crowd, particularly prophet and hairy man extraordinaire Elijah, whose name subtly translates to "My God is Yahweh."

It's important to take a moment here to recognize that ancient Yahweh priests were often not very nice. At the time, virtually everyone worshiped multiple gods—heck, Ahab's king-

---

* The god of the ancient Jews. This write-up uses "Yahweh" because when you start tossing in other gods, like the Baals, things get confusing. Rightly it should probably be "YHWH," since written Hebrew doesn't have vowels and nobody knows how it's actually pronounced. Popular guesses include "YAH-weh," "Je-HOV-ah," and "Ye-HOV-ih." Try freestyling your own!

† To be fair, Yahweh showed plenty of charity and grace, too! It must be admitted, however, that the biblical level of divine mercy was, let's say, wildly inconsistent.

dom was politically strong precisely because it accepted multiple cultures. But Yahweh priests, with their "there are no other gods but me" edict, were not down with that.*

Thus, the Yahweh priests would belittle other gods in the time-honored tradition of middle schoolers everywhere: simplistic name-calling. Elijah, for instance, referred to Baal Shamem ("lord of heaven") as Baal Zevul ("lord of dung")—or, as you may know him, Beelzebub. They even slurred the pronunciation of Jezebel's original Phoenician name—generally thought to mean "Where is the Lord/Prince?"—to something more like "Where is the dung?" Classy stuff.

So Elijah pops up, curses Israel with a drought, lets them deal with that for three years, then shows up again to challenge the Baalites to a god-off. The rules are simple: each side sets up a sacrifice to their god, then waits for their god to set it on fire. Since this story comes to us courtesy of the Bible, the outcome is pretty obvious. Baal's sacrifice stays notably uncombusted, while Yahweh's is instantly hit by a heavenly fireball and goes up like a Roman candle, even after Elijah shows off by dousing it with water.

Elijah then graciously celebrates his victory by murdering the Baal priests. All 450 of them. At least after this truly exhausting amount of homicide, he is polite enough to lift the drought.

Somewhat understandably, Elijah making it rain both water and blood does not endear him to Jezebel, and she promises to kill him in the next 24 hours. He promptly skips town and heads to the mountains, where he runs into Yahweh. Yahweh, being the kindly boss-man that he is, greets Elijah with a curt "What are you doing here?!" and then basically fires Elijah. His final orders are to deliver a few prophecies, then find and train his replacement, Elisha.

Fast-forward a couple years, and Jezebel finds herself in a real estate kerfuffle. Her husband, Ahab, is knee-deep in a sulk-fest because he can't get one of his subjects to sell him his vineyard so that he can turn it into a garden. Jezebel, who has up to this point been portrayed as wily and clever, then concocts an incredibly ham-fisted plot to frame the owner for treason, kill him, and seize the land, even though seemingly everyone is aware of her scheme.† It works, but not before Elijah drops in one last time to wag his finger, tell her she's a bad person, and inform her she's going to be eaten by dogs. Subtle foreshadowing: not one of Elijah's virtues.

The prophet Elisha then succeeds Elijah, who, in characteristically understated fashion, is sucked into heaven by a whirlwind while riding a magic flaming chariot. Elisha, if anything, is even more extreme than Elijah. One of Elisha's first miracles on record comes when a

---

* At least, not most of the time. King Solomon built a bunch of temples to other gods when he married foreign brides, and nobody seemed to really care.

† The Bible also tosses out that she "cut off" the Yahweh priests—which means she either killed them or exiled them. It's tossed in with almost no details, as opposed to the lurid exposés of her other supposed schemes.

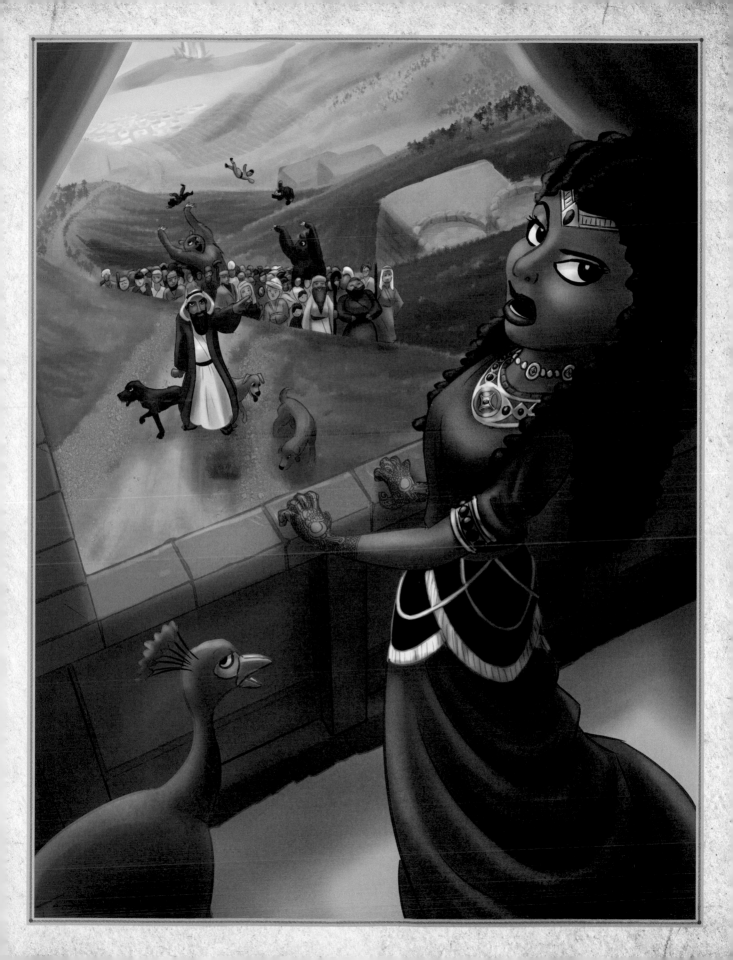

wandering herd of 42 unsupervised children make fun of him for being bald. In return, Elisha summons up two bears, who proceed to tear every single underage youth into bloody strips.

For those keeping track, that is now 492 gratuitous murders attributed to the ostensible heroes of this story, against Jezebel's one.

The story comes to a close when Elisha, on orders from Yahweh, crowns Jehu, one of Jezebel's generals, as king. By this point, Ahab has died in battle and Jezebel's son is on the throne. Jehu promptly starts a coup by stabbing said son in the back, then heads off to take the crown from Jezebel, infamously calling her a harlot in the process.

To her credit, Jezebel doesn't run away. Instead, she calmly dons her best dress and finest makeup and greets the army. Because if you're going to die, you might as well leave a beautiful corpse.

In the fulfillment of Elijah's last prophecy, Jezebel is then thrown from a tower by disloyal servants, trampled by horses, and eaten by dogs. The Bible even goes on to describe how the dogs poop her out, presumably to fit in the aforementioned pun with her name and "dung."

Jehu then proceeds to run the country into the ground. He massacres hundreds more people, including most of Ahab's family, and cuts off ties with other countries. Within a year, he's been conquered by the Assyrians. According to the prophet Hosea, this Assyrian defeat was a punishment from Yahweh for killing Ahab's family—an act that Yahweh had basically ordered him to carry out, by way of Elisha's instructions. Yahweh is, at times, not a very consistent god.

So, at the end, what picture are we left with of Jezebel? She was a strong-willed, devout, surprisingly religiously tolerant woman who built ties with other cultures. If the story of her ham-fisted land grab is true, that's about the worst thing you could say about her—which, let's be honest, is pretty minor in the grand scheme of all the people in the Old Testament. Heck, one could even applaud her initiative in taking the reins while Ahab was being a gloomy gus.

Her real crime, the one for which she has been labeled as the poster child for seduction, was to back the wrong god. Despite the fact that this description fit virtually every person on earth at the time, she was the one to receive punishment—because she dared to open up Ahab's mind to other religions. In the millennia since, this politically pragmatic stance has been repainted as one of the grandest seductions in history. Despite it having brought a degree of peace, stability, and civility to the region unmatched for centuries on either side of Jezebel's era. Arguably, all the way to today.

# Qiu Jin

## (1875–1907, CHINA)

### The Heroine Who Wrote Her Own Destiny

For Qiu Jin,* it was not enough to garner the respect of intellectuals across the country in her fight for women's rights. It was not enough for her to overthrow the Qing dynasty that controlled her country. It was not enough to be considered one of the great poets of the century. Qiu Jin had to carve a place for herself in history. She had to be like her legendary childhood idols, Hua Mulan and Princess Pingyang. She had to be a hero.

And so, in 1907, she greeted the Qing government forces who'd come to arrest her with a hail of gunfire.

It had been a long, winding road from upper-class beginnings to the executioner's block. Instilled with a rebellious spirit from childhood, Qiu Jin moved toward all-out societal mayhem in her twenties, when the Boxer Rebellion shocked China. With her country on the brink of disaster, she could no longer stand by as a housewife. In a move that scandalized her social circles (but not her supportive family), she left behind her conservative husband and her two children to go study in Japan.

In Japan, she radically transformed herself. She took on male clothing and a nickname meaning either "challenger of men" or "emulate male bravery" (depending on the translation). She joined numerous radical Chinese groups operating outside of Chinese borders, including the Triads and the Tongmenghui secret society (which would eventually prove instrumental in overthrowing the Qing dynasty). But most importantly, she became a voice for a new generation of women.

Writing speeches and newsletters in a colloquial style,† she advocated for both women's rights and the overthrow of the government. She spoke out against the practice of foot binding (of which she'd been a victim) and urged women to cease being illiterate slaves to their husbands and start becoming independent workers of their own volition. She tied this directly to her nationalistic jingoism: "Men can no longer protect [China], so how can we depend on them? If we fail to rouse ourselves, it will be too late after the nation perishes."

---

* Qiu was her surname, and Jin her given name.

† This wasn't a small task. Most papers of the time were written in an impenetrably academic tone. By writing on a more accessible level, she made the news of the day and her ideas much more widely available.

When Japan, under pressure from the Qing dynasty, expelled the Chinese dissidents, Qiu Jin became even more radicalized. Thrusting her ever-ready dagger into a podium, she shouted, "If I return to the motherland, surrender to the Manchu barbarians, and deceive the Han people, stab me with this dagger!" Before returning to China, she went to Yokohama to learn bomb-making from Russian anarchists—and almost blew up her room in Shanghai when she returned!

Once in China, she began running a secret rural military training academy. While the secret organization kept up a front as a school for sports teachers, Qiu Jin was hardly low-key about its true nature. Flamboyant, outspoken, and even a bit elitist, she refused to ever again play the part of a submissive woman. This did not endear her to the neighboring country folk, or to her more socially conservative revolutionary comrades. Within months, the rebels' plans for armed revolt had been leaked—her comrades' premature assassination of a local governor certainly didn't help—and government troops were on the way.

But instead of running, Qiu Jin stood her ground. In the same mold as the folk heroes she idolized, she was determined to be a martyr for her cause. She was executed at age 32. Her last words were: "Autumn rain, autumn wind, they make one die of sorrow."

Qiu Jin's death was widely criticized and marked a further decline in popular opinion on the Qing dynasty. The same year she died one of the Qing dynasty's last princesses, **Yoshiko Kawashima**, was born. Once the Qing dynasty fell, Qiu Jin was elevated to the status of folk hero, as she'd always wanted.

## · ART NOTES AND TRIVIA ·

The setting is autumn, in reference to Qiu Jin's final words—which, in turn, were a play on her surname Qiu, the Chinese character for "autumn."

She is seen here cutting a red string around her ankle. This is a reference to the Chinese legend of the red string of fate, which holds that an invisible red string binds two people fated to be together (in the Chinese legend, it's by the ankle; in the Japanese, by the little finger). In cutting it, she's divorcing herself from her husband.

The undone bandages around her feet are a reference to her history with bound feet.

# Yoshiko Kawashima

### (1907–1948, CHINA/JAPAN)

## *The Traitor Princess of Manchuria*

There are few women in modern history whose life story is more of a political hot potato than Yoshiko Kawashima's. A princess of the Qing dynasty during its collapse, Kawashima—aka Aisin Gioro Xianyu, aka Dongzhen, aka Jin Bihui—was alternately a traitorous villain to her people and an iconoclastic heroine who fought for her beliefs, depending on whom you ask. Bottom line, she was a woman caught between many identities: Manchu, Chinese, and Japanese; female and male; soldier and royalty.

All of which makes her biography, frankly, a complete disaster.

The complication of Kawashima's identity started early on. When she was six, the Qing dynasty, of which Kawashima herself was a part, collapsed and the emperor Pu Yi was forced to abdicate—thus ending 2,000 years of imperial rule in China and plunging the country into war between various warlord factions. Her father, in order to secure a Japanese alliance in restoring the Qing to power, sent her to live in Japan. It was there that she went from being known as Aisin Gioro Xianyu to Yoshiko Kawashima.

Even this early on, her biography starts going off the rails. According to many articles and books—many of which inarguably focus on presenting her in the worst light possible—her foster grandfather raped her and she had an affair with her foster father. Subsequently, she married a Mongolian prince, but the union was short-lived. Afterwards, she spent several years in Tokyo in (what many paint as) an endless bacchanal of drinking, gambling, and affairs with partners both male and female.

At some point in her twenties, Kawashima became involved with the Japanese military as a spy, working toward reinstating the Qing dynasty. The stories swirling around this part of her life are equally colorful. An oft-repeated tale is that she seduced a Japanese major at a party (through a shared fetish for boots!), thus gaining a foothold in the spy service. She secured her position as a spy soon thereafter when, disguised as a man, she demonstrated her abilities by sneaking into the offices of a Japanese colonel.*

---

\* The story continued: said colonel found out her identity when he cut open her clothing with a samurai sword and then "conducted a thorough investigation" to determine that he hadn't scratched "any part of her white skin." Yeah. Most of the stories about Kawashima are tinged with this sort of sexual undertone.

If the stories of Kawashima's origins were nuts, they were nothing compared to those from her spy career:

- She disguised herself as a rickshaw driver to sneak Pu Yi, the Qing emperor, out of the city. After several days of hiding him in alleys and stables, she managed to smuggle him to safety, all the while having an affair with his wife, Elizabeth (Empress Wanrong).

- She entered a brothel and pretended to be a Korean prostitute to gather information.

- She made money for herself by taking control of a number of gambling operations and blackmailing her ostensibly staggering number of lovers, one of whom attempted suicide because of her.

- She placed a cobra in Pu Yi's bed to make it look like someone was trying to assassinate him.

- She delivered two camouflaged bombs to Pu Yi, under the pretense that they were from his enemies, and then "discovered" and defused them.

- She married a number of provincial Chinese princes in order to solidify support for the Qing. Shortly after each wedding, she'd slip out and her husband would never see her again.

- At the fourth of said wedding ceremonies, she was stabbed by a Chinese man dressed as a merchant.

- She hired gangs of Chinese thugs to attack Japanese businesses in order to build support for the Japanese.

- She led huge armies, commanding at various times over 5,000 "Rough Riders."

Part of the reason these stories took root was that they were all grounded in some amount of truth. Kawashima did dress like a man the majority of the time.* Japan did frame others for spy-manufactured incidents, thus giving the Japanese grounds to invade China.† As a highly visible supporter of Japan's newly established and widely hated puppet government (Manchukuo), Kawashima was to be a lightning rod for such criticism.

---

\* Her claim at her trial that this was fashion for Japanese women at the time seems to be half-true at best.

† The Mukden incident is the best-known example. In 1931, Japanese agents, posing as Chinese provocateurs, bombed train tracks—though without causing any fatalities—and thus gave Japan a pretext to invade. This maneuver was apparently quite flagrant—almost the entire international community condemned it, and Japan soon thereafter withdrew from the League of Nations.

But was the criticism legitimate? Well, depends on whom you ask. The Chinese and Japanese articles are predictably one-sided, painting Kawashima as either a villain or a hero. The American press of the 1930s viewed her as a dashing heroine but by the 1940s described her as a debauched traitor. Various epithets for her used across the years include "Manchuria's **Joan of Arc**," "The Asian **Mata Hari**,"* and "Eastern Jewel." As most of the contemporary writing on her was wartime propaganda to some degree, it's hard to know what to take seriously.

In 1945, Manchukuo fell to the Chinese, Kawashima was put on trial, and here we find some of the only insight into who she actually was. Traumatized by the poor treatment of her family after Pu Yi was ousted, she viewed her actions in reestablishing the Qing as for the good of China. While she declared herself a Japanese national, her loyalty, she proclaimed, was always to China.

Her appeals fell on deaf ears, and she was sentenced to death. While most accounts agree that Kawashima was put before a firing squad, many describe her being beheaded by swordsmen, and some say she was killed by a mob of hammer-wielding assailants in "the Death of the Little Hammers," an attack reserved for traitors.

Her last line of defense for her reputation, a half-finished autobiography mentioned in death row interviews, seems to have been lost to the ages. One of her last summaries of her life, a quote given to a journalist in her last days, was simply: "Today I am like a flake of snow next to a hot stove."

## · ART NOTES AND TRIVIA ·

Kawashima is here escaping with Pu Yi, after whipping off a Chinese bridal dress. She's followed by a mob of enemies, some wielding hammers and some wielding knives.

In front of the rickshaw is a cobra, a callback to the story of her attempt to poison Pu Yi with one.

She was politically on the opposite end from **Qiu Jin**, also featured in this book. In fact, she was born two months before Qiu Jin's death.

---

* A somewhat silly moniker, given that Mata Hari's cover story was that she was herself Asian.

# Joan of Arc

(1412–1431, FRANCE)

## The Maid of Orleans

We nearly lived in a world without France.

In 1429, France and England were nine decades into what would later be erroneously termed the Hundred Years' War. (It actually went on for around 112.) Due to decades of infighting and generally not having its crap together, France was on the verge of joining Silla, Babylonia, and the Western Roman Empire in the Non-Existent States Club.

This is not hyperbole. France had lost thousands of soldiers in humiliating battles with the English. At the 1415 Battle of Agincourt, despite outnumbering the British by up to six to one (depending on estimates), the French received one of the most severe drubbings in history, losing around 10,000 soldiers to England's 112. Afterwards, many French nobles began supporting the English king, Henry V, to take the throne, which would have effectively reduced France to an English province. Possibly forever.

Into the midst of this chaos strolled Joan (aka Jeanne) of Arc: an uneducated farm girl with a sharp tongue and a sharper sword. With the certainty that came from angelic voices guiding her every move, she led French forces in a string of miraculous victories over the English, thus fulfilling a well-known prophecy. Soon thereafter, she was abandoned by the French king, Charles VII, betrayed to the English, put on trial for heresy, and burned at the stake.

Or so goes the legend. But let's be honest, the legend is total crazytown.

How did a teenage peasant girl even get to the king—were his guards on a smoke break or something? Why did anyone think that the best choice for leading the army was a random pubescent girl who heard voices? And more importantly: how, in the nine hells and seven heavens, did this teenager actually manage to win?

The answer to most of these questions: Yolande of Aragon.

Who, you ask? Well, she would probably be glad you didn't know. You see, Yolande of Aragon, mother-in-law of Charles VII, was one of the craftiest women in French history. Ruler of a great many provinces (she was known as the Queen of Four Kingdoms, although she ran more than that), she shaped Europe's lines of succession for decades through her skillful, stealthy diplomacy. Because of her intense secrecy, even now her influence on events can often only be inferred. But make no mistake: this is the story of two women, one covert and one overt.

Let's start with the matter of getting the king's ear. The prophecy stated that, unlikely as it may seem, a virgin girl from eastern France would rise up and lead the French forces to victory—a description that fit Joan perfectly. Problem is, it also fit a lot of other women perfectly. In the year 1428 alone, 20 people were recorded as having tried to deliver messages from God to the king. But only one was able to get an actual audience, because only one was saying what Yolande wanted him to hear.

Interesting fact about that prophecy, which managed to stand out against the myriad other prophecies of the time: it originated from Yolande's provinces. Provinces known for troubadours, minstrels, and storytellers. Many of whom were employed by Yolande herself.

Expert fortune-telling or 15th-century "help wanted" ad? The world may never know.

Joan's ostensibly miraculous appearance before Charles VII succeeded in kicking the gloomy monarch into action against the English. With the backing of Yolande, Joan was given joint control of the armies Yolande had gathered months earlier. Armies that Charles had up to then been reluctant to use until he'd received word of his assured victory from God, by way of Joan.

It's easy, at this point, to dismiss Joan's role as a mere symbol, a cheerleader recruited to kick-start France into action. In fact, many historians do just that, writing her off as a morale-booster who rallied the troops while operating under a series of possibly schizophrenic delusions. This view of things, however, overlooks the facts. And the facts are that she was a terrifyingly brutal warlord. (Also something the legend tends to leave out.)

Joan started her military campaigns by screaming bloody murder at the English. Literally—from across a river, she'd bellow at them to surrender, lest she kill them. Although they laughed it off, she soon carried through on her threats. As an example, when she sacked the town of Jargeau, her troops went past the point of killing the 700 English troops and went on to kill an estimated 400 disloyal French citizens. Quickly, her reputation for both inspiring her troops and cowing her enemies into submission became her chief weapon. In all, she only fought in 13 battles, whereas upwards of 30 towns surrendered to her without a fight.

But even this ruthlessness doesn't answer the question of how, exactly, a teenage farm girl could be so successful in battle. Many historians assume that other generals did virtually all the work. She is, however, credited by a large number of sources with mastery of cannons, making it difficult to write her off so easily.

How and where a seemingly ordinary teenager became a master of cannon warfare is a matter of much debate (and confusion). The best explanation out there seems to lie in the very fact that she was a commoner. Cannon warfare was relatively new at the time, and the weapons were manned by members of the lower class. In all likelihood, the aristocratic generals who planned out battles would have scarcely talked to such men, and thus would have had little idea of how to effectively utilize the new weaponry. Joan, however, occupied a gray area of being simultaneously a lower-class farm girl and an upper-class general. It makes sense that she would have talked to the cannoneers when no other general would and thus would know how to properly use the things. To be clear, this is speculation—nobody really knows!

In any event, once Joan's cannon-led warfare secured for Charles VII a significant foothold in France, he turned his back on her. Playing it safe after such huge historical losses, Charles VII and Yolande began to parlay diplomatic solutions to secure the English expulsion. Joan, on the other hand, charged forward with a rapidly diminishing amount of supplies and troops. Eventually, on the verge of being captured by the English, she jumped from a tall building, with the aim of dying instead of being taken alive. She survived, however, and was turned over to the (incredibly angry) English, who locked her in chains and proceeded to torture her.

The political farce of a trial that followed showed that Joan was a sarcastic spitfire. The English priests, hell-bent on proving that God was on their side, sought to prove Joan a fraud. When they asked her if Saint Michael appeared to her naked, she replied, "Do you think that God cannot afford to clothe him?" When asked if the saint had hair, she said, "Why should it have been cut off?" Even just getting her to swear to tell the truth was an all-day affair: she refused to join them in even the slightest prayer until she was allowed to confess her sins—for which she would have received absolution, thus invalidating all need for a trial.

Funnily enough, this inquisition mirrored the one she'd received months earlier upon first meeting Charles VII. After lengthy examination of her nether regions to determine that she was, in fact, a virgin, the French friars in charge of determining that she was a legitimate prophet asked her what language her voices spoke. Her reply: "Better than yours." When asked if she believed in God, she answered, "Yes, better than you." In the end, the English found her guilty of a number of charges (most of which amounted to dressing as a man, an accusation that blithely overlooked the fact that a number of female Christian saints had done the exact same thing), and she was executed with extreme prejudice. She burned on her funeral pyre for a full 30 minutes, screaming to heaven for help. Her last recorded word, shrieked at the crowd as loudly as she could muster, was "Jesus."

It would be nice to say that Joan of Arc's exploits brought an end to the Hundred Years' War, but it dragged on for nearly 20 more years. However, in an oblique manner, she did provide the turning point for the war—by making the whole ordeal (including her trial) unreasonably expensive, Joan's actions created friction between the English and their French allies. Yolande seized upon this weakness and used it to turn England's French allies against England, thus finally ending the war.

As for Yolande? She died at a ripe old age, having sent two of her protégés out into the world: Louis XI, the devious "Spider King" of France, and Margaret of Anjou, credited with later debilitating England by helping start the War of the Roses.

Joan herself, having been a public figure for a mere 11 months, slid into the realms of legend for centuries. It was not until much later, when French historians, notably Jules Michelet, wrote passionately about Joan that she was brought back to prominence and canonized as a saint. It is in no small part due to these efforts that virtually every warrior woman written about since World War I—certainly a great many in this book—has been compared to Joan of Arc. She is, to many, the standard by which all others are compared.

## · ART NOTES ·

Joan's flag is a replica of the one she brought into battle. It features Jesus flanked by angels, with the words JHESUS MARIA.

To Joan's right, riding a dragon, is Margaret of Antioch, one of the saints who spoke to her. Margaret's claim to fame was that Satan, in the form of a dragon, swallowed her whole, but then she escaped when her cross caused him gastrointestinal distress.

Lighting the cannon is the Archangel Michael, one of the other angels who spoke to Joan.

In the background, giving orders to archers, is Yolande of Aragon, fittingly obscured in shadow.

# Osh-Tisch

## (LATE 19TH CENTURY–EARLY 20TH CENTURY, CROW NATION/UNITED STATES)

### Princess of Two Spirits

**Y**ou know you're in for a treat when you're writing about someone whose name translates to "Finds Them and Kills Them" in Crow. Osh-Tisch was an assigned-male-at-birth woman[*] and was one of the last of the Crow Nation *baté* (Two Spirit spiritual leaders)—oh, and you can be sure, she earned her name.

She is also far from the only awesome lady in this story.

As a baté, Osh-Tisch lived apart from the main area of the camp and had duties ranging from artist to medicine woman to shaman. She was not just any baté—she was Head Baté in Charge. Contemporary accounts described her as quietly dignified, almost regal.

But during the incident that earned Osh-Tisch her name, she was not acting in her traditional roles at all. Instead, she had taken up arms with her male brethren and gone to war against the Lakota. This act, while, according to Native American historians, not unique in the history of Two Spirits, was so incredibly rare that this author has yet to find a similar story elsewhere.

Osh-Tisch's bravery would have been largely forgotten were it not for a Crow woman named Pretty Shield who spoke of it many years later. While recounting details of the Battle of the Rosebud (a battle in which the Crow fought in a coalition led by the US Army against the Lakota and Cheyenne tribes), Pretty Shield leaned forward and asked: "Did the men ever tell you anything about a woman who fought . . . on the Rosebud?"

Surprised, the reporter replied, "No." Pretty Shield chuckled, remarking that the men "do not like to tell of it." She went on to tell a story of not just one but two take-charge women on the battlefield.

During the battle, a Crow warrior was wounded and fell from his horse. Sensing an opportunity, the Lakota charged forward to collect his scalp. In response, Osh-Tisch jumped off her horse, stood over him, and started shooting at the approaching Lakota "as rapidly as she could load her gun."

Meanwhile, a second woman named The Other Magpie started to scream to create

---

[*] See the sidebar for a long discussion about this terminology.

a distraction. Unlike Osh-Tisch, The Other Magpie (described as pretty, brave, wild, and unmarried) had no firearm. Instead, she had a stick. Not even a particularly good stick either: this was a coup stick.

What's a coup stick, you ask? Well, the supremely brave (and possibly crazy) among certain Native American tribes would use decorative sticks in battle instead of weapons. These were coup sticks. For each hit scored, they'd rack up points and prestige in the world's most extreme game of tag. Hit enough people and your coup stick got to be pretty dang fancy. The Other Magpie's was not fancy. It was a stick with a single feather tied to it.

The Other Magpie, furious because her brother had recently been killed by the Lakota, rode into war with a simple coup stick at her side. Riding straight at the Lakota, she alternated between waving her stick wildly, spitting at them, and yelling, "My spit is my arrows." Yeah.

With the Lakota distracted by this utterly bizarre sight, The Other Magpie hit one of them with her coup stick. A second later, the same guy was dead from Osh-Tisch's bullet, as if The Other Magpie was some sort of supernatural harbinger of death. This act earned Osh-Tisch her "Finds Them and Kills Them" moniker. As the surviving Lakota gave up their scalping mission and scattered, The Other Magpie dismounted and scalped the newly dead Lakota in return. In the end, it was one of only 10 scalps collected by the Crow during the battle. The Other Magpie cut it into many pieces, so that more people could join in the post-battle ceremonial dancing back at camp.

Remember, kids, sharing is caring.

In the years following the Battle of the Rosebud, the Crow were confined to reservations, and it is here that the story starts to get sad. The various missionaries and government agents who visited the reservations were not okay with Two Spirits or anything they considered deviant—which is to say, everything save missionary position with your wife with the lights off. In the late 1890s, this attitude reared its head when an agent named Briskow imprisoned Osh-Tisch and the other batés. He cut their hair and made them wear men's clothing. Various Crow described this as "crazy" and "a tragedy."

The Crow Nation, however, rallied around Osh-Tisch. The tribal leaders did not hold much sway at this point in time with the US government, but they threw their full weight behind her and demanded that Briskow be fired. In short order, he was gone. To the Crow of the time, Osh-Tisch's nature was not only completely accepted but even celebrated.

Unfortunately, harsh treatment from whites was not at all uncommon during this time, and a great many Two Spirits from other tribes ended up committing suicide after being forced into binary gender roles. A Lakota man described the treatment thusly: "I heard sad stories of winktes [Lakota Two Spirits] committing suicide, hanging themselves rather than change . . . after that, those who remained would put on man's clothing."

The handful of recorded interactions with Osh-Tisch support that. In every case, her white contemporaries (who usually referred to her as "him") would ask her questions like why she wore women's clothes. She'd reply that she was "inclined to be a woman, never a man." When they asked what work she did, she said, "All woman's work," and, with no small amount of pride, produced an ornate dress she'd made. Her entire life she tried to explain and normalize what and who she was. Under her leadership, a quiet inter-tribe outreach effort began to emerge, linking all the different tribes' Two Spirits in secret communication in an attempt to facilitate understanding.

Sadly, her efforts were for naught. She is one of the only Two Spirits whose name and story survive to the present day.

After Osh-Tisch died in 1929, the restrictive moral code of Western missionaries took hold in the Crow Nation and became internalized. With no others to take up the role of baté, the institution died out, and its ancient knowledge with it. This happened across almost all Native American tribes. Even though there has been a modern movement to reinstitute the idea of Two Spirits among the tribes, it has been met with great resistance. Modern-day Two Spirits suffer persecution and hate crimes even by members of their own tribe. While everyone agrees that Two Spirits existed, the tradition, wisdom, and acceptance of these roles has been lost to history. It is important to remember and to honor them.

So here's to Osh-Tisch: a bridge between genders, between worlds, between tribes.

## · ART NOTES AND TRIVIA ·

Initially, this entry was going to be entirely on Osh-Tisch, but The Other Magpie just couldn't be left out.

Osh-Tisch is wearing the same outfit as in the one surviving picture of her. This is actually not historically accurate, since she wore men's clothing to the battle. She is portrayed, instead, as she liked to portray herself.

The plants beside her in the picture are a nod to her shamanistic medicine woman role.

Both The Other Magpie and Osh-Tisch have long, luxurious hair. Anthropologist George Catlin described at length how the Crow took pride in their hair.

The Other Magpie is, of course, spitting.

Osh-Tisch is firing a period-accurate Winchester rifle, although the Crow might have been using other guns, like Springfield rifles, at the Battle of the Rosebud.

And as a final aside: the names of Pretty Shield's parents were Kills in the Night and Crazy Sister-in-Law. Which is pretty rad.

## The Term "Two Spirit"

"Two Spirit" is a term likely to trip up a lot of people. Virtually all Native American tribes subscribe to the idea of more than two genders, encompassing identities such as women born as men and vice versa, as well as homosexual, pansexual, asexual people, and the like. "Two Spirit" is most closely analogous to "transgender," but it's not a direct synonym and should not be used in this case, as many Two Spirits take exception to being lumped under, or appropriated by, the term "transgender." So that word's out.

Back in the day, Two Spirits were referred to as *berdache*. This is a term that absolutely nobody should ever, ever use, as its origins are somewhere between the French word for "male prostitute" and the Persian word for "slave." You'll find it a lot in old literature on the subject, but that word's definitely out.

Earlier online drafts of this entry used the terms "male-bodied" and "female-bodied," which some find troublesome, so those are out too. Subsequent drafts used "biologically male-sexed," which some still didn't like. The preferred term as of this writing is "assigned male/female at birth"—which, unfortunately, may not be accurate in this case. Not all native tribes assign gender at birth (some wait as late as four years old), and there's no evidence that Osh-Tisch was ever assigned male by her tribe. However, given that most native children were assigned gender at birth, it seems reasonable to use that language.

Lastly, since each tribe has totally different numbers, kinds, social roles, and even words for said genders, many take exception to even being lumped under the umbrella of Two Spirit. So that word would arguably be out, except there's really no other word to use for the phenomenon.

English is imperfect, y'all!

# The Night Witches

## (C. 1940, RUSSIA)

## The Civilian Pilots Who Became the
## Nazis' Worst Nightmare

The Nazi soldiers on the Eastern Front couldn't sleep. Every night, as they settled into their beds, the same noise would visit them, faint at first but slowly getting louder. It was the whistling of faintly displaced wind, like a witch on a broomstick. Then they'd hear a noisy engine roar to life overhead, and they knew they had mere seconds to scatter before . . . *BOOM*.

Thus did the Nazis come to fear the Soviet 588th Night Bomber Aviation Regiment,[*] known to them as the Nachthexen—the Night Witches.

The Night Witches mark one of the greatest underdog accomplishments in military history. Handed a bunch of slow, flammable trainer planes that had been designed only to dust crops, an all-female group of untrained civilians became one of the most decorated divisions of the entire Soviet military. Flying without armor, guns, sights, radio, cockpits, brakes, parachutes, or virtually any navigation machinery, they dropped bombs on the Germans every three minutes, like clockwork, every night for three years.

And they did this while completely upending Soviet military culture.

The Night Witches were one of three all-female divisions started by flying ace Marina Raskova, and the only one that stayed strictly female. A national celebrity on par with Amelia Earhart even before World War II began,[†] Raskova had the ear of Stalin. He agreed to let her recruit women into the military, seeing their inclusion largely as a morale booster. Raskova fielded over 2,000 inquiries and interviewed all applicants herself. She ended up with a team of civilian volunteers, mostly ages 17 to 26, almost none with military experience. They'd have to be trained.

The instruction was brutal. Due to a severe need for help on the front lines, the recruits had three years of training crammed into four months. They worked 14 hours a day, sleeping

---

[*] Later they became the 46th Guards Night Bomber Aviation Regiment, one of the most elite divisions of the entire Soviet military.

[†] Raskova's main claim to fame came from 1938, when she was 26. Attempting to set a long-distance flying record along with two friends, she ran into trouble when their plane began to ice over. In order to save her friends, Raskova ejected all the plane's spare weight, and then herself. She landed in backwoods forest, where she survived for 10 days before being found by a hunter. When she arrived back in Moscow, she was hailed as a hero.

in a converted school or a recently vacated cow shed, without even the benefit of paper to write down notes.

Their first sortie was disastrous. On one of the first runs, two of their Po-2 bomber craft crashed, killing all four on board. With the women clearly despondent and shell-shocked, their commander sent them back out immediately, giving them an easy target. They carried out their mission swiftly and came back with renewed morale.

As their missions continued, the Night Witches began to develop their own tactics to deal with their lousy equipment. Knowing that their planes had insanely noisy engines, they would cut them well before reaching the target, then glide in so low to the ground they had to speak in a whisper lest the Germans on the ground hear them. The characteristic *whoosh* of the air over their wings was what earned them their name.

Each pilot created custom markings on her plane's wings to use as makeshift "sights"—they had to, since each pilot was a different height. They began using "decoy" planes—while one would glide in soundlessly, another would swing by, engines roaring, catching the Germans' attention and allowing the real attack to go off without a hitch. The bombers' aim was so good that rumors spread among the Nazis that the pilots had been given an experimental serum that gave them perfect night vision.[*]

Some of their innovations even went against regulation. Instead of working only on their own planes, the Night Witches dogpiled whatever plane needed help. This "brigade" system enabled them to turn around a plane in five minutes, allowing them to run 10 to 12 sorties a night. Unable to lift the 50-kilogram bombs by themselves, they loaded the bombs in teams. They would even eat and sleep in their planes so as not to lose any opportunities when there were breaks in the weather. The men didn't do this.

The men didn't do a lot of what the Night Witches did.

Beyond facing the terror of the Nazis' flak cannons, which could easily ignite their cotton-and-plywood planes, the Night Witches had to confront the patronizing attitude of their male comrades. They often heard comments attacking their femininity, like "If you go to the front, no young men will want to go to the movies with you."

With no female uniforms available, they were given ill-fitting men's uniforms and had to stuff their oversized boots with newspaper. They cut their hair short, shedding what was, for many, a source of great pride. And then there was homesickness: many had never left home before, and some were barely even adults.

---

[*] A similar rumor persists to the current day: that carrots improve one's eyesight. This myth was spread by the English to attack German morale and to hide the existence of a secret technology that helped them shoot down German fighters. Since the German diet was low in carrots, they spread the idea that the British soldiers simply had better eyesight due to their carrot-rich diet.

But the Night Witches made their barracks a home. They altered their uniforms to fit better and decorated them with embroidery. They gave each other manicures and new hairdos, decorated their barracks with rugs and pillows, and had dancing and singing contests when the weather was bad. They even, in a total reversal of military policy, referred to each other by their first names.

Simultaneously, they displayed an intense level of discipline. Nobody drank, although they were rationed a regular amount of vodka. (Russia, everyone!) Even when they suffered staggering losses during a July raid, not a drop of liquor was consumed. They were very strict about fraternization and considered wartime romance shameful. This last point, however, was not always enforced—not only were there affairs (both hetero- and homosexual), but there was at least one pregnancy. However, when the commanders regretfully relayed the news of the childbirth to their superiors, they received laughter and congratulations: "This means she bombed the Germans while pregnant! That's amazing!"

By 1944, the Night Witches had established such a tight-knit community that, as a journalist noted, visiting men behaved "as if they were standing on a minefield, not a runway." Yevgeniya Rudneva, an astronomer and poet turned Night Witch, summed up the division's attitude in a letter to her parents: "Now beauty lies not in lipstick or a manicure, not in clothes or a hairdo, but in what we actually do . . . our desire to smash the Germans as quickly and practically as possible makes us beautiful."

By the end of the war, 25 Night Witches had been given the nation's highest honor: Hero of the Soviet Union. Around 200 women had been part of the squadron at one point or another, and only 32 were lost. They flew over 1,100 nights of combat, and each pilot flew over 800 missions. Many of their stories have come from one of their most courageous pilots, Nadezhda Popova, who died in 2013. Of the experience, she later said: "I sometimes stare into the blackness and close my eyes. I can still imagine myself as a young girl, up there in my little bomber. And I ask myself, 'Nadia, how did you do it?'"

There are way too many individual stories of Night Witches to cover here—but you can find many more online at www.rejectedprincesses.com.

# Sita

## (INDIAN MYTH)

---

## *The Princess Who Leapt into a Pit*

**Y**ou are beholding the pinnacle of Indian femininity: Sita, from the *Ramayana*. For those unfamiliar with the Ramayana, it's an incredible (and incredibly long) work of Indian mythology—so here's a condensed version. For 90 percent of the book, it's basically Mario/Princess/Bowser by way of Tarantino. Bad guy (Ravana) kidnaps princess (Sita), and good guy (Rama) goes on bloody rampage for years in order to get her back. Rama kills Ravana, gets the princess back, yay for everyone.

But then there's that last 10 percent of the book.

About five pages after they get home, cut to Rama talking to his advisers. "Advisers," he says, "what are the people saying about me?"

"Oh man, Rama, they totally love you. Way to rock it with killing that demon guy."

"Wait, *everyone* loves me? No way. There's gotta be *someone* who's not on board."

"Well, I mean, there's some knucklehead . . ."

"Well, what's the knucklehead saying?"

"He's saying that Sita totally hooked up with the bad guy, but, I mean, he's a knucklehead."

"Wait, what? People are saying that? Oh crap. Hey, Sita! Baby, I'm sorry, I can't be seen with you. Some guy is saying you hooked up with Ravana. Now, I know you've passed like, my hundred other purity tests, but still. You should go live in the forest for the rest of your life."

So she goes into exile—pregnant with Rama's kid.

Cut to many years later, Rama's having a festival, and two awesome guys show up. They wow everyone, and Rama says, "Oh hey, you two are amazing! Who are you?" They're like, "*Surprise!* We're your twin sons! Also, Sita's alive and in the forest."

Rama replies, "Oh snap! Yeah, that whole thing with Sita was totally my bad. Hey, can we get her in here? I got some smoothing over to do."

Sita shows up, nice and calm. "No, guys, it's cool! Hey, I'll settle this once and for all. Everyone listening? Okay, if I did *not* hook up with the demon guy, may the earth swallow me whole."

Bam, lava, the end.

Now, that's the overview, but if you go into more depth, there's more at play:

- In some versions, Sita was Ravana's daughter in a previous life and was reincarnated as Sita in part to help purge him of evil. (He was one nasty dude.)

- While Sita is generally described as the world's most beautiful human, she was actually fairly supernatural—her birth involved her springing up out of the ground, to be raised as a princess. Thus, when she jumps into the ground at the end, it's a return to her roots (no pun intended).

- She was also a reincarnation of Lakshmi, the goddess of beauty, wealth, and love, while Rama was a reincarnation of Vishnu.

Even taking all of that into account, this author still holds that the reading of "I'd rather jump into a pit of lava than be with you" is a valid one. Your mileage may vary.

Ravana's kidnapping plot began when Ravana's sister unsuccessfully hit on Rama's brother—who promptly cut off her nose instead of just saying, "Not interested." Ravana's sister told Ravana what happened, and he swore revenge. The sister went on to tell Ravana about Sita and how attractive she was, and Ravana got ideas. Gross ideas . . . and it goes on and on. The standard version of the Ramayana is around 600 pages long, and there's a lot worth reading in there. Characters turn night to day by piercing the sky with arrows, there's a bad guy with a chariot pulled by snakes, and a monkey god leaps across the Indian subcontinent while carrying a mountain on his back to resurrect literally everyone in the world.

# Kharboucha

## (19TH-CENTURY MOROCCAN LEGEND)

## The Poet Who Sang Truth to Power

**S**ometimes becoming royalty is far from a reward. Sometimes it's punishment.

Take the story of Kharboucha. Named Hadda at birth, Kharboucha was an illiterate Moroccan poet of the Oulad Zayd tribe who, in childhood, was horribly scarred by smallpox. Refusing to let her appearance hold her back, she embraced the name Kharboucha ("scarred woman") and put her all into singing. She soon created a new style known as al-Aïta ("the Call"), which remains popular to this day. What was so unique about al-Aïta? In a word: protest.

At the time, Morocco was under Spanish and French rule, but the real powers were the regional governors (the *Caids*). Enter Omar Ben Aïssa, our villain. Aïssa proved a decidedly suboptimal Caid, as evidenced by his confiscating the land, cattle, and horses of Kharboucha's tribe. He then topped himself when, in response to Kharboucha singing about said injustices, he massacred the entire Oulad Zayd tribe.

Without a home to return to, Kharboucha began wandering from place to place, singing out against Aïssa. In festivals, gatherings, and marketplaces, she would dub him "eater of carrion"—quite the cultural diss—and advocate open rebellion. Her songs proved popular with tribes all over, which led to Aïssa capturing her and making her his personal singer/jester/prostitute.

Imprisonment didn't quiet Kharboucha in the slightest, though. Even as Aïssa paraded her in front of guests at grand parties, she continued to belt out her songs of protest against him. Fed up with her insolence, Aïssa had her tortured and buried alive. As legend has it, she continued to sing even as she was being buried. Posthumously, her tale spread throughout the region and her songs became more popular than ever.

Now, did Kharboucha actually exist? Probably not. Her story, despite having very specific details regarding places, people, and even dates, doesn't quite hang together. Modern historians consider her an amalgamation of figures like contemporary chanteuse Haja Hamadouia and historic Islamic poet al-Khansa.[*]

---

[*] A contemporary of the Prophet Muhammad, al-Khansa was considered one of the greatest poets of her age. When a man told her she was the greatest poet among those with breasts, she replied, "I'm the greatest poet among those with testicles too." Unfortunately, in the mid-2010s her name was co-opted by ISIS/ISIL/Islamic State on the banner for an all-female "moral police" unit. Lame.

Nevertheless, her legacy as a political firebrand lives on. As recently as the 1990s, a song devoted to her—"Hikayat Kharboucha" by Mohamed el-Batouli and Said Limam—was immediately censored by the Moroccan government upon release. It didn't work, though. Look at the playlist of almost any contemporary al-Aïta singer and you'll find a song devoted to Kharboucha—truly the most fitting form of immortality.

# Marguerite de la Rocque

## (MID-16TH CENTURY, CANADA/FRANCE)

### The Girl Who Lived

here's no more favored pastime for disaffected teens than the hallowed "my family is worse than yours" competition. Although these contests rarely have a clear-cut winner, Marguerite de la Rocque could present a strong entry. For Marguerite was the first European to spend more than one winter in Canada—after her relative Jean-François* abandoned her there, on a barren rock literally called the Isle of Demons.

The crazy thing? She survived and returned home.

Not much is known about Marguerite's life. Although her birth year is unknown, it's clear she was a young unmarried woman who was accompanying Jean-François on an abortive mission to colonize New France (later known as Canada). Why she went along is also unclear—especially seeing as Jean-François was hardly the most reputable or trustworthy individual. He was the sort to soothe his persistent financial woes with piracy, rarely a positive sign.

During the journey, Marguerite had a romance with one of the sailors,† to which Jean-François took none too kindly. Stopping the ship at a godforsaken slab called the Isle of Demons, he ordered Marguerite, the sailor, and Marguerite's servant Damienne—who'd covered up the romantic liaisons—to disembark and then left them all there, with a scant smattering of supplies.

It's worth mentioning at this point that there are two main sources for this story. One, by Queen Marguerite of Navarre, is a gossipy version gleaned, ostensibly, from Marguerite herself. The other, by heartless sycophant André Thévet, is firmly on team Jean-François. Thévet infuriatingly describes the captain as "clever and wise" to punish the trio "without soiling his hands with their blood."

The island—a wooded area replete with wolves, bears, and, in Thévet's telling, demons—was aptly named: the trio could barely sleep at night for the constant howling. Worse still, Marguerite was, in short order, left alone. First to die was her lover, and then Damienne.

---

* He was either Marguerite's uncle, brother, or cousin, depending on who you ask.

† The lover's name is unknown. From his training, one can assume he was a soldier or nobleman, and the fact that his name was kept from official records indicates he was probably of some social standing.

Lastly, she lost the child she'd had with the lover.* This was all within her first year on the island.

And from there, she lived another year and a half by herself. In that time, she hunted bears and deer, probably with one of the four arquebuses (incredibly heavy first-generation firearms) left to them. She survived bitterly cold winters (the island is located in northeast Canada) and the intense isolation of the island by taking solace in religion. Even as she became increasingly convinced the nighttime cries were actually phantoms come to bedevil her, she clutched her crucifix tight and held on.

After two and a half years, in an incredibly unlikely series of events, she was spotted by Basque fishermen and taken back to France. Once home, she befriended the aforementioned Queen Marguerite of Navarre and from there slipped into the mists of history. No official reproach was ever recorded for Jean-François, who lived to be 60 years old. Marguerite herself became a schoolmistress, and beyond that there is no information on the rest of her life—even the date and place of her death are unknown.

---

* She likely became pregnant after being stranded, not before.

# Noor Inayat Khan

## (1914–1944, FRANCE)

---

## *The Spy Princess*

Noor Inayat Khan was, without a doubt, one of the bravest women to ever live. She was a British secret agent during World War II, working as a radio operator in occupied Paris. In fact, working as the *only* radio operator in occupied Paris. The average life span for that job was six weeks, and she lasted almost five months. She escaped the Gestapo numerous times and went out fighting. All this even though everything about her work went against her religious pacifism.

Noor was the least suitable person in the world to become a spy. For one thing, she was a deeply rooted pacifist—her father was a Muslim Sufi who counted Mahatma Gandhi as a personal friend. Their family home doubled as a mystic school. Noor was so deeply invested in Sufism that she outright refused to lie, which you'd think would disqualify her for the job entirely.

On top of that, Noor didn't even like Great Britain! She said as much in her initial interview with the British military, due to her relentless honesty. She told the interviewers that after the war she would devote herself to obtaining India's independence. This is almost like applying to work at a construction site and saying you plan on tearing the building down afterwards.

And she wasn't remotely physically or psychologically suited to be a spy! Prior to the war, she spent her days writing poetry, music, and children's books—she was not exactly body-builder material. In test interrogations, Noor would freeze up in terror and start quietly muttering to herself. Her instructors remarked that she was clumsy and scatterbrained, and that she regularly left codebooks out in the open.

And above that, in the greatest possible sin for a spy, Noor did not blend in at all. Her parents were Indian and white, British and American, royalty and commoner; she was raised Muslim and Sufi; she was born in Moscow and lived in London and France. She was an actual, honest-to-God princess, descendant of Tipu Sultan. She could not have stood out more if her mother had been albino and her father a neon signpost.

But something shifted in her when the Nazis invaded Paris. Seeing German bombs drop on her beloved France stirred up a deep resolve. She signed up for the armed services shortly thereafter.

In short order, she was placed with the British Special Operations Executive, to be trained

NOOR INAYAT KHAN (CONTINUED)

as an undercover radio operator. She flung herself into training, becoming both physically and mechanically skilled in record time. Her eccentricities shone through, though: her radio encryption code was derived from one of her poems, and her code name, Madeleine, was a character from one of her stories. Her clumsy style of Morse signaling was so peculiar that she was jokingly nicknamed "Bang Away Lulu." But despite the misgivings of many of her superiors (most were downright patronizing), she was soon sent to Paris as the first female secret radio operator.

Unfortunately, tragedy struck almost immediately. Barely a week into her Paris assignment, virtually the entire Parisian spy operation was caught in a giant sweep. Noor escaped, but by the end of the SS roundup, she was the only radio operator left in the entirety of Paris. London offered to extract her, but she flat-out refused until a replacement was made available.

What happened next no one expected: she *crushed* it. For nearly five months, she evaded the Gestapo, changing her location, looks, and clothes on a nearly daily basis. On more than one occasion she tricked, evaded, or just plain outran the Nazis. All the while, she did the work of six people, relaying all of the spy traffic for the entire region back to London by herself. She lasted three times as long as the average radio operator.

She was eventually caught, when a double agent betrayed her to the Nazis. She went down as you'd expect a lifelong pacifist would: by punching, kicking, and biting like a wild animal. Then, scant hours into her imprisonment, she made her first escape attempt. She did so by demanding a bath, and insisting that the door be closed (to protect her modesty). As soon as the door shut, she darted onto the roof, nimbly clambering across the tiles, only to be caught again.

Facing the possibility of harsh punishment, she grew outwardly compliant as she fed the Germans lie after lie. All the while, she was plotting another escape, which almost worked— except, just as she left her cell, the British made a surprise air raid. Because of that, the guards did an unscheduled check of the cells, only to find the bars on Noor's window undone and her sprinting across the roof yet again.

She was then reclassified as extremely dangerous, shackled in chains, and kept in solitary confinement. Her interrogations changed from friendly questioning to relentless physical violence. Her prison mates, unsure of who she was, knew her mostly through her nightly weeping. And yet, this woman who had failed her test interrogations so miserably never revealed a single thing. Virtually all of the information we have about her last months comes from the few survivors housed in nearby cells. She would scratch out messages to them on the bottom of their shared food bowl, identifying who she was.

And then one day, she was taken to the Dachau concentration camp, along with three other spies. While her companions were shot almost immediately after arrival, Noor's execu-

tion was prolonged, giving her an extra day that was nothing but hour upon hour of brutal violence. According to the other prisoners, her last word, shouted at the Nazis before she was shot, was "*liberté.*"

Noor Inayat Khan gave everything of herself. She became a pacifist who fought dirty. A klutz who climbed buildings. A Sufi who lied daily. An artist who braved torture. A captive who told nothing.

She was thirty years old.

## · ART NOTES ·

That is the rooftop of 84 Avenue Foch, the building where Noor was imprisoned. The flak going off in the background is a callback to the air raid that thwarted her second escape attempt, and is also supposed to draw the eye to Noor.

Her outfit is what she was caught in—a blue dress with white trim and a gray sweater. The suitcase radio she's using is the same model she used in Paris. Her hand is reaching for the Morse signaling button.

# Empress Myeongseong

## (1851–1895, KOREA)

## The Queen Who Almost Saved Korea

 f you're married, there's a good chance you dislike your in-laws. Maybe they disapprove of you, maybe they're overly controlling, maybe they overstay their welcome. But as bad as you might have it, Korea's powerful Empress Myeongseong likely had it worse—her father-in-law tried to kill her.

And then nearly destroyed the country.

Myeongseong,* better known as Queen Min, was never supposed to be a powerful ruler. An orphan at the age of eight, she was from an unimportant and impoverished noble family, the Min line. The only reason the king's father, Heungson Daewongun,† plucked her out of obscurity to marry his son, King Gojong, was pure political machination: the Daewongun didn't want his political enemies bringing in a bride who could help them seize power. Thus Queen Min—an unconnected and politically unimportant figure.

This plan would backfire spectacularly.

At first, Queen Min faced an incredibly uphill battle. Married to a man with whom she shared little—he liked to party, she liked to study—her position became all the more tenuous when the king had a son by a different lady of the court. After years of trying, Queen Min finally bore him a son too, only for the baby to die in infancy. Despondent over the loss, she began to suspect her baby had been poisoned by the Daewongun.

So she began to read. And read. And in short order, she became dangerous.

Knowing her weak-willed husband wanted to rule independent of the Daewongun, who was still holding on to the throne, she approached Gojong as a political partner rather than a wife. Working in concert with the king, she expanded their power base tremendously, putting her relatives in key government positions. She got her husband's half-brother, whom the Daewongun imperiously referred to as "blockhead," to spy for her. And then she began to legislate.

---

* Myeongseong was a title bestowed on her in death (similar to **Wu Zetian**, who went by "Wu Zhao" in life). The name most often used for Myeongseong, and the one used in life, is Queen Min. Her birth name, believe it or not, is unknown. The closest we have to something to go on is Min Jae-yong, which comes from fictional sources and is unverified.

† Daewongun is a title, usually given to a king's father when he reigns in the king's stead. Heungson Daewongun did just that until King Gojong was 22.

The modernizing policies she brought to Korea were controversial. Long viewed as the "Hermit Kingdom," Korea had recently been forced onto the world stage in response to the colonial ambitions of its neighbors, particularly Japan. Queen Min opened up Korea to Western education, medicine, and technology and started allowing both Japanese and Chinese influence—but also began skillfully playing the two nations off each other. Simultaneously, she began modernizing the Korean military, to prepare it for any foreign threats. This was where she came into conflict with the conservative, isolationist Daewongun.

Although he'd already been forced off the throne by this point, the Daewongun still wielded a quiet and treacherous power. As a testimony to this power, shortly after his forced retirement, explosives went off in Queen Min's sleeping quarters, causing a fire but no injuries. Soon thereafter, Queen Min's closest relatives received an ornate box from a messenger—it too exploded, killing them. Neither incident was directly traced to the Daewongun, but as we shall see, they were both entirely in line with his style of wielding power.

In 1882, members of the old Korean military, outraged over Queen Min's modernization efforts, tried to overthrow the government. Under the aegis of the Daewongun, they attacked police stations, pillaged estates belonging to Queen Min, killed many of her family and supporters, and attempted to kill her. She escaped, and for a time the Daewongun was back in power, undoing as many of her efforts as possible. This ended when she brought in 4,500 Chinese troops, who put the Daewongun on trial in China for treason. As the king's father, though, he was treated leniently, and he returned to Korea in 1885—over Queen Min's strenuous objections.

Unfortunately, all this internal strife weakened the ability of Korea to keep out invaders, and in 1894 Japan took advantage of this by launching the First Sino-Japanese War. China, which had nominally been in charge of defending Korea, was easily defeated by Japan.

With Japan seeing Queen Min as a threat to their plans—and rightfully so, as she was now attempting to leverage Russia against them—her days were numbered. The end came when the Daewongun's allies surreptitiously let 56 Japanese assassins into her palace. They brutally murdered Queen Min, setting her on fire before everyone's eyes. The Daewongun was never officially tied to the murder, and the Japanese government to this day has never admitted involvement. The 56 were arrested, but the Japanese courts pardoned them, citing a lack of evidence.

The next 10 years saw Korea crumble and become a Japanese protectorate. King Gojong, who had over the years developed a deep respect and love for his capable wife, fell into a deep depression and fled to the Russian embassy. With the king a de facto prisoner of Russia, Japan and Russia began warring over who was to take what parts of Korea and Manchuria, resulting in the Russo-Japanese War. Japan won in 1905, and Korea entered a dark period of its history.

In modern days, Queen Min has been remembered as one of Korea's great heroines. Sadly, no photos of Queen Min survive. She lives on only in memory and in song.

# Micaela Bastidas

## (1744–1781, PERU/BOLIVIA)

## The Brains of the Túpac Amaru Rebellion

here's a saying when it comes to war: "amateurs talk tactics, professionals study logistics." Micaela Bastidas was a professional.

In the late 1700s, the areas now known as Peru and Bolivia were awash in terrifying violence as various movements started warring with the Spanish.[*] These were collectively known as the Túpac Amaru Rebellion, named after ~~a 20th-century rapper who faked his death by traveling backwards in time~~ a mestizo who declared himself a descendant of the last Incan king and set about kicking Spanish butt.

The right-hand woman of Túpac Amaru?[†] Micaela Bastidas. She was also his wife.

Now, at this point some may be thinking, *Ugh, this woman is just his historical plus-one.* Oh, you are so very wrong, conclusion-jumpers. Bastidas, the daughter of an indigenous woman and an African man,[‡] quickly proved herself more fearsome, and more capable, than her more famous husband. For while he took the glory, she did all the behind-the-scenes work during the war:

- She managed the supplies, recruited indigenous people, oversaw payments, collected taxes, distributed passports, posted guards, and ran a spy ring.

- She punished and even executed people who didn't obey her commands, like a boss. A really tough boss.

- When a Spanish tax collector came to collect money, she punched him in the neck and kicked him out.

---

[*] The facts of the matter are, as you can imagine, just a bit more complex than "Spaniards suck!" Much of the friction boils down to that classic one-two punch of overwork/taxation by a distant government and underrepresentation in that government. Túpac Amaru tried working within the system for years, petitioning the government and trying to advocate for reform. After that proved as effective as a water balloon in a forest fire, he changed his official stance from "let's work together" to "screw all y'all," forced a local magistrate (at gunpoint) to requisition money for the rebellion, and started killing Spaniards.

[†] Okay, he wasn't actually Túpac Amaru II. The first one was the actual last Incan king. Micaela's husband just renamed himself Túpac Amaru II for PR purposes and may not have been related to Túpac Amaru I at all. Micaela's husband's actual name was José Gabriel Condorcanqui. May that unruffle the feathers of you Latin America historians out there.

[‡] The racial politics of this period are nightmarishly difficult to summarize. Suffice to say, at one point or another, every ethnicity was trying to kill every other ethnicity. Micaela and Túpac envisioned a pan-ethnic coalition of people, but had a hard time getting everyone else on board.

- When an enemy tried tricking her into a trap, she showed up with 2,600 troops and shelled his house.

- When Micaela and her troops captured some Europeans, instead of executing them, she put them to work as accountants and weaponsmiths. How much of this was under threat of death is a matter of debate.

- She'd regularly tear down anti-rebellion decrees from church doors and replace them with her own, like a gun-wielding Martin Luther.*

But if you were to believe the accounts of some Spanish contemporaries, there were few people Micaela was harder on than her husband. Surviving letters have her calling him "lead-footed" in his slowness to provide assistance and threatening to turn herself in to the Spanish if he didn't take things more seriously. She'd vacillate between that and warning him to watch what he ate, fearing he'd be poisoned. Partly this was her, shall we say, managerial disposition—but partly this was just the relationship they had. They loved giving each other a hard time.

In the end, they were overcome, and both Micaela and her husband met incredibly grisly deaths. However, their revolutions didn't stop right there. Rebels in neighboring areas, including other women like Bartolina Sisa and Gregoria Apaza, continued the fight, although they, too, were doomed to failure. Nevertheless, they sowed the seeds of independence—which sprouted in full a little over four decades later when Peru and Bolivia declared independence.

## · ART NOTES ·

Every animated movie needs a cute animal sidekick. Given that they are considered a tasty delicacy in Peru, what more appropriate mascot than a guinea pig? Especially considering that Peruvian guinea pigs are basically beautiful mounds of perfectly coiffed hair.

In the far background, rallying the troops, is Túpac Amaru in the "we're goin' to war, boys!" pose that shows up in almost every statue or portrait of him.

The woman in the background walking toward Túpac is Tomasa Tito Condemayta. She was a Creole woman who led a large number of troops alongside Túpac and Micaela. According to some accounts, Bastidas had a hard time trusting her initially, mainly because she was thought to be a Spanish sympathizer, but one account suggests that Bastidas thought Túpac might cheat on her with Condemayta. Possibly spurious, but worth mentioning.

---

* This was particularly hard for her, as she was a devout Catholic. The church sided with the Spanish, officially excommunicated Micaela, and published notes decrying the rebellion. Regardless, she kept the faith.

# Neerja Bhanot

## (1963–1986, INDIA)

### Heroine of the Hijack

O n September 5, 1986, mere hours before her 24th birthday, Neerja Bhanot turned to see four heavily armed terrorists boarding Karachi's Pan Am flight 73, on which she was chief flight attendant. She dashed to the cockpit to warn the pilots, but was caught by one of the hijackers, who grabbed her hair. Nevertheless, she managed to shout a secret "hijack code" to the cockpit crew—who, according to regulations unknown to any of the flight attendants, quickly evacuated, leaving the 400 passengers and 13-person flight crew at the mercy of the four enraged terrorists.

With the cockpit crew gone, and Neerja now the most senior crew member, she was in charge.

This was far from the first time she'd had to take charge. The previous year she'd been wedded in an arranged marriage, which had gone sour quickly. She'd gone from a life of glamour as a model in India to one of financial, emotional, and even physical starvation in Pakistan—she lost 11 pounds in two months. Despite enormous humiliation and threats of harm, she separated from her husband and fled.

Once back in India, Neerja had worked herself to the bone, regularly sleeping as little as three hours a night as she worked both as a model and as a flight attendant. She was one of the top 80 applicants out of 10,000 for Pan Am's first all-Indian cabin crew. Pan Am 73 was to be their first flight, and it was a job she took very seriously. The night before, when her mother, seeing how sleep-deprived she was, begged her to skip work, Neerja replied, "Mom, duty comes first."

After the pilots fled, Neerja worked to maintain calm. At the orders of the terrorists—who were part of the Libya-backed Abu Nidal Organization—she collected the passports of all the passengers, taking care to hide or destroy the American ones so the terrorists could not target those passengers.

After 17 hours, as sunset neared, a mechanical failure caused the lights in the aircraft to dim and go out. In response, the terrorists opened fire, at which point Neerja threw open the emergency exit.

Instead of saving herself by sliding down the emergency chute, she used her body to shield

MATURITY 4

VIOLENCE V

ABUSE A

three escaping children. She then crawled to a second emergency exit, turning the crank to open it despite having been shot.

She died at the scene, along with 19 other passengers and crew. One hundred others were wounded. The hijackers were arrested in the terminal and tossed into prison.

Her parents received her body on her 24th birthday.

❧

## The Many Heroes of Pan Am 73

In 2016, some accounts came to light that complicated the narrative. In the wake of *Neerja*, a movie based on her life, being released in India, several of the other attendants on Pan Am 73 publicly came forward with their stories for the first time. Emphasizing that their accounts "may differ but the spirit remains the same," they attributed several of Neerja's actions—such as alerting the pilots—to others on the flight. In so doing, they wanted to honor the memory of all their colleagues who worked as a group throughout the crisis. In an interview with BBC News, they stressed that "there was no single hero that day, that crew members not interviewed played an equally important role, and that they want survivors of terror attacks like 9/11 and [the November 2015 Paris attacks] to know that life goes on."

# Boudica

## (C. 20–60 CE, ENGLAND)

## *The Headhunter Queen of Britain*

 t the height of its power, Rome once seriously considered giving up its British holdings entirely. The reason? Queen Boudica, whose brutal revenge spree made her the Roman bogeyman for generations. She killed 70,000 people, burned London to the ground, established herself as the most famous headhunter of all time—and to this day Britain loves her for it.

The first thing to know about Boudica (aka Boudicca or Boudicea) is how little we know about her. We don't know when she was born, how she died, where she died, where she came from, or whether Boudica was even her name (as opposed to a title). However, what we do know, largely from two Roman historians, is enough to earn her a place in the badass hall of fame.

Boudica ascended to power when her husband, the king of the ancient British tribe of the Iceni, died. At the time, Rome was in control of Britain, and the Iceni had voluntarily allied with them. When the king died, he willed half his belongings to the Roman emperor and the other half to his family—thinking that would solve any problems of succession.

It didn't. Instead, the Romans, at the apex of their arrogance, set into action an outrageously poor set of decisions. Try to spot where things went off the rails:

- They did not recognize Boudica's claim to the throne because she was a woman.

- They laid claim to all of the late king's money.

- They also grabbed a ton of Iceni land.

- And said that some money they'd given the late king was a loan, due back (with interest) immediately.

- They publicly flogged Boudica.

- And raped her two daughters.

You can probably tell at this point that the rest of this story isn't going to go well for the Romans.

The amazing thing is, this incident was just another in a series of stupid moves by local

Romans! When Boudica subsequently raised a mob and began marching on the nearby town of Camulodunum (essentially a retirement home for Roman veterans), several other blunders came to light:

- Camulodunum had dismantled its own defenses so more people could build houses.

- The local Roman magistrates had been overtaxing all the neighboring tribes, mostly because they could.

- All the collected money had gone to building a fancy temple, which was effectively a giant middle finger to their subjugated neighbors.

- Lastly, when the Romans got word that some rowdy barbarian lady was acting up, they laughed and sent 200 soldiers to scare her off. The 120,000 men she'd gathered laughed back and killed everyone in the city.

Fun science fact: if you apply a sustained fire to an entire Roman city, you can turn it into a molten pile of sickly red clay. This fact comes to us courtesy of Boudica, warrior scientist of the first century, and the six-inch-thick layer of detritus that is current-day Camulodunum (located several feet below Colchester).

She repeated her experiment with two other cities, including Londinium, the precursor to London. Along the way, her army, which had at this point become a roaming 230,000-man block party, killed an armed Roman legion and around 70,000 civilians and became Rome's worst nightmare. In order to understand how terrifying this was for Rome, one should understand some specifics of Boudica's uprising:

- Her army cut off the breasts of Roman noblewomen, sewed them to their mouths, and hung the bodies or mounted them on spears.

- The Iceni decapitated people as a matter of religious principle, embalming the heads of their enemies and mounting them on chariots. The rest were thrown into rivers (and their skulls are still occasionally found to this day).

- The Roman Empire was huge to the point of unwieldy at this time. Stories of Boudica's untrained mob wiping out Roman veterans left and right raised the specter of uprisings happening everywhere.

- "Moreover," a prominent Roman historian wrote, "all this ruin was brought upon the Romans by a woman, a fact which in itself caused them the greatest shame."

Unfortunately, Boudica's success had largely been predicated on surprise and did not last long. When they went up against entrenched Roman soldiers, the Iceni fell apart. A mere 15,000 Romans were able to rout Boudica's massive army, killing 80,000 in the process. So sure had the Boudican mob been of their victory that they'd brought their families out to the battlefield in wagons—wagons that later pinned them in and prevented them from retreating.

Boudica's final fate is unknown. Some claim she swallowed poison, and others that she was killed in battle. Her story was all but forgotten for centuries, until the rediscovery of documents from Roman historians. After that, she became a national hero of Britain in short order, soon appearing in textbooks, on statues, and in movies.

All this adoration despite the fact that her methods of revenge—religious decapitation—are almost directly equivalent to the actions of more traditionally reviled parties, such as tribal headhunters and religious extremists. Boudica's actions are held up as those of a vengeful heroine, while the aforementioned others' actions are decried as those of deranged villains. Food for thought.

## · ART NOTES ·

Boudica is described as tall, broad, and powerfully built. The outfits and props are all period-accurate. There's some disagreement over whether the Iceni used facial paint, though, so it's only portrayed on her daughters.

The pattern on Boudica's outfit fits the historical description of a many-colored striped garment, which most historians interpreted to be a proto-tartan. Even though the Iceni were located around present-day Norfolk, they were a Celtic tribe and were later pushed out toward areas like Wales and Scotland.

Boudica is said to have released a rabbit from her dress as a fortune-telling omen before one of her battles. The rabbit would undoubtedly make for great comic relief. Presumably along with the mounted skulls on her chariot.

# Artemisia Gentileschi

## (1593–1653, ITALY)

## The Queen of Baroque Painters

5 MATURITY
V VIOLENCE
R RAPE
A ABUSE

rtemisia Gentileschi could go toe-to-toe with any painter of the Baroque period. Look her up in almost any other book, and you'll probably read the phrase "one of the best female painters of the Baroque," but forget that noise: she was one of the best painters of the Baroque, period, full stop. And she got this way by almost exclusively painting powerful women—and getting rather public revenge on her enemies by doing so.

To explain requires a bit of backstory, and here things get rather dark. If you are sensitive to descriptions of public shaming and rape, you may want to skip this entry. But there is light at the end of the tunnel.

Artemisia was a master painter before she could read. The daughter of renowned painter Orazio Gentileschi, she was inducted into the family business early. It was in her father's workshop that she encountered her father's associate, Agostino Tassi, landscape painter and human-shaped pile of garbage. When Artemisia was 17, after many months of attempting to get her alone, Tassi finally succeeded, tossing her down on a bed and raping her.

What follows gets murky. While their initial sexual encounter (Artemisia's first ever) was decidedly non-consensual, after Tassi promised to marry her (although he was already married at the time), they had other, apparently more consensual, sexual encounters. However, after several months of "I swear I'll marry you, baby," Tassi flat-out refused to carry through on his promise.

So the Gentileschis brought him to court.

This trial was a big deal. Over seven interminable months, under the eyes of virtually all of upper-class Italy, Artemisia was subject to drawn-out interrogations. Midwives checked her time and time again to verify that she had been a virgin prior to the incident. She was subjected to torture, being put into thumbscrews and asked the same series of questions over and over, with the misguided goal of illuminating any false testimony.

She didn't crack. She kept her story consistent, raging at Tassi as they put on the thumbscrews, "This is the ring you give me, and these are your promises?!"

Tassi was not nearly so consistent in his testimony, which mostly consisted of an endless stream of inflammatory accusations. He claimed that Orazio had raped his own wife; that Orazio had an incestuous relationship with Artemisia; that Orazio had sold Artemisia to his friends for as little as a loaf of bread. He said Artemisia was "an insatiable whore" and even called his friends in to testify that they'd slept with her. His allegations became so outlandish that the judge started publicly berating him for his staggering flights of fancy.

As if this was not enough evidence that Tassi was history's worst use of carbon, in the trial it came out that he'd been imprisoned twice before—once for sleeping with his sister-in-law, and once for attempting to murder his wife.

In the end, Tassi was found guilty, but his court sentence hardly was fitting: he was given a year of exile from Rome. He only had to serve four months. That does not mean he got off easily, though. Artemisia would see to that.

As the trial was under way, Artemisia began work on one of her most famous paintings, that of the biblical story of Judith and Holofernes. In the story, Holofernes is an invading Assyrian jackhole whom the virtuous Judith seduces. Once he falls asleep, Judith cuts off his head. Virtuously.

In Artemisia's painting, Judith looks conspicuously like Artemisia herself. The gruesomely mutilated Holofernes? Tassi. Moreover, the scene itself, popular during this time, is given a much more forceful interpretation. While, say, Caravaggio's painting of Judith portrays her action as almost effortless, in Artemisia's version there's a clear sense of effort as she saws through Holofernes's body. She even has assistance from another woman, who holds him down while Judith kills him.

This painting made waves and catapulted Artemisia's artistic profile to new heights. She became the first woman to ever enter the prestigious art academy, the Accademia delle Arti del Disegno, where she became buddies with Galileo. She went on to have a long career as a court painter in Florence, Naples, and England. Contrary to the tastes of the time, the vast majority of her paintings (most of which are lost to history) portrayed women as protagonists or as equals to men.

That's not to say she didn't have to work hard—quite the opposite. Despite her fame, she was one of the only women in an overwhelmingly male arena, and there are many records of her having to drive hard bargains in order to get her due. Late in her life she wrote to a friend, "You feel sorry for me because a woman's name raises doubts until her work is seen; if I were a man, I can't imagine it would have turned out this way." Her death was met with the sort of vitriolic comments one might see today in the most misogynistic sub-basements of the Internet.

Artemisia was virtually forgotten until the 20th century—it wasn't until 1991 that she got her first art exhibition! Since then, historians have worked hard to restore her work to a position of prominence, and she has become a modern-day feminist icon.

Tassi, on the other hand, will be remembered forever as a vaguely man-shaped pile of excrement.

## · ART NOTES AND TRIVIA ·

This piece is done in the same high-contrast style characteristic of the Gentileschis' work. The style was pioneered by Caravaggio, whom Artemisia's dad, Orazio, befriended while in jail. Both were colorful characters.

On the bed that Artemisia is ostensibly using for visual reference is her earlier painting of Susanna and the Elders. The painting portrays a biblical story in which a woman is assaulted by men. Lying on top of the painting, also for visual reference, is a sword—the same one used in the Holofernes painting. The sword is angled in such a way as to give Susanna a weapon to use against her assailants, whose faces are obscured by blood. In the context of the piece, the Susanna painting stands in as a proxy for Artemisia herself. In the trial proceedings, Artemisia even said that during her rape she had assaulted Tassi with a nearby knife.

The 1997 movie *Artemisia* actually portrayed Tassi and Artemisia as star-crossed lovers. Ugh.

# Wu Zetian

## (624–705, CHINA)

## China's Only Female Emperor

**M**eet Wu Zetian,* first and only female emperor of China—seen here poisoning her own infant daughter.

Now, that's actually a bit historically inaccurate: the poison was used to knock off her other family members.† Her young daughter she *strangled*, in order to frame her rivals to the throne for murder. It worked. Her rivals—the old queen and the old queen's mother—were executed, and according to lore, they haunted Wu from that point forward.

Now, let's be clear upfront: it's impossible to know if any of this actually happened, because the historical sources on Wu are an absolute trainwreck. Although she's documented by a surprisingly large number of sources, the creators of said documents were, shall we say, not exactly paragons of impartiality. Some authors gleefully recorded her tales of torture and backstabbing, while others—ones she likely bankrolled—could not stop singing her praises. Getting to the bottom of Wu's actual story has been an ongoing struggle for historians for over a thousand years.

After bumping off her rivals, Wu ascended to the position of Emperor Gaozong's main consort. This was unusual in the extreme—having started her political career as consort to Gaozong's father,‡ she was supposed to have entered a convent after the late emperor's death. But even after Gaozong's father died, Gaozong kept her around. She shared power equally with him, even running the government herself when he was sick (which was often). They were referred to as the Two Sages.

---

* Wu Zetian is her post-death name; she was known as Wu Zhao in life (similar to how **Empress Myeongseong** of Korea was renamed after her death and was known by another name in life). "Zetian" means "emulator of heaven," a claim that, if true, would indicate that there's a wild time going on behind the pearly gates.

† Namely, her sister, her niece, and possibly her son Li Hong (although some historians maintain Li Hong died of natural causes).

‡ According to one source, Wu caught the eye of Gaozong's father early on. An anecdote about this period relates how, when she found that the emperor had a stubborn horse whom nobody could tame, she stepped up to the plate. Asking for an iron whip, an iron mace, and a dagger, she said that she would first whip the horse, and then, if that didn't work, hit the horse in the head with the mace. If it still didn't obey, she would slit its throat. The anecdote does not relay the fate of the horse. According to another source, Gaozong's father ignored her and she had to survive independent of his favor. She eventually developed a relationship with Gaozong, who seemed unlikely to take the throne. After many of his older brothers proved unsuitable, however, Gaozong ascended, and brought Wu with him.

She was, even by the most damning accounts, a good ruler, rooting out corruption and helping the commoners.

Once Gaozong died, she took full charge, albeit after some drama around succession. Her oldest son took a swing at ruling, but drastically overstepped his authority and angered others in government, so she drubbed him out of office. She replaced him with his younger brother, who really didn't want to rule. Wu, claiming that the young new king had a speech impediment, proceeded to "speak for him." Shockingly, she spoke for him quite openly.

And so we come to her "reign of terror."

As one might imagine, some government officials were not on board with taking orders from a woman—let alone one as bossy as Wu. She put down their inevitable uprising fairly easily, but now faced with the reality that others were gunning for her, she set about rooting out all of her enemies.

The next three years saw the complete rearrangement of dynastic succession, as she systematically wiped out any and all other claimants to the throne. In one year alone, she destroyed 15 family lines, mostly through executions, trumped-up treason charges, and enforced suicides—in which she summoned her rivals and made them kill themselves in front of her.

That's cold.

How did she drum up her accusations of treason, you may ask? By putting what was, essentially, an anonymous comment box (well, urn) on display. While its ostensible purpose was to help root out corruption, in practice it became a repository for tattle-tale letters, often put there by her spies and secret police. Those who displeased her would inevitably be ratted out by the comment box and then put to the sword—usually their own. This is almost undoubtedly the most hardcore use of an anonymous comment box in history.

Enforced suicide, however, was one of the better fates for those who crossed Wu. Her secret police were not shy about employing brutal torture. In fact, two of them, Lai Jungchen and Wan Gaojun, actually authored a how-to interrogation guide called the *Manual of Entrapment*. Among the poetically named horrors ascribed to them were "piercing the hundred veins," "dying swine's melancholy,"* and "begging for the slaughter of my entire family."

Moral of the story: do not mess with Empress Wu.

---

* This appears to have been conflated in numerous write-ups with the "human swine" torture associated with Lu Zhi, another Chinese empress. The torture, inflicted by Lu Zhi on Consort Qi, involved (gore warning!) cutting the victims' arms and legs off, removing the tongue, and then force-feeding the victims and leaving them to wallow in their own excrement. It is worth noting that copies of the *Manual of Entrapment* that are available online (and thus of questionable validity) do not contain references to extreme torture.

After the three-year "reign of terror," Wu declared a new dynasty, the Zhou dynasty*— and with it, she crowned herself emperor. She was largely able to do this because, despite the horrors she'd inflicted on the nobility, she'd been very good to the people. Her bureaucratic inquisition, in destroying thousands of lives, had rooted out a lot of institutional corruption, and she implemented standards to steer the government toward meritocracy thereafter. She opened up civil examinations to a wider variety of people, making for greater diversity in local and regional governments. From the viewpoint of the people, she was actually a good ruler.

Although she never remarried, she had dalliances with a number of colorful characters. One, described as a man of "unusual ability," was monk† Xue Huaiyi, who frustrated the aristocracy to no end with his casual vulgarity. An example: during a trial on his moral character, Huaiyi barged into the courtroom on horseback, stood around for a bit, then galloped off. While it's uncertain that they were lovers, virtually every history of Wu at least heavily hints that they were. She would have been in her sixties during their relationship. (Go, Wu!)

The other quite literally colorful men with whom she famously spent her waning years were the 20-something Zhang brothers. Two flamboyant men who wore operatic makeup and flashy outfits—many histories depict them in a romantic relationship with the by-then-70-year-old Wu. However, it seems more likely that they were gay (and/or possibly castrated). The Zhangs were party animals, taking full advantage of Wu's good graces to run the government offices like a brothel. Finally, they infuriated others to the point where a group of nobles stormed Wu's palace, cut off the Zhangs' heads, and took control of the government. Wu's response? To gently chide the rebels and go back to bed.

By that point, Wu was tired, worn down from a lifetime of fighting. She renounced her title, forgave her enemies, and soon thereafter, died peacefully.

As previously mentioned, when it comes to Wu, it's nearly impossible to know what was true and what was not. Generations of scholars have done their best to clear things up, and the consensus one gets after synthesizing a lot of writing on her is that, while she was almost undeniably iron-fisted, she was not quite the monster she's often made out to be.

Many of the most diabolical parts of her story, such as the murdering of her own baby, are almost certainly fake. One of the more likely explanations was that the child died of monoxide poisoning, a serious danger due to the charcoal braziers and poor ventilation present at the time. Whether Wu took advantage of the child's death for personal gain is hard to tell. Some histories sprinkle in more detail about her underhanded torture of the deposed queen and dowager queen, with Wu chopping off their limbs and tossing them in a stew. This is almost

---

\* Shortest-lived dynasty in Chinese history! 690–705.

† One telling says that she made him become a monk so that he could be around her quarters without the need for castration. Which actually sounds like it could be true.

certainly untrue. Similarly, the offenses of her secret police are likely exaggerated, although the bureaucratic purges definitely happened.

At the foot of Wu's undisturbed grave rests a large slate. Unlike the slate of her husband, which lists his many accomplishments, hers is blank. As tradition goes, Wu's successor was to decide what to make of her. Nobody could find the words.

## · ART NOTES ·

The throne room is based on ones in the Forbidden City, although Wu would have lived in Daming Palace.

The characters on the baby bottle spell "gold silkworm," a reference to the type of poison she likely used—a slow-acting poison made from the bodies of silkworms. Another source claimed that the poison used was one called "gu," but this was probably just slander, as the language used had connotations of wild sexuality and aphrodisiacs. Quite possibly it would have been one called Zhen (鸩毒), said to be made from the feathers of a rare bird.

Wu was probably much plumper than this, a fact realized too late for the illustration. The beauty standards of the Tang dynasty (which Wu's Zhou dynasty interrupted) preferred full-figured women.

# Arawelo

## (C. 15 CE, SOMALIA)

## *The Greatest–or Worst–Queen of Somalian History*

**D**epending on who you ask, Arawelo was either Somalia's greatest queen, its greatest villain, or its most overzealous circumciser. Or all three.

According to most accounts, by the time Arawelo hit the scene, things in Somalia were pretty crappy. The kingdom had been rocked by decades, if not centuries, of senseless warfare between senseless monarchs—and hoo boy, there was nobody more senseless than Princess Arawelo's dad. The king spent his time deflowering virgins and refusing to eat anything but the fresh marrow of she-goats (perhaps one of the ancient world's weirdest diet crazes). Proper governing, though? Not high on his agenda.

Arawelo, however, picked up the slack. When the kingdom was debilitated by years of severe drought, she and her corps of warrior women would fetch water from faraway spots, thus saving her people. She was clearly doing a much better job than her dear old dad.

But then she officially took power. And here's where things get weird.

There are as many different versions of Arawelo's history as there are tellers of it. In some versions, she led all Somali women in a peaceful seizure of power, grabbing all the weapons while the men were off doing man stuff.* In another version, while out hunting one day, she was raped by a man who soon came to regret it.

In any event, when she took power, Arawelo put women in charge. Reasoning that men had cocked everything up for years† and that women were naturally more peaceful and better suited for governance, Arawelo consigned men to taking care of children and managing the household.

Relegating men to the background took balls—literally. In a move that understandably came to overshadow everything else she accomplished, Arawelo began to castrate men by hanging them by their testicles. Now, the details of this part of the story diverge massively depending on the telling. In some versions, she only castrated criminals, and even then, some-

---

\* The man stuff in question is never specified. Since this book is providing yet another telling, let's say they were playing the world's longest game of Duck Duck Goose. It's in a book now, so it must be true.

† Yes, that's a pun. No, not apologizing for it.

times only metaphorically (by imprisoning them). In other, longer versions, she castrated everyone. Even the little boys.

Of course, one version is the one more often told by men. The other by women. Gold star if you can figure out which is which.

In the latter versions, Arawelo was inevitably overthrown by some combination of her grandson (who'd been hidden away from her) and/or an old man named Oday Biiq ("Wise Coward") who saved his genitals by convincing everyone he had already been castrated. In some versions, after passing himself off as a eunuch, Oday Biiq secretly impregnated Arawelo's daughter, thus producing the grandson who'd challenge Arawelo.

In the years following, one or both of the noncastrated men rose to challenge Arawelo. When Arawelo made ridiculous demands of the male population, such as "bring me a bunch of fruit on the bare back of a camel without using tools!" they outwitted her—in that case, by covering the camel's back in mud and sticking the fruit on the camel. Eventually, they caught her unaware and killed her.

Now, did Arawelo actually exist? Historians seem to think so, but can't confirm any of the particulars, or even the era when she was supposed to have lived.[*] The tale of Arawelo has historically been used by certain factions to "prove" that women can't, or shouldn't, rule. Some even go so far as to use the castration legend to legitimize the practice of female genital mutilation. Thankfully, the image of Arawelo has begun to be rehabilitated in recent years—a movement that has suspiciously coincided with a larger movement against the tradition of female genital mutilation.[†] Imagine that.

## · ART NOTES ·

You can see the women in the background carrying away loads of spears, swords, and bows with them. The men, conversely, are overloaded with children and looking pretty harried.

The child in the basket is the grandchild who would one day come to overthrow Arawelo. In some of the versions, he is hidden in a basket in the reeds by the river—suspiciously like Moses.

The grave of Arawelo, believed to be in Sanaag, is alternately honored and disrespected by female and male visitors, who leave flowers and throw rocks, respectively. This is reflected in the presence of rocks and flowers.

---

[*] In some versions, she's even BFFs with Makeda, the Queen of Sheba—who's generally considered to be a 10th-century figure. History is difficult!

[†] A day after this entry was written, outgoing Nigerian president Goodluck Jonathan officially banned the practice. Clearly this entry should have been written sooner.

# Caterina Sforza

## (1463–1509, ITALY)

### The Tigress of Forlì

he first thing you should know about Caterina Sforza is that her (very apt) surname is Italian for "strength." The second thing you should know is that it friggin' *fit*.

Caterina was born in Renaissance Italy, a place famous for underhanded schemers, debauched nobility, and the pope—but let's not repeat ourselves. The bastard daughter of a mid-tier noble (who, to his credit, loved her to bits and treated her as a fully legitimate offspring), Caterina seemed predestined for the fate of so many women of the time—she'd get married off to cement some political ties, have kids, keep the house tidy, and eventually die in childbirth.

That very emphatically did not happen.

Caterina came to center stage after her first husband passed away. He died of natural causes—it being perfectly natural to die after being stabbed several dozen times. The stabbers in question were the Orsis, a vengeful family who managed to catch Caterina's household by surprise and took her prisoner. Having taken out the rulers of the city (Caterina and her husband), the Orsis figured they had their coup all sewn up. But they forgot about one thing: Ravaldino.

Ravaldino was a fortress outside of Caterina's home of Forlì, and it would come to be central to Caterina's life. She'd won Ravaldino over to her cause some months earlier, when she seduced its persnickety caretaker into leaving his post to join her outside for a spell—and then promptly had him arrested for desertion of his post. It's worth mentioning that she accomplished this feat after riding to Ravaldino several months pregnant.

So, with Caterina held hostage and the family seat under siege, the only thing under her control was Ravaldino, which refused to surrender to the Orsis. Reasoning that the fort commander might relent in Caterina's presence, the Orsis allowed her to enter the fortress and parley with the commander for a limited amount of time. They realized their mistake when she entered the fortress and the drawbridge rose up behind her—as she stood there flicking them off.* Reasoning that she would back down if they threatened her children, the Orsis brought the young Sforzas to the fortress and did just that.

---

\* This was actually not the middle finger, but a Renaissance equivalent called "the fig." You do it by balling your fist up and sticking your thumb between your index and middle fingers. While it's fallen into disuse, certain countries still find it obscene—try it with your friends and see which ones react!

Her response? Appearing on the ramparts, she flashed her nether regions and yelled, "I can make more!"*

They backed down, and soon thereafter she turned the tables. Reinforcements arrived from her allies, and she took back Forlì. Her first order of business was establishing for the benefit of everyone that Caterina Sforza was not to be played with. She executed 80 people—Orsis and collaborators—by ingeniously terrifying methods. While that was the banner headline, the truth was that she was remarkably restrained. Controversially, she forbade her allies to rape and loot in Forlì (which was standard operating procedure). She let the Orsi wives and children live.

Over the next several years, Caterina consolidated her power. She dodged assassination attempts and permanently moved shop to Ravaldino. She refused to let any slurs on her reputation stand—gossip about her and you'd end up either in chains or in the ground.†

The final chapter of her life started with a meeting with Niccolò Machiavelli, of all people. War had broken out between factions to the north and south of Forlì, and Caterina was caught right in the middle. Machiavelli came to convince her to side with the pope's faction, but left humiliated after she politically ran circles around him. The obstinacy she'd shown in that meeting quickly got her on the pope's bad side. He rescinded her right to rule and accused her of trying to poison him. In response, she burned down every building and farm outside the walls of Forlì and prepared for war with the faction represented by the pope and Machiavelli. Soon she was going cannon-to-cannon with one of Renaissance Italy's most brutal nobles, the inspiration for Macchiavelli's *The Prince*: Cesare Borgia.

While Forlì itself folded relatively quickly, Caterina held out at Ravaldino. At night, she'd play music so the enemy forces would think she was partying. Her soldiers would scrawl insults on cannonballs before firing them at Cesare's forces. When the fort was finally breached, Caterina set a wall of explosives on fire to control the flow of enemies and personally fought for two hours, sword in hand. Eventually, some of her allies betrayed her and gave her over to Cesare.

---

\* This account—one of the things everyone loves best about her—is, tragically, almost certainly inaccurate, as Elisabeth Lev points out in *The Tigress of Forlì*. In reality, Caterina probably refused to see them at all, and most firsthand accounts paint her as severely distressed over her kids. The anecdote was probably invented by Caterina's detractors, like Machiavelli, to make her seem like an outrageous woman.

† One of the chief sources of punishable gossip was her secret marriage to the new commander of Ravaldino—a much, much younger man. She was so besotted with him that she became uncharacteristically subservient, deferring to his opinions in matters of government. His de facto reign ended abruptly when he was brutally murdered by a cadre of assassins that included Caterina's own son. In that instant, Caterina's old self came back with a vengeance: she crushed the assassins and imprisoned her own son. Mother and son eventually patched things up, but it took a while.

Cesare, in a series of acts sure to send most readers into a blinding rage, raped her, psychologically tortured her, and kept her in a dungeon for a year. Upon taking the fort, he declared to his forces that "she defended her fortresses better than her virtue"—thus earning the endless sadistic abuse he is now doubtless experiencing in the deepest pit of hell.

Caterina went on to live a quiet existence for the remainder of her years, mostly engaged in legal battles to eke out some small inheritance for her children. She outlived both Cesare and the pope, dying of pneumonia at the age of 46. Speaking of her life in her final years, she said: "If I were to write all, I would shock the world."

# Elisabeth Báthory

(1560–1614, HUNGARY)

## The Blood Countess

irst off: Trigger warnings. All of the trigger warnings. No trigger unwarned. (Okay, fine, it's actually just triggers for gore, violence, rape, incest, and murder. But, um, tread lightly regardless.)

Now then, let's take a step into the life of one of the most vilified women in history. On December 29, 1610, a garrison of soldiers stormed the Hungarian castle of Cachtice and arrested Elisabeth (Erzsébet) Báthory. They accused her of roughly 100 *Saw* movies' worth of torture and took her into custody. As the story goes (and please keep in mind, absolutely *none* of this should be taken at face value), they caught her in the act, finding a freshly buried corpse and a cowering servant, badly beaten but still alive.

The subsequent questioning of over 300 people about the doings of the Blood Countess (as she'd later become known) has put her in the record books as easily the most prolific female serial killer in history, by an order of magnitude. The low-end estimate for her body count (and this was the number given by her closest associates and allies, mind you) was just in the thirties. The high-end estimate was 650 bodies, all of them female servants. The collected testimonials contained a litany of charges against her so vile that they have literally become legend—she would later be used as one of the primary inspirations for Bram Stoker's *Dracula*, and her story has been referenced in hundreds of books, movies, songs, you name it. There were so many charges levied against her that, typed out, it initially took up 10 single-spaced pages. (The list provided here is understandably somewhat truncated.)

So let's make a drinking game of it. The rules are simple: every time you're grossed out, take a shot. Here's hoping you have a full bottle or a strong stomach. Here we go!

According to the surviving testimonials, Elisabeth and/or her closest servant-confidants:

- Kept her servants chained up every night so tight their hands turned blue and they spurted blood.

- Beat them to the point where there was so much blood on the walls and beds that they had to use ashes and cinders to soak it up.

- Beat a servant in Vienna so loudly that her neighbors (some monks) threw clay pots at the walls in protest.

MATURITY 5

VIOLENCE V

RAPE R

ABUSE A

- Strangled a servant to death with a silk scarf (a harem technique known as "the Turkish way").

- Burned her servants with metal sticks, red-hot keys, and coins; ironed the soles of their feet; and stuck burning iron rods into their vaginas.

- Stabbed them, pricked them in their mouths and fingernails with needles, and cut their hands, lips, and noses with scissors.

- Used needles, knives, candles, and her own freaking teeth to lacerate servants' genitals.

- Stitched their lips and tongues together.

- Made servants sit on stinging nettles, then bathe with said stinging nettles. During the bath, she'd push the nettles into their shoulders and breasts.

- Had them stand outside in tubs of ice water up to their necks until they died.

- Smeared a naked girl with honey and left her outside to be bitten by ants, wasps, bees, and flies.

- Kept servants from eating for a week at a time, and, if they got thirsty, made them drink their own urine.

- Forced servants to cook and eat their own flesh (usually from the buttocks), or make sausages of it and serve it to guests.

- Heated up a cake to red-hot temperatures and made a servant eat it.

- Baked a magical poisonous cake in order to kill a rival magistrate, George Thurzó (who was also the guy who arrested her—more on him in a bit).

- Cast a magic spell to summon a cloud filled with 90 cats to torment her enemies. Okay, that's actually kind of awesome.

- Had an ongoing affair with some guy named "Ironhead Steve" (no, really).

- Stuffed five servants' corpses underneath a bed and continued to feed them as if they were still alive.

- Buried victims in gardens, grain pits, orchards, and occasionally cemeteries. Sometimes with rites, often without.

And that's just the charges levied against Elisabeth in her lifetime! After she died, more details were added to the picture:

- She bathed in virgins' blood! (A lie dreamed up centuries afterward. Also would've been nigh-impossible due to coagulation.)

- She was syphilitic from centuries of inbreeding! (Maaaaybe? Seems perfectly with-it in her letters, though.)

- She was epileptic! (Well, she did once mention her eye hurt in a letter . . . ?)

- She was raped when she was young. (Possible but, given scant evidence for it, unlikely. Her powerful position in the world, practically since birth, further complicates this theory.)

- Her aunt Klara was a bisexual or lesbian. (Possible.) The two had an incestuous relationship! (Uh . . . doubt it.) After having numerous affairs, Klara was raped by an entire Turkish garrison before having her throat cut! (Augh, no! What the hell!?)

- She was menopausal, and thus crazy! (If menopause worked like that, the world would have a much smaller population.)

- Her cousin Gábor (whom we talk about later) slept around a lot (true), was bisexual (maybe?), and had an incestuous relationship with his sister Anna (not true), who was herself accused of sleeping with a silversmith (super not true) and being a witch (super ultra not true).

So after all this went down, the sentences went into effect almost immediately. Elisabeth's female "accomplices," all old ladies, first had their fingers torn off with iron tongs, and, once fingerless, were bodily tossed into a large fire. Her one male "accomplice," being less of a participant in the supposed crimes, was shown a tremendous amount of mercy: he was decapitated before they tossed his body into a fire. And Elisabeth Báthory herself was "immured"—which is to say, bricked up into a room in her own castle, where she died four years later.

In conclusion: the Aristocrats!

Well, actually, no. That is not the conclusion. Buckle up, for this entry is about to dump the biggest bucket of cold water on all this malarkey as can possibly be mustered. Based on the evidence and the research meticulously compiled by historian Tony Thorne, there is a case to be made (one which this author believes to be true) that **Elisabeth Báthory is innocent**.

Mic drop.

Now, this is not to say she was a sweet-hearted, blameless victim—she was absolutely not. The overwhelming impression one gets from reading all the available documents (which it is not recommended that you do in one sitting—learn from this author's mistakes) is that she was a take-no-crap kind of lady. Her husband was off at war, and she had to manage an incredibly large estate in his absence. She looked after thousands of servants, governed the local populace, and kept up an amount of property second to none.

And so Elisabeth Báthory needed everyone around her to know one thing, and one thing only: she was Head Bitch in Charge, and she had no time for your nonsense.

Her surviving letters illustrate this beautifully with their overwhelming curtness (even to her husband!). In one of the gems she wrote to an encroaching squatter, threatening him, she ended by saying, "Do not think I shall leave you to enjoy it [settling illegally on my land]. You will find a man in me"—a statement that translates roughly to "I will crush you."

So no, she was not warm and cuddly. She absolutely made life miserable for misbehaving servants (or, more likely, had her head servants do it for her). It is beyond questioning that she beat the hell out of them, and some undoubtedly died from their wounds—she had thousands of servants in an age before penicillin. In fact, scholar Irma Szádeczky-Kardoss claims that the more outlandish tortures (stinging nettles, metal rods, amateur acupuncture) were contemporary folk remedies. Horrifically mean lady? Yes. Cartoon supervillain? No way.

So what happened? George Thurzó—Palatine of Hungary and eminent turd farmer—did.

Now, it's already been mentioned that Elisabeth was powerful, but you need to understand the magnitude of the target she presented: the Báthorys were like the Hungarian Kennedys and had been for centuries. By the time all this went down, Elisabeth's earlier-mentioned cousin Gábor was gunning for the throne (literally starting a war), and Elisabeth was widowed, with more money than God. So Thurzó was all, "Nah, dog, no way I'm letting those two partner up," and decided to take Elisabeth down, hopefully gaining her property and upping his profile in the process.

Now, the details of the plot are a bit murky. Thurzó was a known schemer who'd made a career out of backstabbing people, so a plot of this sort wouldn't be much of a surprise. There's evidence in correspondence with his wife (who kept forgetting to write in code) that Thurzó was moving against Elisabeth over a year before her arrest. He'd been in contact with the local church leaders, who were whipping up the general populace against the Báthorys by telling them stories—stories that would, with minor variations, be repeated over and over in the proceedings against Elisabeth and passed off as "I heard this" but with very few firsthand accounts.

And that's just the cooperating witnesses. In all likelihood—it was standard operating procedure at the time—the members of Elisabeth's household were tortured before testifying. Their testimonials, which are confused and contradictory, lend credence to that. As historian Tony Thorne points out in his exhaustively researched book *Countess Dracula*, it's at times impossible to even tell to whom the witnesses are referring, due to the vagaries of medieval Hungarian pronouns.

The only way to get rid of such an entrenched power as Elisabeth was to catch her committing a horrific act red-handed—which Thurzó said he did, although it took him 24 hours to produce the aforementioned cowering servant and freshly buried corpse. Afterwards, the imprisoned Báthory never had a trial (despite the king demanding one for three years straight). Elisabeth never got to speak in her own defense, and her family records were mostly destroyed. There is very little to go on in determining what sort of a person she actually was.

So, even if she did commit said acts (which is entirely possible, although at nowhere near the scale of the accusations), ask yourself what is more likely: an incredibly outlandish list of violent acts perpetrated by a cadre of old women over decades or an orchestrated persecution against a powerful, harsh, and independent woman—in the age of actual witch hunts!

## · ART NOTES ·

This is one of the more complex pieces. Here's the thought process.

The reader should see through her eyes, as best as possible. Still, you never see her, just a reflection in a dusty mirror. Her expression is meant to be somewhat inscrutable—you can't tell what's on her mind. She's purposely stiff and posed.

Elisabeth has her back turned to Thurzó (in the background, with a feathered cap, in silhouette) bricking her up, with her image caught in her own shadow—symbolizing how her true story has been locked away and obscured.

The whole composition is meant to feel claustrophobic, with her not only caught inside the mirror but also surrounded by the shadows cast from the bricked-up wall.

Her outfit is from a portrait that purported to be of her, but was recently proven not to be. The mirror is a Venetian glass mirror (one of the only types of mirror at the time—each one was as expensive as a battleship!), and the scratches and cloudiness are actually characteristic of that type of mirror.

Elisabeth is washing her hair, a reference to the blood-bathing legends. Is that water reflecting the red candlelight and her dress, or . . . ?

The symbol at the top of the mirror (the dragon) is the actual Báthory family crest, believe it or not. The candleholders are callbacks to that dragon.

Everything on the desk (including the bleeding candles) is related to a different torture rumor. The chest with the small mirror is a scrying box that witches were said to use.

Very barely visible in the darkness of the reflected room, up above a balcony, are a bunch of cats, a reference to the 90-cat curse.

# Malinche

## (1496 [1501]–1529, MEXICO)

### The Maligned Mother of Mexico

ew people can claim the distinction of having their very name become synonymous with a swear word—but Malinche was a rare woman indeed. Alternately characterized as the greatest traitor in the history of North America or a victim thrust into hideous circumstances, even to this day Malinche is a divisive figure.

Our story starts with the arrival of Spaniard Hernán Cortés in 14th-century Mexico. It's worth taking a moment to really describe this loser, as he was one of the more despicable human beings our race has ever created. He was in Mexico only because he'd flunked out of law school, become a sailor, and then mutinied against his boss to claim land for himself like he was playing Monopoly. He had two sets of kids, one legitimate and one illegitimate, and gave both sets the same names. Cortés wasn't even the worst of the conquistadors on that mission, but you get the idea.

It is in regard to his staggering mistreatment of the indigenous peoples that we first meet Malinche. Early on in Cortés's travels, traders give the Spaniards 20 women as (sex) slaves—one of them being Malinche. Cortés gives her to one of his men and promptly forgets about her. Not long after, the Spaniards run across native peoples speaking a language that their translator does not understand, but Malinche does. This earns her a promotion to chief translator and woman number three (out of several dozen) with whom Cortés is cheating on his wife.

Thus begins the ludicrously tortured translation chain of the Spanish conquest: the Nahuatl-speaking people speak to Malinche, Malinche translates it into Mayan, and the Spaniard translator translates the Mayan into Spanish. There were often other local languages involved. Forwards and backwards, backwards and forwards, for months. After a short time, Malinche learns Spanish, but the translation train is pretty tortured for a while.

And the things they have Malinche translate! Once they get to Tenochtitlan—a brilliant lake settlement larger than any European city of the time—they are given a tour of the grounds. Once the tour is over, Cortés tells Moctezuma (aka Montezuma—the leader), in no uncertain terms, that his people are heathens, that the land now belongs to Spain, and that Moctezuma is to tear down the temples and turn them into churches.

And Malinche translates that. How do we know? Because immediately afterwards angry warriors start chasing the Spaniards through the palace, until the conquistadors barricade themselves in their quarters. Shortly thereafter, Cortés, Malinche, and a couple others sneak into Moctezuma's room, where Cortés tells him that he is now a prisoner of Spain. And Malinche translates again!

And it's here that we get some of our only clues as to who Malinche actually was. The reality is, none of her words survived to the current day (it's doubtful she was literate), and we don't even know her real name. Spaniards called her Dona Marina, and Malinche (or Malin-tzin) was probably an adaptation of that name. Funnily enough, the people of Tenochtitlan referred to Cortés only by Malinche's name, due to her being the one to speak for him. Yes, Mexico's famous conqueror did his fell work under a woman's pseudonym. Malinche's history prior to meeting Cortés is largely a mystery (the Spaniards apparently didn't care enough to ask her, or to write down her answer if they did), but the fact that she spoke the royal dialect of Nahuatl indicates she was no layperson—it is likely that she was of the royal lineage of one of the indigenous kingdoms and that she was sold (rather than abducted) into slavery.

The rest of the story plays out in predictably horrible fashion, with the Spaniards laying waste to Tenochtitlan. After the conquest, Malinche is married off to another conquistador and has several children, adding to a prior one by Cortés—all of whom are some of the first mestizos. To Cortés's credit, he awards her a substantial *encomienda* (labor grant—a highly desired reward). Malinche dies young, likely of disease, and in relative obscurity.

As time went on Malinche's name became a deep insult. In the 1800s, a Mexican politician agitating for independence from Spain began mythologizing her as Mexico's greatest traitor. (Ironically, said politician was full-blood Spanish.) In the years thereafter, artists began portraying her as a lusty temptress. Authors inserted her into lurid stories as a villainous contrast to an invented "good girl"—similar to the later stories of the soldaderas (see the entry on **Petra Herrera**).

And that was hugely unfair. First, to label her a traitor to "her people" is like saying Genghis Khan was a traitor to Asia. She was part of one nation (we don't even know which one) and would likely not have recognized the people of Tenochtitlan as hers. Many other tribes (notably the Tlaxacans, who were similarly stigmatized) allied with Cortés to wage war on their common enemies, but history does not give them nearly the same vicious treatment.

Furthermore, "her people" sold her into sexual slavery. She owed them little and had every reason to hate them. And yet, the evidence indicates she didn't even do that. When reunited with her mother late in life in a frustratingly poorly documented meeting, she embraced her and gave her jewels.

Bottom line: Who has the moral authority to judge her? Fate gave her the worst circumstances it could, and she still carved a place for herself with nothing but her force of will. She looked kings in the eye and told them to kneel. She saw the sacrificial altars of Tenochtitlan and lived. She bore the name that felled empires. She is one of the only native people of the period whose name survives to the present day.

Malinche survived. Sometimes that's all you can do.

### · ART NOTES AND TRIVIA ·

All outfits are accurate, save that of Moctezuma. Normally he wore a headdress so neck-crushingly huge that it would have obscured all his people from view, so it got downsized.

Cortés has a scar on his chin (which he got, according to legend, when fleeing from a married woman's husband).

Malinche is here walking a fine line between the two sides. The divider wall upon which she's standing (and the canal itself) is inaccurate—they would not have existed in the middle of one of the main roads—but they're necessary to communicate the idea of her straddling the line between the two cultures.

The looming storm clouds and sunset are meant to communicate the impending horrors to be visited upon Tenochtitlan.

# Ida B. Wells

### (1862–1931, UNITED STATES)

## *Princess of the Press*

ou may know that Rosa Parks was far from the first black person in the United States to refuse to vacate a bus seat for a white person. But did you know that 71 years before Rosa Parks, there was a black woman who refused to give up her seat . . . on the train? This was a woman who put her life on the line for decades to end lynching in the United States. This was a woman who helped found the NAACP. This was Ida Bell Wells Barnett, better known as Ida B. Wells.

Ida was a tough cookie from the get-go. When, at age 16, she lost her parents in a yellow fever epidemic, she rolled up her sleeves, got a job, and worked to keep her siblings out of foster care. When she was 21, the conductor on a train on which she was a passenger ordered her to vacate her seat so that a white woman could use it. Ida refused. When the conductor tried forcibly removing her, she hooked her feet into the chair and refused to budge. When he tore her sleeve in the attempt, she scratched at him and bit him.

When a gang of men finally removed her from the car, she sued the train company—and won. (Although the ruling was later overturned via legal shenanigans.)

But, by far, Ida's most significant achievements were in her anti-lynching journalism.

So let's talk about lynching. Likely the word conjures up images of someone being hanged from a tree. The reality was far, *far* worse than that. We're talking torture that would make **Elisabeth Báthory** or **Wu Zetian** shudder. If you have a weak stomach, you're forewarned—but try to stick with it. It's important that you understand the horror that this woman devoted her life to stopping. During most people's childhoods, these descriptions were constantly censored. This book is not going to do that.

Here are summaries of just a few lynchings that Ida reported on:

- **1892:** Tommie Moss, Henry Stewart, and Calvin McDowell were shot to pieces. (McDowell had fist-sized holes in him.) Moss died pleading for them to spare him for the sake of his pregnant wife. The thing that started this all off was a kids' game of marbles. More on this in a bit.

- **1893:** Henry Smith had red-hot iron brands placed all over his body for 50 minutes, until his torturers finally burned out his eyes and thrust irons down his throat. He was then set on fire, and when he managed to jump out of the fire pit (he was still alive!), he was pushed back in. Someone made a watch charm from his kneecap, and the clothes torn off his body were kept as mementos by some in the 10,000-man crowd. Photographers sold postcards of the event. Gramophone recordings of his screams were sold, like the world's most loathsome ringtone.

• **1898:** Frazier Baker's only "crime" was being appointed a postmaster in a small South Carolina town. His house was set on fire, and when he and his family fled, they were all shot—everyone was wounded, and Frazier and his one-year-old baby were killed. Their charred bodies were found near the wreckage of the house the next day.

• **1899:** Local whites arranged a special train so that more people could attend the mob execution of Sam Hose. He was first tied to a tree, stripped naked, and then mutilated: the mob severed his left ear, then his right. Then his fingers were lopped off and his penis sliced off. Then he was set on fire. As his body burned, the crowd of 2,000 people cut off pieces of him as souvenirs. Bone bits were sold for 25 cents and slices of liver for 10. Even the tree to which he was tied was chopped up and sold.

• **1904:** Luther Holbert and a woman (presumed to be his wife) were forced to hold out their arms as their fingers were chopped off. Their ears were cut off, their eyes poked out, and a large corkscrew was used to bore spirals of "raw, quivering flesh" out of their arms, legs, and bodies. Finally, they were burned to death.

• **1911:** Will Porter was taken to an opera house, tied to the stage, and shot by people who bought tickets for the privilege.

If you need to go look at pictures of kittens for a second, it's understandable. This book will be here.

Back? Good. Now, remember the Moss incident, the one with the marbles? That one is important for a couple reasons: it's the first lynching that really grabbed Ida's journalistic attention (Moss was a friend of hers); it caused a mass exodus of blacks from Memphis (Ida bought a gun and stayed); and it's a useful microcosm through which to examine lynchings as a whole. Now, while it's true that the inciting incident was a kids' game of marbles, the real story was that the three men killed were associated with a thriving black-owned grocery store that was taking away business from a nearby white-owned one. The white grocery's owner was the ringleader behind the mob that led this horrific attack. He orchestrated the terrible murder of three people for . . . basically money.

So Ida got to work. The end result: "Southern Horrors," a seminal pamphlet that blew the lid off lynching myths. Prior to that, the widely believed stereotype was that black men were out-of-control brutes who were constantly a hairsbreadth from assaulting white women—and somehow this was believable to a large swath of the population.

The common wisdom about lynching was that it was in response to black men raping white women. Except that was totally bogus, and "Southern Horrors" proved it. By analyzing a huge number of cases and laying them out in an academic manner, Ida showed that rape had nothing to do with a majority of lynchings, and that most of the time the reason was political, economic, or plain ol' racism in the face of loving interracial relationships.

As you can imagine, this exposé did not win Ida a lot of admirers.

A week after she released her report, a mob broke into the offices of her newspaper, the *Free Speech*, and burned it to the ground while she was traveling. (Yes, they literally eradicated free speech.) The mob threatened to lynch her if she ever returned to Memphis. In response, she looked into returning to Memphis—only to be informed that a group of black men were organizing to protect her should she return. Wanting to avoid a race riot, she stayed away—but kept writing, madder than the devil and twice as eloquent.

Despite ever-present death threats, Ida continued her work for the next 40 years (!) by investigating and writing about lynchings. On more than one occasion, she passed herself off as a widow or a relative of the deceased in order to gain better journalistic access, a ploy that earned one of her contemporaries, who tried the same trick, his own lynch mob. (Thankfully, he escaped.)

And still she would not tone herself down, despite the urging of other activists and even the newspapers that printed her work.

For a good 13 years, she was practically the only journalist investigating lynching. Once others gained interest in the subject—in no small part due to her herculean efforts, which included speaking tours abroad, the establishment of a great many civil rights organizations, and endless reams of articles and pamphlets—she was relegated to a footnote. Despite her massive contributions to the cause, she was almost left off the NAACP's founders list, due in no small part to the desire of some to distance themselves from her forceful, brutally honest language.

In the end, she married a man who supported and advocated for her. Together they had four children, with Ida bearing the first at age 34 and the last at 42. She would even bring her children with her on her speaking tours, declaring herself the only woman in US history to travel with a nursing baby to make political speeches. (She would run for Illinois state senate when she was well into her sixties.) Her entire family got into the activism—when Ida was once feeling despondent about going out to investigate yet another lynching, her son demanded that she do so. "If you don't," he asked, "who will?" When she came around, the entire family was waiting, their things packed, ready to join her on her travels.

And on that powerful mental image, we wrap up the entry.

Ida B. Wells died at age 68, almost done with her autobiography. The last chapter ended mid-sentence, mid-word.

## • ART NOTES •

Ida is depicted here being tossed off a moving train car, although it was definitely stopped when they forced her off. The image is meant to convey her holding on, speeding toward the future, into the light—while the conductor is merely a disembodied leg in the shadows, barely even human.

She is, of course, striking a very animated princess kind of pose. Imagine a musical number happening at that very moment.

The train cars and outfit are period-accurate.

The flying papers represent Ida's reams of writing, with the nearest one being the cover for "Southern Horrors."

Underneath the tree is a cut rope being slowly blanketed by her work. Since illustrating an actual lynching, or even a noose, would be extremely distasteful, this image seemed more poetically faithful to the spirit of her work, without being overly graphic.

The opossum in the tree is a callback to a Loyal League[*] parade float, which featured a black man against a tree with a bunch of dead opossums (possibly meant to symbolize lynchers). It does not seem that Ida was ever directly involved with the Loyal League, but they traveled in the same circles.

The title "Princess of the Press" was an actual title applied to her during her life. The name was partly a reference to Gilbert and Sullivan's *Princess Ida,* a comic opera about a feminist teacher.

---

[*] Although the term has been used to signify a number of different groups, in this case, it refers to a series of organizations that mobilized the southern black vote.

# Phoolan Devi

## (1963–2001, INDIA)

## *The Bandit Queen Who Joined Parliament*

This is not a fun story, but it is an important one. It's the story of a woman who was put through hell, who fought tooth and nail for the right to exist, who atoned for her sins, and who became a leader for the downtrodden. This is the story of Phoolan Devi, the Bandit Queen of India.

Phoolan Devi was born a *mallah*, one of the lowest of the low in the Indian caste system—so low that technically it isn't even part of the caste system. Predestined for an untouchable life of burning dung for warmth and handling corpses, Phoolan was treated as barely human by virtually everyone outside of her immediate family. This included her cousin Mayadin, who came to be her childhood nemesis. He started by swindling Phoolan's father out of his inheritance, then continued by trying to get rid of Phoolan in the traditional way: marrying her off.

But from her first breath, Phoolan would not be cowed, no matter how horrific the act. When Mayadin stole land from her father, she staged a sit-in on the property. She was removed only after Mayadin beat her unconscious with a brick. When, at 11, she was married off to a 33-year-old who raped and beat her, she did the unthinkable: she left him and walked a distance the width of Texas to return home.

Phoolan's homecoming was bitter. Her parents, ashamed that she'd left her husband, told her to redeem her honor by committing suicide. When she approached the police for help with Mayadin's crimes, they beat and gang-raped her. And to top it off, she was soon met at home by endless throngs of men coming to buy or take her services—courtesy of Mayadin and his friends spreading rumors that she was a sex worker.

With nothing else to lose, she began to fight fire with fire. She took a stick and beat the hell out of her unwanted visitors until they left. She showed up at Mayadin's house at all hours, shrieking abuse at him in public. She made it very clear she would not be silenced—and so Mayadin had her kidnapped.

And then, surprisingly, things got better.

The kidnapping did not go as planned. Abducted by a gang of bandits with whom Mayadin was friendly, Phoolan, unexpectedly, found herself befriending the second-in-command, a man named Vikram. They became so close that when the head of the bandits tried to rape Phoolan, Vikram killed him and took control of the gang. Phoolan became his second-in-command. Despite being attracted to her, Vikram made it clear she did not have to sleep with him if she wasn't inclined.

With Vikram by her side, Phoolan quickly established a reputation as a *dacoit* (bandit) to be reckoned with. She learned to handle a gun and joined the gang in robbing trains, kidnapping, ransoming, and the like. She swiftly got revenge on her rapist ex-husband by beating him and then mutilating his genitals. She then revenged herself on the police who wronged her by killing the one who had spread the word that she was a prostitute. Although she was now in charge of a small army of men from higher castes than her, many of them considered her to be a reincarnation of Durga, the goddess of feminine power. Soon enough, so did everyone else.

When word of Phoolan's divine vengeance spread, Mayadin came begging for forgiveness, dressed in rags and offering a plate of money. Despite wanting with every fiber of her being to kill him on the spot, Phoolan let him live. She was only talked down by the combined efforts of her parents and Vikram, the latter of whom she'd gradually come to respect, admire, and even love. They were eventually married, and in his arms she found true happiness.

It was not to last.

The end of Phoolan's happiness came in the form of two brothers: Sri Ram and Lala Ram. The two, both former members of the gang, rejoined it after a recent release from prison. Aghast that Vikram had killed the old boss—who was a *thakur,* a much higher caste than mallahs like Vikram and Phoolan—the two began to plot revenge. One night as Phoolan lay in bed with Vikram, Sri Ram shot her beloved in the head. Then he took her.

The following paragraph is possibly the most difficult-to-read part of this entire book.

Sri Ram brought the blindfolded Phoolan to his home village of Behmai, where a group of men gang-raped her into unconsciousness day after day, for three weeks. At one point, Sri Ram stripped her naked and ordered her to fetch water from a nearby well, kicking her as she went. Eventually an elderly priest from a nearby village helped Phoolan flee, an act for which Sri Ram burned him alive. Phoolan, meanwhile, escaped from Behmai, disappearing into the night.

Seven months later, a small group of people dressed as police officers entered Behmai. After rounding up all the men of the town, their leader got on the megaphone and announced that they had come there for Sri Ram, and that if he was not produced instantly, everyone there would die. It was Phoolan Devi, back from the dead.

In the intervening months, Phoolan had become the boogeyman of rural India. Putting together her own all-mallah gang, she had mercilessly terrorized the unjust. She would castrate rapists and cut off their noses, raid the rich to give to the poor, and free women from slavery. Even mallahs unaffiliated with her took to protecting themselves by threatening that she would show up to avenge them—which she often did. Copycats would pose as her to gain

credibility. No photo had ever been taken of her, and few who'd seen her face were still alive to tell the tale. She was the ruthless reincarnation of Durga. And she'd come back to Behmai.

When the Ram brothers did not appear, Phoolan's men murdered all 22 thakur men in the village, an outrage that led to the launch of a massive manhunt by Indira Gandhi's government. Phoolan dodged armies, grenade-tossing helicopters, and all-out firefights for two years in her search for the Ram brothers. Eventually word got to her that Sri Ram, the chief architect of her misery, had been killed by his brother Lala in a fight over a woman. With her hated enemy dead, Phoolan's rage slowly dissipated and she negotiated her own surrender.

In February 1983, in front of 8,000 cheering fans, 19-year-old Phoolan Devi laid down her arms before portraits of Durga and Mahatma Gandhi and went into police custody. And yet, this was not to be the last chapter of her life.

Even Phoolan herself later admitted that she was half feral when she surrendered. Having never experienced anything approaching the modern conveniences of life, she saw everything new as a threat. Cameras were guns, common English words were insults, and marriage proposals (of which she fielded many) were assassination attempts in disguise. Her paranoia was not totally unfounded—several unsuccessful attacks were made on her life, and when she was diagnosed with ovarian cysts, she was given an unnecessary hysterectomy. The doctor was quoted as saying, "We don't want Phoolan Devi breeding more Phoolan Devis."

Despite her near-complete illiteracy, she negotiated remarkable terms for her incarceration. Phoolan was to serve only eight years, her father was to be awarded the land Mayadin had stolen from him, and her brother was to be given a government job. Even though she ended up serving 11 years without a trial—the Indian legal system of the time was continuously swayed by contemporary politics—she was eventually given a full pardon by a fellow low-caste politician.

Seeing the power inherent in the political system, she too decided to run for office—and won in a landslide. She spent her time in office fighting for the downtrodden and sweeping into prisons unannounced to visit old friends. She married a relatively quiet man whom she referred to in Hindi as "my wife." Her public image was often at the forefront of her mind. In 1994, when *Bandit Queen*, an unauthorized film about her life was released, she protested vigorously and attempted to get it removed from theaters. She hated that it depicted her as "a sniveling woman."

After only five years in office, Phoolan was gunned down in the street, in revenge for the Behmai massacre. There were allegations of a cover-up, or at least severe incompetence, by the investigating officers. In 2014, one of her three killers was sentenced to life in prison.

Many journalists throughout the last years of her life questioned and outright attacked her history—many of the details of her years of banditry have yet to be independently verified. But she always took great exception to anyone assailing the essential truth of her story. As Phoolan lambasted one reporter:

> Do you have any idea what it's like to live in a village in India? What you call rape, that kind of thing happens to poor women in the villages every day. It is assumed that the daughters of the poor are for the use of the rich. They assume that we're their property. In the villages the poor have no toilets, so we must go to the fields, and the moment we arrive, the rich lay us there; we can't cut the grass or tend to our crops without being accosted by them. We are the property of the rich. . . . They wouldn't let us live in peace; you will never understand what kind of humiliation that is. If they wanted to rape us, to molest us, and our families objected, then they'd rape us in front of our families.

The difference between others and her, Phoolan maintained, was that she dared to fight back.

## · ART NOTES ·

The abusive man on whom Phoolan sits has scar patterns in the shape of tiger stripes, as a callback to her reputation as an avatar of Durga, who is often depicted riding a tiger.

Although there is no record of Phoolan having inducted other women into her gang, after saving downtrodden women she often castigated them for not having saved themselves. She was more likely to hand money to other women than to give them a gun. The various women here represent some of the abused whom she helped.

The well in the background is modeled on the one in Behmai by which the 22 thakur men were murdered. The well has crumbling reddish tile around it, which is meant to give the impression of blood as it spills out and pools up around Phoolan.

In the background, the thakur men are being lined up to be shot. Visually, they appear to almost be floating in the reddened area around the well already.

# It Doesn't Have to Stop Here!

There is more information available online on almost every entry you've read here—side stories, concept art, reference imagery—and that's before you get into the new entries that go up regularly for free!

So come with your comments, your criticisms, your corrections, and join us over at

www.Rejected Princesses.com

(Or don't. I'm not going to tell you how to live your life.)

Thanks for reading!

# Acknowledgments

### Thanks go to:

**For helping with every single part of everything:**
Jeremy Porath

**For unwavering moral support:**
Karen Hamilton
Kim Tang
Eileen "Lady Lin" Ambing
Sandra Daugherty

**For making the book happen:**
Alexandra Machinist, Doug Johnson, and the rest of the team at ICM Partners
Carrie Thornton, Sean Newcott, and everyone else at Dey Street
Lily Tillers, Loan Dang, and everyone at Del, Shaw, Moonves, Tanaka, Finklestein, & Lezcano

**For editing help:**
Jonathan Glenn Truitt, Associate Professor of Colonial Latin American History at Central Michigan University (Malinche, Micaela Bastidas, Anita Garibaldi)
Brittany Bayless Fremion, Assistant Professor of History at Central Michigan University (all the North America entries)
Kelly Murphy, Assistant Professor of Philosophy and Religion at Central Michigan University (Jezebel, Yael)
Jeanette Wu (Wu Zetian, Yoshiko Kawashima, Ching Shih, Trung Sisters, Qiu Jin)
Peta Lindsay (Ida B. Wells)
Sara Gaines (Boudica)
Allyson Carr (Christine de Pizan)
Rachael Haigh (Artemisia Gentileschi)
Linda Taba (Yaa Asantewaa)
Raqi Syed (A'isha bint abi Bakr)
Nafees Bin Zafar (A'isha bint abi Bakr)
Jonaya Kemper-Rice (A'isha bint abi Bakr)
Theresa Watterson (Grace O'Malley)
Aubree Katherine Newhall (Mariya Oktyabrskaya, Joey Guerrero, Elisabeth Báthory)
Jon Harris (Jezebel)

**For suggesting entries:**
Arabella Caulfield (Andamana, Keumalahayati)
queenvictoriaroyalty on Tumblr (Alfhild)

Nikita Gadre (Amba)
Silverlady (Anita Garibaldi)
Flavia Saraceni Huber (Annie Jump Cannon)
easyjammin on Tumblr (Arawelo)
Rivka Suparna (Artemisia Gentileschi)
Astrid Phillips Mayer (Elisabeth Báthory)
elegantmess-southernbelle on Tumblr (Princess Caraboo)
an-errant-curl on Tumblr (Christine de Pizan)
changedmamma on Tumblr (Emmeline Pankhurst)
John Owens (Grace O'Malley)
Peter Asberg (Hortense and Marie Mancini, Mary Lacy)
justafakeme on Tumblr (Jara)
Kate Beaton (Ida B. Wells)
Nydia Herrera (Malinche)
grunnels on Tumblr (Malinche)
Asha Dahya (Laskarina Bouboulina)
David Leaman (Marie Marvingt)
Chris K. Layman (Mary Bowser)
Jim MacQuarrie (Mata Hari)
Martin Brennand (Matilda of Tuscany, Wu Zetian)
Chantal Lathanc (Micaela Bastidas)
Irene Kim Asbury (Empress Myeongseong)
serenada on Tumblr (Nanny of the Maroons)
Wendi Milasi (Nellie Bly and Elizabeth Bisland)
Laurie Scott (Noor Inayat Khan)
Jeremy Porath (Nzinga Mbande, Qiu Jin, Tomoe Gozen, Tomyris, Trung sisters)
Terri Drake Imhoof (Phoolan Devi)
Jean Choi (Pope Joan)
B. M. Matthews (Rani Lakshmibai)
crawd on Tumblr (Olga of Kiev)
Stacey Adams (Sybil Ludington)
kitsunechan on Tumblr (Wallada bint al-Mustakfi)
Alyzee Morales (Xtabay)
Jasmine Faelyn (Yaa Asantewaa)
Jane Onwuchekwa (Yaa Asantewaa)
charlape on Tumblr (Yael)
Sara C. (Yoshiko Kawashima)

# Bibliography

### Khutulun

Polo, Marco. 1875. *The Book of Ser Marco Polo the Venetian: Concerning the Kingdoms and Marvels of the East*, vol. 2. Translated by Sir Henry Yule. London: John Murray.

Weatherford, Jack. 2010. "The Wrestler Princess." *Lapham's Quarterly*, September 27. Accessed June 14, 2014. http://www .laphamsquarterly.org/roundtable/wrestler -princess.

### Tatterhood

Carter, Angela. 2012. *Angela Carter's Book of Fairy Tales*. London: Virago Press.

### Agnodice

Grant, Mary, ed. 1960. *The Myths of Myginus*. Translated by Mary Grant. Lawrence: University of Kansas Press.

### Te Puea Herangi

King, Michael. 2008. *Te Puea: A Life*. Auckland: Penguin Group New Zealand.

Parsonson, Ann. 1996. "Herangi, Te Kirihaehae Te Puea." In *Dictionary of New Zealand Biography*, vol. 3. Updated October 9, 2013. http://www.TeAra.govt.nz/en/ biographies/3h17/herangi-te-kirihaehae-te -puea.

### Moremi Ajasoro

kwekudee. 2014. "Ife People: Ancient Artistic, Highly Spiritual, and the First Yoruba People." Trip Down Memory Lane, September 14. http://kwekudee -tripdownmemorylane.blogspot.ca/2014/09 /ife-people-ancient-artistic-highly_14.html.

Ogumefu, M. I. 1929. *Yoruba Legends*. London: Sheldon Press.

Ragan, Kathleen. 2000. *Fearless Girls, Wise Women, and Beloved Sisters: Heroines in Folktales from Around the World*. W. W. Norton & Company.

Ring, Trudy, Robert M. Salkin, and Sharon La Boda. 1994. *International Dictionary of Historic Places: Middle East and Africa*, vol. 4. Abingdon, UK: Taylor & Francis.

### Sybil Ludington

Bohrer, Melissa Lukeman. 2007. *Glory, Passion, and Principle: The Story of Eight Remarkable Women at the Core of the American Revolution*. New York: Simon & Schuster.

Dacquino, V. T. 2000. "Sybil's Story." From *Sybil Ludington: The Call to Arms*. Fleischmanns, NY: Purple Mountain Press. http:// ludingtonsride.com/history.htm.

Johnson, Willis Fletcher. 1907. *Colonel Henry Ludington: A Memoir*. New York.

Patrick, Louis S. 1907. "Secret Service of the American Revolution." *Journal of American History* 1.

### Kurmanjan Datka

Kakeev, A., et al. 2002. *Tsarina of the Mountains: Kurmanjan and Her Times*. Bishkek, Kyrgyzstan: Ilim.

### Andamana

Mathilda. 2008. "The Guanches of the Canary Islands." Mathilda's Anthropology Blog, March 10. https:// mathildasanthropologyblog.wordpress .com/2008/03/10/the-guanches-of-the -canary-islands/.

Whiting, William B. 1875. *Andamana: The First Queen of Canary, Ancestress of the Family of Eugenie, the Late Empress of the French, and Her Remarkable and Successful Coup d'État*. New York: Edward O. Jenkins.

### Mary Seacole and Florence Nightingale

Robinson, Jane. 2004. *Mary Seacole: The Most Famous Black Woman of the Victorian Age*. New York: Carroll & Graf.

### Gráinne "Grace O'Malley" Ní Mháille

Chambers, Anne. 2003. *Ireland's Pirate Queen: The True Story of Grace O'Malley*. New York: MJF Books.

### "Stagecoach" Mary Fields

Cooper, Gary. 1977. "Stagecoach Mary: A Gun-Toting Black Woman Delivered the US Mail in Montana." *Ebony*, October.

Dow, Luella. 2009. "On the Road: Women Mail Carriers Celebrate Century and a Half of Service." Cheney Free Press, May 22. http://www.cheneyfreepress.com/story/2009/05/22/neighborhood/on-the-road-women-mail-carriers-celebrate-century-and-a-half-of-service/5921.html.

Drewry, Jennifer M. 1999. "Mary Fields: A Pioneer in Cascade's Past." *Footsteps*, March-April. Reprinted at Cascade Montana. http://www.cascademontana.com/mary.htm.

Hazen, Walter. 2004. *Hidden History: Profiles of Black Americans*. St. Louis: Milliken Publishing Company.

Shirley, Gayle. 1995. *More Than Petticoats: Remarkable Montana Women*. Helena: Falcon Press.

### Yennenga

Schwarz-Bart, Simone, and André Schwarz-Bart. 2002. *In Praise of Black Women*, vol. 2, *Heroines of the Slavery Era*. Madison: University of Wisconsin Press/Modus Vivendi.

Sheldon, Kathleen E. 2005. *Historical Dictionary of Women in Sub-Saharan Africa*. Lanham, MD: Scarecrow Press.

### Annie Jump Cannon

Veglahn, Nancy. 1991. *American Profiles: Women Scientists*. New York: Facts on File.

### Wilma Rudolph

Smith, Maureen M. 2006. *Wilma Rudolph: A Biography*. Westport, CT: Greenwood Press.

### Alfhild

Druett, Joan. 2000. *She Captains: Heroines and Hellions of the Sea*. New York: Simon & Schuster.

Killings, Douglas B., ed. 1905. *The Nine Books of the Danish History of Saxo Grammaticus*. Translated by Oliver Elton. New York: Norroena Society. Reprinted at Online Medieval & Classical Library. http://omacl.org/DanishHistory/book7.html.

### Calafia

Montalvo, Gaci Rodrigues de. 1992. *The Labors of the Very Brave Knight Esplandian*. Translated by William Thomas Little. Binghamton: State University of New York, Center for Medieval and Early Renaissance Studies.

### Keumalahayati

Clavé-Çelik, Elsa. 2008. "Images of the Past and Realities of the Present: Aceh's Inong Balee." *International Institute for Asian Studies Newsletter* 48, Summer. http://www.iias.nl/sites/default/files/IIAS_NL48_1011.pdf.

Sufi, Rusdi. 1994. "Laksamana Keumalahayati." In *Wanita utama Nusantara dalam lintasan sejarah* (*Prominent Women in the Glimpse of History*), edited by Ismail Sofyan, M. Hasan Basry, and Teuku Ibrahim Alfian. Jakarta.

### Marie Marvingt

Lebow, Eileen F. 2002. *Before Amelia: Women Pilots in the Early Days of Aviation*. Washington, DC: Brassey's.

"Flying Not the Sport for Women." 1910. *El Paso* (TX) *Herald*, December 6.

"Red Cross Aeroplanes." 1914. *Fergus County* (Lewiston, MT) *Democrat*, March 31.

### Iara

Benedito, Mouzar. 2013. *Understanding Brazil, the Country of Football*. Translated by Phil Turner. São Paolo: Liz Editora.

"Brazilian Folklore #1: The Tale of Iara." Not Blue, Nor Red. http://motorcyclles.tumblr.com/post/77640457917/brazilian-folklore-1-the-tale-of-iara.

Duende, Daniel. 2008. "Brazilian Myths and Haunts on the Lusosphere—Part 1." GlobalVoices, October 15. https://globalvoices.org/2008/10/15/brazilian-myths-and-haunts-1/.

Tunks, Jeanne. 2001. "Brazilian Music and Culture: An Internet Tour." *Social Studies and the Young Learner* (National Council for the Social Studies), 14 (2): 14–15.

### Jane Dieulafoy

Adams, Amanda. 2010. *Ladies of the Field: Early Women Archaeologists and Their Search for Adventure*. Vancouver: Greystone Books.

### Tin Hinan

Glacier, Osire. 2013. *Political Women in Morocco: Then and Now*. Trenton, NJ: Red Sea Press.

Robinson, Marsha R. 2012. *Matriarchy, Patriarchy, and Imperial Security in Africa: Explaining Riots in Europe and Violence in Africa*. Lanham, MD: Lexington Books.

"The Tomb of Tin Hinan, Desert Queen of the Tuaregs." 1968. *Look and Learn*, December 14. Reposted August 6, 2013, at Look and Learn: History Picture Library. http://www.lookandlearn.com/blog/26338/the-tomb-of-tin-hinan-desert-queen-of-the-tuaregs/.

Wilde, Lyn Webster. 2000. *On the Trail of the Women Warriors: The Amazons in Myth and History*. New York: Thomas Dunne Books.

### Hatshepsut

Cooney, Kara. 2014. *The Woman Who Would Be King: Hatshepsut's Rise to Power in Ancient Egypt*. New York: Crown.

### Emmy Noether

Dick, Auguste. 1981. *Emmy Noether, 1882–1935*. Translated by H. I. Blocher. Boston: Birkhauser.

### Ka'ahumanu

Mellen, Kathleen Dickenson. 1952. *The Magnificent Matriach, Ka'ahumanu, Queen of Hawaii*. New York: Hastings House.

### Katie Sandwina

Fair, John D. 2005. "Kati Sandwina: 'Hercules Can Be a Lady.'" *Iron Game History* 9 (2): 4–7. http://library.la84.org/SportsLibrary/IGH/IGH0902/IGH0902d.pdf.

Foulkes, Debbie. 2010. "Katie Sandwina (1884–1952): Circus Strongwoman." Forgotten Newsmakers, December 14. https://forgottennewsmakers.com/2010/12/14/katie-sandwina-1884-%E2%80%93-1952-circus-strongwoman/.

Pednaud, J. Tithonus. n.d. "Sandwina—Woman of Steel." The Human Marvels. http://www.thehumanmarvels.com/sandwina-woman-of-steel/.

### Gracia Mendes Nasi

Brooks, Andrée Aelion. 2002. *The Woman Who Defied Kings: The Life and Times of Doña Gracia Nasi—a Jewish Leader During the Renaissance*. St. Paul, MN: Paragon House.

### Sayyida al-Hurra

Duncombe, Laura Sook. 2015. "Sayyida al-Hurra, the Beloved, Avenging Islamic Pirate Queen." Jezebel, March 3. http://pictorial.jezebel.com/sayyida-al-hurra-the-beloved-avenging-islamic-pirate-1685524517.

Glacier, Osire. 2013. *Political Women in Morocco: Then and Now*. Trenton, NJ: Red Sea Press.

### Matilda of Tuscany

Fraser, Antonia. 1989. *The Warrior Queens*. New York: Knopf.

Nieuwenhuijsen, Kees C. n.d. "The Assassination of Godfrey the Hunchback." http://www.keesn.nl/murder/text_en.htm.

## Moll Cutpurse
Middleton, Thomas, Thomas Dekker, and Jennifer Panek. 2011. *The Roaring Girl: Authoritative Text, Contexts, Criticism*. New York: W. W. Norton & Company.

## Nellie Bly and Elizabeth Bisland
Goodman, Matthew. 2013. *Eighty Days: Nellie Bly and Elizabeth Bisland's History-Making Race Around the World*. New York: Ballantine Books.

## Trung Trac and Trung Nhi
Fraser, Antonia. 1989. *The Warrior Queens*. New York: Knopf.

Rigden, Stephen. 2007. "Who Was the Warrior Woman, Le Chan?" Around the World, March. http://www.phespirit.info /places/2007_03_vietnam_1.htm.

Tran, Tuyet A., and Chu V. Nguyen. n.d. "Trung Trac and Trung Nhi." Viet Touch. http:// www.viettouch.com/trungsis/.

Womack, Sarah. 1995. "The Remakings of a Legend: Women and Patriotism in the Hagiography of the Tru'ng Sisters." *Crossroads: An Interdisciplinary Journal of Southeast Asian Studies* 9 (2): 31–50.

## Yaa Asantewaa
Agyeman-Duah, Ivor, and Osei Boateng. 2000. "Yaa Asantewaa: A Woman of Iron." *New African* 391 (December): 40.

Black History Pages. n.d. "Nana Prempeh I (1870–1931)." http://www.blackhistorypages .net/pages/nanaprempehi.php.

Boahen, A. Adu, and Emmanuel Kwaku Akyeampong. 2003. *Yaa Asantewaa and the Asante-British War of 1900–1*. Accra and Oxford: Sub-Saharan Publishers and James Currey.

Brempong, Arhin. 2000. "The Role of Nana Yaa Asantewaa in the 1900 Asante War of Resistance." *Le Griot* 8.

McCaskie, T. C. 2007. "The Life and Afterlife of Yaa Asantewaa." *Africa* 77 (22): 151–79.

Wilson, Tracy V., and Holly Frey. 2014. "The Yaa Asantewaa War of Independence." Stuff You Missed in History Class (podcast), June 25. http://www.missedinhistory.com /podcasts/the-yaa-asantewaa-war-of-.

## Gertrude Bell
Adams, Amanda. 2010. *Ladies of the Field: Early Women Archaeologists and Their Search for Adventure*. Vancouver: Greystone Books.

Frey, Holly, and Tracy V. Wilson. 2012. "Gertrude Bell: The Uncrowned Queen of Iraq." Stuff You Missed in History Class (podcast), November 19. http://www .missedinhistory.com/podcasts/gertrude-bell -the-uncrowned-queen-of-iraq/.

## Eustaquia de Souza and Ana Lezama de Urinza
Vela, Bartolomé Arzáns de Orsúa y. 1975. *Tales of Potosí*. Edited by B. C. Padden. Translated by Frances M. López-Morillas. Providence: Brown University Press.

## Mary Bowser
Abbott, Karen. 2014. *Liar, Temptress, Soldier, Spy: Four Women Undercover in the Civil War*. New York: HarperCollins.

## Pope Joan
Boureau, Alain. 2001. *The Myth of Pope Joan*. Chicago: University of Chicago Press.

Greer, Mary K. 2009. "Papess Maifreda Visconti of the Guglielmites—New Evidence." Mary K. Greer's Tarot Blog, November 7. https:// marygreer.wordpress.com/2009/11/07 /papess-maifreda-visconti-of-the -guglielmites%E2%80%94new-evidence/.

Kirsch, Johann Peter. 1910. "Popess Joan." In *The Catholic Encyclopedia*, vol. 8. New York: Robert Appleton Company. Reprinted at New Advent, http://www.newadvent.org/cathen/08407a.htm.

Rustici, Craig M. 2006. *The Afterlife of Pope Joan: Deploying the Popess Legend in Early Modern England*. Ann Arbor: University of Michigan Press.

### Nwanyeruwa

Birrell Gray Commission. 1929. "This is Emena Okpobo, speaking of the carnage at Utu Etim Ekpo Public Records Office in December, 1929." http://web.archive.org/web/20060907035421/http://jhunix.hcf.jhu.edu/~plarson/syllabi/122/reading/igbo/igbo.htm.

Evans, Marisa K. n.d. "Aba Women's Riots (November–December 1929)." BlackPast.org. http://www.blackpast.org/gah/aba-womens-riots-november-december-1929.

Falade, Kayode. 2013. "Ikot Abasi: Celebrating Heroines of Aba Riots." National Mirror Online, August 3. http://en.africatime.com/nigeria/articles/ikot-abasi-celebrating-heroines-aba-riots.

Zukas, Lorna Lueker. 2009. "Women's War of 1929." In *International Encyclopedia of Revolution and Protest: 1500 to the Present*, edited by Immanuel Ness, 3634–3635. Malden, MA: Wiley-Blackwell.

### Mary Lacy

Guillery, Peter. 2000. "The Further Adventures of Mary Lacy." *The Georgian Group Journal* 10: 61–69. http://content.historicengland.org.uk/content/docs/research/marylacyweb.pdf.

Jonklaas, Owen. 2014. "Mary Lacy, the Female Shipwright." Tall Tales and True: Stories from My Family Tree, April 12. https://familyhistorytales.wordpress.com/2014/04/12/mary-lacy-the-female-shipwright/.

Stark, Suzanne J. 1996. *Female Tars: Women Aboard Ship in the Age of Sail*. Annapolis, MD: Naval Institute Press.

### Josefina "Joey" Guerrero

"CIA Analyst Edward Hauck Dies at Age 72." 1996. *Washington Post*, June 28.

"Joey Gains Citizenship After Long Struggle." 1967. *Carville Star*, vol. 28 (2), November–December.

Johnson, Thomas M. 1951. "Joey's Quiet War." *Reader's Digest*, August.

"A Letter from the Publisher." 1953. *Time*, August 24.

"News of Former Carville Patients." 1964. *Carville Star*, vol. 24 (2), November–December.

Schexnyder, Elizabeth. 2009. "Joey G. Remembered." *Carville Star*, vol. 64, June.

### Chiyome Mochizuki

Hayes, Stephen K., and Mike Lee. 1984. *Legacy of the Night Warrior*. Burbank, CA: Ohara Publications.

### Nana Asma'u

Heath, Jennifer. 2004. *The Scimitar and the Veil: Extraordinary Women of Islam*. Mahwah, NJ: Hidden Spring.

Mack, Beverly B. and Jean Boyd. 2000. Excerpts from *One Woman's Jihad: Nana Asma'u, Scholar and Scribe* (Bloomington: Indiana University Press). Reprinted at Women in World History, http://chnm.gmu.edu/wwh/p/214.html.

Razainc. 2015. "Nana Asma'u: Leader of Women's Rights in Islam and West Africa." Loonwatch.com. April 6. http://www.loonwatch.com/2015/04/nana-asmau-leader-of-womens-rights-in-islam-and-west-africa/.

Tasmeem. 2012. "Nana Asma'u-Scholar, Poet, Community Leader, Educator." Mosaic: Recognizing Extraordinary Muslim Women, July 3. https://mosaicofmuslimwomen .wordpress.com/2012/07/03/then-nana -asmau-scholar-poet-community-leader -educator/.

Wadlow, René. 2015. "A Pre-history of Boko Haram: The Long Shadow of Usman dan Fodio." Toward Freedom, February 9. http:// www.towardfreedom.com/30-archives /africa/3808-a-pre-history-of-boko-haram-.

### Julie "La Maupin" d'Aubigny

Burrows, Jim. 2008. "The Adventures of La Maupin." http://www.eldacur.com/~brons /Maupin/LaMaupin.html.

Gardiner, Kelly. n.d. "The Real Life of Julie d'Aubigny." https://kellygardiner.com/ fiction/books/goddess/the-real-life-of-julie -daubigny/.

Malcolm, Robert. 1855. *Curiosities of Biography: or, Memoirs of Wonderful and Extraordinary Characters*. London: R. Griffin.

### Nanny of the Maroons

Gottlieb, Karla Lewis. 2000. *The Mother of Us All: A History of Queen Nanny, Leader of the Windward Jamaican Maroons*. Trenton, NJ: Africa World Press.

### Xtabay

Preuss, Mary H. 2005. *Yucatec Maya Stories: From Chen-Ja to the Milpa*. Lancaster, CA: Labyrinthos.

Triay, Mario Diaz. n.d. Excerpt from *Guia Turistica de la Peninsula de Yucatan, La tierra de los Mayas* (*A Tour Guide of the Yucatan Peninsula, Land of the Maya*). Reprinted at Merida (Mexico) Tourism Office, http:// www.merida.gob.mx/turismo/contenido /cultura_in/xtabay.htm.

### Tomoe Gozen

Tyler, Royall. 1991. "Tomoe: The Woman Warrior." In *Heroic with Grace: Legendary Women of Japan*, edited by Chieko Irie Mulhern. Armonk, NY: M. E. Sharpe.

### Empress Theodora

Atwater, Richard, trans. 1927. *Procopius: Secret History*. Chicago: P. Covici.

Browning, Robert. 1971. *Justinian and Theodora*. New York: Praeger.

### Rani Lakshmibai

Devi, Mahasweta. 2010. *The Queen of Jhansi*. Translated by Sagaree Sengupta and Mandira Sengupta. Calcutta and New York: Seagull Books.

### Mariya Oktyabrskaya

Sakaida, Henry. 2003. *Heroines of the Soviet Union 1941–45*. Oxford: Osprey.

### Yael

Judges 4–5. In *Holy Bible: New International Version*.

Rymanover, Menahem Mendel. 1996. *The Torah Discourses of the Holy Tzaddik Reb Menachem Mendel of Rimanov, 1745–1815*. Translated by Dov Levine. Hoboken, NJ: KTAV Publishing House.

Watts, Joel L. 2010. "Judges 4.17–22: The Rape of Sisera?" Unsettled Christianity, December 22. http://unsettledchristianity .com/judges-4-17-22-the-rape-of-sisera/.

### Wallada bint al-Mustakfi

Adarsh, K. R. 2005. "Woman of Distinction: Wallada Bint al-Mustakfi: The Poetess of Andalus." *Al-Shindagah* 67, November– December. http://www.alshindagah.com /Novdec2005/woman.html.

Bat-Shimeon, Miriam. 2011. "Wallada bint al-Mustakfi." Miriam's Middle Eastern Research Blog, April 11. https://awalimofstormhold.wordpress.com/2011/04/11/wallada-bint-al-mustakfi/.

Segol, Marla. 2009. "Representing the Body in Poems by Medieval Muslim Women." *Medieval Feminist Forum* 45 (1): 147–169.

*Ada Lovelace*

Moore, Doris Langley. 1977. *Ada, Countess of Lovelace: Byron's Legitimate Daughter*. New York: Harper & Row.

Morrison, Philip, Emily Morrison, and Charles Babbage. 1961. *Charles Babbage: On the Principles and Development of the Calculator and Other Seminal Writings*. New York: Dover Publications.

*Laskarina Bouboulina*

Demertzis-Bouboulis, Philip. 2001. *Laskarina Bouboulina*. Spestai, Greece: Museum Bouboulinas.

*Ching Shih*

Murray, Dian H. 1987. *Pirates of the South China Coast, 1790–1810*. Stanford, CA: Stanford University Press.

Yuan, Yung-lun. 2011. *History of the Pirates Who Infested the China Sea from 1807 to 1810* (1831). Translated by Karl Friedrich Neumann. London: Cambridge University Press/Oriental Translation Fund.

Yuan, Yung-lun. 2016. *Record of Pacifying the South China Seas*. Translated by Jeanette Wu.

*Christine de Pizan*

Adams, Tracy. 2014. *Christine de Pizan and the Fight for France*. University Park: Pennsylvania State University Press.

Carr, Allyson Ann. 2011. "Diction as Philosophy: Reading the Work of Christine de Pizan and Luce Irigaray to Write a Hermeneutics of Socially Transformative Fiction-Mediated Philosophy." Institute for Christian Studies.

Hindman, Sandra L. 1984. "With Ink and Mortar: Christine de Pizan's Cite des Dames." *Feminist Studies* 10 (3): 457–83.

*Harriet Tubman*

Clinton, Catherine. 2004. *Harriet Tubman: The Road to Freedom*. Boston: Little, Brown.

*Anne Hutchinson*

LaPlante, Eve. 2004. *American Jezebel: The Uncommon Life of Anne Hutchinson, the Woman Who Defied the Puritans*. San Francisco: Harper San Francisco.

*Petra "Pedro" Herrera*

Fuentes, Andres Resendez. 1995. "Battleground Women: Soldaderas and Female Soldiers in the Mexican Revolution." *The Americas* 51 (4): 525–53.

Salas, Elizabeth. 1990. *Soldaderas in the Mexican Military: Myths and History*. Austin: University of Texas Press.

*A'isha bint abi Bakr*

Heath, Jennifer. 2004. *The Scimitar and the Veil: Extraordinary Women of Islam*. Mahwah, NJ: Hidden Spring.

Spellberg, Denise A. 1994. *Politics, Gender, and the Islamic Past: The Legacy of A'isha bint abi Bakr*. New York: Columbia University Press.

*Olga of Kiev*

Cross, Samuel Hazzard, and Olgerd P. Sherbowitz-Wetzor. 1953. *The Russian Primary Chronicle: Laurentian Text*. Cambridge, MA: Mediaeval Academy of America.

*Agontime and the Dahomey Amazons*

Alpern, Stanley B. 1998. "On the Origins of the Amazons of Dahomey." *History in Africa* 25: 9–25.

Araujo, Ana Lucia. 2011. "History, Memory, and Imagination: Na Agontime, a Dahomean Queen in Brazil." In *Beyond Tradition: African Women and Their Cultural Spaces*, edited by Toyin Falola and Sati U. Fwatshak, 45–68. Trenton, NJ: Africa World Press.

Edgerton, Robert B. 2000. *Warrior Women: The Amazons of Dahomey and the Nature of War*. Boulder, CO: Westview Press.

### Mata Hari
Shipman, Pat. 2007. *Femme Fatale: Love, Lies, and the Unknown Life of Mata Hari*. New York: William Morrow.

### Josephine Baker
Baker, Jean-Claud, and Chris Chase. 1993. *Josephine: The Hungry Heart*. New York: Random House.

### Dhat al-Himma
Kruk, Remke. 2014. *The Warrior Women of Islam: Forgotten Heroines of the Great Arabian Tales*. London: I. B. Tauris.

Lyons, M. C. 1995. *The Arabian Epic*, vol. 3, *Texts: Heroic and Oral Storytelling*. Cambridge: Cambridge University Press.

### Alice Clement
Smith, Bryan. 2003. "Alice Clement: The Detective Wore Pearls." *Chicago*, December 1. http://www.chicagomag.com /Chicago-Magazine/December-2003/The -Detective-Wore-Pearls/.

Undine. 2015. "Alice Clement of the Chicago P.D." Strange Company, April 6. http:// strangeco.blogspot.ca/2015/04/alice -clement-of-chicago-pd.html.

### Shajar al-Durr
Duncan, David J. 1998. "Scholarly Views of Shajarat al-Durr: A Need for Consensus." *Chronicon* 2 (4): 1–35. http://www.ucc.ie /chronicon/duncfra.htm.

Nicholson, Helen J. 2004. *The Crusades*. Westport, CT: Greenwood Press.

Smith, Bonnie G. 2008. *The Oxford Encyclopedia of Women in World History*. New York: Oxford University Press.

### Amba/Sikhandi
Buck, William, trans. 1973. *Mahabharata*. Berkeley: University of California Press.

### Khawlah bint al-Azwar
Heath, Jennifer. 2004. *The Scimitar and the Veil: Extraordinary Women of Islam*. Mahwah, NJ: Hidden Spring.

Pauw, Linda Grant De. 1998. *Battle Cries and Lullabies: Women in War from Prehistory to the Present*. Norman: University of Oklahoma Press.

Qazi, Moin. 2015. *Women in Islam: Exploring New Paradigms*. Chennai, India: Notion Press.

Waqidi, Muhammad ibn 'Umar. 2005. *The Islamic Conquest of Syria: A Translation of Futuhusham: The Inspiring History of the Sahabah's Conquest of Syria*. Translated by Mawlana Sulayman al-Kindi. London: Ta-Ha Publishers Ltd.

### Princess Caraboo
Gutch, John Matthew. 1817. *Caraboo*. London: Baldwin, Cradock, and Joy.

### Anita Garibaldi
Sergio, Lisa. 1969. *I Am My Beloved: The Life of Anita Garibaldi*. New York: Weybright and Talley.

### Tomyris
Rawlinson, George, trans. 1862. "Herodotus: Queen Tomyris of the Massagetai and the Defeat of the Persians Under Cyrus." Excerpt from *Herodotus: The History* (New York: Dutton & Company) at Fordham University, August 1998. http://legacy.fordham.edu /halsall/ancient/tomyris.asp.

### Emmeline Pankhurst

Bartley, Paula. 2002. *Emmeline Pankhurst*. London: Routledge.

### Marjana

Lyons, Malcolm C., trans. 2010. *The Arabian Nights: Tales of 1,001 Nights*. London: Penguin Books.

### Mai Bhago

Kohli, M. S. 2003. *Miracles of Ardaas: Incredible Adventures and Survivals*. New Delhi: Indus Publishing Company.

Raju, Karam Singh. 1999. *Guru Gobind Singh: Prophet of Peace*. Chandigarh, India: Ratna Memorial Charitable Trust.

### Hortense Mancini and Marie Mancini

Carroll, Leslie. 2008. *Royal Affairs: A Lusty Romp Through the Extramarital Adventures That Rocked the British Monarchy*. New York: New American Library.

Goldsmith, Elizabeth C. 2012. *The Kings' Mistresses: The Liberated Lives of Marie Mancini, Princess Colonna, and Hortense Mancini, Duchess Mazarin*. New York: Public Affairs.

### Nzinga Mbande

Cross, Robin, and Rosalind Miles. 2011. *Warrior Women: 3000 Years of Courage and Heroism*. London: Quercus Publishing Inc.

Fraser, Antonia. 1989. *The Warrior Queens*. New York: Knopf.

Lienhard, Martín. 2008. "Queen Njinga's Milongas: The 'Dialogue' Between Portuguese and Africans in the Congo and the Angola War (Sixteenth and Seventeenth Centuries)." In *Afrimericas: Itineraries, Dialogues, and Sounds*, edited by Tiago de Oliveira Pinto Ineke Phaf-Rheinberger. Madrid/Frankfurt: Iberoamericana/Vervuert. Reprinted at http://www.buala.org/en/to-read/queen-njinga-s-milongas-the-dialogue-between-portuguese-and-africans-in-the-congo-and-the-an.

Stapleton, Timothy J. 2013. *A Military History of Africa*. Santa Barbara, CA: Praeger.

### Hypatia

Damascius. 1993. "The Life of Hypatia." In *The Suda* by Damascius, translated by Jeremiah Reedy. http://www.cosmopolis.com/alexandria/hypatia-bio-suda.html.

Grout, James. n.d. "Hypatia." Encyclopedia Romana. http://penelope.uchicago.edu/~grout/encyclopaedia_romana/greece/paganism/hypatia.html.

Richeson, A. W. 1940. "Hypatia of Alexandria." *National Mathematics Magazine* 15 (2, November): 74–82.

Scholasticus, Socrates. n.d. "The Life of Hypatia." In *Ecclesiastical History* by Socrates Scholasticus. http://www.cosmopolis.com/alexandria/hypatia-bio-socrates.html.

Whitfield, Bryan J. "The Beauty of Reasoning: A Reexamination of Hypatia of Alexandria." *The Mathematics Educator* 6 (1): 14–21. http://math.coe.uga.edu/tme/issues/v06n1/4whitfield.pdf.

### Jezebel

1 Kings, 2 Kings. In *Holy Bible: New International Version*.

Gaines, Janet Howe. 2000. "How Bad Was Jezebel?" *Bible Review*, October. http://www.biblicalarchaeology.org/daily/people-cultures-in-the-bible/people-in-the-bible/how-bad-was-jezebel/.

Hazleton, Lesley. 2007. *Jezebel: The Untold Story of the Bible's Harlot Queen*. New York: Doubleday.

### Qiu Jin

Ono, Kazuko, and Joshua A. Fogel. 1989. *Chinese Women in a Century of Revolution, 1850–1950*. Stanford, CA: Stanford University Press.

Rankin, Mary Backus. 1975. "The Emergence of Women at the End of the Ch'ing: The Case of Ch'iu Chin." In *Women in Chinese Society*, edited by Margery Wolf and Roxane Widke. Stanford, CA: Stanford University Press.

## Yoshiko Kawashima

"Asian Mata Hari Is Faded Beauty." 1948. *Spokesman-Review*, March 19.

Crowdy, Terry. 2006. *The Enemy Within: A History of Espionage*. Oxford: Osprey.

"Daughter of Chinese Prince Helps Japan." 1933. *Berkeley Daily Gazette*, February 23.

"The Jap Cinderella Who Stabbed Us in the Back." 1942. *Milwaukee Sentinel*, April 12.

"The Japs' 100-Faced Spy Master and His Masquerading Mistress." 1942. *Milwaukee Sentinel*, February 1.

"Manchuria's Joan of Arc." 1934. *Berkeley Daily Gazette*, January 10.

Shao, Dan. 2005. "Princess, Traitor, Soldier, Spy: Aisin Gioro Xianyu and the Dilemma of Manchu Identity." In *Crossed Histories: Manchuria in the Age of Empire*, edited by Mariko Tamanoi. Honolulu: University of Hawai'i Press.

## Joan of Arc

Goldstone, Nancy Bazelon. 2012. *The Maid and the Queen: The Secret History of Joan of Arc*. New York: Viking.

Manning, Scott. 2011. "How Was Joan of Arc So Skilled with Cannons?" Historian on the Warpath, December 12. http://www.scottmanning.com/content/joan-of-arc-cannons/.

## Osh-Tisch

Lang, Sabine. 1998. *Men as Women, Women as Men: Changing Gender in Native American Cultures*. Austin: University of Texas Press.

Linderman, Frank Bird. 1972. *Pretty-Shield: Medicine Woman of the Crows*. New York: John Day Company.

Roscoe, Will. 1988. *Living the Spirit: A Gay American Indian Anthology*. New York: St. Martin's Press.

Roughgarden, Joan. 2004. *Evolution's Rainbow: Diversity, Gender, and Sexuality in Nature and People*. Berkeley: University of California Press.

Williams, Walter L. 1986. *The Spirit and the Flesh: Sexual Diversity in American Indian Culture*. Boston: Beacon Press.

## The Night Witches

"Audio Slideshow: Night Witches." 2009. *BBC News*, November 2. http://news.bbc.co.uk/2/hi/in_depth/8329676.stm.

Garber, Megan. 2014. "Night Witches: The Female Fighter Pilots of World War II." *The Atlantic*, July 15.

Markwick, Roger D., and Euridice Charon Cardona. 2012. *Soviet Women on the Frontline in the Second World War*. New York: Palgrave Macmillan.

Martin, Douglas. 2013. "Nadezhda Popova, WWII 'Night Witch,' Dies at 91." *New York Times*, July 14.

Noggle, Anne. 1994. *A Dance with Death: Soviet Airwomen in World War II*. College Station: Texas A&M University Press.

Smith, Annabelle K. 2013. "A WWII Propaganda Campaign Popularized the Myth That Carrots Help You See in the Dark." Smithsonian.com, August 13. http://www.smithsonianmag.com/arts-culture/a-wwii-propaganda-campaign-popularized-the-myth-that-carrots-help-you-see-in-the-dark-28812484/.

## Sita

Buck, William, trans. 1976. *The Ramayana*. Berkeley: University of California Press.

## Kharboucha

Glacier, Osire, and Valerie Martin. 2013. *Political Women in Morocco: Then and Now*. Trenton, NJ: Red Sea Press.

Harmach, Amine. 2009. "Aux origines du personnage de Kharboucha." Aujourdhui.ma, January 2. http://www.aujourdhui.ma/maroc/culture/aux-origines-du-personnage-de-kharboucha-90066.

## Marguerite de la Rocque
Boyer, Elizabeth. 1983. *A Colony of One: The History of a Brave Woman*. Novelty, OH: Veritie Press.

Thevet, André, Roger Schlesinger, and Arthur Philips Stabler. 1986. *André Thevet's North America: A Sixteenth-Century View*. Kingston, Ontario: McGill–Queen's University Press.

## Noor Inayat Khan
Basu, Shrabani. 2006. *Spy Princess: The Life of Noor Inayat Khan*. Stroud, UK: Sutton Publishing Ltd.

## Empress Myeongseong
Cummins, Joseph. 2006. *History's Great Untold Stories: Larger Than Life Characters and Dramatic Events That Changed the World*. Washington, DC: National Geographic.

Lee Bae-Yong, Ted Chan. 2008. *Women in Korean History*. Seoul: Ewha Womans University Press.

## Micaela Bastidas
Walker, Charles F. 2014. *The Tupac Amaru Rebellion*. Cambridge, MA: Belknap Press of Harvard University Press.

## Neerja Bhanot
Bhanot, Harish. 1985. "A Father Reminisces." *Hindustan Times*, October 5. http://neerjabhanot.org/father.htm.

Bharathi, Veena. 2014. *Ordinary Feet, Extra-Ordinary Feat*. Delhi: Quills Ink Publishing.

Bhattacharya, Brigadier Samir. 2014. *Nothing But!* vol. 5, *All Is Fair in Love and War*. Gurgaon, India: Partridge Publishing.

Moran, Megha. 2016. "Inside a Hijack: The Unheard Stories of the Pan Am 73 Crew." *BBC News*. http://www.bbc.com/news/world-asia-35800683

## Boudica
Dio, Cassius. 1914. *Roman History*. Translated by Earnest Cary. Cambridge, MA: Harvard University Press. http://penelope.uchicago.edu/Thayer/E/Roman/Texts/Cassius_Dio/62*.html#1.

Fraser, Antonia. 1989. *The Warrior Queens*. New York: Knopf.

Tacitus, Cornelius. 1876. *The Life and Death of Julius Agricola*. Translated by Alfred John Church and William Jackson Brodribb. https://en.wikisource.org/wiki/Agricola.

## Artemisia Gentileschi
Christiansen, Keith, and Judith Walker Mann. 2001. *Orazio and Artemisia Gentileschi*. New York: Metropolitan Museum of Art.

Garrard, Mary D. 2001. *Artemisia Gentileschi Around 1622: The Shaping and Reshaping of an Artistic Identity*. Berkeley: University of California Press.

## Wu Zetian
Dien, Dora Shu-fang. 2003. *Empress Wu Zetian in Fiction and in History: Female Defiance in Confucian China*. New York: Nova Science Publishers.

Guisso, R. W. L. 1978. *Wu Tse-T'ien and the Politics of Legitimation in T'ang*. Bellingham: Western Washington University.

Rothschild, N. Harry. 2008. *Wu Zhao: China's Only Woman Emperor*. New York: Pearson Longman.

## Arawelo
Affi, Ladan. 1995. "Arraweelo: A Role Model for Somali Women." Somali Peace Conference, Paris (October). http://www.mbali.info/doc384.htm.

Ali, Abukar. 2006. "The Tale Behind Women's Circumcision." About the Horn, January 5. http://sayidka.blogspot.ca/2006/01/tale-behind-womens-circumcision.html.

Chait, Sandra M. 2011. *Seeking Salaam: Ethiopians, Eritreans, and Somalis in the Pacific Northwest*. Seattle: University of Washington Press.

Mohamed, Farah. 2012. "Queen Araweelo: A Short Story of a Somali Hero, Queen Ebla Awad (Araweelo)." Somali Media Network, June 1. http://www.somalimedia.com/queen-araweelo-a-short-story-of-a-somali-hero-queen-ebla-awad-araweelo/.

Mukhtar, Mohamed Haji, and Margaret Castagno. 2003. *Historical Dictionary of Somalia*. Lanham, MD: Scarecrow Press.

Said, Shafi. 2006. "The Legendary Cruelty." Incoherent Thoughts, March 23. https://shafisaid.wordpress.com/2006/03/23/the-legendary-cruelty/.

Zabus, Chantal J. 2007. *Between Rites and Rights: Excision in Women's Experiential Texts and Human Contexts*. Stanford, CA: Stanford University Press.

## Caterina Sforza

Lev, Elizabeth. 2011. *The Tigress of Forlì: Renaissance Italy's Most Courageous and Notorious Countess, Caterina Riario Sforza de Medici*. Boston: Houghton Mifflin Harcourt.

## Elisabeth Báthory

Thorne, Tony. 1997. *Countess Dracula: The Life and Times of the Blood Countess, Elisabeth Báthory*. London: Bloomsbury.

## Malinche

Karttunen, Frances. 1997. "Rethinking Malinche." In *Indian Women of Early Mexico*, edited by Stephanie Wood, Robert Haskett, and Susan Schroeder. Norman: University of Oklahoma Press.

Lanyon, Anna. 1999. *Malinche's Conquest*. Crow's Nest, New South Wales: Allen & Unwin.

Truitt, Jonathan Glenn. 2010. "Courting Catholicism: Nahua Women and the Catholic Church in Colonial Mexico City." *Ethnohistory* 57 (3): 415–44.

## Ida B. Wells

Giddings, Paula. 2008. *Ida: A Sword Among Lions: Ida B. Wells and the Campaign Against Lynching*. New York: Amistad.

## Phoolan Devi

Devi, Phoolan, Marie-Therese Cuny, and Paul Rambali. 2003. *The Bandit Queen of India: An Indian Woman's Amazing Journey from Peasant to International Legend*. Guilford, CT: Lyons Press.

Weaver, Mary Anne. 1996. "India's Bandit Queen." *The Atlantic*, November.

# About the Author

In a past life, Jason Porath worked as an animator on films such as *How to Train Your Dragon 2* and *The Croods*. During lunch one day, he and his coworkers had a competition to see who could come up with the most unlikely candidate for the animated princess treatment. Jason took the idea and ran with it, and here we are.

Jason lives in Los Angeles, where he enjoys exploring abandoned buildings, building tesla coils, and singing a lot of karaoke.

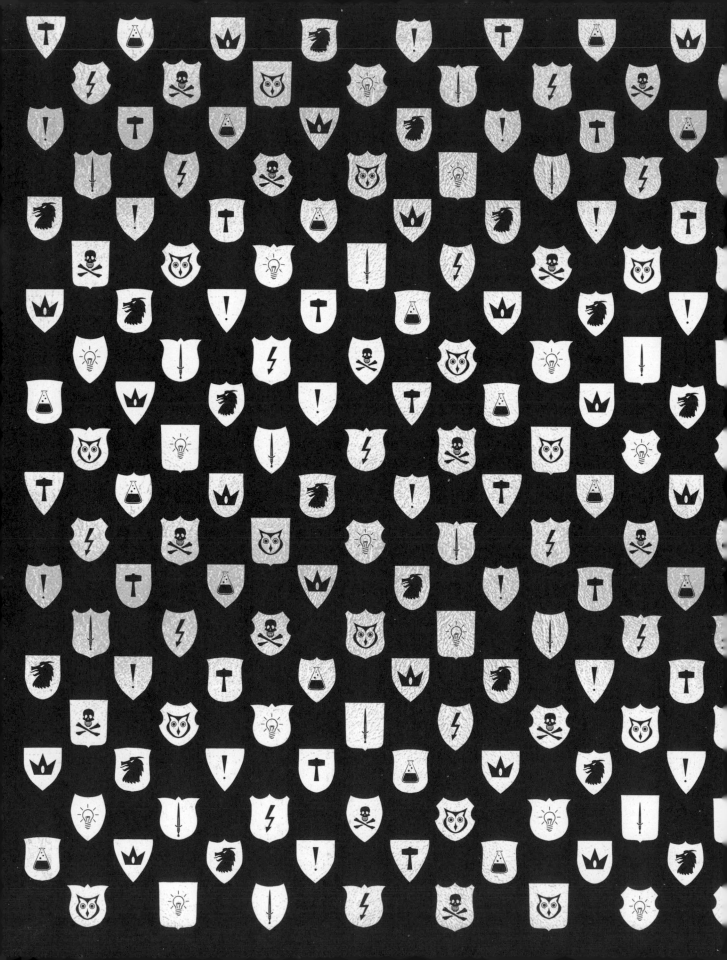